By Gladys Hasty Carroll

Novels
AS THE EARTH TURNS
A FEW FOOLISH ONES
NEIGHBOR TO THE SKY
WHILE THE ANGELS SING
WEST OF THE HILL
CHRISTMAS WITHOUT JOHNNY
ONE WHITE STAR
SING OUT THE GLORY

Collected Short Stories
HEAD OF THE LINE

Nonfiction
DUNNYBROOK

Sing Out the Glory

GLADYS HASTY CARROLL

Sing Out
the Glory

Boston · Little, Brown and Company · Toronto

Published simultaneously in Canada
by Little, Brown & Company (Canada) Limited

PRINTED IN THE UNITED STATES OF AMERICA

To
my daughter Sally
who has lived all her sixteen years
on a narrow, sweetfern-bordered lane
along which three hundred years of American history
have passed
leading to today and tomorrow

Author's Note

ALL THE CHARACTERS IN THIS STORY
ARE IMAGINARY, BUT HAVE ROOTS IN
THE REALITY OF LIFE IN
MANY AMERICAN COMMUNITIES

Sing Out the Glory

I

I HAVE yarn to spin, colors to blend, a pattern to weave, and edges to bind securely for the preservation of the whole. I cannot promise that the yarn will not be loose, the colors too pale or too strong or ill-matched; please be tolerant of the workmanship. The wool is of the best quality, clean and sturdy, springy to the touch, native grown, product of snug shelter, rocky pasture, and the narrow sweetfern-bordered lanes which wind forever between the all-but-forgotten beginning and the unforeseeable end.

In my basket the carded and rolled shearings, all alive and billowing, are heaped bottomside up. I attach the top roll to the spindle and strike the great wheel with a wooden pin. It begins to turn, and I am startled by my own temerity in setting it in motion.

There were two hills, which we called mountains. One was higher than the other, and from a spring near the top of the higher leaped a brook which, when it tore into our valley and broadened, we called a river, as the Abenaki Indians did. We called it by its Indian name, the Assabenbeduc. The Indians were here when the Scots and Englishmen came. Through our ancestors we know them as friends, tall teachers of the science of survival in the wilderness. There were not many of them in the valley, and

3

even fewer of us at first, with fish and birds and deer and bear sufficient for all. Sufficient, that is, to fend off starvation — which was as much as they or we presumed to ask of their Great Spirit, our Puritan God. Beasts on the mountains, fish in the stream, never-failing springs of fresh water, a forest of virgin pines hundreds of feet high and straight as a plumbline dropped from heaven; these were provided for any man who had the strength and skill to make a clearing for his family and bring his provision into it. Those who lacked this strength and skill, others struggled to extend their own to cover, in pity and forbearance. It was necessary to be strong and wise, necessary also to be kind, for we were human beings inhabiting a land which had no need of us, or felt none.

One day, many miles away, cattle came ashore from a ship which had crossed the sea from Denmark. The news swam up our river like salmon racing to spawn, followed, along the river's bank, not long afterward by three of these docile creatures, their sharp hoofs cutting in the half-frozen ground the rude trail which was to become the valley road. On their backs they carried the grain to feed them until grass grew. That spring white men spread fertilizer on their land and spaded it in before they dropped their seed. Red men sat by, watching, shook their heads and grunted amusement. That summer the white men's corn had longer and fuller ears; their potatoes were larger and more to a hill. They dug holes below the frostline in which to store all this corn and these potatoes.

The winter was the cruelest we had ever known. We built huge fires to melt cakes of the frozen earth and chinked the cracks in our log walls with mud. A cow became a member of the family which owned her and slept where they slept, welcome for her body heat and for the

4

warm, frothy milk she would give in the morning. Red men, cold and hungry, sometimes came to sit by the cabin fires, to eat and to take home a little food, but their wives and children, like the hedgehogs and rabbits, kept hidden. Spring was late, and when it came, many Indians had died. There were left chiefly the old and tough, and of the old, Time is the conqueror.

In spring, the river often overflows its bank and floods the valley floor, enriching the soil of its meadows. From the windows of cabins clinging to the high instep of a mountain's foot, we looked out one morning for the first time at the blue waters of a lake crowded with bobbing blocks of silvery ice, and rubbed our eyes at a miracle which later, from many enactments, became a commonplace of spring.

The fog is never commonplace because it cannot be predicted. We are only ten miles from the coast, and at any time of day or night a gray sea-turn may glide in, cooling and thickening the air until we say that we can cut it with a knife, bringing us the taste of salt, the smell of seaweed and scalefish and shellfish, the sound of the waves beating against the cliffs and of great, mournful horns blowing to warn the coastwise ships. The fog which rises from the river has no color, no texture, no taste, smell, or sound. It is sheer vision, a vision of purity, a slow, mesmeric, inexorable erasure of the slate. You see fog mushrooming along the river's course. Gently, it obliterates the alders tangled on the banks, wipes out the road. Buildings without foundations, trees without trunks, hang in the air like mirages. Sun may be shining brightly on them, or rain drenching them, or stars twinkling above or among them. Slowly the fog reaches higher and spreads. Ridgepoles, small topmost branches, and your own dooryard vanish.

5

There is nothing left now but shining mist. It is all, and you float on it, utterly alone, as one imagines he might in empty space if flung off by earth; as the mind does, drifting into sleep; as the spirit must, having escaped its mortal frame.

The river fog takes our world away, over and over, often when we least expect it. In a little while, it gives it back, or returns us to it. But we never find it quite as it was before. The clock has kept on ticking. Time has passed, and time is the changer.

The story of the last Indian — or the last few Indians — to run silently over the mountainside, shoot the small rapids of the Assabenbeduc, chuckle at the white men's curious pursuits, lift up long arms and pray, has not been preserved. Indians, Scots and Englishmen lived here side by side for several years. Then the record begins to speak only of white settlers — as if some fog, having taken away the valley, returned it without the Indians who had lived through the Coldest Winter. That there was no conflict, no savagery, is sure; for, as I said, the white men's children down through many generations have known them as friends, tall teachers who could not themselves learn new ways, and who were outplayed by Time and Nature in the grim game for which no man has yet learned the winning combinations. The Indians are gone from the valley and, as a separate race, from most parts of our country, but their marks are plain in every American history and geography book, and in the culture of the nation. The blood of the American Indian flows in the veins of many who bear English, Scotch, Irish, or French names. It flows in mine.

The cattle were followed into the valley by sheep, and more land was cleared for the planting of grain and flax.

6

The air was stirred increasingly by the whir of wheels. Spinning wheels, flax wheels, cart wheels, water wheels. Livestock and the grain ground at a mill called the wolves down from the north. At night the sight of their bared teeth outside the cabin windows made the children draw closer to the hearth. The women longed to light a second candle, but sang and prayed instead. The men took muskets from the wall, opened the door, and fired. The wolves shrank back but howled around the barns all night. On winter mornings there was blood on the snow.

The children ran up like steps, despite the many stillborn babies and the fevers which took off older ones. Frame houses were built, shingled, and clapboarded; all much alike, with a great central chimney, a large room on either side of it, sometimes three small rooms across the back, and a loft overhead where boys slept on straw and cornhusks with comforters for cover. Bridges across the river opened the way for land to be cleared and houses built on the other side.

And all the time the fogs came and went, taking the valley away, returning it, taking it away.

One day our world came back threaded with the smell of war. Horses were hurried from their stalls and hard-ridden by men going to meetings. Even the cows grew restive, knowing they would be milked late or by women's unaccustomed hands. Sheep huddled and watched with anxious eyes. The muskets were taken down from kitchen walls, placed against men's shoulders, and carried out of sight down the road. Neither they nor the men came back, if at all, for a long time. That was at stake which meant more to valley men than stock or seed or shelter or even the present welfare of their families. Women and children

7

must plow and sow and milk and grind and bar out wolves as best they could. Men had liberty to defend, freedom to win, and a new nation to establish, for their own future welfare, and that of those they loved and who would come after them. These great duties took them a far piece, into land strange to their feet, and into danger. . . .

The fog lifted. Most of our men — not all — came home.They had aged ten years, though they had not been gone that long, and our women had aged more. The youngest child had grown tall. But there was a new fire in every eye. We had our liberty; freedom had been won; and the new nation had been born. The musket hung again on the wall. The fields and the women became fertile. In spring evenings we sat together on the door rock and listened to the peepers from the marshes. On summer nights there was no sound but the whippoorwill's, the running water, and the wind in the pines; sleep was deep. In fall the stacked corn rustled; barn lofts were full of fodder for the creatures; the darkness of cellars was strong with the scent of vegetables, apples, pork in salt brine, and cider foaming at the bunghole. In winter the fish were locked under the ice, cordwood was drawn down from the mountains on sleds pulled by oxen, harnesses mended, hot bannock spread with fresh butter, and mush dipped into bowls to be sweetened with molasses and drowned in milk. Lamps had replaced candles. A woman could sew as well as spin after supper. It was good to be alive, and we were grateful.

Until then our religion and education had come from the Bible, brought from the kitchen shelf to the table each bedtime, and read aloud by the member of the family who could read best. This, the prayers of a traveling preacher who sometimes stopped at one door or another to ask for a night's lodging, the example and the precepts of the elders, the lessons of the mountains, river, sky, woods and fields day in, day out, kept us in contact with God and in tune with our place and time.

But a fog drifted away, and we knew that we wanted to worship as a community, must learn more than was yet known in the valley. We built a church with pews and a pulpit. The next traveling preacher who asked for lodging stayed with us for years. We built a one-room school, with pegs for hanging children's jackets, shawls, and caps, a shelf to hold the water bucket and dipper; it had a chimney, and a shed behind for the firewood. The preacher became the teacher also.

Another fog, and, as it dissipated, the grave, gaunt face of Abraham Lincoln seemed emblazoned upon the soft blue valley sky, his words to issue from the higher mountain and be echoed from the other like rolling thunder. The old, the women, and the children looked up from the work to which they bent from sunup to sundown, and listened.

. . . Our fathers brought forth on this continent a new nation, conceived in liberty, and dedicated to the proposition that all men are created equal.

Now we are engaged in a great civil war, testing whether that nation, or any nation so conceived and so dedicated, can long endure. . . .

It is . . . for us to be here dedicated to the great task remaining before us . . . that this nation, under God, shall have a new birth of freedom — and that government of the people, by the people, for the people, shall not perish from the earth.

9

Valley men had fought and were fighting to preserve the union of this nation. They had fought at Shiloh, Manassas, and Antietam, had caught fevers in Southern swamps, been wounded at Gettysburg. Now they went on to be killed at Cold Harbor, or taken prisoner and confined to Andersonville.

If slavery is not wrong, nothing is wrong.

Valley men went with Sherman into Atlanta, Savannah.

Fondly do we hope — fervently do we pray — that this mighty scourge of war may speedily pass away. Yet, if God wills that it continue . . . so still it must be said, "The judgments of the Lord are true and righteous altogether."

Men are not flattered by being shown that there has been a difference of purpose between the Almighty and them. To deny it, however, in this case, is to deny that there is a God governing the world.

Valley men were among the Union troops which occupied Richmond, and there the President, lonesome Abe Lincoln, met them.

It is not merely for today, but for all time to come, that we should perpetuate for our children's children that great and free government which we have enjoyed all our lives. I beg you to remember this . . . in order that each one of you may have, through this free government which we have enjoyed, an open field and a fair chance for your industry, enterprise, and intelligence; that you may all have equal privileges in the race of life, with all its desirable human aspirations. It is for this the struggle should be maintained, that we may not lose our birthright . . .

10

A few days later, as azaleas bloomed in Charleston, General Robert E. Lee offered his sword to General Ulysses S. Grant. General Grant would not accept it. This War Between the States had been a war between brothers, and it was over. The Generals sat down together and wrote words on paper:

Each officer and man will return to his home . . .

When valley men reached home, lilacs were budding there, and the apple trees.

In the new peace the valley vibrated with machinery. A railroad passed so near that we could see the smoke of the engines and hear their whistle in the night. An old man, listening, said, "I wisht I was aboard of her, a-goin' to England." We had mowing machines and sewing machines, sawing machines and parlor organs; springs were deepened to become wells and pumps were put in them; fireplaces were sealed and stoves set up. Girls no longer wove the sheeting for their bridal beds but walked downriver to the cotton mills where they could earn money to buy it, and to buy pans for their kitchens, crockery for their chambers, feathers for their hats, and bright bits of gold for their ears. Boys went west on the railroads, even as far as the Klondike, in eager search of more gold than the girls saw any use for. Other boys went to sea, fishing off the Grand Banks, or much farther east, or rounded Cape Horn and crossed the Pacific. Some came back soon, some were gone a long time, some never came back. The girls walked upriver from the mill every night and sat on door rocks after supper, waiting, listening for the tread of the boys who had gone away. When the horses had been stabled, the hand was off the lever, the foot was off the treadle, the supper fire had burned low, there were still no sounds but the natural valley sounds; the peepers or the whippoorwill, the running water, the wind in the pines, the rustle of the stacked corn.

A pink sunrise, a ruddy-gold sunset. Days of scudding rainclouds. A warm winter, an early spring, a field of grain so tall a child could be lost in it. A sudden frost, blackened acres, rust on the potatoes. A good woman dead, a baby born. Flood and drought. A great tree felled, a log riding to mill to become boards for the floor of a new house; a delicate seedling unfolding its twin leaves, stepped on by a cow, crushed, yet by the next morning standing straight again, reaching toward the sun. . . . The fog taking it away, returning it, taking it again, returning it; and with each return it was changed a little. Something familiar disappeared, or something intangible but challenging had been added. Over and over, we had a new world.

I say "we" because it has been so often described, in so much detail, that I feel I saw it all from the beginning. Even from the Day Before Man, when the mountains were thrown up and a spring spouted out near the top of the higher one.

But there came a time when I not only saw. I was. I, and a Boy, in a world so new that it was not yet inhabited by anyone else.

I had been floating on a silver mist for what seemed like an eternity but may have been only an hour by the clock. I was too young to read the time. Then I had seen the floor of our back porch, the long steps down from it, the wide, black crack in the bottom step which was a plank laid on the ground. I opened the kitchen door, sat on the stool, and watched each separate green blade of grass return to its accustomed place. When I could see the wheel ruts in the yard, I crossed the porch and sat on the top step to watch the trees come back. Their trunks, always the first to go, were likewise the first part of them to come again.

From the still hidden branches, a voice said, "Hullo, there."

I did not answer. I did not know the voice was speaking to me. I did not know this was the Beginning. I waited.

"Can you talk?" the voice asked.

I looked around, but could see no one.

I said hesitatingly and very low, not to disturb anything and not to make a foolish mistake conspicuous, *"I can talk."*

"Good. So can I. What's your name?"

The voice was speaking to me. Me, myself. It was astonishing.

I said, "Althea."

"Althea what?"

I did not know. If I had ever known, I had now forgotten.

I said, "Just Althea."

"Nonsense. Everybody has two names."

So in this world everybody had two names. I thought, I have to get another name.

"What are your names?" I asked.

"Perry is the one that counts. Ever heard of anybody named Perry?"

I had heard of the Elder, of course. Elder Perry was God's messenger to the valley. People were always saying that. They went to church on Sunday to get their message from the Elder. If anyone was sick he brought messages to the house. He had come several times with messages after the tree fell on my father last winter. The Elder had bright eyes, a shiny head, and a long white beard which covered his top buttons so that you could not tell whether they were buttoned or not. He walked very slowly, with a cane. His shoes were thin and soft and had neither lacings nor buttons. But this could not be the Elder speaking. The Elder could not climb a tree. The Elder's voice was like his shoes, old and thin and soft. Besides, the Elder did not have two names. As Mr. Kerensky was Mr. because he brought us needles and thread and remnants of cloth and ric-rac braid in a red cart, Elder Perry was Elder because he brought us God's messages.

Only the stars and God were higher than the trunks of trees. Stars were silent . . . but God had been known to speak. Did God have two names now? I clasped my hands. I knew I was God's child. Perhaps in this new world we were all to have Perry as a second name.

"Am I — Althea Perry?" I asked eagerly.

The voice laughed.

"Maybe," it said, "but I doubt it by a long sight."

Then the sun came back. From a small blue patch of sky infinitely far away it looked down a mist-walled shaft and shone bright and clear upon the first of our row of dooryard maples. The branches and twigs were wet-black, lacing the wet-green of the leaves like penciled lines on a crumpled green paper. In the string hammock which my older sisters had hung by chains from high branches for the purpose — I thought — of eluding me, a boy lay on his side with his head on his crooked arm, and one leg in rolled-up overalls hanging over the edge.

His hair was the color of the sulphur and molasses

14

which my mother mixed for us in the spring. It was curly and where the sun touched it, it gleamed like the gold of the Klondike. His eyes were the blue of the new sky. A new sky is bluer than any other sky, the bluest blue of all. He was smiling at me, and did not stop.

I knew then that if Perry was his name and not everybody's name, it was not my name, for we were not alike. At our house all the hair was dark and straight, all the eyes were gray or brown, and when the people I knew smiled it was a sudden thing and quickly passed. This boy who kept on smiling was a stranger.

I tried to think what to say to him. I wanted to watch him while he spoke.

I asked, "How did you get up there, Perry?"

He laughed again.

"Perry is the important name. You aren't supposed to use it too much. Might get worn out. I use Owen for every day."

"How did you get up there, **Owen**?"

"Climbed, of course."

He rolled over on his back, with his arms raised and his hands under his head, his knees hunched. He was looking up through the leaves, smiling at the leaves now. I could see the cleft in his cheek. His face was nearly as brown as ours, but his bare arms and legs were almost white.

I waited.

"I must say," he remarked finally, "this is some country. You see trees so tall you think they must reach to the moon, and you think you will go climb one to see if it does. But the first ones you come to are so prickly you can't climb them, so you keep on walking until you find some that don't prickle, but as soon as you start up, you find they are too sticky to climb. So you keep on walking and all of a sudden something wraps around you and you can hardly see from one tree trunk to another. Then you can't see a hand before your face. You keep on walking, bumping into things, and then you aren't bumping into things, so you try to run. And all of a sudden — smacko! You've whammed into something so hard it almost knocks you out. You fall down and watch stars for a while. Then they go and you're still all wrapped up in this funny blanket. You guess maybe it's fog. You crawl up to what hit you and find it's a tree that neither prickles nor sticks. So you climb it hoping to get above the fog and find out where you are. You don't find out where you are. But what do you find? You find a hammock waiting for you. A nice, comfortable hammock! . . . Do hammocks grow in all the trees? Or is this a hammock tree?"

"That is a maple tree," I said. "I think. Lucy and Edith put the hammock there."

"Who are Lucy and Edith?"

"My sisters."

He turned over on his side again, and was smiling down at me. The sun had widened the shaft until it had disappeared altogether. The orchard, the road, the mountains, and the alders on the riverbank had all come back. Everything which had been here before was here again, as far as I knew; and the Boy and Me, besides.

"They must be bigger than you."

"Much bigger."

"Then I'll bet they have two names. I'll find out at school what their other name is. Then I'll tell you what yours is. Would you like that, Althea?"

"Yes. Are you going to school?"

"Sure. As soon as it starts. Next week, I guess."

16

"I want to go to school."

"How old are you? Four? Five?"

"Four."

"Then you're not old enough."

"How old are you?"

"Almost thirteen. But they'll let you go to school when you're six."

"How can I get to be six?"

He laughed again.

"Just wait, Althea."

"I've been waiting. If you are going to school, I want to go to school."

I stood up. I had many feelings, all of them new and strange. A bird seemed to be fluttering inside me. I could not tell whether he was a sad or a happy or a frightened bird. I sensed that he was all three and I imagined him very small and very blue, as blue as the sky and Owen's eyes. I thought that his breast must be the color of the mist, and that under each wing was a scarlet brush-stroke.

I said loudly and clearly, "I want to go where you go, Owen."

I saw his eyebrows lift into sunlit tents. His eyes, studying me, twinkled with surprise and pleasure, but they were not startled. There was a gentle calmness all through and around him, radiant and serene. He was not as unaccustomed, I saw, to inspiring adoration as I was to proffering it. No bird fluttered in the cage of his heart. He carried no cage. His heart had open windows and wholly happy things flew freely in and out.

His mouth moved to form words.

Then my mother opened the door, came out on the porch with an armful of rugs and a broom.

"For goodness' sake, Althea," she said, "if you're bound

to pretend, do you have to do it so loud? Anybody'd think you were talking to somebody on the mountain!"

I watched her spread a rug and sweep. Seeing her made me afraid that only I could see and hear Owen, or even — worst of all — that I had imagined him. After a minute, I forced myself to look up. He was still there, still smiling at me, swinging his leg over the side of the hammock.

I said, "I was talking to somebody in the tree."

"Somebody in the — oh, you must have made a friend of a treetoad."

She glanced at me in faint amusement, and spread another rug. Her face was thin and yellowish-brown. It had no other color in it.

She said, "It's nice since the fog," and stood looking across the field.

"There is a little bit of it left on your hair," I told her. "Right next to your face."

She put up her free hand to her ear and shrugged her shoulders.

"That's not fog," she said. "My hair's turning white. First time you've noticed it?"

She began to sweep again, harder and faster than before.

When she stooped to fold the rug, I said, "I wasn't talking to a treetoad. I was talking to Owen."

"Mmm. Who's Owen?"

I knew. I could answer her.

I said, proudly, "Owen Perry."

She straightened and stared at me.

"Owen Perry! Now where did you get an idea like that? Did you stay awake after I put you to bed last night?"

I did not remember, but I shook my head. What did last night matter now?

I said, "He's in the tree. Can't you see him?"

18

"Which tree?"

She sounded unbelieving still, but excited. Her eyes gripped mine as sometimes her hands did my shoulders.

"The one with the hammock in it," I stammered. "Owen's in the hammock," I cried. "Look and see, Mother. Look and see!"

Her eyes let go of mine and we both turned our faces up.

Mine must have been beseeching.

Owen was swinging his other leg over the side of the hammock. His black shirt was as wet as the maple branches. His hair stood up like a jay's crest. His quizzical smile had become a friendly, apologetic grin.

"Good morning, ma'am," he said. "I'm coming down now. Should have come before, only I thought I might scare you, before Althea got us introduced."

He swung from his hands like a monkey, reached with his boot for a lower branch, balanced on it, bent and grasped it, swung again, and was on the ground. He rubbed the wet bark off his hands, against the seat of his overalls, and came toward us, smiling at me exactly as he had at first, and smiling at my mother in that other polite way.

"I guess I got lost in the fog," he told her. "I've heard folks say that, but I didn't know what they meant before. So when I bumped into this tree I climbed it to see if I could find out where I was. But I couldn't see anything. And I still don't know just where I am."

"This is Brad McIntire's farm," said my mother. She sounded cold. "Are you — the boy that's visiting the Elder?"

"I'm the Elder's grandson, Todd Perry's boy," nodded

Owen. He sounded proud. "Only I don't think we've come to visit Gramp. I think we've come to stay."

"Is that so?" said my mother noncomittally. "Well, you can see the Elder's place from here if you look in the right direction." She pointed. "To get there you have to go down the lane and turn right, cross the bridge that'll be on your left and then turn left until you come to the first road turning off to the right. You wandered some ways seems like, and it's most dinnertime. Come in, Althea, and wash. Your father and the girls'll be back from market any minute. They'd have been here an hour ago but for the fog."

She picked up her rugs — she had never let go of the broom — and went with short, hard steps into the house, leaving the door open behind her.

Owen and I were alone again. Almost. I had never been so near to a boy before. His wet shirt clung to him like skin and I could see his breathing. He had thrust his thumbs into his pockets. His fingers looked supple and strong, with broad, flat, close-clipped nails. He stood with his feet wide apart, as I had seen my father stand, but it did not give him the planted look it gave my father. He seemed braced to spring.

He said, "I'll bet she's a tiptop housekeeper!"

"Who?"

"Why, that mother of yours!"

His voice rang with enthusiasm. He was so close that I had to tip my head far back to see his face. It shone like his hair. He was a golden boy.

I could not forget my mother's coldness toward him. It puzzled and hurt me.

I said, "I'll bet your mother is — just as —"

I stopped because I could not repeat the words he had

20

used. He waited a minute, smiling down at me as if he understood what I was trying to do, though I did not, and appreciated it without needing it.

"Mine?" he asked then, cheerfully. "I haven't got a mother. Never have had, as far back as I can remember. You're lucky you've got her, and don't you forget it. . . . Go in and wash, like she said, even though you do look clean as a whistle. I have to cut along now."

He pulled a thumb out of his pocket, gave me a quick wave, and moved away.

"Owen —"

He turned back.

"Will you ever come again?"

"Come again? Sure. Why not?"

"Before the world goes away again?"

I saw him saying my words over in his mind. Suddenly his whole face smiled. He came back then and touched me lightly with one finger.

"Just wanted to see if you're flesh and blood," he laughed. "Thought you might be elfin. You mean, before another fog rises, don't you? Well, yes. I should hope so. I hope you don't have them every day. So long, Althea. Be good now. Go right in and wash."

"I will."

I would always do whatever he told me. I went at once to the door.

"Althea!"

I turned eagerly. He was not yet far away, but far enough so that he looked smaller.

"I've got news for you. Your other name is McIntire. You're Althea McIntire."

He laughed and vanished.

I went slowly into the kitchen. I was Althea McIntire.

My mother was the same as always, except that she was quicker. She took down a roller towel and tossed it to me, telling me to wipe my feet with it; they were bare. With the other hand she opened the oven door and took out a pan of biscuits. There was warm water in a wash basin in the black iron sink. As I stood rubbing yellow soap over my arms and hands, she brushed off the back of my dress and told me I should have known better than to sit down when the step was wet. Then she put a clean towel over the roller and went back to the stove. I could smell new potatoes cooking, salt pork crisping, and green apple pie cooling on the table. I stood washing and washing, in a dream.

My father came in, with egg and butter boxes full of tea and sugar, saleratus, and cream of tartar, bottles of flavoring, and a striped bag of candy for me.

Lucy was right behind him, carrying a jug of molasses and a shoe box tied with string.

Edith had new shoes on her hands, as if her hands were feet. She was waving them and clapping the soles together. The toes and sides were black and very shiny, and they had gray cloth tops with black buttons.

"Brad, why in the world did you let her get patent leather?" scolded my mother. "First time they get wet they'll crack. Be a sight before Christmas."

"What she wanted," my father answered.

"Have to rub 'em with vaseline," my mother told Edith. "Every single morning."

Edith put the shiny black toe of one shoe against her cheek.

"Why have they got new shoes?" I asked, from far away.

"School starts next week. Girls can't go to school bare-footed. Not my girls, anyway."

22

"I have to have new shoes," I said. "I'm going to school next week."

"You'll go to school when you're old enough," said my mother. "And not before. That won't be next week. Now sit down, all of you. Dinner's about spoilt."

"I'll be old enough next week," I said, working my way onto my chair.

My mother's eyes flashed.

"Contradict me, will you, miss?"

My father touched her arm.

"Let it go, Martha," he said. "She don't know when next week is. She means she'll be old enough some time."

He put food on my plate.

I had not meant to contradict my mother. I was only thinking aloud. I knew that when Owen went to school, I would be old enough to go to school. It was as sure as if it had already happened, like the brook springing out of the mountain, the first cows, the Coldest Winter, the wars, and the wheels.

I ate my dinner that day, as I lived for nearly two years, apart with Owen in a walled garden entirely our own, into which no other person could intrude and into which only a few were ever invited.

I did not know or even wonder where Owen had been before he came to me. I remained entirely unaware of all that caused my parents and our neighbors a quick and growing anxiety — later proved justified — until it was explained to me long afterward. But what was known to them — though then unknown to me — is a part of this story which must now be told.

The Perrys had been among the first settlers in the valley, along with the Dennetts, Carters, Fernalds, McIntires, Browns, and a few other families who had since died out or moved north to other settlements. Among the five families which could recall no other home than the valley, there was a closeness of sympathy born of long association and frequent intermarriage. Elder Perry's mother had been a Dennett. Of all the babies born to Ephraim and Abigail Dennett Perry, only Daniel lived to grow up, and at the age of eighteen he answered the call of Abraham Lincoln and went South with the Union Army. He was gone and rarely heard from for three years. When he returned, he brought a wife with him, a city girl.

Ephraim had been a prime mover in the building of the valley church, and one of its strongest supporters. Daniel had gone to Sunday School there, and later sung in the choir. Now it had been closed for two years for want of a preacher. Our only religious gatherings were kitchen prayer meetings. Daniel, whose heart and mind had been open to the call of Abraham Lincoln, was now open to the call of the Lord. He decided to devote himself to study for the ministry. To his parents this was an answer to all their prayers in kitchen, field, and chamber. To his wife it was a confession of weakness, of a desire to be supported by his father and to escape the responsibility of providing his own family with comforts which did not exist in any isolated valley between two wooded hills. She stayed with Daniel long enough to bear a son, then went away, taking the baby with her.

Daniel did not follow them. By that time he was Elder Perry, preaching twice on Sundays and holding midweek prayer meetings, seasonal all-week revival meetings. The valley had no money with which to pay him a salary. His parents gave him food and shelter as long as they lived. After that he kept warm with the wood he cut in the hill pasture, ate what he grew in his garden and gathered in his orchard and from the fields and woods, and was grateful for the fresh meat valley men brought to him when they butchered — and the salt pork from their tubs of brine, the dish of pudding or plate of pie or loaf of bread the women sent in to him from their Saturday baking. Each year he spotted big trees ready for cutting in his pasture — enough of them to sell for a hundred dollars, which he kept in a sugar bowl and drew on for his tax, his church contribution, and any medicine he might need to send to town for. One year recently he had spotted enough trees to bring two hundred dollars and put a hundred-dollar bill into an envelope which he carried pinned to his undershirt. He told his neighbors where it was, and said it was to cover the cost of his last illness and burial.

Elder Perry was a good and simple man, profoundly patient and infinitely kind. That his neighbors regarded him as only so much better than themselves as an Elder should be is some indication of the qualities of character he had taught so well, by precept and example, that they were accepted in the valley as a matter of course, the natural inheritance, in varying amounts, of all God's children.

But one day, shortly before the fog which brought Owen to me, the nostrils of valley men and women flared to the scent of a new and sinister element in the atmosphere. A strange man and a boy were seen in the morning sitting with the Elder on his door rock; in the afternoon they were seen climbing his pasture hill, and again coming out of the woods toward his house. That night Hester Dennett (the eldest of three unmarried Dennett sisters) hurried over to Carters' with one of her velvet cakes and urged Frank to take it to the Elder, to find out what was going on. Frank returned with the report that the man and the boy were still there and might be for a long time. The boy had gone to bed. The man sat by the Elder's kitchen stove, in shirtsleeves, smoking, and told Frank that he was Todd Perry, the Elder's son.

"Ma died before I got my growth," said this man who called himself Todd Perry, "but she told me about Pappy here, and where I was born. I always meant to come back, but you know how young bucks are. I got married. My wife died when the kid was born and then I had him to raise, so I put him out to board and went to Texas building railroads. By ——, that's a wild country down there. Many's the time a rattler's sung behind my heels when I set on the side of the bed pulling my boots on. I've had enough of that, I can tell you. So I picked up the kid — he's most big enough to look after himself anyway — and come home to shake down with Pappy here and see what I can do for him."

This way of talking was strange to the valley. It was very strange to hear the Elder called Pappy.

But the Elder sat by, nodding and smiling.

"It is good," he told Frank. "Good to have my son and grandson with me."

Everyone knew that the Elder's bride had named her son Todd for the wife of the martyred President, but the old ones, peering out when the stranger set off for the first of his many Saturday walks to town, said he in no way resembled Rose Perry. The light-minded Rose had been small and red-haired, with pearly white skin, freckles, and a little, licking tongue. He certainly did not resemble the Elder, who was small and pale. The stranger was as big, dark, and rough as the fear and suspicion his presence aroused in the valley.

They waited to see him come back, late that night. He and Bill Brown came together.

"Look at him," they said. "Pitchpoling from one side of the road to t'other. Bad as Bill."

But everyone knew that tomorrow morning Bill would be in church, eyes swollen from crying, and ask to be prayed for; then he would go home and throw full bottles into the river; his children would hop in excitement to hear them splash. From Monday through Friday he would do the best he could by his family, though his best was not good enough to keep them warm in winter, or properly fed and clothed; Bill was weak in body and spirit. The valley waited to see whether the stranger was as bad as Bill, or worse.

Only the Elder felt no fear or suspicion, sheltered by his sublime faith in the wisdom and goodness of God by Whom all is ordained, and Whose ways pass all understanding.

Only the Elder . . . And I, with Owen in the garden.

The fact that my sisters put on their new shoes and began going away with lunch pails in the morning, coming back in the afternoon, had no more significance for me than when they had gone berrying in the long summer days. I waited for Owen, and next week.

I sat on a grassy bank where the goldenrod and wild blue asters were already blooming, and held in one hand a letter, in the other two pennies with which to buy a stamp for it. It was warm, and the pennies stuck to my palm. I was looking up at the sky, which was bright blue, and two small white clouds — only two — floated lazily on it. I thought they looked like sailboats on a sunlit sea, though I had not yet seen the sea, but only smelled it, nor sailboats except in pictures. The boats had names. One was *Owen,* and the other *Althea.* They were quite close to each other, and would soon be joined.

"Well! What you doing here?" he asked.

I looked around at him, delighted but not surprised, and started to scramble to my feet.

"Is it next week?" I asked eagerly.

He put his hand lightly on my head and stopped my scrambling. He threw himself on the bank beside me.

"Why do you ask that, Althea McIntire?"

"Because if it is I have to go get my shoes on. Girls can't go to school without shoes, my mother said. They haven't got me new shoes yet, but Daddy polished my old ones. They look almost like new."

"You want to go to school, do you?"

"Oh, yes."

"Why?"

"Why — because you go to school."

He laughed and pulled one of my braids gently.

"You have to have a better reason than that. It's no sense for anybody to go to school unless they want to learn things."

"I want to learn things. I've learned my name. It's Althea McIntire."

"That's good. But in school you would have to want to learn to write it." He took the letter out of my hand and pointed. "Like somebody else's name is written here."

I stared, fascinated.

"I want to learn to write it," I said at last, on a long, outgoing breath. "I want to learn to write your name, too. *Owen Perry.* I want to learn to write your name first."

He laughed again. I loved to hear him laugh. Then slowly the laughter went away except for the twinkle in

28

his eyes. I loved that twinkle on his serious face. He took a pencil stub from his pocket. I loved to see him reach into his pocket and take something out.

"I've got a surprise for you, Althea," he said. "This is next week, and school is right here today, and Teacher doesn't care about shoes. Can you do this?"

He drew an *O* on the back of the envelope, lightly, and passed the letter and pencil to me.

"Don't press down hard," he said. "We're going to have to erase it. This paper doesn't belong to us."

I made a mark, and he showed me how to erase it lightly. Whether serious or laughing, he did everything lightly.

"Try again," he said. "All the way around until you come to where you started." He put his hand over mine, to guide it. "See? That's an *O. O* is the beginning of my name."

I studied my *O* with deep pleasure.

"Look up, Althea," he exclaimed. "Those two little clouds! They've come together!"

He sounded surprised that they had come together. I was not surprised. I had known they were bound to come together. I began to make another *O*.

"Look up," he said again.

I lifted my eyes reluctantly from the paper.

"What do they look like to you, Althea?"

"Like two sailboats together," I said. "Upside down."

"Can you draw them? Like this?"

He drew them, and I copied his drawing.

"Now do you know what you've done? You've made the second letter of my name. You've made a *W*. To write my name, first you make an *O*. Then you make a *W*."

My achievement astonished me. I sat on the bank making *O's* and *W's* and erasing them. The sun was hot and the drying grass smelled sweet. There was no sound except from a bobolink in the meadow. Owen lay beside me with his chin in his hands. The mailman came and took my *O's* and *W's,* but I knew by then that I could always make more, whenever I wanted to and wherever I might be. Owen broke off little sprays of goldenrod and tucked them into my hair behind my ears, wove them into my braids.

He said, "You look pretty. Everything in the valley is pretty. The valley is the nicest place I've ever seen. You know what I think? I think heaven must be like the valley."

I thought so too.

When I went home, my mother asked, before she looked at me, "Where have you been? The mailman went long ago."

I said, "I've been to school. It's next week. Teacher didn't mind because I wasn't wearing shoes. I can make *O's* and *W's.*"

Now she was staring at me.

"There's no school today. It's Saturday. Who put that goldenrod in your hair?"

"Owen . . . He says heaven must be like the valley."

"More like the Garden of Eden after the snake moved in."

I was rummaging in the cupboard for a paper bag, and climbing up to reach a pencil kept with hatpins and corset stays in a broken-handled pitcher on the pantry shelf.

"See," I said. "*O* is like this — And *W* is like this. . . . *O* and *W* are the beginning of Owen's name."

I sat at the kitchen table making my marks on the torn brown paper, only half-aware of the buzz behind me and above my head. My mother was repeating what I had said. Edith was snickering and pulling at the goldenrod. Lucy was admiring, and saying she guessed Mrs. Carter would be surprised at me, and that there was not one thing to show Owen Perry was not a nice boy; handsome, too.

"Handsome is as handsome does," said my mother.

"Well, wasn't it handsome of him to teach her how to make letters like that, at her age?" asked my father, who had come in for his dinner.

"Time," snapped my mother, "will tell whether it's a good thing or the devil's works. I'd rather she learnt to write her own name."

"I'm going to learn that, too," I said. "As soon as I can write all of Owen's. Owen says it's no sense for anybody to go to school unless they want to learn things. I want to learn lots of things."

It was always a schoolday in the garden where I lived. I learned, on our porch steps, to make the rest of the letters in Owen's name; I learned there, too, the name of the place where the sun goes down, how different old wood smells from new wood, that a hedgehog is also called a porcupine and does not throw his quills, that the earth is a big ball, that the stars look small only because they are so far away. There was always playtime in the garden, too. Owen pushed me in the rope swing hung from an apple-tree branch, sending me out over and over again— but always there when I came back. He raked the bright maple leaves into piles for me to jump in, to bury myself in. When I was tired, he raked them into piles again and put them into grain bags from the shed.

One late afternoon he passed as I stood in the yard watching my mother take clothes off the line.

"Hi, Althea," he said, not stopping.

31

"Wait," I cried. "Aren't we going to school?"

"It's too cold to have school today."

I could not deny that it was very cold. The trees were bare and the sky was gray.

"We could have it in the barn. It's not so cold in the barn. In the hay."

He came into the yard a little way, but said, "I don't think your mother would want you to go to school in the barn. Would you, Mrs. McIntire?"

"Can't we, Mother? I *have* to go to school. I've started to learn to write my name. You said you wanted me to learn to write my name."

My mother dropped a handful of clothespins into the basket and said, "Oh, go into the kitchen. Both of you. I'll be there in a few minutes."

Into the kitchen!

"Come on, Owen," I cried.

But he said, "Let's help your mother get these clothes in, first. They're beginning to freeze."

It was no use. Valley men and women could not help liking Owen. Though I did not know then that he had other schoolmates than myself, he had many, and all alike loved and admired him. In the spelling matches he was always chosen captain; in the school yard, in whatever game was played, he was the leader; in drop-the-handkerchief every girl wanted to leave the red bandanna at Owen's heels though he usually dropped it to a boy because the boys ran a better race. If he showed special attention to a girl it was one to whom other boys paid none. His teacher, Mrs. Carter, said he was bright and quick at his studies; she said he was as mischievous as any, but that his mischief was neither vicious nor destructive, amusing even to her, so that she often had to stiffen her face to keep from smiling when she reprimanded him. The day he piled the entry full of cordwood from the shed so that the only way to get into the schoolhouse was through the window by which he had come out, she told him to clear a passageway and he did so. After school she told him to take the wood back where he had found it and he did so, whistling, though cordwood sticks were heavy for a boy his size, heavier to put where they belonged than to play a trick with. He was careful, she noticed, not to scar the entry paint. When he had finished, it was dark and they were alone. She took the black walnut ferrule from her desk, and told him to hold out his hand. He extended it, readily, meeting her eyes with an impish grin.

" 'Here I stand,' " said he, " 'before Miss Blodgett. She's going to strike and I'm going to dodge it.' "

She burst into tears and had to turn her face away.

"Oh, now, Mrs. Carter," Owen said, "don't do that. I was trying to make you laugh. I didn't suppose you'd cry. Stop it now, and go ahead and hit me. I wouldn't dodge. I was only fooling. . . . What are you crying for? I don't mind your hitting me. I've been hit a lot of times harder than you could hit."

She did not doubt this. Biting her lip, she put the ferrule back into the drawer.

"I can't strike you, Owen."

"I wish you would. I'd feel better. I've bothered you a lot."

"Well, I can't. You haven't bothered me nearly as much as you've helped me, since you came. Because of you, I hardly ever need the ferrule any more. Maybe that's why I can't use it."

"I ought to have been building the fire for you this

morning, instead of piling cordwood. I'll come early every morning this winter and build it, if you'll let me have the key. I'll sweep out, too. And wash the blackboards."

She took the key from the purse which hung by a silver chain from her belt and handed it to him. They went outside silently, and Owen locked the door. Then he took her books and papers and walked with her to the Carter place.

On the way he talked about the constellations in the sky. She knew the names of some of them. He told her the names of others.

Going up her lane he said, "I like these lanes with people living at the ends of them. I never knew there was a man like my grandfather, and people like the other people in the valley. I'm pretty lucky to be here. I ought not to make trouble for people like you. If I do, you ought to throw me out."

"Nobody who appreciates the valley will be thrown out of it," Mrs. Carter answered. "You are a good boy, Owen."

She told the others later, "I couldn't say more than that and I couldn't say less."

By now they were convinced that the Elder did not know what the stranger did on Saturdays. Poor Mattie Brown, running wildly across the field and through the woods to the Fernalds with the baby in her arms and Agnes dragging the twins, sobbed out as soon as she could get her breath, "It's two of them now!" or "It's two of them again! Both fightin' mad! They're a-stavin' up everything they can pull loose!" The Fernalds were used to having Mattie and her children spend Saturday nights in their shed chamber. Mattie had always baked her beans early, to be prepared, and left before daybreak Sunday morning to go home and pick up, patch up her belongings and Bill's. She said Todd was never there when she returned, and Bill never seemed to recall that he had not come home alone. Valley people supposed that the stranger let himself into the Elder's house long after the Elder was in bed and asleep. On Sunday morning he came to church with the Elder, very spruce in a blue coat with brass buttons and a pale silk necktie with a stickpin in the shape of a horseshoe. He lounged in a back pew and sang the hymns louder than anyone else, though people noticed that he did not know the words without the book. They admitted that he had a good, strong voice, but they resented the sanctimoniousness of his face, combined with a curious gleam in his eye, when Bill Brown made his flushed and downcast weekly appeal for his neighbors' prayers.

"There's a hypocrite," Hester Dennett told her sister Susan. "A complete hypocrite if I ever saw one. And I don't mean poor Bill. *He*'ll bear watching."

He was being watched.

It must be understood that the people of the valley then were a clan. What one of them knew they all knew; though some might know more than others of this or that, it was only a matter of degree. Whatever was entirely unknown to one was equally unknown to all. They shared a common religious, historical, national, social, educational and experiential inheritance. Isolated from the rest of the world since their word-of-mouth record began, they had become accustomed to going out into it from time to time; but having it — or any part of it — come in and settle with them was like having the ground cut from beneath their feet, so that they did not know which way to step.

35

It seemed a pity that the valley's first stranger was Todd Perry.

Not far behind him came others.

The fields provided the valley's everyday food supply. The forested mountains were the source of its water, its shelter, its meat, its beauty, and its wealth; enough for all forever, if carefully husbanded and frugally used. For more than two centuries, our mature trees had been selected with care, cut down by farmers, drawn by ox teams to Carter's Mill, and sawed to the dimensions needed by the owner for building or repair or to be taken out of the valley and sold.

One Sunday Bill Brown told Mattie, "I hadn't ought to get myself so mixed up. There's suthin' I got to remember, only I can't. Seems like somebody is a-coming here, somebody told me. Now who in tunket was it?"

The next day they came, two elegant gentlemen with mustaches and gold watches big as turnips, riding in a top buggy behind a sleek, lively little horse. The rug their feet rested on, as they rode, looked like fur and was the color of chimney bricks. They had a fringed shawl over their knees. They sat in the Brown dooryard and talked with Bill about the trees in his pasture. They gave him a cigar and looked hungrily at the mountains. As the ground was frozen but the snow had not yet come, they drove across the field to the edge of Bill's pasture and sat there talking while he stood in his barn doorway smoking his cigar. On their way back through the yard, they told Bill that the man who had talked to him on Saturday would be out soon to "go over the lot" with Bill and make him a cash offer for his trees.

The man who came on Tuesday had a big, soft, black mustache and bare, ruddy cheeks and chin. The elegant gentlemen's mustaches had been very small, with the ends waxed and twisted into sharp points, like slate pencils across their upper lips. Valley young men were all clean-shaven, valley old men so bearded that only their fore-heads, eyes, and cheekbones shone out among their white or hoary locks and whiskers. When these strangers who wore only mustaches had been and gone, though their faces, figures, and voices vanished, their mustaches, whether big and soft or small and sharp, floated on the empty valley air like the disembodied smile of the Chesh-ire Cat.

But the man who came on Tuesday was back again on Wednesday with another who looked enough like him to be his brother, though Bill said the name of the first was Peters, and of the second Anthony. They told Bill that the elegant gentlemen, the Anson Brothers, owned a sawmill which did not have to stay in one place and depend upon mill rights to running water, as Carter's Mill did, but was portable and operated by steam like railroad engines. It did not wait for logs to be hauled to it along the road, but was set up in the woods, near the trees to be sawed. Peters's work was to do the buying and set up the mill. Anthony was the sawyer. Both were Canadians, only lately come down from Nova Scotia. Bill counted for them the number of trees in his pasture which were ready for cut-ting. Mattie said he should have reserved enough of them to put new sills under the barn, but Peters offered him such a high price if he would sell without reservation that Bill said he could buy beams for the underpinning if he had to before his other trees were large enough to cut.

By Friday night the agreement had been made, the money passed, Peters and Anthony had made arrange-ments to board at the Fernalds', and on Saturday Peters

37

took Bill to town in his democrat wagon. They picked up Todd on the way. It was quite a luxury for Bill and Todd to ride out of the valley behind a high-stepping horse. The horse, Mattie said, when she reached Fernalds', was a smart critter to find her own way back to the Browns'. It was freezing cold out and Mr. Anthony insisted that Mattie and the baby have his room. "The bed's clean," he smiled. "I wasn't here last night, so it hasn't been slept in. I'll shake down on the kitchen couch, if that's all right with you, Mrs. Fernald." Then he asked Della if she would put fresh sheets on Peters's bed for the other Brown children. "I'll pay for their washing," he said. "I don't think Pete'll get this far tonight. If he does, I'll send him to the barn. Good enough for him."

Della Fernald, sixteen, looked at him out of deep brown eyes and said, "I'll be glad to, Mr. Anthony. It's mighty nice of you to feel this way for Mattie and the young ones. There won't be any charge for the washing. I'll do it myself. I love — I just love to wash and iron. . . . Don't you call it mighty nice of Mr. Anthony, Ma?"

Della's mother told my mother later that she could not deny it, though she did not sleep a wink that night for fear of what might be left in her beds after the Browns had gone, and went in there the minute they left to go over the quilts and featherbeds "with a finetooth comb." Luckily, she found no unwelcome visitors, but she could not rest until she had told both Della and Mr. Anthony why she had never put the Browns in her spare room before. For one reason, she did not dare, and for another it had never seemed necessary as Bill, by himself, had never undertaken to walk to town in the coldest weather.

"Now that he has companions," said Lottie Fernald, "and a horse to haul them, he may go every Saturday all winter, for all I know. I'm not stony-hearted. God knows I'd do anything I could for Mattie. But if I ever see a bug in a room of my house, I'll burn everything in the room quick as I can throw the stuff out of the window and set a match to it."

With Della's tear-filled eyes fixed on his face, Mr. Anthony said gravely, "I don't wonder, Mrs. Fernald. I should have thought of that. By next Saturday the mill will be set up and Peters will be gone. The horse will be for my use, and will not take Bill to town. I hope we'll have some snow before then, and that Della will go with me for a sleigh ride in the evening."

"It was wonderful to see," Lottie told my mother, "how fast Dell's tears dried up."

The women laughed together about this, but were agreed that Della must not ride outside the valley, and must be home before the sun went down. Though Bert Anthony was young — and handsome if you could forget his mustache — and though the fact that he neither drank nor condoned drinking, as well as that he had offered his protection to Mattie and the children, was greatly in his favor, still he was a stranger out of the wild north country to which presumably he would return when his work in the valley was done. Did not every honest man go home after work? And who could imagine what a home would be in the wild north country?

The snowstorm came. The mill was drawn in by four span of horses with huge, hairy legs, and set up in Brown's pasture. Two pair of the horses went out and returned, each drawing on sleds a small tar-papered shack. From the one window in each shack the faces of small children peeped as they passed. They had red cheeks and black, beady eyes. Bert Anthony said that these shacks were the

39

Frenchmen's camps, which followed the mill. The Frenchmen were the choppers, and wherever they went they
took their families with them. Who could imagine living
in a tar-paper shack in Brown's pasture in the dead of
winter?

Big pines at the edge of the pasture came screaming
down. Hardwood was cut to make the steam which ran
the saw. Todd was fireman, because he said he had done
this work on railroad engines. Eddie Fernald had the job
of marking the width and thickness of each board as it
came off the saw, before it dropped into the pit. Smoke
rose from the stack, the steam was up, the saw purred,
but snarled as it bit into the log. A pile of red sawdust
started and grew. The whistle blew shrilly at seven, at
twelve, at one, and again at five. Valley clocks began to be
set by the sawmill whistle.

But the day Owen and I cooked our Sunday dinner on
the marsh ice, there was no smoke, no snarl, and no
whistle. We had had subzero weather for three weeks,
but the night before a high wind had blown the ice clear,
and that day the weather had moderated slightly.

Owen had come over as soon as he changed his clothes
after church, and asked my mother if he might take me
on a sled to the marshes. He said he had apples and potatoes in his pockets, and we would build a fire and roast
them for our dinner. He promised that he would not take
me out of sight of the house. He reminded my mother
that she need not worry even about the main thread of
the marsh brook, as the ice was so thick everywhere that
the men were going to meet on the pond the next day with
ox teams, to cut and haul the blocks they would store in
their icehouses against the summer's heat. It was Owen's
habit to make these promises and explanations, but they

40

had become unnecessary. Though my mother did not understand why he wanted to spend time with me rather than with my sisters who were about his age, she had accepted it as a fact and was not suspicious of him. While Owen buttoned my leggings, she wrapped biscuits and fried fresh pork in wax paper, put them into a bag with some cookies, poured cocoa left over from breakfast into a bottle, and gave us an old pan in which to warm the cocoa, tin cups from which to drink it, and a long fork for holding the meat over the fire.

As we left she said from the doorway, "You see that her skirts don't get too near the flame, Owen."

He smiled and promised, "I will, Mrs. McIntire. Hang on tight, Althea."

I was whirled away as if in a chariot, which seemed to speed over the hill and across the meadow under its own power, with Owen racing ahead. The top layer of light snow spread like fans on either side of me, and embroidered my red mittens in feathery designs as I held tight to the side rails of the sled. The sun made a blinding glitter around me, but in the distance the frozen marshes had a bluish cast, reflected from the sky. Fascinated, I watched them come nearer until they were beneath me, and I rode in and out among the tufts of stiff, brown grass.

Owen held my chariot still until I had stepped from it and stood beside him.

A frozen world is not a dead world. It is alive and radiant, but still and pure and completely peaceful.

"Now we will get wood for our fire," Owen said.

We were at a side of Brown's pasture where no trees had yet been cut. We went in among them and Owen took a hatchet from his belt. He struck off small branches with neat, quiet clips and filled my arms with them, then filled his own.

"Does it hurt the trees to be cut?" I asked.

He shook his head.

"It's like when Gramps cuts my hair. I do it easy. It doesn't hurt."

"I don't mean this. I mean cut down. All down."

He shook his head again.

"I wondered about that too. I asked Gramps. He says, not if they're ready. He says if trees are old enough to be cut down, they're ready. Like people, he says, that have lived a good life are ready to die because it's the only way to get to live with God."

"Do trees go to live with God when they're cut down?"

"No. I said trees are ready to cut down when they're big enough, like good people are ready to die when they're old enough. Trees go to live with people. People go to live with God."

I rubbed my shoulder against a tree.

"Trees can live with me standing up," I said.

"Sure. But they can live with you in the floors you walk on, too, and in the roof that keeps the snow off you while you sleep, and in the chairs where you sit and the table where you eat and write. In your sled, even. . . . But this part we're going to burn is just the trimmings."

He knelt on the ice and I knelt beside him. I could feel its cold through my leggings. He made a nest of small pine boughs, took dry chips from his pocket and made a heap of them on the boughs, placed short pieces of wood crisscross on top. I placed my wood crisscross too.

"See," he said "We're making X's."

He took apples and potatoes from his pockets, brushing off bits of bark, and we tucked them in around the bottom of the pile. He struck a match against the side of his high boot and held the flame cupped between his hands until it grew strong. I marveled that it did not burn him.

The flame looked big inside his hands. It looked small when he laid it among the chips. It lay there, shielded from the wind, and flickered several times. I thought it might go out. But it reached a curl of birchbark and turned the edge of it red. The center of the curl became transparent. Then the whole curl leaped and ignited a pitchy piece of pine. A minute later the boughs were crackling, and long flames ran up all round like the sides of a fiery bowl.

I jumped up and down with delight.

"Don't get too close," Owen said.

He put his hands on my shoulders to hold me back. We stood looking at what we had made. I felt it hot on my face as I had felt the ice with my knees.

"It's like a thought," Owen said.

I waited.

"A thought in a person's mind," said Owen. "It might be a good thought or a bad thought. It might just drift out and disappear, the way sparks do. Or you might keep it in your mind while it grows bigger and hotter, like the match, until you can't hold it any longer, and put it in a place where you want it to burn better because you want to see what it can do. Outside it looks small, as if it couldn't do anything. But if it sets something else afire, and that something else sets something else afire, then it has done a lot. You may not know how much for a long time. Because once a thought catches on, nobody can put it out. It isn't like a fire that way. It —"

He broke off. He did not think I understood. He picked me up and put me on the sled, ran across the ice, pulling me behind him, sliding on his heels, letting me fly past him, and pulling me around in swift, flying circles.

At last he stopped and laughed.

"There's frost on your nose," he said.

Our fire had burned down to coals. He dug out the potatoes and apples to cool, set the pan on the coals and poured the cocoa into it. Sitting on my sled, I held the fork to which he had fastened a piece of meat. He made a fork from a branch to heat his meat on. The fat dripped onto the coals and sizzled. The cocoa began to steam. He pulled the pan off and poured cocoa into the tin cups, spilling some and getting soot on his mittens. The smell of hot food on the winter air was better than the smell of hundredleaf roses in June. A crow cawed. . . .

We began to eat and, as if it were a signal, as if the raucous bird had called her, a girl came out from among the trees onto the ice.

She was almost exactly my size but somehow I knew that she was older. Her cheeks were as red as the fire and her black hair hung in matted strands around it. She wore no cap, her coat was ragged, and her hands were bare, chapped with cold, and grimy.

She was coming toward us and kept on coming until she was close to us. Then she pointed at herself, smiling, and said, "Marie."

Owen said, "Hi, Marie. I'm Owen. And this is Althea."

She made some strange sounds, waving her grimy hands.

I said, "I think you are a witch. Get off my ice. Go away."

She stood there laughing.

Owen said, "She's no witch. She's a girl like you. What she said was nice. What you said wasn't very nice, was it? You hungry, Marie?"

He cut open a potato with his jacknife and gave it to her. She bobbed her head, made more strange sounds, and began eating the potato, soot and all.

"What she says isn't nice. She doesn't say anything. She can't talk."

"Maybe she thinks we can't talk because she can't understand us. But you can tell when anybody says nice things. It shows in their faces. She's hungry. Watch now. Want this, Marie?"

He cut his slice of meat in two, put half inside a biscuit and gave it to her.

"See her face light up, Althea?"

I couldn't see anything on her face but soot and crumbs. She made more sounds.

"Why can't she talk like us?"

"Why can't we talk like her? It isn't our way, that's all. Nobody ever taught us. She must live with the choppers. She's a French girl."

"I'm an American girl," I said proudly. He had taught me that himself.

"She's an American girl too. She's French the way you're Scotch."

"She doesn't belong in the valley."

"Oh, yes, she does. While her father is chopping wood in the valley."

He gave her an apple and a cookie. They were smiling at each other. In a place that I could not touch, I hurt.

I asked, "Do you like her like you like me?"

"I don't like anybody else like I like you. I don't like anybody else like I like anybody else. But I like everybody that's nice."

"You said she was nice and I wasn't."

"I said what she said was nice and what you said wasn't.

That's different. Everybody says something that isn't nice, once in a while. But if you stop thinking it, you stop saying it."

Marie held out her empty hands and Owen gave her another cookie.

I didn't like cocoa unless it was warm and mine had grown quite cool.

I said, "She can have the rest of my cocoa."

"Give it to her, then."

I held it out. She took the cup and drained it. It must have tasted very good to her for as she returned the cup to me, she crouched beside the sled and kissed my legging-covered knee. When she turned up her face, I could see the light on it through the soot from the potatoes and apples. She was making sounds, and I thought she was saying thank you, though I did not know why it took her so long.

I said, "You're welcome," and tried to smile at her.

"Good girl," Owen nodded. "Look, you stand up a minute, while I give Marie a ride on the sled. Eat your dinner now. You haven't eaten much of anything."

I stood up. He motioned. Marie laughed and lay on her stomach on the little sled, her long thin legs waving. Owen sped up and down the ice, letting the sled go ahead of him on the turns and spinning her around as he had spun me. Her laughter danced across the marshes and echoed back from the woods. When I am excited, I am very quiet, but excitement made her laugh. It sounded like suddenly shaken sleighbells.

I ate my meat and biscuit. There was only one cookie left and I did not eat it.

When they came back I gave it to Marie, to make up for the cocoa which I had given to her only because I did not want it.

46

She jumped up, snatched the cookie, laughing, and pointed at me and at the sled, looking at Owen.

"She wants you to ride now," he said. "You women will be the death of me. Get on."

Marie ran toward the woods.

"Is she going home?" I asked.

"I guess so."

"I understand her when she laughs."

"Sure, we all laugh in the same language. I like to hear people laugh, don't you?"

I had never thought about it. But at the first whirl I began to laugh because Owen liked to hear people laugh and because Marie — if she should hear it — would understand it. Laughing in the whirls felt good, and I laughed in every one.

When we came back to where the fire had been, it had gone out. Marie was coming back across the ice. She had a handful of red berries, as red as her cheeks, and gave them to me.

I said, "Thank you."

She did not understand the words, but bobbed her head and laughed, so I laughed too. Owen laughed with us, throwing his head back. Marie ran laughing across the ice. At the edge of the woods, she called back, *"Merci! Merci!"* and disappeared.

"What did she say?" I asked Owen.

He was putting the cups, fork, and sooty pan into a paper bag.

"I don't know. It doesn't matter."

"I know what she said. She said 'Thank you.' "

"How do you know?"

"It was the same sound she made whenever we gave her anything."

He looked at me with respect.

"Golly, I guess you're right, Althea."

On the way home I said, "We had a good school today. We learned that everybody laughs in the same — the same —"

"Language," he shouted back. Then he stopped and came back to me where I sat on my sled in a great expanse of snow turned pink by the setting sun. "Yours is the prettiest, though, Althea. You laugh the prettiest. Maybe because you're the luckiest." He tightened the scarf under my chin.

I knew I was very lucky.

Valley men told Bill Brown, "They're chopping trees up there that haven't got three quarters of their growth. You noticed?"

Bill nodded. He said he guessed those Frenchmen were all too handy with an ax. He had mentioned it to Eddie Fernald. Eddie said he thought some of the logs coming into the mill were pretty small.

A few days later valley men asked Eddie, "What's going on up there in Bill's pasture? You must be marking down mighty small figgers. The Frenchmen chop everything they come to. What you getting out, beanpoles?"

Eddie shrugged.

"I spoke of it to Bert last night. He says that's the way Bill sold it. Everything but the ground."

"He meant lumber fit to cut. Any fool would know that."

"Maybe. But the Anson Brothers are no fools. Neither was Peters, when he wasn't drunk. Bill sold 'em everything there but the ground. Bert's orders are to saw everything he can. They use the small stuff for boxboards.

Hardwood goes to keep up the steam and heat the choppers' camps. You sure get ahead faster when you strip as you go. We'll be through on Bill's by the end of the month."

Frank Carter, my father, and other valley men saw a gleam in Eddie Fernald's eyes which had never been there before. They turned away, perplexed. When the mill went out of Bill's pasture, and the stacked boards had been hauled away, nothing was left there but the ground, not even one big seed pine from which small pines might grow. Bill had only his rundown farm and the money the Ansons had paid him. The money would not last Bill long. His family's suffering in the past was mild beside what it would be in the future.

But they had money now. Bill bought a new cookstove for Mattie, a pair of horses for himself, new coats and boots for all the children.

The Elder's way of life also improved. Todd had worked every day at the mill. The Elder now had a chunk stove to warm his East Room where he slept, and a new suit for preaching. Todd bought a driving horse to take Bill and himself to town on Saturday; on Sunday, he took the Elder to church.

When the mill moved out of Brown's pasture, it moved into Fernald's.

Valley men asked, "Are you going to let them take everything but the ground on yours, Eddie?"

Eddie grinned. The gleam was brighter in his eye. His pasture was twice the size of Bill's, and had many times as much lumber.

He said, "No papers have been passed yet. I don't know just what I'll do. Mill's closing down till next winter, anyway. It's only setting here till snow comes again."

"You'd better save enough to build a piece onto the barn to hold your riggings. Don't do 'em any good to be left out to the weather the way they are."

Eddie said he knew that all right. He said he guessed he knew as well as anybody else what farms needed.

He startled the other men by adding, "What a farm don't need is woods. Another thing it don't need is mountains. Another thing it don't need is rocks."

Eddie knocked his cap back on his head and thrust his thumbs under his suspenders.

Frank Carter told him, "Man that knows his farm don't need rocks ought to dig 'em out of his land, same as I have. Any I can't dig out, I blast out."

Eddie said something about places where there were no rocks to be dug or blasted out. Nobody knew what he meant. Nobody gave it much thought.

After a minute's silence, my father said, "A farm needs water. Without the mountains for it to run out of and down from, and without trees to hold it in the ground, where would you get it?"

"Some places," Eddie said mysteriously, "they get it from away down under. Comes spouting up from a hundred feet below, pure as if it had been boiled. And the land so flat and the air so thin and dry and clear you can watch a ball game forty miles off."

They would have thought he had been drinking if they had not known that Eddie was not a drinking man.

"We better go over to Bill's," Frank told my father. "Talk to him about that underbrush that's strewed all over his pasture."

There is a time of year after the frost goes out of the ground and before the leaves come on when there is greater danger of forest fires than at any other season except the end of a hot, dry summer. Before that time came valley men had bunched and burned like cornstalks the brush the mill had left behind. Now there was left, where the Brown pasture had been cool and dark with trees great and small, only jagged stumps shining like picked bones in the sun.

Now there was left in the Fernald house only Eddie and Lottie. Della had stood up with Bert Anthony before the Elder to be married, and with Bert had gone north. They would be back, Lottie said, by time to saw again. But Lottie was lonely without Della. The only near neighbors she had were the choppers' families whose camps had followed the mill into the Fernald pasture; and Lottie said shortly, "I have no truck with them."

It was spring, and I could print not only Owen and Althea, but the name of anyone whose name I knew, because I had learned the alphabet. Wherever Owen took me, he carried a small book, a scratch pad, and a pencil. He had borrowed the small book of Mrs. Carter. It had a picture in color on each page, and words beneath it. The picture on the first page was of a little girl in a sunbonnet. She was running along beside blue water, and the sun was rising out of the water. The words said, "Good morning, dear." It was the sun and the blue water, the sky and the golden sand, greeting a little girl at the beginning of everything, before mountains and springs, before people and cows and wheels and wars, before parents and sisters, sleds, sawmills, and Frenchmen; but only an instant before Owen. I was that little girl and it was Owen I was running to meet. Somewhere beyond the edge of the picture there was a tree, and Owen sitting in it. I had spied him and was running toward him, while the sun

51

in the sky and the waves on the beach called, "Good morning, dear."

I understood now that Mrs. Carter was Owen's teacher, as he was mine, and that the school in which Owen studied was in many ways unlike the schools in which he taught me. He described it to me as we sat on stone walls, tying together, with everlasting, the mayflowers we had picked at the edge of the woods; or waiting for a mother robin to leave her nest so that Owen could hold me up to count her eggs — for now I could count, also.

I asked, "When will I go to that school?"

Owen did not know. He said my mother would decide. He thought perhaps I would go in the fall, since I could read and write and count.

I asked my mother when I would go to Mrs. Carter's school, and she said, "When you're six. That's soon enough to start the rounds. All you've had so far is mumps on one side."

I did not know what she meant. It was not important to me. I was richly content to stay exactly as I was for another year or forever, with no change anywhere. But change is everywhere and constant; there is no hiding place where it will not sooner or later show itself.

Owen came into the yard with masses of pond lilies, their long stems wound around his arms. He slid them off onto the grass, pumped a wooden tub full of water, and showed me how to loop the stems so that the blossoms would float on the surface.

"See?" he said. "That's how they looked in the pond where I found them. It is a round pond away over in the woods. From all sides, almost to the middle of it, the lilies grow thick. The center is like the blue hub of a wheel, or like a blue saucer."

"I wish I could go to the pond."

"It's too far. Your legs are too short. So I brought the pond to you." He was leaving the center open, like the blue hub of a little wheel, or like a little blue saucer. "Now smell, Althea. Put your cheek against them, shut your eyes, and breathe deep."

I floated with the lilies. I was on the pond, away over in the woods.

When I lifted my head, blinking, he rubbed his hand dry on his overalls and wiped my face and forehead.

"School is like that," he said. "When your legs are very short, it comes to you. People bring it. The wind and the sun, trees, flowers, birds, animals, everything brings it to you. When your legs are longer, you go to the school that's nearest. For us, that's Mrs. Carter's school. It has books and maps and blackboards and a globe that is round like the earth with pictures of all the countries of the world on it. Lately Mrs. Carter has got a big chart that tells what is beyond the earth — the stars that are suns, and the stars that are planets."

He said Mrs. Carter was a fine teacher. She made people want to read the books she had, and study the maps and charts, and work out hard problems on the blackboard. She taught people all she knew, and then she told them they should go to another school farther away to learn more than she knew, and said that by and by they should go to a school still farther away to learn still more.

"How does she know there is more to know, if she doesn't know it?"

"Same as you know there is more to know than you know."

"How does she know where the other schools are, so far away?"

"She has been to one. For two years. In the village. It is called an Academy. She says she couldn't stay long enough. She should have stayed four years. And she has read about colleges. They are the farthest away, and teach the most."

"Did anyone ever go to one?"

"Nobody we know. But doctors have been to them, and lawyers, and some ministers, and the people who wrote the books we study. Mrs. Carter says I should go there."

"Why?"

"I don't know. But when you go to school, I think she will tell you you should go there."

"Why?"

"I don't know that, either. But I think she will say so."

"I will go if you go. Will you go, Owen?"

"Maybe. I'm thinking about it. Trouble is — I don't want to leave the valley."

"I don't either. Let's not leave the valley."

"Well, we won't very soon, anyway. There's a lot more yet the valley can teach us. There are other schools beside Mrs. Carter's in the valley, Althea."

Three boys, passing, called to Owen. They were all bigger than he. One was Ted Carter; the other two were choppers' sons, brothers of Marie, Pete and Joe Luneau. Ted had a thick brown glove on his left hand and was punching it with a ball. They wanted Owen to play a game with them in the field across the lane where the grass had been cut.

They said other boys were coming into the field from up the road.

"Climb on my back," Owen said to me. "Hang on tight.

54

I'll put you up in the tree hammock. You can watch the game from there. I'll be back soon."

He left the pad and pencil and our little book with me, but I did not use them. I sat for a long time watching the boys throw the ball, hit it with a slab of wood, and run. I could see that Owen, though he was the smallest, could throw the ball hardest, hit it the farthest, and run the fastest. This made me very proud, but when I was sure of it, I looked down at my lily pond and imagined that in its blue center there was a flat boat on which a little house was built. I lived in it, with Owen. I baked a cake for him in a tiny oven, frosted it pink and sprinkled it with coconut. I poured milk for him from a tiny pitcher. We sat on the side of the boat to eat, with our feet touching the cool water. He sang a song to me, very softly, and I lay half asleep with my head on his shoulder. The fragrance of the lilies was all around, and the tight web of their strong stems was like an invisible wall protecting us from whatever lay beyond it.

Then I heard him laugh, and opened my eyes. He was sitting cross-legged on a branch beside me.

"So this is what you do while I get six home runs, and win the game! Sleep! A great mascot you are!"

"I knew you'd win the game. I saw you throw the hardest and hit the farthest and run the fastest. I wasn't sleeping."

"What were you doing, then?"

"Thinking."

"What about?"

I was silent.

He took a penny from his pocket, tossing and catching it. "A penny for those thoughts."

I sat watching him until I knew what I could say.

55

"I'm thinking — what other schools are in the valley beside ours, and Mrs. Carter's?"

I suppose it was a long way, even for Owen, from baseball to school. He grew sober, and as the laughter slowly left his face, so did the flush from exercise in the heat. Up where we were it was cool and quiet. I waited. We were sitting on the boatside, with our feet in the water, and I had baked him a cake. . . .

He said every person was a school where other people studied to learn that in some ways all people are alike, but in more ways each person is different from any other. Every house was full of living books.

He said the Dennett house was a very important school because it had not only people in it, but history. He said the Dennetts had been the first family in the valley to move out of a cabin into a house with five rooms and a loft, with clapboards and many windows. Before the Revolutionary War they had built the house in which Miss Hester, Miss Susan, and Miss Mary lived now; the big, black house with a chimney at each of the four corners. The house was full of strange things the first Dennetts had brought home from all over the world; shelves and cupboards and drawers were full of these strange and beautiful things. Miss Mary knew where they all came from and could tell stirring tales of Dennett adventures on great ships and in foreign ports. Miss Susan was more interested in books, papers, old letters, and other records of our own country, the United States. She kept them in trunks and read them over and over. Miss Susan supplied the information. Miss Hester used it. Miss Hester was the lecturer. She came to Mrs. Carter's school sometimes to watch the flag pulled to the top of the white pole, and to hear the children give the salute.

56

"You'll learn the salute, someday, Althea. *I pledge allegiance to the flag . . . and to the republic for which it stands; one nation . . . , indivisible, with liberty and justice for all.*"

Owen said these words low, but slowly and distinctly. They sounded like magic words to me. I did not know what any of them meant, but the sound of the free-running brook was in them, and of wind in the pine trees, and of marching feet.

I asked, "Are they magic words?"

"They're better than magic. Miss Hester tells us what they mean, when she comes to school. Mrs. Carter says Miss Hester told her about things like that when she was a little girl. They mean —"

"I didn't know the Dennett sisters were ever little girls."

"All women were little girls once, silly. Same as all little girls are going to be women."

"Lucy and Edith and I are going to be the — the McIntire sisters?"

"You are the McIntire sisters, aren't you?"

"Well, not . . ." I looked at him helplessly. My throat began to swell and burn. I knew that the Dennett sisters were old and lived together alone. "They're old. I don't want to be old with Edith and Lucy. Without any father or any — any —"

He seemed to know what was in my mind.

"Don't worry," he said. "You won't."

He sat looking across at me, and his eyes said the same as his words.

Then he went back to where he had been when I interrupted.

"Anyway, I didn't mean when Miss Hester was a little girl. I meant when Mrs. Carter was a little girl, Miss

57

Hester was the teacher, like Mrs. Carter now. Miss Hester taught her about this country we live in, how big it is, and how it won its independence, and can't be divided, because we are the United States. In the beginning there were only thirteen states, so there are thirteen red and white stripes in our flag, but now there are forty-six states, so there are forty-six stars in our flag. You could count the stripes, Althea, but there are more stars than you could count yet. That's how many states there are. More than you could count. All united. Because we chose our own government and wrote our own Constitution, and believe in liberty and justice for all. Liberty is being free. And justice is being fair. That's what the flag means. That's why we salute it. Because men have fought and died for it, and would again."

"How does the salute begin — that I will learn?"

"*I pledge allegiance*. That means I promise to be true."

"I pledga legions."

"*To the flag.*"

"To the flag."

"*I pledge allegiance to the flag.*"

"I pledga legions — to the flag."

"That's good, Althea! That's good!"

A breeze stirred the leaves about our heads and the sun came through in soft splotches. I sat in an imaginary boat on a transplanted lily pond, in a hammock high in the branches of a maple tree which overlooked the whole farm of my father and his father and his father's father, the whole valley from mountain to mountain, and for the first time was aware of a land stretching away in all directions beyond the mountains, of other mountains and valleys and fields and roads, and of people in many ways unlike valley people but all alike in that they had a flag which

58

meant being united and being free and being fair; a flag for which men had died, and would again. It was my land and they were my people. It was my flag. I had promised to be true to it, and Owen had said, "That's good, Althea."

Later he told me there was still another school in the valley. Besides our school, and Mrs. Carter's school, and the school of people, and the school of history, there was the church school where the Elder was the teacher and taught the book of God.

"Of course every good school teaches that," Owen said, "but the church has to teach it to the other schools first and all the time, or they wouldn't know it."

"You haven't told me about God. Tell me."

"I guess I haven't told you because you know as much as I do. I didn't know anything about Him until I came to live with Gramp. I felt things about Him, but I didn't know things about Him. I had never been to church or read the Bible. I heard a little of it read aloud each morning in school, and we repeated the Lord's Prayer; but nobody talked about it. I didn't know what it meant. Gramp reads from the Bible every night and explains it to me. On Sundays he explains it more."

"My father reads the Bible every night. But he doesn't read it out loud. He doesn't explain it."

"It's hard to read and explain, unless you know how. Gramp knows how. But your folks live by it as much as they can. So do the Carters and the Dennetts, and lots of other people in the valley. Even Bill Brown."

"Bill Brown gets drunk. God doesn't like for people to get drunk."

"So Bill wishes he wouldn't. He tries not to. Gramp

says God loves Bill for trying not to, even if he does. Gramps says a craving for drink is a cross some men carry, and there must be some reason why they have to carry it. He says everything that happens, and everything we do or don't do has a reason; a good reason, though often we can't see it, and good will come even of evil in time, but it may be a long time. Everything is according to God's plan, Gramp says, but we don't know what the plan is. We only know it must be good, because God made it."

"Did God plan for Bill to get drunk when He doesn't like for people to get drunk?"

"He must have, because Bill does. Maybe He planned it that way so other people in the valley would see what it does to Bill and his family, so other people in the valley would try to help them. Maybe someday something wonderful will happen that never would have happened if Bill hadn't been the way he is. Gramp says God made each of us the way we are, and all He expects is that each one of us should do as well as he possibly can. Gramp says He doesn't expect birds to swim or fish to fly, or He would have taught them how."

"Maybe someday He will."

Owen nodded.

"If you can believe that, Gramp would say you've got the faith that can move mountains."

I looked across the valley. Would anyone want God to move the mountains, standing there strong and dark and green, growing bluish toward the top, and rimmed in gold from the sun?

Owen followed my glance and my thought. He touched my hand and shook his head.

"Not that kind of mountains, Althea. Mountains of trouble. Mountains of fear. Mountains of ignorance.

60

Mountains of evil. Gramp says they get big, like when you roll a snowball across a field, when people don't know God well enough to trust Him. If we trust Him enough, they disappear."

I knew then that I trusted Him, because I could not even imagine bad things that big. Bill Brown, drunk, was bad, but he was only man-size, he was drunk only on Saturday night, and I had never seen him that way. Trouble was to make you cry, and I did not cry often and I had never cried long. Fear was feeling afraid, and I had never been afraid more than a minute; a little fear like a squeak of a mouse that ran away, like a splinter in my thumb which someone took out with a sewing needle. I did not know what ignorance was. Bad things were small. Only good things were big like the mountains. Trusting God was like being with Owen in a boat on a lily pond, or high in a tree; nothing but good could come there.

"I trust Him," I said complacently.

Owen nodded.

"Sure. I guess all children are born trusting, and nobody has ever taken it away from you. Don't let them, either."

"You trust Him, don't you?"

I was surprised that he did not answer at once. He looked off over my head, across the field and the river, to the ridgepole and chimney of his grandfather's house. For the first time since I had known him there was no twinkle in his eyes. His lips were hard against his teeth.

"You trust Him, don't you, Owen?" I repeated urgently.

"I try," he said at last, still not looking at me. There was something like hoarseness in his voice. "Mostly I do. But sometimes —"

He broke off, giving his head a shake, and smiled at me.

61

"Don't forget, Althea," he said, "I wasn't born in this valley, like you. I'm older, and I'm just learning some things you've always known. It'll take me a while, Gramp says. We'd better go down now. I'll get you going good in the swing before I leave. You can let the old cat die, and by then I guess you'll have to hyper to supper."

I thought, "Owen has three ways of talking. The way he brought with him, and the way we talk, and the way he's learned from the Elder and Mrs. Carter and Miss Hester and all the books."

As I climbed into the swing I said, "I like to have you to come back to."

"What do you mean by that?"

"After you push me. When I get far out, I want you to wait and push me again. I don't like to let the old cat die. It feels too empty. It feels like the end of things."

"I'll push you five times," Owen said. "Then if you don't want to stop, push yourself with your feet whenever you can touch the ground. You can keep going by pushing with your whole body, too, in the air. You don't have to let the old cat die. After I give you a good start, you can keep going as long as you want to."

I counted the pushes, one by one. After the fifth one, he said, "Here I go to supper. Good night, Althea!"

From far out, I looked down on him jumping from the bank into the lane.

I called, "Owen! Who cooks your supper?"

He answered, "My father. Now the mill isn't running. He's a good cook, too. Gramp says he's getting fat on the meals he gets this summer. We're going to have fried pickerel tonight. I caught four this morning when it rained. They bite best in the early morning when it rains."

62

He waved and disappeared.

I began to lean far backward as the swing went out and forward as it went back, and kept going so well that I had not once touched my feet when Lucy called from the window that supper was ready. My father, coming from the barn with full milk pails, set them down to stop me in midflight.

"You're quite a swinger, Allie," he said, "for five years old."

I told him, "Owen taught me."

"You and Owen are great friends, aren't you?"

I nodded, walking beside him toward the porch.

"Well, I guess he's a good friend to have," my father said quietly.

The goldenrod and wild asters turned the roadside blue and yellow again. Mrs. Carter's school reopened, and I found that I could swing myself high enough to see the flag blowing in the wind above the trees.

"I pledga legions," I said over and over, "to the flag. I pledga legions to the flag. I promise to be true, to be true, to be true. I pledga legions."

One Saturday Owen brought the flag in its canvas bag, saying Mrs. Carter had told him he might. He spread it on the grass under the blue October sky. I counted the stripes. I learned to count the stars. Owen said that the blue of the flag was for the truth we knew, the wonder of being free, the duty to be fair; the red of the flag was for the courage we must show; the white of the flag for the purity of our belief in God and of our wish and need to be guided by Him in all we did as citizens, as states, and as a nation. I learned about the republic for which it stands. . . . *I pledge allegiance to the flag . . . and to the*

63

republic for which it stands. . . . Owen said our country was a republic because we had free elections in which we chose the men who ran the government and made the laws in a city where great buildings were gleaming white with gilded domes. He said the name of this city was Washington, for the First President of our United States.

"Is the White City, Washington, very far away?"

"It seems far now. Maybe because we've never been there."

"Will we go there someday?"

"We should. Everybody should. Because it's our capital. It belongs to us."

"We will go," I said confidently. "Someday."

After that, when I was swinging high, I often saw, beyond the red, white, and blue of the schoolhouse flag and over the top of the higher mountain, the pillars and domes of a white and gold city, my capital, named Washington for my First President.

"I pledga legions to the flag," I sang. "I will be true, I will be true, to the flag and to the capital and to the republic for which it stands. I will be free. I will be fair. I will be good. I pledga legions . . ."

But it soon grew too cold for swinging. Snow came, and the mill started up. It was a dark and noisy winter in the valley. Outdoors there was the crash of trees, the whine of the saw, the spewing of black smoke, and the shrill whistles which hung on the air long after the sound had died away, and again long before it burst out again. Indoors the women talked all day; they talked to each other face to face as they ran in and out on anxious visits; they talked to each other by twisting a handle to make sharp, jangling signals and speaking into a black hole which they

64

called the mouthpiece, for a telephone line had been strung from house to house; they talked to themselves. In the long evenings they talked to the men, and the men talked, too, more than they ever had before. Never before had so much been happening that valley men and women could do nothing about but talk! Words became a substitute for muscles, which they would have preferred to use, but which in this emergency were useless.

Women refused now to set their clocks by the whistle. They hated the whistle.

"It is another snake," said my mother. "Like they lay in the rock piles where the biggest raspberries grow. Even when they're still and you can't see them, you can't forget them, for that's just when they hiss. It's better to keep watching for them, so you'll see when they raise their ugly heads. . . . Lottie, are you going to let them strip your pasture like they done Brown's?"

"I can't do anything about it." Lottie's voice came thin and small through the storm into our kitchen. "Eddie says it's up to them. He sold everything to 'em. Even the ground. He got a good price, I guess. He won't tell me how much."

"Didn't you have to sign before he could sell?" demanded my mother.

"Course I did."

"Then you was a fool to do it. I'd have died first."

"Sometimes I wisht I had."

"Where's your spunk, Lottie? You used to have a-plenty."

"You don't know how Eddie is lately. He struts around like an old turkeycock. Don't hear a word I say. All I've got to be thankful for is that Della's home, for company. She don't feel very well, though. She's expecting."

65

After a minute my mother said, "I suppose she is expecting something good. If she is, she's the only one of us that seems to have any reason to. I feel as if the big mountain was rumbling, ready to explode at any minute and wipe us all out. Might be just as well if it did."

"You mustn't think that way, Martha. I try not to. Sometimes, I can tell you, seems as though I don't know which way to turn. But the Elder says the Lord will help us if we ask Him."

"The Lord," snapped my mother, "helps them as helps themselves. And nobody is helping themselves around here but the Anson Brothers. They've got their snouts into the valley as if it was a trough. Question is, where they'll be uprooting next."

This question was in the mind of every valley man and woman. Bill Brown, the ne'er-do-well, sold every stick of wood in his pasture right down to the ground; there would be nothing worth cutting on it again for fifty years, maybe a hundred, maybe never. Surly Eddie Fernald — suddenly become bright-eyed, close-mouthed, a strutting turkeycock — had sold his pasture right down through to China. If land belonging to the Anson Brothers was left littered with tops drying to tinder, who would have a right to clear it? If it was left uncleared and the sun found a whisky bottle there to shine on long enough in the early spring, or if lightning struck there in the late summer, the valley might become a blazing caldron. And when the mill left Fernald's pasture, where would it go?

In yards and barns, along the road and lanes, tramping by twos and threes through the snowy woods on Sunday afternoons and touching a tree here and there as they might the head of a good dog or a gentle child, each man told the others that no tree should be cut until it was

66

ready for cutting, that without trees the valley would be a desert canyon where no one could live; and what good then would money be? But they all knew Bill Brown would once have agreed, and Eddie Fernald before Bert Anthony came there to board. The mill would not leave the valley without cutting more than two great gashes through it, if the Anson Brothers had their way. They felt besieged and wondered if there was a third weak spot in their ranks, a third man who from stupidity or greed, or both, would open a postern gate to the enemy. They listened not only to one another's words but to the timbre of the voices, and watched the eyes to see whether they shifted, to gauge the degree of determination.

In one another's kitchens and back and forth over the wire, women said, as my mother did: "He'll never ask me to sign. He knows better. I'll die before I sign. He ain't even thinking of it. I'd know if he was." Some spoke as if they were shooting off guns, which was my mother's way; others grimly, doggedly; others low and sadly. But there was not a wife in the valley who did not know that when you married a man you had to live with him or leave him. In all the years, the only woman who had ever left a valley man was Rose Perry, and she had never been a valley woman. To live with a man one sometimes had to endure worse than death; they all knew that. The first time Bill Brown had come home drunk after he was married, and beaten Mattie until she got away and ran to the house of her mother, Mattie had sobbed all night in her mother's bed like a child with a long nightmare. In the morning when he came for her, she saw him coming and hid up-chamber.

"Mat!" called her mother sternly from the foot of the

stairs. "Bill's here. He wants you. He says he'll never touch another drop."

"I don't believe him."

"Whether you do or not, you married him. He's brought your coat. Come down and put it on."

Mattie, wide-eyed and dewy-cheeked then, her body and legs thin and straight but her breasts beginning to fill out for the first of the big brood to come, crept to the head of the stairs and stood there trembling.

"Marm, I'd ruther die," she whispered.

"Maybe you had," replied her mother calmly, "but a woman can't always have her druthers. Come down here."

She knew she sounded as if she had no heart, but, as she told my grandmother afterward, her heart had swelled until it seemed to fill her whole body and was pushing so hard to get out that she throbbed with pain from the top of her head to the soles of her feet.

When Mattie reached her, she said low, "Next time start sooner. But unless your mind's made up to go back when he's over his jag, don't come where I am."

Mattie's mother never forgot, as long as she lived, how Mattie looked that morning going into the kitchen where Bill stood and letting him put her coat on her as if she were a wax doll that had been laid too close to the stove where the heat had taken the color from her face and twisted her vacant smile into a grimace.

"But 'twas best," Olive Waite said years later, as my grandmother sat beside her deathbed. "Mattie learnt. She had to. It never's been as hard again for either one of us, though it's been hard enough. What you can't change, you got to put up with. You don't change anything by turning your back on it."

The women knew, though they would not admit it,

that there was a limit to their capacity for directing the courses of their lives, if none to what they might be called upon to bear.

The darkness of that winter and lateness of the spring was less from storms and the sawmill blasts of smoke and steam than from the clouds of suspicion which enveloped every house. The more that was said, the less anyone trusted his own ears. The more valley people tried to draw together, the farther they drew apart. All they knew of one another became insignificant beside the one uncertainty, the assurance which no one could give or accept.

"I hope to the Lord them Frenchmen don't spend another summer here," Lottie Fernald fretted. "They've had me scart to death ever since they moved into the pasture. You know they never step without a lighted pipe in their mouths."

"I guess I'd have been scart if they'd stayed in ourn after it was all cut off," said Mattie. "Specially if nobody had been in there to clean up the brush." She added proudly, "That was one thing Bill did see to. He got the menfolks to help him clear that all out and burn it before the frost ever left the ground. And the minute the mill moved, he drove the Frenchmen after it. Wasn't no mind to have them hanging around. Course Bill has the say-so there, seeing as he still owns the ground." Then, because she felt sorry for Lottie, who had done her so many neighborly kindnesses, she did not leave these words to stand alone, but went on, "Bill says can't anybody step into the woods anywhere without stumbling over a parcel of them young ones. For mercy's sake, how many them little tramps is they?"

"Eight in one shanty, and eleven in t'other," Lottie answered. "Luneaus, all of 'em."

"My soul! And I think my five is a grist!"

"That's besides the ones that's growed up. Bert told Della the little one they call 'the Old Head' is Napoleon Luneau. Nobody knows how many wives he buried. One he's got now don't look any older than the other woman, Bert says, the one that lives in the shanty with the Old Head's oldest boy, the one they call Robi. But the Old Head's got three more boys bigger'n he is, all chopping with him and Robi. But Bert says there's nineteen over there under fourteen years old, a lot of 'em babies. Della walked over by the shanties last Sunday, with Bert, and she said there was some rolling around in the snow, not big enough to walk."

"Imagine that! Wouldn't you think they'd get their deaths of cold?"

"Would, if they was like other folks."

"Must be nigh onto thirty of 'em, eating and smoking and going to bed and getting up, all in two one-room shanties."

"Don't bear thinking on."

"None of the young ones go to school, do they?"

"There, Liz Carter says one day two or three or maybe five or six of them'll come. Be waiting with Owen when she gets there. Barehanded, and their feet wrapped up in pieces of shorts bags. They might stay all day with nothing to eat but what the other ones give them out of their dinner pails, or they might go off as soon as they've et what food they can scrounge. Maybe she won't see 'em again for a month, and in between-times she may have another bunch altogether once or twice. Sometimes they bring one that can't hardly toddle, and squalls until they lug it off."

"I should think she'd get the truant officer after 'em.

Just as leave not have 'em underfoot, most likely. I don't suppose they can learn anything."

"Liz says of course they can't, not understanding a word said to 'em, and nobody understanding a word they say."

"Sound like a litter of puppies. Only not so smart."

"Liz says you can't tell whether they're smart or not."

"Anybody with a brain in their heads would learn to talk right before they was fourteen years old."

"Well, I don't know. They're Frenchmen. Della says the babies act smart enough. She says they look cute rolling in the snow."

"Well, that's like puppies. All I can say is I hope I never have grandchildren that look like 'em! One they call Pete has come down once or twice to play with Jimmy, but with Agnes right around I put him out on his ear in a hurry, I can tell you. You may think I'm forehanded. Agnes is only eight. But I'm taking no chances, in case they stay around here. . . . Don't a one of 'em ever come to church, I notice."

"Oh, no."

"Heathens, I suppose."

Whatever was said that year in the valley was repeated to others, who repeated it to others, until it had gone the rounds and became the material for cross-reference. Much of it was repeated in later years, and is still repeated here, for changing reasons and with changed emphasis.

The one place where valley men and women found brief escape from their gnawing suspicion, spreading resentment, and agonizing anxiety was in church. They flocked there every Sunday morning as into a fortress. Men who had fallen into the habit of going only in dull seasons now went regularly, giving rides to those who had been

71

accustomed to walk. Women who had felt they should stay at home with small children now took the children with them. My mother took me.

Between my mother and father in the democrat wagon, with Lucy and Edith on the seat behind us, I rode each Sunday out of our yard, down the lane, and along the main road where until then — strange as it seems now — I had never been. I saw only what was close to me, perhaps because in such new and strange surroundings I did not dare to look afar; but more, I think, because a child has an intuitive wisdom which tells him that he cannot encompass everything at once, cannot evaluate what is distant until he knows well what is at hand, cannot attempt to reach the horizon until the path from his own door is trod as confidently by dark as by daylight. I saw the horse's hindquarters arch and spread as he pulled his load, and when the hill was steep, he lifted his tail to give him the final spurt of energy which took him over the crest. Going down the other side, he pushed back into the breeching to brake the rolling wheels. Pony was a workhorse and old; he went slowly. I saw snowbanks gray from spattered mud, and out of them ran little brooks fiery with light. A soft, low branch of a giant pine hung so near that my father could flick it with the tassel of his whip; the green of it was so dark it had a purplish cast. A baby pine, growing beside it, seemed pale and delicate by comparison, but it would be mighty in its time, its parent then long gone. In the shadow of a ledge, the ice had not melted but was as thin as the glass of a water tumbler — and someone's foot had broken through it. If I could have knelt by this opening, I would have seen inside a grotto with silver walls, a silver bed with rubies and sapphires in the headboard, a silver table with a crimson velvet cloth, and Owen

72

and Althea sitting by it, drinking hot, golden porridge from tiny silver bowls.

Then we rounded a curve and the church was in front of us. It was always familiar. There seems never to have been a first time when I saw it, like a great white box with a slant roof, four small-paned windows set into each side, and a narrow chimney jutting out of the gable end. It was as simple as the house a child draws on a slate or a piece of rough paper, and if smoke was coming out of the chimney it curled gently like the smoke a child draws. We approached from the west, and if the sun was shining — as it seems always to have been — the church was limned in gold, with the light which had passed through the east windows coming through the west windows to greet us, and all surrounded by the blue mat of the sky — for the valley ran east and west, with the mountains to north and south.

The driveway was cut into a sandy bank, always hollowed out just below the grass roots of the turf at the top. Here Pony made his greatest effort, with tail lifted and ears laid back. From here to the board fence behind the church he went on momentum. My father sprang down, hitched him to the fence and blanketed him. My father ignored the small iron step, like a trivet, on the side of the wagon. My mother's foot sought it by instinct, barely touched it; she reached the ground like a leaf on a breeze. My sisters felt for it with first one foot and then the other, and half-fell off. I could put both feet on it, and then I jumped, unless my father came back to lift me down. My mother stood laughing at us, never so young-looking and pretty as on a Sunday.

Together we climbed the three steps to the long, unroofed porch which we called the platform, and crossed to

73

open one of the doors on either side of a high window which had in it all the colors of the rainbow, but darker shades than those of a rainbow. The door always stuck a little under my father's hand. He went in first, and waited until we had passed him in single file, then closed it behind us. The door, opening and closing for us, and for others after us, let in a small blast of fresh air and sent a slight tremor through the still room, which smelled of paint and damp plaster, of Sunday School books, hymnbooks, oil in the lamps, wood smoke, and split-pine knots; of the mothballs and spices in which Sunday clothes were kept through the week, of Florida water and bay rum. It was the Sunday smell, the church fragrance, the perfume, I assumed, of heaven. My mother guided me first into our pew and sat beside me — I suppose to be sure that I was quiet. She need have had no concern. I wriggled back on the narrow, wooden seat, and sank into the deep-piled comfort of placid, respectful human silence, softly pointed up by the crackle of the fire in the stove at the back, the rustle of clothing, and an occasional long, outgoing, muted sigh as one after another felt the burdens of the week slip from him.

Before us was the pulpit on a platform across which had been laid a single strip of worn, ingrain carpet. Above was the colored glass window. Behind the pulpit a small sofa in black horsehair with roses carved on the frame stood against the white wall. On one end of this sofa sat the Elder. I fixed my gaze on him. My eyes always drew his, and before he covered his eyes with his hand, they twinkled down at me as Owen's twinkled.

When the gold hands of the clock on the wall reached 10:30, Mrs. Carter slipped onto the organ stool, and the Elder came forward to the pulpit. As the music of the

Doxology stole out, grew, and spread through the room, we all rose and — as it seems to me now — both doors flew open without sound or jar. Beyond them the fields were like green satin, the trees were full of bloom and birds, outside was as peaceful and beautiful as inside, the two flowed freely in and out; the church had overcome the world and made it its own, like the prodigal returned home. Through each door drifted a semicircle like a new moon, or half of my mother's wedding ring; behind the Elder's head they met and fused into a halo which followed him as he moved.

The Elder's voice was for the most part low and gentle. Understanding little of what he said, I learned of the love of God from his tone, of the age of God from the translucence of the skin drawn tight over his forehead, cheekbones, and hands, of the eternal health of God from the almost boyish color in his cheeks and lips, and of the majesty of God from his ink-black, long-tailed coat, his gray-and-black pin-striped trousers, but especially from the heavy gold chain which, threaded through a buttonhole, hung in two loops between the pockets of his white piqué waistcoat. His beard was now close-cropped and concealed nothing. He had nothing to conceal. He was whole, immaculate, and glowed with godliness.

To me, to sit before him was like being in my garden with Owen, the garden no one else could enter.

To valley men and women, it was as if the fog had lifted, leaving the valley as it had been when they were children, before any stranger had come into it, before they had known suffering, fear, suspicion, and resentment. Here Anson Brothers did not come, nor Luneaus, nor sawmill whistle, and young trees grew serenely to great age.

Owen was among us, but Owen belonged to us; wherever he had come from, he was now a valley boy. Bert Anthony sat in the Fernald pew, but that was proper for he was Della's husband and took the place of Eddie, the only valley man who had not shown his face in church for a year now; a man should sit in every pew, and Bert was the man in Fernalds'. Todd Perry sat beside Owen, in the farthest back pew near the stove, and kept the fire. Todd, though intimate with no one but Bill Brown, was no longer thought of as a stranger. Since he had come before the Anson Brothers, Luneaus, or Bert Anthony, before the destruction of young growth, he had been here for a great while, as the valley now counted time. Besides, he claimed to be the Elder's son and perhaps he was. Certainly he took good care of the Elder; worked steadily, provided food and even cooked it himself, had put a stove in the Elder's bedroom, a long-tailed coat on the Elder's back, and a gold chain on the Elder's vest. Saturday night backsliding was forgiven him as it was forgiven Bill, who had now had to be forgiven more than that. Neither Todd nor Bill ever missed a Sunday service, and a man who always came to Sunday service, though his past be cloudy and his weekday sinning grievous, must surely feel need of redemption and would ask to be led in the way of the Truth and the Light.

Toward the end of his sermon, the Elder always came from behind the pulpit, and stood at the edge of the platform, his voice suddenly rising until it was larger than himself. All drowsy or wandering eyes snapped back to fix upon his face, pupils dilated. Arms upflung, he spoke with the roll of thunder, the boom of cannon, the reverberation of great waves against a cliff. The voice came less from the Elder than from the sky above the roof over our heads, and we knew then that God was as mighty as He

76

was majestic, as stern as He was kind, as terrible in His wrath as He was tender in His sympathy and understanding. When one did as well as he could, though he be adrift on a sea of trouble, God's hand would bear him up and God's patience with his weakness would be everlasting. But let one of His creatures lose the way for want of effort to seek it — follow the road the Devil had built instead of the rough trail blazed by the ax of God, close his eyes to God's presence and his ears to God's word — then surely he would be recalled, made penitent, and redirected; for *The Lord thundered in the heavens. . . . God thundereth marvelously with his voice. . . . And it is turned round about by his counsels. . . . He causeth it to come, whether for correction, or for his land, or for mercy. . . . Great things doeth he which we cannot comprehend.*

The Elder's arms returned to his sides. He moved back quietly and stood behind the pulpit, folding his hands upon the big open Bible from which the fringed ends of a gold and a crimson velvet ribbon hung and clung together.

"Beloved," he said softly, "Oh, my brothers and my sisters, God said unto Job, 'Now men see not the bright light which is in the clouds, but the wind passeth, and cleanseth them. Fair weather cometh from the north.' Beloved, whom the Lord loveth he chasteneth. . . . Let us pray in the name of Jesus Christ, Saviour of mankind."

He raised one hand, reaching toward and above us, and it seemed to cover us all.

Now may the Lord watch between thee and me while we are absent one from another. Amen.

The Sunday service was always closed with these words, in this tone. It was so the day the bolt struck, when only he and Owen had felt it; even though they did not yet know its force, they knew enough to have shaken the faith of anyone with less schooling than had been the Elder's in his seventy-five years of prayer and study.

Owen was shaken. When we moved toward the aisle that day, after the benediction, and I looked back at him then as I always did, I saw the white line around his mouth.

He stood alone beside the stove. His hand was on the cover lifter but he was not moving it. He was not smiling at me as he always had. He was not even looking at me, or at anyone or anything. His face was toward the window, but I knew he did not see it, nor what lay beyond it. And there was that white line around his mouth.

The Elder stood on the right side of the open door, as always, taking in his warm grasp the hand of each as we reached him. For many years I knew which hand was my right only by placing myself mentally so that I faced the big elm which grew close to the church platform, and felt the Elder's hand enclose mine.

"Good day, Brother Brad; the back of winter is broken, isn't it? The frost will soon be out of the ground, and we must look to our fences to be ready for first pasturing day . . .

"Ah, Sister Martha, I see you have worn your hat instead of your shawl. Your ears must have tingled a mite on the ride up, but it is warmer now, for the sun is high . . . And here is your Lucy. How tall she is growing! And Edith, nearly the same size, for all she is younger! It is almost as if you had twins, Sister Martha. And little Althea, besides.

"I know you thank God for these blessings."

He stooped to me.

"I am glad you are old enough to come to church, little Althea. God bless you."

Standing on tiptoe, I whispered, "Do you ask God to bless Owen, too?"

"Owen? Oh, indeed I do. Many times every day."

"But now," I whispered, "he looks so sad."

The Elder's glance followed mine.

"Yes," he said. "Yes, child. He does. I know he does. He is."

"Does God know, too?"

"God knows."

"Then why does He let it be?"

"The Lord trieth the way of the righteous, my child. He that trusteth in the Lord, mercy shall compass him about. The Lord redeemeth the soul of his servants, and none of them that trust in Him shall be desolate. I have been young, and now am old; yet have I not seen the righteous forsaken. Go forth, child, with a light heart into this beautiful morning, for the earth is the Lord's and the fullness thereof."

But on the sunny platform my mother was saying to my father, "Where's Todd? He wasn't in church, was he?"

My father shook his head.

"I don't believe he's sick. The Elder didn't mention him. He always prays for the sick."

My father said nothing.

As the Browns joined us, my mother asked Bill, "You see Todd last night?"

Bill chewed his underlip.

"He don't know," Mattie answered for him. "I just asked him. That is, he knows they started out together. He can't remember leaving town. But I know he came into our yard on shank's mare, and he'd been going it that way

79

for some time, by the looks of his boots. I guess wherever Todd is, his horse and buggy's with him. Unless he rolled off into a ditch."

"Then how'd the Elder get up here this morning?"

"He rode with us, that's how he got here," Lottie Fernald put in triumphantly. She could not conceal her satisfaction that someone beside Eddie had become the talk of the valley. "He started to walk, but we overtook him and picked him up."

"The boy was with him," said Bert, "but the boy wouldn't ride. Said we didn't have room. I told him we'd make room, but he wouldn't ride."

We stood looking at one another. Everyone seemed to be on the platform moving together in a kind of daze toward the wagons. Owen and the Elder were alone in the church. I went back as far as the door, but no farther. Up by the stove, at the far end of the empty room, the Elder stood with his arm around Owen. I thought the Elder was praying. But after a minute my quick ears caught his words.

"Your father is not far away. Don't grieve so, my boy."

Owen made a sound like a sob or a choke.

Then he said, "I don't believe he is my father. I don't believe it. He can't be. . . . But then how am I your grandson? And I am, Gramp."

"You are my grandson," the Elder assured him steadily. "And whoever or wherever your earthly father is, your heavenly Father is always with you."

The emptiness of the room filled up with peace.

"Oh, here you are, Althea," said my mother loudly. "I didn't know where you had run to!"

At her voice and her clicking step on the platform, the Elder and Owen looked toward us.

"We're waiting for you folks," she called in, smiling at them. "We want you to come have dinner with us."

"Well, that is kind of you, Martha," the Elder said, "but I think —"

"Now don't put me off. You haven't eaten with us for a coon's age, Elder Perry, and Owen never has. We've got a roast of pork to go with our beans, I put raisins in the brown bread, and you can have your choice of three kinds of pie, to say nothing of molasses doughnuts and as good a spice cake as I ever made. I'm all ready for you but making the tea and dishing up; so come along. I warn you my feelings'll be hurt if you don't."

"Well, we don't want to hurt your feelings, Martha," the Elder said slowly. "Do we, son? We'll come, and thank you."

"Good. Here's Brad now with the wagon. Edith, you come in front with us. I'll take Althea in my lap —"

"No need, Martha, no need. The boy and I'll walk down."

"Walk? The idea! You get right in with Lucy. Brad, cramp the wheel."

"You get in, Gramp," Owen said in a low, tight voice. "I'll walk."

"I'll walk with Owen," I said, taking his hand. It was cold, though the day was warm.

He bent suddenly, caught me up, and put me on my mother's lap. He felt stiff, and still did not meet my eyes. He looked only at his grandfather.

"I'm going home, Gramp," he said. "I've got to."

He started off running, crossed the road, and disappeared into the woods.

My father looked after him.

"Thought the boy said he was going home."

"He did," the Elder answered quietly. "He will. But by a roundabout way. He likes the woods. They are a great comfort to him. He seeks God there, I think."

"Don't help anybody much to go through Brown's pasture lately," said my father. "Nor Fernald's."

"But Owen will soon be through Brown's," the Elder said, "and come to yours. You have fine big trees in yours, Brad. What are sometimes called cathedral pines."

"Only a few of mine are ready yet for cutting."

"And what there are Brad will take down himself," my mother said. "Luneaus'll never touch an ax to a tree of ours."

"Well, now," the Elder said mildly, "Brad is young and strong enough to take down his own, and he knows how. I used to do it, but not for a good many years. They say the Luneaus are good choppers. I had Mr. Luneau go through mine with me two, three weeks ago, to see the ones I've marked for cutting. I thought he might take care of them for me when they're through on Fernald's." He cleared his throat. "If he does, I may mark a few more."

"Bert Anthony says they're all through there now. Must be. Nothing more than a witherod left standing. Mill shut down yesterday, he said."

My mother caught her breath.

"Where they going next?"

"Bert said he didn't know. Said he hadn't spotted anything else for Ansons. Hasn't seen the Ansons lately. Live away north in New Hampshire, Ansons do, he says."

"Then I hope to the Lord," said my mother fervently, "I hope to the Lord they take their old mill and all that goes with it nearer t' home."

"Bert's wondering whether he'll follow it out of here.

He says Della hates to leave the valley and he's taken quite a shine to it himself."

Nobody mentioned Todd on the way home, or during dinner. In the excitement of the news that the mill had shut down and probably would leave the valley, taking Frenchmen and shanties with it, Todd and Owen seemed forgotten. But I remembered Owen, and could not eat for thinking of the white line around his mouth, the choking sound he had made, and the stiffness of his arms when he lifted me into the wagon. My mother noticed that I did not eat, asked, "What's the matter with you, Althea?" but was satisfied that my forehead did not feel hot when she touched it. My father said that as soon as the mill was gone, valley men would clear the brush off Fernald's pasture, without asking permission. He thought pine would seed-in from the other lots in time, though it would be a good many years. In the meantime, my mother said, the Brown and Fernald pastures would be barren, and berry bushes would spring up thick. She supposed Browns could make out to live on blueberries, with what else they could rake and scrape, when their bag of money was all spent; she could remember Bill's older sisters huddling grate- fully inside her mother's open oven door on a bitter win- ter day, waiting for the "lend" of a sack of corn meal and a basin of molasses, saying, "We'll bring it back, Mis' Pat- terson, when we gits some more. We ain't got nuthin' now to git with, but we hopes when huckyberries comes —"

"It'll be different, though, for Fernalds, if *they* ever hit the bottom of the barrel. That must be an awful holler sound, and they're not used to it. I don't see but Bert and Della will have to leave sooner or later. That little farm with all the growth cut off will never keep the roofs tight and feed two, let alone five — or maybe a dozen, way

Della's starting out! . . . Well, looks like we're all through, so step right into the sitting room, Elder Perry. You visit with Brad while the girls and I clean up here."

"Your dinner was delicious, Martha. Especially the dried-apple pie. But I think now —"

"There, I guess one thing men don't cook, when they're doing for themselves, is pie. You wouldn't have a second piece, though. I didn't think you et very heavy. You'll find some bananas on the desk in the sitting room. You like bananas?"

"Oh, yes. Yes. But I think I should be going now. Owen —"

"Oh, don't worry about Owen. That boy'll always land on his feet. You and Brad have a little talk. Then he'll hitch up and take you home." She had him through the door and into the platform-rocker. "Brad'll be here in a minute. He's just getting his pipe. Always has a smoke after Sunday dinner. Here's this week's paper you can look at, if you want to."

She came back into the kitchen and told my father, low, "Now see what you can get out of him about Todd. Something must be up." Then: "Edith, you carry. Lucy, scrape and stack. Althea, you're going to have a nap. Now don't say you're not sleepy. You're going to have a nap anyway."

I was not sleepy, but I was glad to creep into my cot in the alcove off my parents' room, and be alone. I closed my eyes and tried to think my way into the garden. It was like trying to recall a dream. I tried and tried, but I could not get over the wall or through the gate. My legs were too short for one, my shoulders too wide for the other. Big, slow tears ran down my cheeks. They soaked my pillow, and tasted salt.

84

When my father came in from the barn after taking the Elder home, I was sitting on the dark backstairs, for I had heard him drive away and come back and I wanted to hear what he might say about Owen, as one longs to hear even the name of a loved one long in another land; but I did not want them to see me and ask why I had cried.

"What did you find out?" my mother asked at once.

"All they know, I guess," my father answered. "Not much. Todd drove off yesterday afternoon. Said he was steak-hungry and would bring back a slab. Took Bill with him. And Todd hasn't come back yet."

"If that's all, what's Owen taking on so for? Only wonder is it hasn't happened before. Owen must know well enough what Todd goes for. He wasn't born yesterday. With the mill shut down, Todd may be on a week's spree, like Bill was once or twice."

I heard the couch squeak as my father sat down on it to change his shoes.

"One thing," he said — "the boy feels as if it's shaming his grandfather."

"As if anybody'd blame the Elder for what Todd does!"

"Another thing — they had kind of a scare this morning."

"What scared 'em?"

"You know that hundred-dollar bill the Elder always has pinned to his undershirt? This morning he thought 'twas gone."

"*Gone!* My soul and body! Don't he sleep in his undershirt?"

"Sure. But he takes his bath and puts on clean clothes Sunday morning. Generally, he does it after breakfast, right before church. But today, some reason, he woke up early, and made up his mind he'd just pull on his pants and heat some water and then wash up and change. After he got his clean undershirt on he reached into the one he'd took off, to onpin the envelope. And 'twasn't there."

"My soul and body," my mother breathed again.

There was no other sound in the kitchen but the ticking of the clock.

"Well, he s'arched," said my father in his deep, easy voice, "and he s'arched, even though, he said, he knew there was no place that envelope could be except inside his dirty undershirt. But it was gone, pin and all, and the shirt not tore. So he give up and got dressed and started some breakfast. When Owen come down, they set down to eat, because, he said, Todd's always late Sunday morning, it being one day he can sleep late, the Elder said; so they don't wait for him. And while they was eating, that envelope being on his mind, the Elder mentioned it to Owen. He told me that was a great mistake, because the boy knew what the Elder didn't — and that was that Todd hadn't come home. The two worries together got the boy all hared up, and nothing the Elder could say after that amounted to much, long as the hundred-dollar bill was gone and Todd was gone too. But the Elder said Todd didn't take it; didn't see how he could have anyway; the Elder knew he had it on him when he went to bed, and Todd had been gone since the middle of the afternoon. He told the boy he knew he didn't take it, in case he was afraid the Elder had such an idea, and the boy just went off outdoors crying. . . . Anyway, when we drove into the yard, the boy come running out and told him he'd found the envelope under the bed, and the bill was in it. The Elder looked awful puzzled, said he didn't see how it had got onpinned, and I told him he must have onpinned it without thinking when he took the shirt off, before he washed. Anybody does a thing like that sometimes. And the Elder's getting along in years."

I heard my father get up and open the entry door. He was putting on the frock he wore to milk in, whistling softly and tunelessly between his teeth.

My mother asked suddenly, "Brad, you think it did happen so? You don't think the boy took it for himself, and got so scared he give it back?"

The whistling stopped. So did the beating of my heart.

"NO," said my father, louder than I ever heard him speak before or afterward. "I don't know *how* it happened. But how could the boy have took it? And if that boy is a thief, I'm a thief, and the whole valley is a den of thieves!"

His milk pails clanged together, and the door into the shed slammed behind him.

In the silence which followed, I sat as if frozen; but after a little, when my mother began moving about, taking things from the cellar cupboard, I tiptoed back to my bed. The alcove was always dim. I could not tell there, even at midday, whether the sun was shining, though when it rained I heard it clearly like little feet above the slanted ceiling. There was no sound of rain that day, but it was growing dark. I lay floating as on the fog when it thickened, waiting to be carried on to what was better or to be brought back to what was good and familiar. Somehow I knew that the garden had vanished and I should never find it again.

"Wake up, Althea," my mother called cheerfully, opening the door at the foot of the stairs. "Owen's here. He's brought you something. He's waiting on the porch with it."

I slid onto the floor and put on my shoes, but could not find the eyelets and went downstairs with the lacings dragging. My mother smiled at me, holding my coat.

"I guess you'll be surprised," she said. "The things that boy thinks of! Take this."

She gave me a preserving jar.

On the porch it was not quite dark. There was still a pink line along the horizon to the west.

Owen sat on the top step with a pail between his knees. It was a small, blue-banded pail — the kind that lard was sold in.

"Come see, Althea," he said, without looking up.

The pail was nearly full of water and tiny black fish were swimming in it.

"Little fish," I said.

"Minnows. Six."

"Where'd you get them?"

"Caught them in the river. I fixed a net."

"What you going to do with them?"

"You can have them if you want. I asked your mother to give you a jar to put them in."

"Wouldn't they rather be in the river?"

"No. Because big fish would eat them."

"Oh . . ."

We sat together in the chill spring dusk, watching the minnows dart about and wheel, against the bright tin of the pail.

"What do they like to eat?"

"Your father'll know."

My father, who had said, *If that boy is a thief, I am a thief, and the whole valley is a den of thieves.*

I asked, "Has your father come home yet?"

88

"No. . . . Althea, you remember who was the first President of the United States?"

"The one our white city was named for. Washington."

"George Washington. That's right. He was one of our greatest Presidents. So was Abraham Lincoln. So was Theodore Roosevelt. Theodore Roosevelt was President when you were born. I've been reading about him. Books I borrowed from Miss Hester. Washington died a long time ago, and so did Lincoln. But Roosevelt is still living, and he might be President again. He might be elected President this fall. If he gets nominated. You have to get nominated first."

"How do they do that?"

"They make a lot of speeches in great halls, telling people what they'll do for the country. Other people make speeches for them, saying what good Presidents they would be. We *know* Theodore Roosevelt would be a good President, because he was before. If I was a man, I'd vote for him. He's a great man."

"What's he like?"

"Well, he loves this whole country. He knows it from one end to the other. He was born rich and sickly in New York City but he was strong enough to make himself get well, and he has hunted and fished all through our Maine woods and in New York mountains, and been a ranchman in the West; so you see he is brave and knows how to work. He graduated from Harvard, the best college in the country, and has written books. He was Police Commissioner of a wicked city when he was thirty-seven years old, and made everybody keep the laws. He was Acting Secretary of the Navy when our battleship *Maine* was blown up in the harbor of an island called Cuba which was under the

89

control of Spain. He resigned, and organized a company of Rough Riders (sometimes called Teddy's Terrors) and fought in Cuba with it. When he brought it back he was the most popular man in America. He became Governor of New York, then Vice President of the United States, then President when he was forty-three. . . . You see, Althea, there are a lot of people in this country who work all the time to help rich people get richer; they don't seem to care what happens to poor people. And there are a lot of other people who think all rich people are bad and all Big Business is bad; they think the workingmen ought to have as much money as anybody. So the two groups fight each other to get a President who will fight for them against the other side. Theodore Roosevelt knows that businesses can't be run without a lot of money; if we didn't have big businesses we wouldn't be a great country; and anyway, we're a free country; we all have a right to make as much money as we can, if we want to. But it's against the laws to steal it, and everybody has a right to as good a living as he can make, within the law. That includes the workingman, of course. Teddy Roosevelt is for a square deal for everybody. He said, 'More than that no man is entitled to, and less than that no man shall have!' He's for all the people and that's the kind of President we need. . . . I'd like to be like Teddy Roosevelt."

I had never heard anybody say so many words without stopping.

I asked, without knowing why, "Has he got a mother? And a father?"

"He did have," Owen answered. "Good ones." After a minute he added, "But his father died when Teddy was nineteen, and his mother when Teddy was twenty-six. Even his wife died the same time as his mother. He'd hardly started then all he was going to do. But he went right ahead after that. Nothing could stop Teddy."

"Does he live all alone?"

"Gracious, no. He married again." He looked at me for the first time, and smiled. "He married somebody he had liked when she was a little girl."

I put my chin on his arm and watched my fish, though it was quite dark now and I was not sure whether I saw the fish or only remembered them. We were not in the garden; we were out in the cold world. But we were together. Owen was strong and brave, and I was content.

"Do they have children?" I asked.

He laughed and put his arm around me. It was not stiff. "Sure. Quite a whopping lot. Two girls and four boys."

"What are their names?"

"The girls are Alice and Ethel. Colors have been named for them. There's a shade of blue that's called Alice blue, and a shade of pink that's called Ethel pink. One of the boys is named Theodore for his father. The other three boys have kind of funny names. They're Kermit, Archibald, and Quentin."

I sat counting in my mind.

"How many children does that make?"

"Count to four for the boys. Then count two more for the girls."

I counted to four, and counted two more.

"Six," I said gravely. "And that's how many minnows are in the pail. I'm going to call them like Teddy's children. So I'll remember. Then we can name our children for Teddy's children. Alice, and Ethel and —"

"Theodore. Call him Ted," said Owen. "Kermit. Archibald. Quentin."

We had been swept out of the garden by swift currents,

91

but for a little while hid in a quiet cove while the waters of a great country and an unfathomable world swirled past us. Owen would be President, I the wife he had liked when she was a little girl, and we sat in the dark naming our children. Slowly he poured the contents of his lard pail into the preserving jar I held with both hands.

In the kitchen my mother was ringing Lottie Fernald's number, two longs and three shorts. She rang it several times.

"That's funny," she said. "They must all be there . . . right at suppertime."

She rang again, and Della answered.

"Ma's upstairs," she said in a muffled voice. "Wait a minute." When she came back she said, "She can't come now, Martha. She says she'll call you when she can."

Della sounded as if she had been crying.

Lottie did not call back that night.

The next morning Mattie Brown came running up our steps and into the kitchen.

"Have you heard, Martha? The Fernalds are moving away!"

My mother dropped into her rocking-chair, her hands gripping the arms of it.

"I guess you hadn't. I didn't dare talk it over the telephone. Bill went over to see Eddie about something last night, and he was putting stuff into crates in the shed. Said he'd been planning it some time, making boxes and crates and sorting out tools Sundays while the rest of 'em was at church. Said he knew Lottie'd take it hard, with Della the way she is, so he didn't say anything to her until he had to. But he told 'em all yesterday as soon as they got home. He's been reading up about the prairie country out West, and made up his mind what he wants is a ranch somewhere in Wyoming or the Dakotas where he can raise cattle. Says this is the time of year to get out there and look around. So he and Lottie's starting tomorrow. When they get their place, Bert and Della is to ship their stuff. If they're not back in a year, Della's to sell the farm. But she and Bert can stay on it till then if they want to."

"Starting tomorrow," my mother repeated, staring at Mattie.

"Ain't that just like a man? Couldn't stand letting Lottie get used to it, so she's got to strike out without getting used to it. Poor soul, I'll bet she's most crazy, and Della too. Lamps didn't go out over there till daybreak this morning. I kept getting up to look. I don't suppose any of 'em got a wink of sleep, any more'n I did. Be a wonder if Della don't lose her young one out of this."

"Poor Lottie," my mother sighed. "I'll have to go over and see what I can do to help."

"I'm going with you."

They were gone all day.

When my mother came back, Lucy had made a cake, and she and Edith had cooked supper. We were sitting at the table. My mother washed her hands and sat down in her place. Edith brought her a cup of tea. She put milk in it and stirred. She looked pale and tired, but her eyes were bright.

"Of course you've heard about the Fernalds," she said to my father.

He nodded.

"That your cake, Lucy? Looks light and nice. Don't cut it. I'll take it over to Lottie's tonight. You'll have to come, Brad. We're going to have a surprise party for them. Mattie left before I did, to call up all around. It's the least we can do, and all we can do."

93

She said Lottie and Della had been in a dreadful state when she got there, and no wonder. First, my mother and Mattie had fixed them doses of spirits of ammonia and put them to bed. My mother marched herself out to the barn where Eddie and Bert were hammering, gave Eddie a good long piece of her mind and told him not to make another sound for two hours even if he had to leave for the Dakotas in what he stood in. Then she and Mattie cleaned up the kitchen, planned the party, and had dinner ready when the womenfolk woke up. My mother took some to the men in the barn, and told Eddie that after he had eaten he could hammer himself to death if he wanted to. Back in the kitchen, she and Mattie undertook to cheer up Lottie now that she was rested. They told her she need not worry about Della, for they would look after her as they would one of their own daughters. They pretended to envy Lottie her chance to see the country, with no housekeeping to do for weeks and weeks. They told her she was going to be a pioneer woman, and wondered if she would learn to ride horseback astraddle. They promised that if ever she was in a rodeo, they would be on hand to see it if they had to walk to get there. All together they washed and ironed Lottie's clothes, and cooked up food enough to feed her and Eddie for three or four days on the train.

"We made quite a frolic of it," said my mother. "Lottie feels as much better as a woman could in such a fix. Now you menfolks'll have to do your part by Eddie. He's mad as a hatter from what I said to him about what he's done to the valley and the way he's treated Lottie. I had to get it off my chest. But now you'll have to smooth him over, for Lottie's sake. Besides, he was a good neighbor enough for forty years, until he took this streak. No use sending

94

him off mad, if we're never going to see him again. What's done is done. After they're gone and the mill's gone and the Frenchmen are gone, we can settle down once more, God willing. All we've got to do is put our best foot forward tonight. It won't take long, because they've got to get to bed. Bert's taking them to the station bright and early."

She put on her second-best dress, the garnet cashmere with the black braid trimming. My father changed into his suit and the gray percale shirt he wore to church. As they sat in the wagon, Lucy handed up the cake, covered with a white cloth.

"You've got a little money with you, Brad?"

My father nodded.

"They'll probably pass the hat, but don't give more than a dollar. Eddie Fernald's milked enough out of this valley already. But there, I'm bound I'll never say another word for or against him. He'll get what he deserves out there on them prairies, I don't doubt. The Lord have mercy on poor Lottie, though, that never done anybody any harm."

The next day there was a strange hush all through the valley, as always in a house the day after a funeral. It was not broken by my mother and sisters starting the spring housecleaning. They worked without speaking except to ask a question or to give a brief reply. The sound of scrubbing brushes and of brooms sweeping up the wet, shredded newspaper which had been scattered over the parlor carpet had a mournful sound, and the antiseptic smell of yellow soap flooded the house and drifted through the open doors and windows, wiping out the familiar fragrances of food and smoke and kerosene, even of new grass and bursting leafbuds and split wood beside the chopping block.

95

Big braided rugs from the chambers and the sitting room hung on all four sides of the drying yard. The parlor chairs and marble-topped table tilted oddly on the uneven ground beside the driveway. The rugs had been beaten soundly with my mother's whanging, heavy wire weapon. The red upholstery of the chairs had been brushed and sponged, the table's top scrubbed and its base polished.

I stood and looked at them.

"Where are we?" the chairs asked, bewildered. "What is this place to which we have been brought?"

"Am I of no use?" asked the table, like wind in a crack. "Have I no home? Does no one need me?"

"Why hang we here?" murmured the rugs. "Is there a reason for all we have endured?"

"There must be a reason," I answered gently. "Let me think . . . there is a reason. You are to make a hall. Wait. I will show you."

The rugs became rich draperies covering alabaster walls. The space between two of them turned into folding doors. The table was on casters and, by leaning my whole weight against it, I pushed it through. The marble gleamed in the light of the sun, reflecting softly the rosy color of the draperies. I had to lift the chairs, one at a time, on my back. As I rolled them into a line before the table they bumped my head, elbows, and knees. I stood panting, rubbing my bruises.

"See?" I said. "I waved my wand, like Cinderella's god-mother. Now you are a hall. A great hall full of people, waiting to hear a speech."

I ran to the porch for the minnows, and put them on the table. I took my place behind the table, spread my hands as the Elder did in church, and addressed the multitude.

96

"Most of our great Presidents are dead," I shouted. "But one is living, and he must be our President again. He went to college, and he made a wicked city good. He won a war. He is for all the people. He is like Owen. Do you want Owen for your President? Well, you will have to wait while he goes to college. While you are waiting you must have a good President, one who is for all the people. Do you want the trees to stop being cut down? Then vote for Theodore Roosevelt. He will say enough trees have been cut down. He will say, 'Let the rest of the trees stand.' " I held up the preserving jar. "Bad men have cast a spell on his children. Do you want to give him back his children? Then vote for him and make him President. Their names are Alice, and Ethel, and Ted and Kermit and —"

My mother came through the folding doors.

"What are you doing, Althea?"

The multitude vanished. The draperies became rugs, and the parlor furniture stood awkwardly in the middle of the drying yard. Sleek little fish darted round and round inside the jar I held.

"I — I was making a speech," I said.

"A speech!"

She was beginning to unpin the rugs.

"For President Roosevelt."

"For President — wherever did you hear of him?"

"From Owen. Owen told me." I carried the minnows back to the porch. Then, seeing that she went on unpinning rugs as if she had forgotten me, I stood tall and repeated what I thought she would be most pleased to know. "Vote for President Roosevelt, and he will say enough trees have been cut down," I proclaimed. "He will say, 'Let the rest of the trees stand.' "

She looked around, and it seemed to me that I had again waved a magic wand, and that the laughing astonishment, having softened and brightened her thin face, was spreading all through the valley; as if a strong, great, and good man were at that instant being elected President, and the mill would be gone when anyone went to look for it. Lottie was on her way home to take care of Della, Todd had come back with presents for Owen and the Elder, even the trees which had been cut down would spring up tonight; and in the morning a red, white, and blue flag with stars and stripes would be flying from the top of every one.

But valleys and countries are not made secure by magic, trees cut down do not rise again, and flags do not fly unless pulled skyward by human hands.

I heard footsteps and thought, without looking to see, that the minnows had disappeared and any minute now Alice in a blue gown would come dancing along the lane, followed by Ethel in pink, and after them Quentin, Archibald, and their brothers would come rolling hoops.

But these footsteps were slow and heavy. Bert Anthony was turning into the yard.

He saw my mother among the rugs and furniture and touched his cap, but did not smile.

"Brad 'round?" he asked.

"Down behind the barn," she told him. "Moving the pigpen. Fine day, isn't it? I suppose the folks are some distance off by now. You and Della get over the party all right?"

"Oh, yes."

He went on, without stopping, past the barn.

She called after him, "Anything the matter, Bert?"

Whether or not he heard, he did not answer.

My mother stood uncertainly for a minute, then stooped and picked up a pile of rugs. As she passed me on the porch, she said, "Go down and ask if anything's the matter. If there is, I want to know it."

I went unwillingly. If anything was the matter, I did not want to know it. My head swam with all the reversals of the last few days. I had learned too much too fast. I wanted to sit alone in the sunshine and listen to the grass.

Behind the barn my father and Bert stood facing each other.

"It never rains," said my father, "but it pours; does it?"

"If anything is the matter," I said, "Mama wants to know."

Neither man noticed me more than as if I had been a bird.

"You could have knocked me over with a feather," Bert said. "I couldn't make head or tail of what the Old Head was trying to say, so Robi started in. He can talk a little better than the Old Head, but not much. First I didn't think he could mean what it sounded as if he meant, but he did. They've just got back from Ansons', and the whole thing is sewed up. They're smarter than I ever gave them credit for. Smarter than I am. See, I haven't been paid for two months either, but I thought Ansons would clean up before they moved the mill. Now I'll never see a penny of it. . . . But I guess I'll make out some way. This other business, though . . . I didn't know what to do, only to tell the Luneaus to hold off until I'd talk with you and Frank Carter."

"Dummed if I see what you *could* do," my father said, "or I, or anybody else."

It was plain to me that something was the matter.

"Mama wants to know," I shouted, bursting into tears.

The tears did not surprise them. My father put his hand on my head. I felt him sigh.

"It's a good thing she wants to know," he told Bert, "because she's got to, whether or no. Can't be any secret about this. We better go up to the house."

He picked me up and carried me in, Bert trudging behind us.

"Is she hurt?" my mother cried.

"Her feelings, I guess," my father said. "You know how young ones are. Let her cry it out." He put me on the couch, and I lay there sobbing. "No time to bother with her, Marthy. We've got trouble here."

"What now, for the Lord's sake?"

"Sit down and take it easy. You tell her, Bert. What you told me."

I grew quiet to listen, to find out why I had been crying. Bert's words were halting, but no one else spoke until he had finished.

He said that the Luneaus had stopped by, after being away for several days, to tell him that they would want him to saw for them next winter, that they had taken over the mill and horses from the Anson Brothers — who owed them, taken all together, a good deal of money. They had showed him their deed to the Fernald pasture on which the mill, the horse barn, and the camps set. They showed him also the deed to the lot they were going to saw next summer. It was a deed from Todd Perry to the Luneaus — a deed to the whole Perry place, lock, stock, and barrel. Todd had told them, two weeks before, when the papers were passed, that the Perrys would be moving out the day the mill shut down. That was the day the Luneaus started for New Hampshire to settle with Ansons about the mill.

They were surprised to see smoke coming out of the Elder's chimney when they came back, and Owen leading the cow to the river to drink. They wanted Bert to find out how soon the Perrys would be leaving, because Robi and his family wanted to move in before planting time; the Old Head's second boy, Girard, was fixing to get married and needed Robi's camp.

"See, Marthy, if it's legal," my father said gently, "it means the Elder must have deeded the place to Todd. Todd's sold it right out from under him, and high-tailed it back to wherever he come from."

"It's legal," Bert said. "Luneaus are smart. They had the title checked. It was all clear. The deed is stamped and notarized and witnessed, and all the rest of it. They're on their way now to the County Seat to have it recorded."

My mother, usually so quick to speak, had not said a word, but sat looking from one man to the other, with her hand at her throat. Now she opened her mouth, but sound did not come easily. The men waited.

"That — is — the meanest," she said — "the meanest, downright dirty — most devilish — and of course them varmints never said one word to the Elder —"

"The Old Head says *he* did," Bert told her. "Says the Elder showed him over the lot and pointed out the biggest trees."

"Oh-h-h, what a dastardly trick! The Elder was just showing him the trees he wanted cut to get the money he has every year for his medicines and suchlike!"

"Chances are the Old Head didn't know what the Elder was saying," Bert suggested. "Any more than the Elder could make out what the Old Head was saying. And that's just what Todd counted on, when he got the two of them together. You can't tell much about Frenchmen, even if you

101

work around them for a long time; but some way I don't believe the Old Head or the boys, either, knew what was going on. They thought all the Perrys were moving out."

"Anyway, hadn't been the Luneaus, would have been the Ansons or somebody else," said my father. "If the Elder put it into Todd's hands, he was bound to lose it unless he died before Todd could get aholt of the money it would bring."

"Oh, you two can talk till you're black in the face," cried my mother suddenly. "You can palaver it over and smooth it out, but you can't make it any different'n 'tis." She stood up. "You brought that mill here, Bert Anthony, and you brought them Frenchmen. You've sawed two of our good lots right down to the ground, had that Satan of a Todd Perry hanging around to keep your fire going for you. You've filled this valley full of stench and sawdust, got Della Fernald in a fix and drove her folks off out West; now your Luneaus have took everything the poor old Elder's got, even the roof from over his head. Next thing, I suppose, you'll be for stabling the horses in the church and sticking boards in the schoolyard. That's what we get for letting foreigners stop here in the first place, instead of riding them out on a rail. That's what the Elder's got for having so much faith. Well, I can tell you I haven't got any faith in anybody I haven't known since they were born, and less than I did in them I have. So don't try to pull the wool over my eyes!"

"Now, Marthy," my father said. "Marthy —"

"She's mad," Bert told him. "I don't wonder."

My mother looked from one face to the other. When she spoke again, it was in an altogether different tone.

"What's to become of the Elder? And that boy?"

"They can stay with us," I said urgently. "Can't they stay with us, Mama?"

"They can stay with *us*," Bert offered. "We've got all kinds of room. Della would be glad —"

"Can't they stay with us, Mama?"

"They can stay wherever they want to. There isn't a house in the valley that wouldn't take them in and folks share their last crust with them. . . . But none of us has got much, and to leave the house where he was born and always lived, see it filled up with ones that don't talk so you can understand 'em and don't even go to church, see his pasture look like Brown's and Fernald's do, be *dependent* — it'll kill the Elder. He won't live out the year. You know it, Brad."

My father shook his head. His hands were spread on his knees. He looked down at them helplessly.

I thought, There must be something we can do.

My mother said, "And . . . And who is going to tell him?"

The clock ticked, but labored as if it might stop and then there would be no movement anywhere.

"Seems as though," my father said at last, "it would come best to him from Owen."

Bert nodded.

"That's what I was thinking. They're pretty close, I've noticed. The boy could put it better than anybody else. . . . I might as well go over now and break it to Owen."

He stood up, and my father with him.

"I'll go along," my father said. "I'll visit with the Elder — tell him how Eddie and Lottie got off — while you get Owen where you can talk to him."

They tried to square their shoulders.

103

"What an awful thing," my mother said, "to have to tell a young one — or an old one —"

"That boy's got a lot of man in him," said my father. "He'll stand up to it some way."

They were pulling on their caps. My mother followed them to the door.

"Bert," she said piteously, "I didn't mean anything I said about you —"

"Forget it, Martha. I know you didn't."

"I'm just — half out of my mind. You're a good man. Dell's lucky to have you. I hope you'll stay in the valley and — sink or swim with the rest of us."

"I aim to," Bert Anthony replied steadily.

When my mother came back into the kitchen she told my sisters, still as mice by the back windows, "I'm ashamed of what I said about him. Not a word of truth in it. Nothing that's happened is his fault. He's one of us now, whatever comes."

Then she sat down beside me on the couch and pulled me tight against her.

"And so's your Owen, Allie," she said. She had never called me Allie before, though my father did sometimes. "No matter who he is or where he came from. We're rid of Todd, whatever he's cost us. And somehow, some way, some time we'll be rid of the Frenchmen. But Bert and Owen belong to us, they're our kind, and we'll stand by them through thick and thin. Don't you worry, Allie."

"I'll try," I promised, knowing how hard she was trying.

I went outside and changed the minnows' water, fed them, watched them; but I could not talk to them. I went into the barn and let the cows take grain from my hand with their soft, slippery lips. Chewing, they gazed silently at me, and I gazed silently back. I went behind the barn

104

to see the new pigpen, but it was empty, only half-finished, broken off in the middle like everything else. The clock of my world had stopped.

When it grew dark, I went into the house and stared at the table set for supper.

"Wash your hands, dear," said my mother. "Your father ought to be here any minute."

He came as I stood at the sink. I heard my mother run into his arms, but I did not look at them.

"It seemed," she said, low, "as if you'd never get here."

"I only stayed about an hour. Then we kind of run out of talk. Bert and the boy hadn't come back. They went over to the brook to get some cowslip greens, they said."

"How was the Elder?"

"Same as always. Talked about the Fernalds. Didn't speak of Todd. As I was leaving, he said maybe we might have a prayer."

"Has he ever done that before when you called in?"

"No."

"Who did he pray for?"

"That was kind of an odd thing, too. He prayed for the people in the valley to feel closer together."

"That'll come to pass. Have to."

"He didn't mean only us. He said, 'Oh, Lord, Thou knowest that, with whatever tongues we speak, we are all Thy children. Let Thy countenance to shine out of every face. Teach us to be patient with one another, to love one another, putting up no barriers, that we may grow in grace. Thou art the Father of us all.' "

After a minute, my mother took off a kettle cover and set a plate of steaming biscuits on the table.

"After what I've heard this day," she said, "it seems to me a barrier has been raised here that even the Lord can't take down. Pretty soon the Elder'll hear it too. Poor, sweet old soul."

But as I sat at the table, stirring my bowl of apple sauce, I prayed: *Let Thy countenance shine. Teach us to be patient. Teach us to love. Help us, God. Take care of the Elder. Take care of Owen.*

I believe that the others were praying too, but I did not know what they were praying for. No one spoke all through the meal, or during the cleaning up. The weekly paper, which had come that day, lay in its wrapper on the stand between the windows. My father did not open it. Instead, though it was not Sunday, he smoked his pipe, sitting bent forward with his elbows on his knees.

My mother was shaking out a clean nightdress for me when we heard steps on the porch. My father opened the entry door. Bert stood there with Owen, Frank Carter, and two of the Luneaus.

"Well, come in," my father said loudly. His chair almost fell over as he kicked it out of the way with his foot. "Come in. Girls, clear the stuff off that couch. Make some room here. Set down, all of you —"

"This is Mr. Luneau," Bert said, looking strangely at my mother. "And his boy, Robi."

She said nothing. Her hands were behind her, gripping the edge of the table.

The younger one put a long finger to his mangy black fur cap. He looked very solemn. The old one wore a felt hat, warped out of all shape by sweat and weather, pulled low over his little black eyes which snapped from one face to another and here and there around the kitchen like a squirrel's. He was grinning from ear to ear. His face was small, and so thin that the bones pushed out the dark skin. He had no teeth at all.

The old one was the first to sit down, on the end of the couch. Owen, his cap in his hands, sat down beside him.

"Owen," said my mother sharply, drawing a chair from beneath the table, "come sit here."

"Aw, he all right," exclaimed the old one. He struck Owen on the back, and laughed. His laugh was like a cackle. "Me, I t'ink he one good man." He waved his arm. "*Tous, tous bons hommes.* Me, I t'ink —"

"*Vous quietez-vous, la Tête Vielle,*" rasped Robi Luneau.

The sounds were strange. All had sat down now except my mother and Robi. The kitchen was full of men sitting forward on couch and straight chairs, their faces dark blots against the lamplit walls. Robi stood in the corner beside the entry door, his thumbs thrust into his belt and his fingers loose over his pockets as if covering guns. He reached higher than anything else in the room except my mother's shadow, which ran up onto the ceiling. The air was heavy and still, as it is before a thunderstorm.

Owen's whole face was as white as the line around his mouth had been Sunday morning. I wanted to go to him, to get between him and the Old Head, and put my arm around him. I looked at my mother and saw that she was frightened, as frightened as valley women had been when wolves howled at their cabin windows. Owen looked stern, he looked frozen, but he did not look frightened. I stayed with my mother, and smoothed her skirt.

After a minute of the startled silence which followed Robi's rasp, Bert said:

"Well, Brad . . . Owen and I talked. Then we went over to see Frank. He went with us to the Luneaus. This is how it is, you see. The Luneaus bought the Perry place of Todd. They thought it was his to sell, and 'twas."

"Gramps deeded it to him last summer," Owen said slowly.

I would not have recognized his voice. It sounded as if he were talking in his sleep. His eyes were fixed on my father. Sometimes he stopped for a minute or two, and we all waited. "I'd have prevented it if I could . . . but I couldn't. He was being good to Gramps, and made out as if he would have to go away when the mill went. Gramps didn't want . . . us to go. So he told Todd the place would be his . . . and after him I was to have it. He signed the papers, and they both acted very pleased. . . . I want all of you to know I never trusted . . . Todd. Six months or so before we came here, he took me away from a family that boarded State children. I'd been in two or three different homes like that, 'far back as I can remember. I'd never seen him before, but he *said* he was my father. And the State must have thought he was . . . or they wouldn't have let me go with him. We went and stayed for a while with my mother's folks, in Pennsylvania. They'd never seen her husband, and hadn't heard from her for years before she died. She was working in a railroad restaurant in Texas when she married Todd Perry. . . . Todd told everybody she died when I was born. But she didn't. The family she boarded with wrote to her folks that she died in 1900, and that would make me twelve years old now. I'm *fourteen*. What I think is, my father died after I was born, and then my mother married this man, and the time came when he thought maybe he could cash in on my father's name. . . . My mother's folks didn't take to him much, so we left there and drifted around in a number of different cities, getting closer to Maine all the time. He drank a lot, and when he was drinking he was ugly. But other times he could be as nice as pie, same as he was here to Gramps. . . . He used to teach me games. One was to see if I could take things out of his pockets without his feeling me. I got pretty good at that, and it didn't lead up to what he thought it would. You know that bill Gramps thought he'd lost last Saturday night? I've taken it out of his shirt every Saturday night for weeks and put it back as soon as Todd had come in and gone to sleep. I was afraid Todd would get it if I didn't. But last Saturday night he didn't come back, so he didn't wake me, and Gramp woke up early and found it gone. I didn't know what to do then."

The Old Head watched Owen closely, admiringly, while he talked. Now he struck him on the back again.

"Aw, what he say, *je ne sais pas*," he shouted. "*Mais*, me, I t'ink he one good man."

"I'll say the same," agreed my father.

Bert nodded.

"Owen's been carrying a lot of responsibility alone. It's a good thing he's learnt how, because he's got more to carry now. But there's ways we can help him out some. After I told him what the Luneaus told me, he said a way had to be found to keep his grandfather from finding out what Todd had done. He wondered if they wouldn't wait to saw the lot until the Elder — well, if they wouldn't let it stand as long as he lives. He said if they would just cut the big trees the Elder wants cut each year, he would get a job in town and send them money so they could pay the Elder for them; that way he would have money for the taxes and his medicine, same as he always has."

"That figures," my father said. "He always gives me the money to pay his tax bill when I pay mine. I could hand it back to the Luneaus. I guess I could get the tax collector to make out a bill to him, just for the looks of it. . . . But —"

He looked at Robi and his father.

"Owen thought the Luneaus would help him out if they could. He's got pretty well acquainted with them, from playing ball with Joe and Pete. I started thinking how we could make it some easier for them to wait to take over the property. We went over to Frank's and he said he was willing to let the Luneaus do any valley sawing there is to do. Frank says his boy Merton has taken a job at the foundry in town. That leaves Frank alone at his mill, and he says he's willing to shut down in favor of the Luneaus, if they can make out that way. They say they think they can."

"They can?" said my mother incredulously. "They will?"

She felt for a chair and slid into it, pulling me into her lap. I could feel her breath on my ear.

My father's eyes had not moved except between Robi and the Old Head.

"That's quite a thing," he said, "for any man to do. You fellers have got a good deal invested in that mill and in the Perry house."

The Old Head, grinning broadly, poured out French like a shower of hailstones.

"What does he say?" asked my mother. "Can anybody tell?"

"What does he say, Robi?" asked Bert.

Robi shrugged and spread his hands.

"He great one for talk," he said. "He say he have great love for *ce garçon là*, like his own, great sorrow for men old like him wit' one son only and he bad one. He say he like *ce patrie ci,* he want to stay in it, be good friends. Dat *Tête Vielle,* he alla time too much heart, too much tongue."

"So — what do you say, Robi?" asked my father.

Robi shrugged again.

"Bert, he knows," he said. "I have told him."

My father looked at Bert.

"Robi told us he is not old like his father," Bert said. "Robi has to look ahead. He has many brothers and sisters, as well as a big family of his own to think of. He likes the valley and would like for the young Luneaus to grow up here. But he wants them to grow up like Owen and other valley children. The older ones have lived in camps and worked hard since they were knee-high to grasshoppers. They want something better for the rest. Want them to live in houses with brick chimneys and cellars underneath, with well water and barns for their cows, and fields to have gardens in. Want them to stop moving around all the time, stay where they can go to school and learn something. He says they are all out of money now, but it won't take much to carry them through until winter. If they could get enough chopping and sawing to do between now and then so they could buy a lot to saw, even if that's out of the valley they could move the mill for the winter and bring it back in the spring. But Robi wants the school-age children to stay here. And his brother Girard needs a place to live when he gets married next week. He says if there's any way all that can be fixed, he can wait for the Perry place until the Elder's through with it, long as Owen pays the tax. But he don't see how it can be fixed."

My father cleared his throat.

"We'll fix it," he said. "Some way. Got to. It's only our fair share."

111

Bert smiled. It was the first smile except the Old Head's in the crowded room that night.

"That's what I told him. I told him Luneaus had as much to learn about the valley as the valley had to learn about Luneaus. Frank here started us off by turning over to them whatever sawing there is to do. On the way back here we stopped in to talk with Della. She agrees with me that we can do one of two things. Either we can let Girard and his wife have the rooms in the east end that her grandparents used when they were alive — there's a bedroom and a sitting-room and a little kitchen with cupboards and a sink — or, if the Elder should be lonesome after Owen goes, and he wanted us, she and I would move over with him, and Robi and his family could move in where we are; maybe they could let Girard have the east end, too."

After Owen goes . . .

I slipped off my mother's lap and went to him, squeezing in between him and the Old Head but not to separate them. I rested a hand on the knee of each. The knee of the Old Head's pants was rock-hard with pine-pitch. Owen seemed not to notice me, but the Old Head put his rough dark hand over mine and cackled softly, "Ah, *La petite. La jolie petite fille.*"

"What would Eddie and Lottie say to that, Bert?" asked my father.

It was my mother who answered.

"They'd better not say anything," she cried out. "If they was still valley folks, they'd know it was the least they could do. I don't see why Dell even needs to tell them. They told her and Bert they could have the Fernald place for a year. It's up to them now how they use it."

"That's so," my father agreed. "Then that'll fix you up

for the next year, anyway, won't it, Robi? If you get enough chopping to do this summer, that is. Well, you can have the job of putting into boards any trees I've got that's big enough to saw. There's quite a lot in my pasture. I'll see the rest of the folks in the valley and find out what they'll do about theirs. The Dennetts have a big stand of lumber at full growth, and I think they'll let you have it. Only thing, you understand, we don't any of us want to hurt what's still growing. You can fell so as to save that, I guess, can't you?"

"Luneaus," rasped Robi, "one t'ing dat we know it, dat how to fell trees." He took his thumbs out of his pockets, flashed his first smile at his father, and pulled off his cap. His teeth were white as milk in his brown face; his long, dark hair curled over his ears. *"C'est bon,"* he nodded. "Okay. *C'est bon, la Tête Vielle.*" He slid to the floor as if he were made of rubber, his back against the wall and his hands clasped around his sharp knees. His head rested on one side, in the corner, and he closed his eyes.

"Ho! Ho!" shouted the Old Head. He jumped up, so suddenly that I kept from being pushed off the sofa only by clinging to Owen, and danced a jig in the small space, waving his arm and snapping his fingers. "Robi say, '*C'est bon!*' Ho! Ho! *Nous sommes tous les amis. Maintenant,* the old man, he keep he house. We Frenchman, we chop. We live good. We laugh, we love. *Les enfants,* they learn. *Tous hommes, tous la même chose. Mon Dieu, c'est bon.* We go now."

He hopped around the circle, shaking hands.

When he reached my mother, she stood up. I saw her take the Old Head's grimy hand in both her pale ones. There were tears in her eyes.

"Here in the valley, Mr. Luneau," she said, "when

neighbors get together in the evening, we have something to eat and drink. I suppose it's the same where you come from? Wait while I make some coffee. Edith, get some doughnuts from the crock. Lucy, you bring up a custard pie."

"*Café? Pie?*" he cried. "*Tu es une bonne femme. Très jolie, aussi.*"

He tapped his chest.

"*Moi, Napoléon.* Napoleon, me."

"Napoleon," smiled my mother through her tears, measuring coffee. "I am Martha."

"Mart'a," cackled the Old Head. He spun around and hit my father on the back. "Your woman, Mart'a, she one fine woman." He pushed at Robi with his foot. "Robi! *Dormez-vous? Hey-lá! Café!* Pie, *aussi. C'est bon, n'est-ce pas?*"

Robi opened one bright eye, like pushing a black button through a slot, and said, "*Oui, papa. Oui,*" indulgently. Then he sat straighter and asked my father how many feet of lumber he thought he had ready for cutting. All the men welcomed the familiar topic. Their voices grew strong and they spoke easily. The coffee began to bubble and the cheery smell of it spread through the room. Chairs were drawn up to the table, and the men sat around it, my mother with them. Lucy and Edith brought milk and doughnuts to Owen and me, and stood in the pantry with their own. The talk was loud and I could not understand it.

"Are you going away, Owen?" I whispered.

"After school closes."

"Will that be a long while?"

"A little while."

"Will you ever go to school after that?"

"Oh, yes. I'll go to school in town. To the Academy. I promised Gramps."

"Can you go to school, and earn money too?"

"You bet I can."

"And go to college?"

"Sure."

"After you go, will you ever come back to the valley?"

"Of course I will. . . . *Sh.* Listen to what they're saying."

"I can't understand it."

"You don't have to understand the words. Listen to the voices. We mustn't forget this. Something's begun here tonight that's going to last and make big changes. We don't know how big."

I listened. It was late, and I was very sleepy.

"It sounds like a good thing," I whispered.

"It is. A wonderful thing."

"But it came out of a bad thing."

"Remember when I told you Gramps said that's how it is. He says good will come even out of bad, in time, because it's all according to God's plan. Gramps always knows that. So he isn't afraid of anybody or anything. He knows the Lord will provide."

"Isn't it you and the rest of them that's providing for the Elder? I thought —"

"And who put it into their minds to do it?" asked Owen. "It's a chance He's given us, and we're taking it. It'll do us all as much good as it'll do Gramps. And what Gramps hears about it'll make him mighty happy, even though he doesn't know it all. He's been wanting everybody in the valley to come together. He has grieved — listen, now —"

My mother was saying, "If need be, come next winter,

115

one of your children can stay with us while you're gone, Napoleon. Maybe two."

Frank added, "I don't doubt Liz and I could take a couple. Mert will have to stay in town through the week in bad traveling, when he works there. They could use his room."

"Aw, *c'est bon*," cried the Old Head. *"N'est-ce pas, Robi?"*

I thought, Maybe Marie will stay with us. We will give her a bath and she can wear one of my nightgowns and sleep with me. We'll listen together to the rain on the roof. . . .

I must have fallen asleep then. I remember nothing more about that night.

It seemed to me when I woke the next morning that Owen had already gone. As our garden had vanished forever in an instant, so a fog had risen as we sat on the couch in that dim-lit, noisy, crowded, happy kitchen and when it went away it had taken him with it.

I was not lonely, nor sad. I knew that he would come back to me from time to time. I felt sure that some day he would come and take me away with him. I would be his wife. He would give me a house to keep and I would work in it every day while he was not there, waiting for him to come at night. I could hear his step. I recognized his whistle. We would have children and give them the names of Teddy Roosevelt's children. But we were not old enough for that yet. Before that we had much to do and much to learn. He was doing his part. I would do mine. I took care of the minnows. I asked my mother to let me wash the breakfast dishes every day. I asked Lucy and Edith to show me how to make my bed. I polished my own shoes on Saturdays, and on Saturday nights took my own bath. I must have seen Owen at church, but I do not remember it. The Owen I saw there must not have been the Owen I carried in my heart.

The first time he came back to me, the roses were blooming at the end of the house. I sat beside them, dressing my doll, fastening a pink bud at her waist with a safety pin. He came up the bank and sat with us.

"I washed her dress myself," I said.

"It's nice and clean."

"I ironed it too."

"You've learned a lot lately. You'll be learning fast now. You'll go to Mrs. Carter's school in the fall."

"You won't be there."

"No. I finished yesterday. I'll be in the Academy."

"Will I go to the Academy?"

"Of course you will. And to college too."

"I don't know. My mother never said."

"She doesn't know about college yet, maybe. She'll want you to go when you're old enough."

"I want to go to the Academy with you."

He laughed.

"You're always in such a hurry, Althea. You have to go to Mrs. Carter's school first. You have to do a lot of other things."

"I know. I wash the breakfast dishes. I make my bed and polish my shoes."

"That's good. Will you do some other things too, for me?"

"Yes. What other things?"

"Three things. Bert and Della are going over to stay with Gramps after I leave. Della and Gramps will

117

be alone all day. They may be lonesome. Will you go over and spend a day with them sometimes?"

"Yes, I'd like to do that. If my mother will let me."

"I think she will. Probably Della would come to get you, and Bert will bring you home. That's one thing. Another thing, will you play with Jimmy and Agnes Brown if they come over? They're a little older than you but not much. I think you'll be in Jimmy's class when you go to school. You can write and read better than he can now. Maybe you can help him. If he could read and write better, he wouldn't cause Mrs. Carter so much trouble, and he'd get better marks. Agnes is smart, but she isn't happy. She thinks nobody likes her. Could you like her, do you think?"

"Do you like her?"

"I kind of like her. She's a good girl. She can't help it that she isn't pretty."

"I'll like her, if you want me to. And help Jimmy. And play with them. I'd like to have somebody to play with."

"You'll have them. And you'll have Robi's children when they come out of the woods and move into Fernald's. That's the third thing. Robi's children will be just across the field from you. Maybe your mother won't want you to go over there until she knows Robi's family better, but they will come over here. Will you let them take turns on your swing? They've never had a swing."

"I'll push them," I promised, "like you pushed me when I was little. I'll let them ride down the hill from the barn in my express wagon. I'll show them where the strawberries are, when they get ripe."

"That's good," Owen said. "They're things I'd do if I was here. I'll think about you doing them. I'll bet you'll find Agnes will help you with your schoolwork, too, same as I would, and the Luneau kids will push you in the swing when it's your turn, and they'll bring you raspberries and blackberries from deep in the woods where your mother wouldn't let you go for fear you would get lost. A Luneau would never get lost in the woods."

"And pond lilies?" I asked, remembering.

"And pond lilies. I'll bet you anything the Luneaus will bring you pond lilies when they bloom again. . . . You said 'when I was little,' Althea. You're getting bigger all the time, aren't you? I see your mother has let down the hem of your dress. Your hair is longer and heavier. What color do you think your eyes are?"

"Gray?" I asked. I knew they were not brown. Lucy's and Edith's were brown, like my mother's. People said I looked like my father, and his eyes were gray.

"They used to be, I think. Now they're changing. They're getting darker, and kind of purplish. Like dark pansies. . . . It's because you're getting bigger that you can do so many things. The next time I see you you'll be doing things you can't do now. Next fall maybe they'll let you help pull the flag up to the top of the pole at school. It's fine to put up the flag. Remember how it looks in the sky above the schoolhouse?"

I nodded.

"Wherever I am," Owen said, "I think I'll see it flying over the valley."

He stood up, pulled me up, and kissed me on my mouth, there by the hundredleaf roses.

"We're going to do all we can for the valley, Althea," he said. "We're going to do great things before we're through. Because whatever we do for the valley, you know, we do for the country, for the country is just one valley and one mountain and one city and one prairie after an-

119

other, over and over and over. And all its people are our people."

He said, "I'm going now," and kissed me again, and was gone. I was alone with the limp doll and the roses and a hummingbird which darted in and out of the syringa bushes.

I had been little, but I was growing bigger. I, who had been helped to read and write, would help Jimmy. I, who had been kissed, would love Agnes. I, who had been swung, would swing the Luneaus. My hair was growing longer and heavier, my eyes turning purple. I blinked, and circled each braid with a thumb and forefinger. It was nice to be pretty; it was better to be good. I who had watched the flag which others had pulled up, would soon be helping to pull it up, to keep it flying over the valley, this beautiful valley, this patch of the closely stitched quilt which was our country; my country and Owen's, and the Elder's, Della's, the Browns', the Luneaus', and Mrs. Carter's.

Owen had said that we were going to do great things.

I got down on my knees beside the roses and asked God what I should do first.

He said, *First, see the glory that is here.*

I looked at the glory. It was in the sunset over the smaller mountain, in the rosy light which lay along the face of the higher mountain; in the sound of the river flowing steadily toward the distant sea which I had not yet seen but only smelled; in the dark tops of the pines; in the grass just now tall enough to stir in the evening breeze; in the planted fields, in the wheeltracks of the lane, in the cows coming slowly up from pasture, heavy with milk, in the rooflines of houses and barns and sheds. It was in all we had built here, all that had been but would not be again, all that would come which we could not yet imagine; in what we remembered and what we dreamed of; in what we were born knowing and what we would learn.

Now sing it out, He said. *Whatever you want to live and grow, sing of it. Not only with your voice, but with your heart and hands. . . . You might begin by setting the table for your mother.*

I knew that only God can answer prayers. But the voice I heard was Owen's.

I I

THE valley farmer liked to be alone. So did the valley woodsman. Alone with one tool was best: the spade, the hoe, the scythe, the fork, the hammer, the ax, the bucksaw, the crowbar. In this company he was both student and master, apart with the sweetly submissive object of a passion which age and experience did not diminish but, rather, increased in intensity. The wooden handle was part of himself, a longer arm satin-smooth and shaped for searching out the soft crannies in stone, the warm folds of sleeping land, the pulsing veins of slowly rising sap; secrets which only he might discover and invade. The edge of steel, the pointed tines, the rod of iron were made sharp and strong not for rude assault but for exquisite delicacy of approach, and he used them with a deft tenderness impossible to his blunt fingers in direct contact.

A man and his tool, alone in a broad, bright field or a shadowy forest, served only himself and his love, under God; and only God observed him. The sounds he made were muted to low murmurings or gentle, clicking laughter by the immensity of earth and sky which surrounded him. The tree came sliding down and was cradled in moss at his side. The stone was pushed aside and fitted into a pattern. The turf was overcome and the dark loam looked up with soft, smiling eyes. The dew-wet grass went over singing, in splendid swathes, to lie in curving lines; and when he tumbled and tossed it, it twinkled at him, threaded with gold. The seed he sowed put down roots, put out leaves and buds; and when each bloomed he saw it as a new and special miracle. He knew then that, since what he had belonged to no other, he would build and maintain a fence around it, and, foreseeing winter, would make a shelter to protect it, laying the shingles snugly, row on row.

Next best to being alone with a tool in his hand was being alone with the creatures of his barn. He liked a horse which would not step on plants as he went up and down the furrows pulling a cultivator; a horse which stopped when he heard "Whoa," stood until he heard "Giddap," and kept on going until he heard "Whoa" again; a horse which surged with a will into the harness for a long, hard pull and tossed his head with satisfaction when it was over. Such a horse drank gratefully from a shallow stream and a man's thirst was half-quenched before he raised his own can of ginger water to his mouth. Such a horse needed no shouts, no whip, but stood quietly to be curried, brushed, and shod, moved over at a touch to let a man walk into his stall, was blanketed when he had to stand long in the cold, was rubbed down when the sweat stood like white foam on his sides, and sometimes wore a straw hat to shade his eyes from the sun and his head from its heat, with sprays of sweetfern tucked into his mane to keep off flies. A good cow waited for a man at the pasture barn at milking time, was motionless while a man sat with his forehead pressed against her rump to take away the weight of her bag, stared at him serenely as she chewed her cud in the dusk. A good sow ate hungrily, snuffled in a pleased way when her back was scratched, did not lie on her litter, and had a new pen often so that all but her snout was clean and her skin was a pinkish color under the silver bristles. A good hen laid a brown egg and cackled when she had done it, did not hide her laying place, snapped up as if they were gold nuggets the kernels of corn warmed in the kitchen oven on frosty mornings, kept her nestful warm for three weeks' hatching-time, covered her brood snugly at night and in the daytime taught them to scratch where angleworms curled beneath the topsoil, thereby showing a man where to dig bait quickly on a rainy day. A good dog rounded up heifers in the fall, protected sheep and fowl from the tramps of his species, could smell a rabbit, did not bark when the fish were biting, lay at ease by a man's chair until the bone on the plate was clean of meat. A good cat lived in the barn lofts and cellars, prowled along the beams, sat like a statue on a jutting stone of the foundation, pounced on the mice, battled the rats, and was rewarded by streams of warm milk directed straight from the cow's teat into her open, scarlet mouth. A man and his creatures held the forest back, cleared the field of stones and kept it clean of bushes, provided food and fuel for a family, worked together from sun to sun, were rarely separate except in sleep. In barn, field, or forest, the creatures thought as often of mankind as did the man, which was not often. In sleep both dreamed of the day's work done and the coming day's work to do.

The farmer's and the woodsman's wife also liked to be alone. When menfolk were neither in the house nor in the yard, when the children were in school or playing out of sight and sound, and the baby was asleep upstairs, then — unless two women lived in one house, sharing one kitchen — and only then a woman was ruler of her small domain. She heard her own footsteps, her own voice in song, heard herself rattle the dishes, heard the clock tick, the board creak, or the frozen nail snap. She raised a window or stepped to the door to breathe the clean, outside air, to hear the birds sing, or to smell the new boards, the wet leaves, the drying sweetgrass. She went into the yard to pin clothes on the line or to pour dishwater into her flower bed, and paused to look at the sky or the wind in the apple tree. She spoke to hens burrowing under the lilac bush; she kept Rhode Island Reds and thought they looked like geraniums in full bloom from a little distance. Back in the house, she ran a steel comb through her long hair, smiled at herself as she put up the coils with tortoise-colored pins and side and back combs, murmured with faint mockery, "Well, I look neat but not gaudy," put on a white apron, and sat down to sew, humming through the pins she held between her teeth.

But a woman differs from a man in many ways. Characteristically, she is rarely long absorbed by the impersonal. The mind of the valley man's wife, briefly freed of duty to concentrate on the hourly needs of her family, of its constant demand on her attention and ministration, first refreshed itself on beauty — the beauty of freedom and silence, of fragrance, of birds and flowers, sky and wind, of her own hair and eyes and mouth and clothing. Then her thoughts danced off to people; what they had done, were doing, might do. Those who had died, how best remember them? Those who were ill, how make them better? Those who were miserable, how make them happy? Those who were happy, why were they so? Those who were haughty, how take them down a peg? Those who were shy, how give them confidence? Those who were ignorant, where could they be instructed? Those who were wise, how share their wisdom? Those who were cruel, who could make them kind? Those who were unfair, how teach them justice? Those who were afraid, how give them courage? Those who were bad, how rid them of evil? Those who were good, how reward them? Those who were lazy, how put them to work?

When a valley woman's mind had dwelt on these subjects, she came to conclusions. She concluded that her beloved dead were best remembered and honored by efforts to make a better world, beginning with her own household, extending to her neighborhood, and as far beyond that as she could reach; that her man and other men had had a long time to make a better world and done very little about it, apparently either because it suited them as it was or because they did not consider that it could be improved; that a woman's influence was slight except through her children. Adults would always remain much as they were, whether happy or haughty, cruel or wise, lazy or good, but there were no limits to the possibilities of the young.

"The children," she said aloud, breaking her thread, "are our only hope."

If there was still time, she went to the telephone or ran across the field, and found another woman with whom to share this opinion. They looked through mail-order catalogues for lists of books, exchanged patterns, borrowed newspapers, made out lesson plans for Sunday School, and hurried home to teach their little girls how to bow and how to tie their ribbons, how to spell and multiply, to make their boys sit down at the kitchen table and memorize, or fill a tub and take a bath.

"You're going to have chances your father and I never

had," each mother said. "If I have to work my fingers to the bone. If I have to take a whip to you."

They did not know exactly what they were doing, but the time for it had come, and they were bound to do it.

The farmer's and the woodsman's child liked to be alone. He could and often did spend happy hours walking in and out of a mud puddle, feeling the wet clay ooze slowly up between his toes, examining his footprints, digging small ditches with a stick and watching the water trickle into them, stopping them up with wooden or stone dams, studying intently the widening circles on the surface of water into which he had tossed a stone. In bitter cold, he would climb a frozen snowbank, jump from it, climb and jump again, methodically, a hundred times, then go into the woods to a patch of ice he knew and run and slide on it, back and forth, until the sun went down. He knew where mayflowers and lady's slippers hid, the special taste of the fruit of every kind of apple tree — Red Astrachans, Green Porters, Striped Porters, Maiden's Blush, Russets, Snowflakes, Sweets, Baldwins, Blue Pearmains — and of ivory pips, checkerberries, blacksnaps, sweetfern seeds, wild pears, and the sweet end of a stalk of timothy; when hickory, beech, or hazelnuts fell he heard and reached them ahead of the squirrels. He could smell weather brewing. His nose was of great value to him, and served him best when he was alone. If he had been dropped blindfolded out of the sky into the valley he would have known instantly and exactly where he was, as well as the weather condition there, without the use of any other sense than that of smell. The brook or the river or the pond was on his right, the mountain or the sawdust pile or the swamp on his left. The ocean, though miles away, was at his back, and before him there was a barn and chimney smoke. In no two places could he be so surrounded — only one. With eyes uncovered and hands unbound, he sniffed everything he saw or touched, not to identify but to enjoy it. The smell of an apple, a sun-warmed berry, a fish, a newly dug potato, or a pink-lined mushroom was as delicious to him as its taste; of a board pile, a leather thong, or a ragged brush soaking in turpentine more interesting than any use he could make of them; of a flower more beautiful by far than its color or formation. But the country child cared less for flower fragrance than for heartier odors. He preferred the clean tanginess of ferns, the dark mystery of swamps and mud, the sweat of a horse's harness, the exhilaration of running water and ice, the muskiness of frost-blackened plants, barn cellars, and holes in the ground. He knew that every stone, even, has a different smell from any other, as well as a different sound when it is struck.

Paddling and jumping, listening and sliding, watching, touching, and smelling his solitary way along narrow paths, beside still or lively waters, under pines which sang to him and hardwood trees which talked to him with rustling leaves or creaking branches, he was often late to school or church or neighbor's house or home again.

Like his father, he was endlessly content, often enraptured, when he and his world were alone together, and, until the sun slipped over its rim, took little account of time. Unlike his mother, he did not think, while alone, of himself, but became almost bodiless, mindless, fusing with trees and air and sky and water and ice and moss and cold and stones and mud and juniper until he lost consciousness of his own personality and of any need or desire peculiarly human; even less did he think of or wish for the company of his own kind, or feel concern about past, present, or future.

Yet, once he had aimlessly rounded a curve or slowly pulled his weight to the top of a hill, and saw ahead of him the manmade structure to which he had been sent, a consuming eagerness and curiosity transformed him, his eyes strained to pierce the walls, and he began to run toward it as fast as his flailing legs would carry him.

In the valley district school by the fall of 1915 there were twenty pupils, ranging in age from four to sixteen. My sister Edith was the oldest, and helped our teacher, Mrs. Carter, with the little ones. Beside us two McIntires, there were fourteen Luneaus — eleven of them the children of Napoleon, who lived now on the Perry place; three of them the children of Robi, who with his brother Girard had bought the Fernald farm after Ed and Lottie moved out West — five Browns, and five Daleys, who with their father Sean from northern Ireland had lately moved into the old Burnham house, until then unoccupied for many years.

Mrs. Carter had not had so many pupils for a long time and never of so many different backgrounds. For thirty years she had taught valley children named McIntire, Brown, Carter, Fernald, Burnham, Harvey, Nason, Clark, and Hersom, as she had gone herself to the valley school with McIntires, Burnhams, Harveys, Carters, Browns, Fernalds, Clarks, Hersoms, and Nasons. The ancestors of all of them had been born on one side or the other of the dotted line between England and Scotland; they themselves had been born between the two hills we called mountains, under the valley schoolhouse flag, and all went to the valley church to receive God's messages from Elder

Perry. Of them all, she alone had gone beyond the valley school, and she only for two years. All the boys, when they left the valley school, had worked on their fathers' farms until they had farms of their own, or had gone out of the valley to do other kinds of work and to make their homes in other places. The girls had either stayed on with their parents, or married and gone to live with the parents of the boys who were learning to be farmers; as young Elizabeth Hersom had married Frank Carter at the end of her first year of teaching, and gone to live with him and his parents and his unmarried older sister Cora, in the white house across the road from Carter's Mill. She was the wife of a man she had always known, and her parents had known his parents. For a long time it had seemed that no day in the valley would ever be very different from the day before, that any change which came would be so gradual as to be all but imperceptible.

Then Owen Perry had finished at the valley school and entered the Academy in town. That summer, the Carter sons left their father's mill to work the foundry, Robi and Girard Luneau moved their families into the Fernald place, and the Luneau mill, run by fire and steam, did the sawing Carter's Mill had done by water power. Frank Carter enlarged his herd of cows and Cora had more butter to make. That fall, seven Luneau children entered school. They had never been to school before and at first they were all in the primary class with Forrest Brown — though only Germaine was five years old, as Forrest was. Marie, Armand, Albert, Rose, Joe and Pete Luneau were six, eight, nine, ten, eleven and twelve when they first came to school. That was the first year I went, but because Owen had taught me to read and write, I was in Jimmy Brown's class, though he was a year older than I.

The Luneau children had never before been with the rest of us except, now and then, to play. They had been born under the Canadian flag. Their mother spoke only French, their father mainly French with a smattering of English. They did not live as we lived. They did not go to our church. But our parents had come together to keep as serene as his earlier ones had been the last year of the life of Elder Perry. And we children came together at school.

At first all the Luneaus had seemed as alike, except for size, as seven ponies, colts, and young horses, and as different from the rest of us. We included them naturally enough in recess games, but in the schoolroom we laughed behind our geography books when big Pete read haltingly, "Dis is a boy. Dat is a girl," tall, unkempt Rose stood at the blackboard drawing *A* and *C*, Joe sat calmly picking his nose while Mrs. Carter tried in vain to make him understand that here on the map was the State of Maine and she wanted him to draw an outline of it on his paper.

But before the snow came that year, Pete and Joe were living at our house while their parents had gone in a westerly direction with the sawmill. Albert and Armand were staying with the Carters, sleeping where the Carter sons had slept a year ago. The three aging, unmarried Dennett sisters had had an airtight stove set up in the chamber which was their summer guestroom and Rose and Marie Luneau slept in the fourposter under a canopy, with Germaine on the trundle bed beside them. In the beginning they had all been scrubbed in wooden tubs in the sheds of their winter homes, had their heads washed in kerosene, and put on clothing given to them by their winter mothers. Then, gradually, they had learned to live in plastered, painted, wallpapered rooms like wild birds in cages with doors they could unlatch at will. But even when they were free, they no longer liked to stay dirty; when they came in out of the cold, it was pleasant to find that the wind did not follow them; they slept well in their separate rooms, no more than two in one bed and if there were two the bed was wide. It seemed strange to them for a few weeks, no doubt, as they seemed strange to us, but they were always cheerful. There had never been loud laughter in the Carter, Dennett, and McIntire houses until the Luneaus came.

From being startled by their laughter, we grew to laugh more spontaneously ourselves. My father said Pete was as good as a man with the stock and at the woodpile. Joe worked well, too, while he was working, but he often dropped his pail or his ax and disappeared, fleet as a rabbit into underbrush. Pete was my father's favorite, but my mother loved Joe; he sometimes put his cheek against her arm, and he smiled up at her through his curly black eyelashes whenever she stood near him. The Dennetts said Rose took to housekeeping like a duck to water; she went through that whole big old house every Saturday like a whirlwind and in a room where she had cleaned you could not find a speck of dust. The Dennett sisters took their noon dinner every day out of a kettle Rose kept on the back of the kitchen stove; they said they did not know what she found to put in it, but there was always enough, it was delicious, and it never tasted twice alike. When Miss Mary had taught her to brush and braid her little sisters' hair, fasten the ends of the braids with elastic and loop them up with narrow red ribbon, she knew how to brush her own, tie it back at the nape of her neck with a wide red bow, and let the dark "masses down like a mantle over her shoulders."

Now when Rose stood at the blackboard we did not laugh at her size as she carefully made *B*'s and *D*'s. Edith thought with envy of how the Dennett sisters praised her cleaning, how beautiful she was, how soon she probably would be married because she was so beautiful, such a good housekeeper, and looking womanly already. Agnes and Jimmy begged her to bring a kettle of her soup to school and treat us all. One day she did. I stared at her, wishing I had crisp curly hair, slept under a canopy, had little sisters to watch over and tend.

Before the end of their first year at school, Pete and Albert had been promoted to my class and Pete was ahead of the rest of us in the arithmetic book, though reading was still difficult for him and I helped him with the lesson every night. As for Armand — Armand had left Jimmy and me far behind. He was in a class by himself except in arithmetic. In arithmetic, he worked with my sister Edith and did it faster and more accurately than she did, though she was thirteen then and he only eight years old. Mrs. Carter said she had never had a pupil with such a head for figures as Armand's. She said that even at the supper table he was hungrier for figures than for food, and did accurately in his head long sums she had to put on paper; and when he had measles that winter, he was delirious for two nights and added, subtracted, multiplied, and divided at the top of his voice, hour after hour. It was Armand who told me that the largest unit named was a decillion. It seemed to trouble him that, after that, one had to speak of so many decillion, which could become awkward if one tried to count, say, the grains in a sawdust pile.

That summer when the Napoleon, the Robi, and the Girard Luneaus came back from living with their small children in the camps which followed the mill, Elder

Perry had died. Bert and Della Anthony had built a little house of their own in a field which had belonged to Della's parents, Ed and Lottie Fernald. So the Robis and the Girards moved into the Fernald house, and all the Luneau children we knew went with Napoleon and Annie to the Perry house. After that, the Luneau women never followed the mill again, and the children lived at home with their mothers; but Rose worked on Saturdays and holidays for the Dennett sisters, as Pete did for my father. Armand still spent many days and nights at the Carters'! He called Frank and Cora "Uncle Frank" and "Aunt Cora," but he always called Mrs. Carter "Teacher."

The Luneaus, even the older ones who spoke little English, now belonged to the valley and were a part of it. Those who had been to the valley school, and Girard's fat, pretty, tidy little wife Aurora, who had lived in the village before she was married and gone to the village school, seemed so little different from the rest of us that we were startled, when a village minister began to hold Sunday afternoon services in the church which had been closed for six months, to find that none of the Luneaus came to them. My mother promptly asked Joe the reason, when he dropped in for a glass of the filling she was making for pumpkin pies. Joe could not explain it, but soon after he left, Aurora ran across the field to explain it for him, much as Rose was already explaining it to the Dennett sisters.

"You see, Mrs. MacIntire," confided Aurora with eager little gestures, "we belong to a different church. We are Catholic. We became members of that church as soon as we were born, all of us. So we cannot go to yours."

My mother saw no sense in that, and said so. There was only one church here, and nothing that was said or done in it could do anybody anything but good. She had never seen a Catholic church. She did not know where there was one. She did not know much about the Catholic faith, but if she lived where there was only a Catholic church she would go to it. The Luneaus had lived in the valley for two years and not gone to any church. She thought that was too bad.

"Oh, but we have all been married by the priests," smiled Aurora, "and read the lessons and letters sent to us by them, and said our prayers. Annie and Lena and I count them off, night and morning, on our rosaries. All the children study the catechism Sundays. We have kept as close to our church as we could. And now — now we are going to have our own place to go to church and our own Father. Is it not wonderful? It will be in the town. My father and my uncles have been working toward it for a long time, ever since they came from Canada. Now Girard and his father and brothers are going to give the lumber for the church and all our men will help to build it. It will be ready before the mill goes out again, and then — if you are up in time —" she laughed merrily — "then you will see us all riding down to early mass! And won't we be a roadful?"

We were all up in time, that first Sunday morning they went. It was not yet daylight, and they had lanterns on their wagons. They did indeed make a roadful, and the sound of their voices and the creaking of the heavy wheels were like the frogs when they are noisiest on a summer night.

"Don't see why they think they have to have a service while most folks are asleep," said my mother.

"It's their way," my father observed mildly. "Have to admit it gets the day off to a good start. Folks used to say,

135

'Start airly and get home airly.' It's a free country, you know, Marthy."

"Yes, but it'll seem funny, come Christmas time, if we can't have all our young ones together around the tree in the church here."

"Oh, I shouldn't wonder if they can all come to the Christmas tree."

That was how it worked out. They went to their church to worship, as we went to ours. But whenever we had a supper or a concert or a Christmas party at the valley church, the Luneaus came. The women brought food, the children recited and sang songs — Joe and Marie had fine voices to sing — and after the first Christmas party they were invited to, when all their children, like the rest, received gifts of rag dolls and Teddy bears and little carts, the Luneau men always provided the handsomest tree they could find to bring from wherever they were sawing. They whittled out tiny boats and muskets, too, as they sat, womanless, in their camps on November nights, and little wooden crosses which their women at home painted with silver or goldleaf and tied onto long ribbons so that every girl in the valley had one to wear around her neck.

Each fall more little Luneaus joined us at school, until, as I have said, in 1915 there were fourteen of them there, with five Browns and two McIntires. We had played and studied together, and taught each other so many lessons, indoors and out, that we no longer felt there were any important differences among us. Armand Luneau read and studied history and geography with us, but while we struggled with fractions Mrs. Carter had brought in textbooks in algebra and geometry for him. My sister Edith and Rose Luneau were even closer friends than Agnes and I, or at least more inseparable, for they often slept together in one house or the other, and my mother never allowed me to go often or to stay long at Browns'. Jimmy Brown and Albert trailed Albert's brothers, Pete and Joe, wherever they went, and Forrest Brown trailed too, but always lagging behind the other four because he was so much younger, and short-legged like his father. The Brown twins, who were five that year, burrowed in sandbanks with Napoleon's three youngest, Désirée, Alexandre, and Maurice, and Robi's three oldest, Yvonne, Robert, and Leo, as if they were one flock of chickens. The valley had made room for the Luneaus, and they had found their places and fitted in.

But that year the Daleys came, having moved into the old Burnham house in which my mother had been born and had lived until she was married. The place had been sold at auction when my grandfather died, to city people who stripped the house of its paneling, staircase, and cupboards, and never came back. We heard that the Daleys had not bought it, but only rented it for the summer. We were surprised when they were still there in the fall, and the children began coming to school.

They were not like any children we had ever known. Indeed, we were not sure they were children. But neither were they like any grown people we knew. We half-doubted that they were people at all.

Hannah, though not the oldest, was much the biggest. She was, at thirteen, the tallest pupil in the school and had the broadest shoulders. Her face was long and all her features were large except her eyes, which were narrow, almost colorless slits with lashes to match her strawlike hair worn parted in the middle and hanging over each big ear in a braid tied near the end with twine string. Her dresses were Mother Hubbard aprons, lengths of calico sewn together at the sides and hemmed, with a square neck and with two patch pockets, but with no sleeves or belt. One was dark gray and the other a faded blue. Her bare arms were so long that her big hands hung nearly to her knees. She never smiled at us nor spoke to us, but at recess stood staring at our games as if they were senseless gyrations. We felt that she watched our feet as we played, rather than our faces.

"The way we do ants," Jimmy said to me uneasily.

Charles, who was the oldest of the Daleys, scarcely reached Hannah's elbow. The second sister, Kathleen, two years younger than Charles, was taller than he; and Dennis, four years younger than his brother, was quite as tall and much more substantial. Charles was altogether extraordinary. His nose, his ears, his knees, his fingers, and his bare brown feet were tiny and pointed. He ran like a rabbit, in long soaring hops. Sometimes we thought he flew. His hair was red and stood up in a thatch like a bluejay's. Every inch of his skin which showed had several freckles. He was as talkative as Hannah was silent, but his voice was both soft and highpitched, and he never seemed to be talking to us. He chattered to Kathleen and his little sister, Julie, and even sometimes to Hannah, who only nodded or shook her big head; but most often he was chattering to himself, or to trees, flowers, stones, and running water. He talked so fast and in such an odd way that we could not separate one word from another.

Kathleen, though tall, was very slight. She was plain-featured, but extremely lithe and graceful, and had black hair which hung around her face like a mane. We were as fascinated by Kathleen as we would have been by a young fawn come to school — and could get no closer to her. She liked high places, and was always peering down at us from swaying upper branches, or from the top rail of a fence on which she stood as sure-footed as if it had been a floor. Her skirts were torn at the hems from climbing, and the rags clung to her slim ankles or blew out like coarse lace in the wind. Her eyes were as big and blue as Hannah's were narrow and colorless, but had no more expression. They were like glass discs, or twin pools left after a rain and reflecting only the sky.

Julie, hardly four years old, was a female Charles without his wiriness or activity. Wherever Hannah was, there Julie was planted like a freckled lily trying to hide in a thornbush. In the schoolroom she sat hour after hour behind Hannah's elbow, never stirring, hardly blinking, never even asking permission to go to the pail to dip up a drink of water. In the schoolyard, where Hannah stood Julie sat, her doll's hands folded as if she had no need or wish to move. We had been told that Hannah was the only mother Julie had ever known, for their mother had died when Julie was born. We supposed that through the week, Hannah was Julie's father too, for Mr. Daley worked on the railroad and was at home only Saturday night and Sunday. The rest of the time the children stayed alone in a house without inside finish, stairway, or cupboards, at the end of a road along which no one else traveled. We shuddered to think what it must be to have Hannah Daley for both mother and father.

Dennis was dark like Kathleen, but in no other way resembled his sisters, his brother, or anyone else we knew. Dennis had a swarthy skin, a thickset build, a slow, heavy tread, and a surly expression. He was a creature of moods, but not of many. He was always somber and often belligerent. He threw the stones Charles fondled and talked

139

to at the birds Charles loved; and if Charles chattered at him protestingly, he threw stones at Charles.

"Can you stop him, Hannah?" Mrs. Carter asked, finding she had no control over Dennis once he was beyond the door.

Hannah shook her head.

"But he might *kill* a bird! Or even Charles!"

Hannah shook her head again. She seemed entirely unconcerned, as if neither the birds nor Charles were of interest to her. Whether they were or not, we gradually learned that there really was no need for concern while birds and Charles were Dennis's target, for they were fleet and Dennis a poor shot. Dennis was also poor at stick-knife, though he played it by the hour, so savagely that he often cut his hands, his trousers, and his feet. Dennis was poor at everything except geography and drawing. Even in geography he could not remember the capitals and largest cities, or imports and exports — perhaps because he scorned to try — but he knew every body of water, every river and mountain range in the world, and could name and draw them, giving their depths and heights and courses as easily as we could describe the valley. With the stub of a pencil or a blunt wax crayon racing furiously across a sheet of yellow scratch paper, or with a piece of chalk held lengthwise and then sidewise against the blackboard, he made mountain ranges wooded at the base, barren toward the top, and crowned with snow, oceans on which we saw the tides coming in, lakes which rippled, rivers which came down in waterfalls from the hills and broadened in the low land. As he drew, he seemed to feel alone. When he turned and saw us staring at what he had drawn, he glared at us threateningly and lunged back to his seat to set his geography book like a wall against us.

The first words I ever heard Kathleen say of her own accord — of course she replied sometimes to Mrs. Carter's questions — came out in a little cry one stormy recess when we had to play inside, and Dennis was drawing the Himalayas on the board.

"I *will* climb them! . . . Dennis! . . . I *will!*"

He shot one angry look at her and swept the board clean.

"Not them, you won't," he growled. "See? There's nothing there."

And nothing was there, of all that had been a moment before. Dennis had given us the Himalayas, and Dennis had taken them away. It was black magic. Tears filled Kathleen's empty blue eyes and glistened on her thin face.

The French Luneaus had brought merriment into our quiet valley. The Irish Daleys brought an element for which we had no name then, but which I now recognize as mysticism. Both enchanted and repelled by it, trying to escape it but irresistibly drawn toward it, we were caught in a web so silken-fine that we did not know it had been woven. We only knew that while the Daleys puzzled us, made us uncomfortable, they were always with us even when we could not see them — as if at any moment a boulder might become Charles, or the squirrel running along a branch above our heads might turn into Kathleen. We saw Hannah's face in the full moon. And we believed that if one of us alone should ever meet Dennis in a lonely place, that one would vanish forever.

Wherever young Browns, McIntires, or Luneaus went that fall, we went by twos if not by sixes. On Halloween not one of us would step outdoors. We sat in our kitchens smelling the smoking candles inside the grinning gargoyles we had made of our fathers' pumpkins, and shivered at our own daring. Even on an ordinary day, no child would run an errand unless another child went with him. This was not easy for busy mothers to understand. My mother, who had only me to send — for my oldest sister, Lucy, now worked in a store in the village, came home only week ends, and my second sister, Edith, was nearly woman grown, doing a woman's work — was especially exasperated.

"Call up Browns'," I begged. "See if Agnes and Jimmy won't come over and pick with me."

"They'd have every cranberry there is there picked before you had a cupful, and I want to make at least three mock-cherry pies."

"But I can't go alone, Mama. I *can't.*"

"You did last fall. A dozen times. You said you liked to. And slow as you are, you *did* pick clean."

"But now I can't, Mama! I can't go alone!"

"I don't know what in the world is the matter with that young one," she said to my father. "She acts as if she was bewitched."

He gave me his slow, kind smile.

"Joe's going over to Carters' with a cow right after dinner. As he comes back, maybe he can pick up Agnes. I guess there's cranberries enough ripe for two girls to pick."

"But how will Agnes get home?" I cried. "She can't go *alone.*"

"She can go with Joe when he goes home tonight."

"Of all the foolishness I ever heard," my mother scolded. "Right here in the valley in broad daylight!"

I sat on the step, waiting for Agnes. But when Joe drove into the yard in the democrat wagon, with Daisy tied to its tail, it was not Agnes beside him with her lard

142

pail in her lap, fastened to her belt by its bail, but Jimmy who swung his lard pail above his head and jumped over the wheel before it had stopped turning.

"Goin' cramb'rin'?" he asked.

His voice was low, next to a whisper, and I knew why. The Daleys must not hear where we were going, for of course they knew that cranberries grew along meadow ditches, out of sight of houses.

I nodded and picked up my basket.

We walked as softly as Indians over the hill.

"Where's Aggie?" I murmured.

"Tendin' the baby. Baby's sick, and so's Ma. Ma's sick because she got so mad last night. Pa come home ravin'. First time he has sence last summer. She sent us over to Robi's, but she didn't dast go and take the baby, he was so hot and feverish, and it was rainin' cats and dogs. So she made out to stay there, but Pa broke up two chairs slammin' 'em aginst the walls, and it tore off great hunks of plaster. Trouble is, she's scairt of him, she and Ag."

"You scairt of him?"

"Naw. Nothin' to be scairt of. After he's busted somethin', he lays down and goes to sleep. Next mornin' he's good as gold. But she's still mad as a wet hen. So mad she's sick."

"Gee, you're brave, Jimmy. I'll bet you're not even scairt of the Daleys."

"Naw," he said again, but without conviction. After a minute he added, "They're different, though, some way. They're queer. Best stay away from them, that's all. Best keep a sharp eye out."

We had reached the cranberry beds, and knelt in one. Jimmy began scraping the berries off by the handful, but

143

I picked one at a time, in my slow way, and still I fumbled. They all ran together in a red mat. I could not focus on them because I had to keep looking around and behind me and the sun was blinding bright on the marshes where the water had risen after last night's rain.

"I'll tell you what," Jimmy said suddenly. "You pick and I'll watch. After you get your basket full, I'll pick and you can watch." He sat back on his heels. "Nothin'll move around here that *I* don't see, you can bet on that," he boasted.

Instantly each separate berry came clear before my eyes, crisp and bright and *true*. I began picking, and the berries dropped into my basket, bouncing like red marbles. The sun was warm on the back of my neck. The air was rich with the smell of frost-blackened potato-tops drenched by the rain and beginning to dry. A kind of singing started up in my heart.

I had never been alone with Jimmy Brown before, nor with any boy except Owen. And when I had been with Owen I did not know yet what it was to be afraid. Now I knew, and Jimmy understood it, and was protecting me. I was safe. No one knows the joy of being safe until he has been afraid. Fear is all the worse when one does not know what it is he is afraid of, and the relief from blind, unreasoning fear is exquisite.

I said, "I'm glad it was you who came, Jimmy — instead of Agnes.'"

"Yeah. A girl can't do much. 'G'inst a thing like this. . . . You better not come out like this any time, any more, without me."

"I won't . . . Oh, I won't."

I picked for a while in silence. I could hear Jimmy twisting, behind me, to look in all directions at once.

After a while he said, "Worst trouble with them, they don't do anything anybody else does the way anybody else does. If ever they'd play ball, or drop-the-handkerchief, or go fishin', or even talk so's you could make 'em out, you might think . . . But no. They don't act like kids. Don't act like anything human. . . . Wonder what Mrs. Carter makes of 'em. Ask me, she's as muddled up as anybody else, but most of the time she acts as though they was folks, don't she?"

I nodded. It all seemed far away now. I was picking cranberries in a sunny meadow, and Jimmy was watching over me. It was like the time when women used to go to church between men who walked fore and aft with guns. No harm could come anigh.

From time to time I looked at him from the corner of my eye. He was tall for ten, and though he was slight, muscles already stood out on his upper arms, below the rolled-up sleeves of his blue shirt, and on his bare legs, below the buckled band of his knickers. His hair, the color of maple syrup, had not been cut for a long time and curled in the heat around his ears and above his eyes. His eyes were gray and cast a steely glint on his thin, brown, hard young face.

I liked that steel, that hardness, because it was not a quality to be seen in a girl — no girl should want it — and because it was directed not against me but in defense of me.

"If they had ever played anything, they wouldn't be the way they are," he said, when we had been quiet for a long time.

And later, "Or you might say, if they wasn't the way they are, they'd play. . . . Kids ought to play sometimes."

145

"If anybody could get 'em to play," I ventured, "do you suppose —"

He shrugged. "No use," he said. "Besides, who'd want to try it?"

I had filled my basket. I had enough cranberries for three pies. They would not even need looking-over before they were washed. I motioned to him to take his turn at picking, and sat where he had sat, where he had flattened the brown third crop of meadow grass. I was snug in the place he had made for me; so safe and snug and oddly happy that I could not remember to watch the stone wall, the scattered trees, the edge of the woods, the sky, for lurking Daleys. My gaze kept coming back to Jimmy, the sweat stains spreading across his shoulders, his quick hands roughly stripping the vines and filling his pail with red and green and white, ripe berries and leaves, unripe berries and threadlike worms.

He said, "I guess I've got enough. Don't know as we've got sugar to cook with anyway."

He came and lay beside me on his stomach with his chin on his folded arms. After a while he rolled over and dropped his head in my lap. I stared down at him. He smiled, then closed his eyes and sighed.

"It feels so nice here," he said. "Can't be Daleys are anywhere near."

Filled with wonder, I separated the matted curls around his ears and across his forehead, and felt them cling to my nine-year-old fingers.

Miss Hester Dennett was saying to Rose Luneau, in the great Dennett house where they were dusting books and cleaning bookshelves together — Miss Hester was very particular about the order of her books — "I must get over

146

to school someday soon. There are many of you there this year, aren't there?"

Rose laughed.

"So many," she said, "the little ones, they have to sit on the floor. Only that little Julie Daley, she will not. Beside her big sister Hannah, she is, all the time."

"Seems strange that family has lived on the Burnham place six months now, and I have never clapped eyes on one of them. They don't come to the valley church. Do they go to yours?"

Rose shook her head.

"Father Ribère, he drove up one Sunday to see them, but their big dog he come at him before he can turn in, and make his horse afraid. The Daley man, he is in the yard and do not try to help Father with the horse and the dog, but only stand there with arms cross and watch. Father, he try to greet him but he do not answer, that Daley man. He stand like stone. It is how all the Daleys stand when they are still. Father, he came to our house afterward and we make lemonade for him. He say when we tame the Daleys he try again. I think he mean the dog, but the dog we have never see. I cannot tell how it is possible to tame the stone."

"The man may be stone," said Miss Hester. She had no reason to suppose that any man was otherwise than stone, unless putty in some strong woman's hands and even putty hardened with time into whatever form it had been given. "But not the children. All children have warm hearts and eager minds and must be made to want to use them. I wonder if the Daley children were born in this country."

Rose spread her hands. She did not know where they had been born. She doubted if they had been. To her, who knew so well the rosy color, the waving arms and legs,

147

the fragrance, the soft helplessness, the utter reality of the newborn, it seemed most unlikely that any Daley had ever been so blessed.

"What do their faces look like when the flag is unfurled at the top of the pole?" Miss Hester asked. "Or — I suppose you haven't noticed."

"Yes," Rose said. "Yes. That, I have. It is no different. It do not change. *Maintenant* — can you believe? — often they do not lift their heads to see it."

Miss Hester's eyes dwelt lovingly on Rose's bright, puzzled face.

"You *have* noticed, dear child," she said. "You — and the other children in your family — you always lift your heads to see it, don't you?"

"It is so beautiful. Of course," Rose answered. "It is proud and strong and kind. And it is ours now."

"Ah," said Miss Hester. "That's it. It protects you. And you will protect it. To do so we must all be proud and strong and kind. You and your family understand that. But the Daleys don't. Even though they may have been born under it, they do not understand it. It must be that no one has ever taught them what it means, or they would love to lift their heads to see it. . . . Yes, I must go to school some day very soon."

The Carter horse was hitched to our barnyard fence, and Mrs. Carter sat by the kitchen table with my mother and Edith.

"I felt as if I just had to talk with somebody," she was saying. "I'm about at the end of my tether. Edith, here, has more idea than anybody else what I'm going through, because she's there to see. I don't know what I'll do after you're through in June, Edie. I — I really think I'll hand in my resignation after this year. There's a lot more work

148

for women up home since Frank shut down the mill and started dairying, and Cora isn't getting any younger —"

"Resign!" repeated my mother. "You mean stop teaching, Liz? Oh, you can't do that —"

"Why, Mrs. Carter," Edith cried, "you've always —"

"It just seems like always to you, Edie. It hasn't been. There were teachers before me and there'll be teachers after me. Younger teachers have new ideas, and they have training. They've been to Normal School. I don't really know how to teach and I'm — I'm getting old."

"You're just three years older'n I am, Liz Carter, and that's not old," declared my mother. "Whether you know how to teach or not, there never was a better teacher than you are, and every child that's been to you will say so. I know what you've done for my girls. Look at what you did for Owen Perry. They say he's going like a house afire down there to the Academy. Lucy keeps hearing folks tell how he's right to the top of his class. And who but you could ever have taken up all the Luneaus when they couldn't even talk, and got them to reading out of books, and writing too, and doing arithmetic like Armand does? Say you don't know how to teach! What's got into you, Liz?"

Mrs. Carter looked at Edith.

"Haven't you told your mother what I'm up against?"

Edith shook her head and burst into tears. She was always quick to cry.

"I haven't said anything," she sobbed. "None of us say anything. We don't know what to say. Even I don't. And I'm the oldest."

"Poor Edie," Mrs. Carter said, her lips quivering. "I know you worry. I see it every day in your face. And it isn't right. I don't want my children worrying in school.

149

They should be happy learning things together, the way we always were, Luneaus and all, until — until —"

"Until *what?*" demanded my mother.

Mrs. Carter took hold of herself. She felt she must, for Edith's sake.

"Until the Daleys came, Martha," she said quietly. "Those Daleys are *strange*. They've lived in the valley six months now, and they've been in school two months, and nobody knows them. It begins to look as if nobody will or can know them. They can read and write and figure, but I don't know where they learned that. *I* can't teach them anything. I can't even teach the other pupils while they're there. Everybody watches the Daleys, but the Daleys hardly ever do anything really worth watching. We watch them partly because we are afraid of them, and partly because we can't help it — it's an awful fascination — it's as if they're under a spell and they've put us under a spell. The children think — I don't suppose they put it into words, but they think — and sometimes I think — that Charles Daley is a leprechaun, and Kathleen is a flying squirrel, and Julie is a toadstool, and Dennis is a demon, and Hannah is a witch —"

My mother said, "Nonsense." She looked sharply at Edith. "Is *that* why Althea won't go anywhere alone lately?"

Edith nodded, looking with desperation at her teacher.

"Of course it is, Martha," said Mrs. Carter. "And it isn't nonsense. If you spent five days a week with them — or even one day — you would know how we feel. Speaking to those Daleys is like shouting down a rain barrel. Touching Hannah or Julie is like touching a block of wood. You couldn't touch Charles or Kathleen any more than you could touch a will-o'-the-wisp. And nobody would

150

dare to touch Dennis. But get away from them you can-not, if they are where you are. Forget them you cannot. Might as well try to get out of a fishnet when the top has been gathered up and tied. . . . What I feel, Martha, the children feel a thousand times more acutely, because that is what it is to be a child. . . . The Daleys came to school to be taught; whether they know it or not, what they need most to be taught is how to listen, how to respond, how to communicate, how to give, how to receive, how to be *peo-ple*. But I've tried, and I can't do it. I can't even protect the children from them and from the — the weird atmos-phere they create. *Don't* you suppose some younger, better-trained teacher could do what I can't?"

"No, I don't," snapped my mother. "Don't suppose any such thing. Not for a minute. Seems to me that the trou-ble is you and the children have kept this all to yourselves too long. No wonder you did, though; it sounds so daft. But if it's so, it's so, and if it's so you've got to have some help with it. School's all right, but school can't do every-thing. Why don't those young ones come to church? Are they Catholic?"

Mrs. Carter shook her head.

"If they were Catholic, they'd go to church like the Lu-neaus do, and I'm sure they don't. They don't go any-where except to school. I don't know why they come there so regularly, unless they have heard of truant officers. They just stay up there in and around that house with no inside finish and no stairs, and Heaven only knows what works go on! Alone all the week — and what their father is I can't imagine —"

"Well, we've got to make it our business to find out," my mother said. "I'll talk this over with Mattie. She'll be thankful to know what is the matter with Agnes and

151

Jimmy and Forrest and the twins, same as I am to know what Edith has been mooning about and why Althea's acting so skittish. You can't fight blind. Soon as we can, Mattie and I'll go over some Saturday to pay a call on the Daleys and ask 'em to come to church. Then if they don't, we'll make Brad and Bill go and talk to the man. People that act like demons and witches and — what did you say? Toadstools? I can't for the life of me see how anybody could act like a *toadstool!* — are people without religion. And until people know they need that, there isn't much good anybody can teach them."

Jimmy Brown thought the Daleys needed to learn to play. Miss Hester thought they needed love of country. Mrs. Carter thought they needed education. My mother thought they needed the valley church. Father Ribère thought they needed Catholicism. But there was something else which had to come before any kind of planned instruction could penetrate the defensive entanglements they had built up and were steadily extending; but nobody yet knew this, much less what it might be.

Mrs. Carter had been gone some time when I came in for a pan into which to turn out my cranberries for looking over. My mother, getting supper, asked if I had forgotten how to pick clean. I said with dignity that I thought they should be looked over before they were washed, and went back to the porch step to do it. I knew the berries were clean, but I wanted to be where I could see Jimmy standing at the shed door, watching my father and Pete sort potatoes, waiting for Pete to be ready to go home because I had asked him not to go alone.

It did not occur to me to wonder why, having felt safe in Jimmy's protection, I feared for him to be alone in our enchanted valley, but I was fascinated by the realization that I could worry about Jimmy Brown or — for that matter — about anyone except myself and, now and then, my mother. Did this mean that I loved him? I knew that my mother worried about my father when he was long out of her sight, which could only be a symptom of unreasoning love, for nothing could happen to my father. But I had loved Owen and never worried about him. What was this I suddenly felt for Jimmy which I had never felt before?

From the corner of my eye I watched him swinging on the shed door, twisting the rusty hook which hung from it. I was in agony lest my father should tell him to get off before he broke the hinges, for I had been told long ago, and he was heavier than I. I thought that if anyone in my family should speak to Jimmy as if he were not an honored guest, I should never forgive myself if I did not rise and say, "If you cannot be polite to Jimmy, I can't stay here." But if I did not stay at home, I did not know where I could stay. From time to time he darted a glance at me, and each time I felt my face grow hot and had to lower it over the pan in my lap.

At a great distance I heard the telephone bell, but did not count the rings, and was vaguely surprised when my mother began to speak in her telephone voice. She did not say much, and there were long pauses. What she did say ran aimlessly up and down the windy tunnels of my mind.

"Hullo? . . . Oh, yes, Liz. . . . Who? *Eddie?* . . . Oh, my soul and body! . . . Dell can't go, can she, the way she is? . . . No, of course not, but I didn't know but she'd feel as if she had to go see how her mother's fixed. . . . My land, she *has* — this quick? Well, what do you think of that! . . . Does seem as though, don't it? . . . No, I can't take it in. . . . Well, I'm sure I'm glad you did,

Liz. Let me know when you hear anything more, and I will you. . . . No, poor soul, there's nothing we can do for her now, but looks like later on there'll be plenty of chance. . . ."

The telephone rang again. Jimmy was going toward the pump. Suspenders held up his knickers and I studied the brown X across his back, glad he could not look at me unless he turned. He stepped onto the curb and began to move the handle up and down. Now I could see the side of his face with the sunset light on it.

"Mattie, have you heard?" asked my mother. "Why, Eddie Fernald dropped dead last night out there in North Dakota! . . . Lottie sent Del a telegram. Liz Carter stopped in at Del's a little while ago and Del told her. Liz called me as soon as she got home. . . . Why, no, 'course she can't, way she is. Anyway, it took Ed and Lottie a week to get out there. . . . No, no, burial will be out there, Lottie told Del. Said she knew Eddie would just as soon. He liked awful well out there, I guess, some reason. . . . Well, yes, I do, Mat. She put that right in the telegram. Told Del she was going to start home soon as the funeral. Going to put everything they had into somebody's hands to sell for her when they can, and she's coming home as fast as she can. . . . There, I hope so. I don't doubt she'll be as glad to see the valley again as we will to see her. But as time goes on — nothing to live for but Del and the young ones — poor Lottie, I don't know what she'll do with herself. Awful to be a widow at her age. She'll be an old woman in a few years, and still she may live for thirty. . . ."

I could hardly remember Ed and Lottie Fernald, who had lived in the valley before the Luneaus . . . before Owen spoke to me out of a tree . . . before Pete came to

154

stay with us that winter . . . before the Daleys . . . before Jimmy had sat behind me while I picked cranberries, guarding me, and then put his head in my lap. . . .

She'll be an old woman in a few years. . . . Not I, not I! I was young, young, young! My wheel had only begun to turn. Everything everywhere was new. Even my own dooryard was new, for Jimmy was walking toward me, across it, bringing a dripping tin cup. I watched him, wondering. . . .

He asked, when he reached me, "Want a drink?"

I nodded, but could not move, and he held the cup to my mouth. It was ice-cold, and I drank until it was empty, looking up at him over the rim, suddenly unembarrassed and unafraid.

"It's good water," he said solemnly.

I nodded. It was the best water I had ever tasted.

He smiled at me and I smiled back. Pete came out of the shed. Jimmy hung the cup back on the side of the pump, and ran to catch up with Pete. He did not look at me again, but he was doing what I had asked him to do. I sat listening to their footsteps, growing fainter, and a star came out above the pump.

At supper my mother told my father about Eddie Fernald.

I was thinking of Jimmy.

Later, in the chamber I had shared with her since Lucy went away to work, Edith told me that the next day my mother was going to get Mattie Brown to go with her to call on the Daleys and ask them to come to church. She repeated what my mother and Mrs. Carter had said.

I thought, "While his mother is away, maybe Jimmy will come over here. But Agnes would have to come with him. And Agnes would have to bring the twins and Forrest and the baby. That wouldn't be the same as it was today. I wonder if it will ever be the same again as it was today."

Edith said impatiently, "Althea, are you listening? Mother thinks if the Daleys went to church they wouldn't be — the way they are."

I said dreamily, "Jimmy says if they could play games, they wouldn't be the way they are."

"Well, I can't imagine 'em playing games," Edith said, blowing out the light. "For that matter, I can't imagine 'em in church, either. *I* think they ought to be put on an island where nobody else is. I heard once about an island in a lake in New Hampshire where somebody put all the rattlesnakes in New England. They couldn't swim, so they couldn't leave the island, and that's why we don't have rattlesnakes any more."

"I don't mind snakes," I said. "Jimmy would kill one, if he saw one, quick as a wink."

"Well, I don't like 'em, dead or alive," said Edith from the dark beside me. "They make me feel the way the Daleys do, only not so much. That's why I think an island is the best idea."

"If we only had an island in the middle of the river," I said, "we could take them over there in Frank Carter's boat."

I fell asleep thinking of the Daleys cast up on a desert island, and Jimmy and me looking over at them from the safety of the riverbank. Across the swift dark current, Hannah and Julie stood motionless, like figures cut out of rock; Kathleen flew from tree to tree; Charles ran up and down the bare face of a cliff and his ears stood high above his head, twitching; Dennis was spearing fish for their supper — but these were strange fish, for the tip of

156

his spear ran red. Jimmy lay with his head in my lap and smiled up at me.

"There wasn't any island," he said. "So I made one. Last night. It's a present. A present for you. Instead of a ring for your finger."

"I like it better," I told him softly. "Much better. Now you and I can pick berries together. We can climb the mountains and slide on the hills and wade in the brooks and go to the pond for lilies, and never, never, never need to look behind us."

But that was only a dream.

My mother came back discouraged from the call she and Mattie Brown had made on the Daleys.

She told my father at supper, "What an afternoon I've put in! Hustled to get through my Saturday work in time to hitch up and take Mattie over to the old place — and the road up in there is so gutted out I didn't know but it would pull a wheel off, and the bushes have filled in so that they kept slapping Pony on both sides so I had all I could do to hold him down to a walk. By the time we got into the dooryard, we were all shook up, and then it was an awful shock to me to see what condition the old house is in, and juniper coming up all through the field. I hate to think how that place has gone back since I lived there.

"There was nobody in sight, and no sign anybody had been around for years, only there was a sound of chopping in the shed. It was ghostly, that's what it was. We didn't dare get down out of the wagon, just sat there calling, 'Anybody home?' and my voice didn't sound like my own. It fair squeaked. After a while, a boy came to the shed door with an ax in his hand, and at the same identical instant, I swear, another boy's face popped out of a window frame (no glass in it now) up under the ridgepole of the barn; a big girl and a little girl were standing in the front door of the house, and another girl came out of the woods where the pasture used to be. Not one of them moved after our first glimpse of them, and not one of them spoke a word. They just stared at us as if they'd never seen our kind before. Like we would at creatures from another planet.

"I told them we'd come to ask them to come to church tomorrow afternoon. I said the service was at two o'clock, and that they must know where the church is. I said we'd all be glad to have them, and there would be organ music and singing. They didn't say aye, yes, or no, nor even nod or shake their heads, ary one of 'em. The big girl and the little girl acted stone-deaf. The boy in the top of the barn had a silly grin on his face the whole time. The one in the shed door had his head down like a bull and held his ax as if he might take it to us any minute. The girl that had come out of the woods was too far away for us to make out her expression, but she looked as if she'd been left there by gypsies.

"Finally I asked, 'Is your father here?' I had to ask three times, louder every time, and then the boy in the shed door growled, 'He's a-comin', and you better get out before he does.'

"So we *got* — not because I was scared, so much, by that time, as because I was so mad I wanted to lay hands on every one of 'em — give that big girl a good shake, throw a rope around the one at the edge of the woods, take the ax away from the one in the shed door and hit him a clip with the broad side of it, and drag the grinning one down out of the loft by the seat of his pants. No *wonder* Liz Carter is at her wit's end! . . .

"Now, Brad, you're not saying anything, but I will **not**

158

be bamboozled that way. I want you and Frank to go over there tomorrow morning and lay the law down to that man. Tell him we're not going to leave his pack of young ones to grow up savages, even if he is. Tell him we want them in church at two o'clock sharp, and we'll see what we can do with them there. Because if they don't straighten out and straighten out quick, I'm going to report him to the State for neglect, and some Saturday night when he comes moseying in he'll find they've all been shipped off to where they'll get straightened out. I mean what I say, Brad. You know what I am when I take the bit in my teeth. I'm not going to have Liz Carter resign and the valley school ruined by five young hoodlums from nobody-knows-where that don't know anything because they won't learn anything."

So, since Mrs. Carter was at her wit's end and my mother had taken the bit in her teeth, my gentle father and silent Frank Carter dutifully stormed the Daley fort that Sunday morning. They walked over together — to spare horses and wagon wheels — and found Mr. Daley sitting on a rotting doorstep, moodily smoking his pipe.

"Morning," said my father. "Nice day. . . . Your name Daley?"

"It is indeed."

"Heard you folks had moved in here. Where my wife grew up. Her old home place. . . . I'm Brad McIntire. This is Frank Carter. His wife teaches the school. Where your young ones go. . . . Womenfolks have been talking it over, wishing they'd come to church today. . . . Maybe you could come with 'em, first time, anyway. . . . Elder Leighton from the village preaches for us. He's pretty good. . . . Service starts at two o'clock."

Mr. Daley spoke at last.

"Start it any time you want to, for all of me. We won't be there."

My father and Frank looked at each other. My father cleared his throat.

"Everybody in the valley goes," my father said mildly. "Except the Luneaus. They're Catholic, and have their own church in the village."

"That may be your business," replied Mr. Daley, "but, bejabbers, it's not mine. We have nought to do with churches."

He stood up and advanced a few steps. There was threat in the set of his shoulders, the curl of his fingers, and the way he looked out under his knotted eyebrows. Mr. Daley was a brawny man.

My father, though small in stature and mild, never backed away from anyone.

He held his ground and said slowly, "I take it your young ones are your business. They're not mixing in very well. All the womenfolks want is a chance to help them out. Way they're growing up, alone, they may get into trouble."

There was a long silence after this. Mr. Daley's face grew crimson, his eyes bulged, his breath came fast and hard, he swung his arms. My father and Frank tried to judge whether he was working up a terrible fit of anger or fighting to keep it down.

Finally words came in a jerky growl.

"My young ones are my business. How they grow up is my business. If they get into trouble, that'll be my business. And I'll thank everybody to keep their noses out of it. I brought them here to keep them away from folks. It's folks that cause all the trouble. Mostly folks like you that's forever poking in where they're not wanted. The law forces me to send my young ones to school. I abide by the law. But there's no law that says I have to send them to church, and that's the *last* place I'd send them. I never went to church, and if my wife never had she'd be living today. . . . There is a thing for you to chew on. I'm a lone man because my wife went to church. She belonged to a church, heart and soul. And her church told her she had to have children. She had to have all the children she could. That woman was the world and all to me, and I watched her kill herself in twelve years, having five children that lived and four that didn't. Now she's gone, there's nothing left for me but work, and nothing worth working for. Every day is a year long. If one of them children even steps inside a church door, I'll thrash him within an inch of his life. He'd be in trouble before I was through with him, I'll warrant. So put that in your pipes and smoke it."

My father said gently, shaking his head, "Awful too bad. Thinking the way you do of her. But, thinking the way she did, she wanted her young ones to go to church, didn't she? And different churches teach different things, you know. . . . Besides, you can't keep her young ones away from folks. *They're* folks, and they're together. They're teaching each other, one way or another. You sure what they pick up that way is right?"

Mr. Daley made a choking sound, went into the house, and slammed the door. My father and Frank walked quietly home again.

After church that afternoon, as my mother sprang into the wagon, she said, "Well, they didn't come, did they?"

"I told you they wouldn't," my father reminded her.

My mother pressed her lips into a thin line.

"I'll give them one more week," she said. "Then I'll

161

talk with Liz, and if they haven't shown any signs of straightening out, I'll write to the State."

"Better leave them alone," my father said. "They're bad off enough as 'tis. If they can stand it, seems as though we could."

My mother did not answer, which was her way of admitting that perhaps he was right. It was not Edith's or my place to speak. But as we rode slowly and silently toward home, we could feel the chill threat of a long, dark winter, and I knew Edith was thinking, the same as I, "He spent only a few minutes with one Daley. He doesn't know what it is to live day and night — even in our dreams — with five!"

The next day we felt a new flicker of hope. Rose Luneau told Edith that Miss Hester was coming soon to teach the Daleys the meaning of the flag.

"She tell me" — Rose said — "she say, They then have the warm heart. They be proud of it, and kind. They laugh and talk. Like us. They no more stone. No more knife, *jamais*. Dennis, maybe he draw nice picture of the flag, *n'est-ce pas?*"

When the bell rang to call us together Tuesday morning, the boys started their daily race for the canvas bag which hung from a hook in their entry.

But Mrs. Carter said from the doorway, smiling, "Let's wait a little, boys. Miss Hester is coming to see us, and you know she likes to watch you raise the flag."

All the usual morning exercises waited for Miss Hester, and the usual schedule was changed. We began at once with geography classes, and Mrs. Carter asked Dennis to draw a contour map of New England and the Atlantic Coast covering the whole front board while the rest of us recited. Dennis worked swiftly but in wondrous detail, as

162

always. Between watching him and watching for Miss Hester, we had such difficulty in putting our minds on what was printed in the big, thin books that at last Mrs. Carter told us to close them. She sent Charles, Hannah, Kathleen and several others to the blackboard along the east wall to make the Atlantic Ocean there, and to draw ships coming from England and Ireland toward where Dennis was drawing the North American East Coast. Those of us still in our seats snickered because Hannah's ships looked like big washtubs with smokestacks and Charles's and Kathleen's sat on the tops of waves as if resting on windrows of ice. But they kept on making ships as if they would never have enough, and finally had ships traveling in both directions. In the meantime, Dennis had finished and was back in his seat, staring blackly at his bare desk, and Mrs. Carter was chalking in a tiny flag here and there along the coast he had drawn, and a little way inland. After she drew each flag, she had one of us come up and print in a name.

"Jamestown," she said. "Where the first people from England landed. Plymouth. Where the first permanent settlement was made. Those people came in the good ship *Mayflower*. Put *Mayflower* on the side of one of your ships, Charles, because yours are sailing ships and so was the *Mayflower*. Hannah's ships, with the smokestacks, came later; some of them, like some of the sailing ships, came from Ireland, and I suppose Mr. Daley was on one of them. . . . Boston. . . . New York (then New Amsterdam — its first settlers came from Holland). . . . Philadelphia, the Quaker City. . . ."

We were all caught up in the panorama of ships straining across stormy water toward the hills and valleys and rivers Dennis had drawn, and we too were scrambling ashore, planting little flags, building cities. All but the Daleys.

I raised my hand.

"There were Indians on the shore when we came," I cried. "Wearing fur blankets. And on one of the ships there were cows from Denmark. The first cows we ever had."

"That's true," smiled Mrs. Carter. "Would you like to draw the Indians in, Althea? And, Hannah, let Julie make the cows on one of the ships. I'm sure Julie can draw a cow."

But Julie would not even take the chalk which Hannah stolidly held out to her. Charles and Kathleen had tired of making ships and were making castles, animals no one had even seen, strange plants, and funny little people all over the ocean floor, changing the Atlantic into a puddle of stagnant water where refuse is thrown to rust or moss over into grotesque forms. Dennis continued to stare at his desk as if avoiding the awful sight of what others did with chalk on blackboards. We could see the pulse beating heavily in his neck, and it seemed to throb out hoarsely: "They spoiled it all when they came with their flags and their names. It was beautiful when there was nobody there. It is ugly now. In a minute I shall snatch it away from them. It's mine. They shan't have it to spoil."

"All take your places, please," said Mrs. Carter bravely. "Let's talk a little now about why people came in ships to the wilderness which this continent used to be, why people kept on coming after the cities were built by others, why many people still come from other continents and countries to live here, why many people who cannot come long to come and live in the United States of America? *Why?* . . . Who can tell me why? . . . Rose?"

"For the freedom," said Rose. She was pink with delight that she knew.

But Dennis was scowling at his desk, Charles was kicking Kathleen across the aisle between them, and Hannah and Julie sat pushed together like a large and a small lump of unrisen dough.

Mrs. Carter nodded at Rose and tried to smile but her lips trembled.

She said yes, that the first settlers had come here to find freedom as a way of life, freedom to worship God each according to his own belief, freedom of opportunity to make a good world for children to grow up in. She said part of this continent belonged to England, part of it to France, part of it to Spain, part of it to Holland; but that all the people who came here to live became Americans, and all thought that, far from their parent countries, they could plan their own lives and the future as they wished, without interference from across the ocean. But while these settlements were young, she said, they needed help from their parent countries, just as children do from their parents. And so they grew up. By and by they knew they were grown up, but their parents did not know they were grown up because they were too far away to see.

All the time Mrs. Carter was talking, I thought she was going to cry.

Then the door opened and Miss Hester walked in.

Miss Hester, though old, was very vigorous. Her face, under a little black hat, was long, brown, and weatherbeaten as the prow of a Viking ship. Her full black skirts rustled magnificently, and when she unbuttoned her coat a metal mesh bag like a big bright pocket swung by a chain from the belt at her waist. She wore black silk gloves, and when she took them off we saw the veins on

165

the backs of her hands raised like blue ropes, and the knuckles of her fingers twisted by years into powerful knots.

"Children," said Mrs. Carter gratefully, "this is our Miss Hester, as most of you know. Miss Hester Dennett. She has lived in the valley all her life, and members of her family were among the first white people to make their homes here. She knows more about this part of our great country than any other person. We might say that she *is* our history."

"Have one of them read from the Bible, Elizabeth," said Miss Hester in her crisp, dry voice, as she seated herself on the green chest in which we kept the globe. "Then I will hear their prayer. That was the beginning here. It will always be the beginning of everything that lasts. God is, was, and ever shall be."

Mrs. Carter called Edith to the desk and handed her the open Bible. Edith began to read aloud and, though the words were familiar, I did not know what they meant. I watched Miss Hester's face and saw the meaning there: that every one of us was important in God's sight, because he had in him something peculiarly his own to contribute to a Great Plan for life on this earth, that great round ball sheltered by Miss Hester's skirts like a flock of chickens by their mother's wings. Did it — did it mean the Daleys, too? Yes, said Miss Hester's face authoritatively, it does mean the Daleys too.

I wanted to look at them, for it seemed to me they must suddenly be transfigured, but I could not take my eyes from Miss Hester until she bowed her head when Mrs. Carter said, "Now let us pray."

Our voices came out as one strong, young voice . . . *Hallowed be Thy Name . . . Thy will be done, on earth*

as it is in heaven. . . . Deliver us from evil . . . Thine is
the Kingdom, and the power, and the glory, . . . Amen.

Miss Hester said, "Amen . . . Amen."

Then she rose, stood squarely in the center of the spare floor before us, and began to speak. There was no quiver in her voice. It was crisp with knowledge, dry with courage, and steel-bright with pride.

She told us about the Abenakis, how savage they had been against their enemies, but how the small tribe which lived in the valley when we came had received us as friends because we had met them as friends, had remained our friends, and their chief had become a Christian through the teachings of one John Eliot.

"When their chief died," said Miss Hester, "he was buried on the mountain, and we call him Saint Aspinquid as the Indians did, because he was a great and good man."

She told us about the first houses and the first cows, the first war, and the first flag with thirteen stars for the thirteen original states in our Union. She told us about the Declaration of Independence, the Constitution, the Bill of Rights, the exploration and settlement of the West, the coming of the machines and of settlers from many different countries, the differences in way of life between the North and the South and how those differences, great as they were, were not great enough to separate us. She told us about Lincoln and the Emancipation Proclamation and the Gettysburg Address, and the steadily growing number of stars in the flag. . . .

"This country belongs to the people," said Miss Hester. "We elect our own officers. We make our own laws. No man or small group of men tells us what to do. We are responsible for ourselves. We give ourselves more freedom than is the lot of any other people on earth, and yet we do

167

not permit unlicensed freedom, freedom which would do injury to others. We have freedom under God, which is the freedom to be good and to do good in all the ways we can find; not the freedom to be evil and to do harm to others, which is *not* freedom under God, and which is not freedom in the long run but the worst kind of slavery."

She told us nothing we had not heard before many times in the valley, but she told it in a way which made us see it all coming about, step by step, made us feel that we ourselves were a part of every period in our nation's history; and she poured out the truth and the wisdom on which our nation was founded, by which it had grown great, like water from a spring. We drank thirstily, and the more gratefully because its taste was familiar and we knew it to be crystal clear.

"Bring me your flag," said Miss Hester, looking at a boy she had never seen before.

It was Charles Daley. He brought it.

"Take it out of the bag," said Miss Hester. "Careful! Don't let it touch the floor. Never let the flag touch the floor or the ground. It protects us. We must protect it. I'll hold this end. You hold the other."

She looked at a girl she had never seen before.

"Come and count the stars."

Hannah came and counted them, touching each with one big, blunt finger. Julie stood behind her like a foreshortened shadow.

"Forty-seven."

"You missed one," said Miss Hester. "There are forty-eight now. The one you skipped may have been your own state. The State of Maine. What is your name?"

"Hannah Daley."

"Hannah Daley, this valley is part of a great tract of

land which once belonged to the Commonwealth of Massachusetts. When it became the State of Maine, a new star had to be sewn on every flag in the country. Every state has its own special personality, its own assignment of duties according to its history and its location on the map, and is as dear to those who live in it as ours is to us. Never skip a star in this blue field, Hannah. It may be your own. And whether it is or not, it is priceless. United we stand. . . . Now we shall go outside. *You* may carry the flag." She waved a small brown, blue-veined hand at Kathleen.

"When you carry this," she said, "you carry our heritage. It is as much as a child can do. When you are older, you will add to it."

We followed Miss Hester and Kathleen to the yard. It was November, and no one had told us to put on our caps and jackets, but we scarcely felt the biting wind.

"Fasten it to the rope," Miss Hester said to Dennis. "My joints are old and stiff. Yours are young and lissome. . . . Once this flagpole was the tallest, straightest tree in my father's pasture on the side of the mountain. When the schoolhouse was built, he had the tree cut down and peeled off the bark and painted it. It was a great day in the valley when this pole was in place and we raised a flag to the top of it for the first time. I can just remember it. Some of the women had tears running down their faces.

"My father said, 'Old Glory. . . . There she waves.' . . . What is your name, boy?"

"Dennis Daley."

"Dennis Daley, raise the flag of your country."

It went to the top of the pole, and the icy wind flung it out. The sky, which had been November gray, turned to pearl around it, and the colors glowed. Old Glory, there she waved; our Stars and Stripes . . .

"Symbol of our freedom under God," said Miss Hester. "Men have died for it, and their women have lived for it and it alone. The past has been given to us. The future we must build, as others built our past. Give your pledge of allegiance, children."

She stood as straight as a soldier, with her hand hard against her bosom. Our hands went to our foreheads.

"I pledge allegiance to the flag . . . and to the republic for which it stands; one nation . . . , indivisible, with liberty and justice for all . . ."

But Miss Hester's voice did not place her usual exclamation point at the end. Our gaze came down from the flag, now so magnificently unfurled, and sought her face. We looked where she was looking, at the Daleys. Hannah and Julie stood like stones, staring across an empty field. Kathleen and Charles were watching a crow on the bare branch of an elm tree at the corner of the yard. Dennis was scowling at the ground, fists thrusting out the pockets of his knickers, of which the strap at one knee had given way, letting the leg of it slip nearly to his ankle.

"I must go now, my dear," said Miss Hester quickly to Mrs. Carter. "May God bless you, and bless your children."

She hurried off along the rutted road. We stared after her, and for the first time in our lives she looked old to us, old and mortal, hurrying toward death. She grew smaller and smaller until she became like a frost-blackened leaf blown down the hill out of our sight.

We turned numbly to Mrs. Carter, who said nothing. Her head was lowered and her shoulders seemed stooped as she went through the door into the schoolhouse. We followed, but not at all in the spirit of the children of

170

Hamelin, more as the people of Hamelin watched them disappear.

The Daleys would not play. They would not learn. They would not go to church. They would not even look up at the flag. All those we trusted had come, tried their cures in vain, and gone away. We were again alone with Daleys, shut in with Daleys. The winter ahead looked dark, bitter, and interminable. The fire in the stove was nearly out. Mrs. Carter took off the cover and stirred the dying coals with a bent and rusty poker. We shivered.

That afternoon my mother was not at home when we came from school. There was a note from her, propped up against the red sugar bowl on the kitchen table, saying that she was spending the day with Della, and telling Edith what to cook for supper. I did not like the way Edith fried potatoes; she let the edges get black. I did not like her biscuits; they were too tall and hard; my mother dropped out biscuits from a big spoon and they were as soft as cake, with crisp, golden tops like frosting. I especially disliked Edith's scrambled eggs. She used an egg-beater and made them like a mass of slippery custard. The white of the egg was the best part, and I wanted to be sure it was there. When she had supper ready, and had strained the night's milk, the three of us sat down at the table, but the room seemed empty. I was not hungry, and sat listening to the clock tick.

Suddenly there was a better sound, the quick tap of my mother's footfall on the porch steps. She came in with cheeks as pink as a girl's, from the cold; said, "My, something smells good, Edith!" pulled off her gray hood and shawl and hung them behind the stove, went to the sink to wash her hands. She asked from there, as she splashed, "Did you remember to pick up the eggs, Althea? Good

171

girl! How many?" The roller squeaked as she drew on the towel. Her cup rattled against the saucer as she poured her tea. Her chair scraped across the floorboards as she pulled it back from the table. Now she was in her place, and all the parts of my life fitted in around her, so that I, too, could come to life for the first time since morning.

"My goodness," she said. "Second meal I've had today that I didn't cook myself! Dell was saying that when she was your age, Edith, she couldn't cook a thing but fudge. That's what come of Lottie's spoiling her the way she did, I thought to myself. All I said was that you and Lucy could get a meal together as well as I could before you were twelve years old, and so'll Althea. . . . Did you get a saltfish today, Brad? That's good. I've had a hankering for a piece of toasted saltfish for a week now. Always feel that way, come November. . . . Dell said she thought the trouble was her being an only child. That's why she's wanted another one as quick as she could have it after Wayne. Poor young one, she's had her hands full, though, looking after one before she'd really got the hang of keeping house. I don't know what Lottie's going to say, when she gets there, to see how yellow the sheets have got that she left for Della when she went out West. And the way Dell fades her colored clothes is a crying shame. She has got so she can cook, though. She made a corn chowder this noontime that was as good as I ever eat, and she had an apple pie that was all right, too, though I think sugar on piecrust is gilding the lily. She's neat around the sink, and that's something to be thankful for. Lottie never could stand a sink smell any more than I could. But the paint in the bedroom and parlor and all upstairs hadn't been washed since they built the house. It's lucky I got over there to scrub today. Wayne's fingermarks was all over

172

everywhere. As I told Dell, I don't see how hands that size could travel so far and carry so much dirt. She admitted she didn't do any spring cleaning this year, she felt so miserable at the time. Now of course she hadn't ought to do any reaching. Bert had a fire going in the parlor today. Tonight he's setting up a stove in what's going to be Lottie's room, so I'm going back tomorrow to clean up there. They had a letter from Lottie today, said the funeral would be Sunday (last Sunday, that is, of course) and she'd start Monday and figured she'd be here Friday night. That'll give us just about time. I'll bring Dell's curtains home tomorrow and do them up for her. I must say I'm glad Lottie'll be here with Dell this time when there'll be Wayne to look after as well as the rest. I only hope she'll be equal to it, so I can tend to my own business for a while."

She dipped blueberry sauce into a dish for me, and it tasted good because she had dipped it. She split and buttered a biscuit for me, which was softer because she had split and buttered it.

I slid into a half-dream, hardly conscious of my mother herself, but deliciously aware of what had happened to the rest of us and to the room since she came into it. Edith looked less plain, even pretty, with the anxious frown gone from between her eyes; there were lace-edged ruffles over her shoulders. My father, eating quietly, listening, looked young again, untired. His thinning hair lay in waves on either side of the part, and I knew how he had held his left hand against the ends as he peered into the little mirror in the tin comb-case, and drawn the dripping black comb upward with his right. The lamplight was bright on the red sugar bowl, on the checked cloth, on the bone-handled knives and forks and coin-silver spoons, soft on the steeple clock, the black stove, the braided rug, the crisp, cretonne cover of the couch. Beyond the windows there was nothing but velvet dark, curtains enclosing all this brightness, this softness which was our own.

I thought, When I marry Jimmy Brown, he will come here to live. I will never live anywhere but in this house. Then he will have everything we have, and his eyes will stop darting around so fast, like a weasel's.

I did not think of the Daleys again until we were back at school the next day. Then I realized afresh that here we could never forget them, but only for us did they exist. The village minister and the village priest were far off in their village. Miss Hester had gone back to her old books and papers. Our mothers were remembering only that Lottie Fernald was coming back to the valley, our fathers only that she was coming without Eddie. In our desperate need, we were deserted. The Daleys had been set off on a barren island, but we were confined there with them. Angry, sucking currents swirled through the bottomless pits which surrounded valley children for seven hours every day and separated us entirely from the snug shelter of the mainland where the grownups lived. Even Mrs. Carter seemed now as much a child, in her helplessness, as any of us, and, in a hopeless way, we made faint attempts to protect her by massing ourselves between her and the Daley Five, concealing Dennis and his knife, distracting her gaze from Hannah's and Julie's blank stare, covering with our solid footsteps the sound of Charles's and Kathleen's pattering here and there.

"If we can only hold it off," I said low to Jimmy on the way home Friday afternoon. "Whatever it is, maybe we can *push it down*. Can't we?"

He shook his head.

"We can't," he said. "It's nothing you can get hold of, *to* push. I don't know what's going to happen, but something's going to happen. It's got to."

He kicked grimly at a small stone, trying to dislodge it, but the topsoil had frozen the night before and there had been no sun all day to melt it. He kicked so hard that I knew it must hurt through the thin, twisted sole of the boot, which was too large for him and turned up sharply at the toe like the point of a ski. I felt the hurt myself.

Edith and the Luneaus had gone ahead of us. Agnes, with the twins and Forrest, was somewhere behind. Nobody knew where the Daleys were. We two seemed to be alone. I put both hands on his arm, raising myself on tiptoe, and kissed his cheek.

He drew back sharply and looked at me. I tried to smile, but something new flashed in his face which stiffened my lips and made me drop my eyes. Suddenly his arms were around me, his whole body pressed hard against mine, his cold nose inside the plush collar of my jacket.

He was whispering in a kind of dry sob, "Oh, Allie! . . . Allie! . . . Allie —"

If I had been frightened for an instant, I was frightened no longer. I clasped my hands behind his back, holding him as much as I could as if he were a baby, cradling him, supporting him.

"All right, Jimmy, dear," I kept whispering. "Everything's going to be all right, Jimmy."

Then, from the bushes beside us, a hoarse voice said, "You — make — me — sick."

Jimmy let go so quickly that I almost fell. He shoved me aside with one arm, turning me enough so that I saw what he was seeing.

Dennis Daley stood there in the shadow, a ragged cap

pulled low above his eyes, his mouth curled in a sneer, his knife open on the palm of his hand.

Jimmy lunged a few steps toward him, one shoulder hunched and his fists raised.

"You shut up," he growled. "You leave us alone. You blasted, black —"

Dennis did not move a muscle.

"Jimmy's mad," he chanted tonelessly, "and I'm glad, and I know what'll please him; a bottle o' rum and a sugar plum, and a pigtailed kid to squeeze him."

Jimmy's face turned dark red. His mouth twisted, clamped on one side and open on the other. Foamy drops ran out of it, and the words, "You con-founded rattle-snake —"

Dennis snorted, still without moving a muscle.

Jimmy lunged toward him again.

I screamed, "Jimmy! His knife —"

With Jimmy's first blow the knife went flying. The boys were the same age. Dennis was taller and heavier-set, but Jimmy was quicker, more wiry. Jimmy was the first to go down, but he clutched Dennis's leg with a vicious twist, and they were down together, rolling over and over in the bushes, punching, grunting and cursing.

I jumped up and down, screaming, "Jimmy! Jimmy! Jimmy!" and my screams echoed back from the dark hills, down from the stretched gray tent-top of the empty sky, and up from the frozen ground. Alone in this silent arena, Good Knight Jimmy Brown was fighting a duel to the death — I thought — for me, against the personification of evil.

But then, as if from the mountains, down out of the sky, and up from the ground reinforcements came swarming. There seemed to be dozens and they were all Browns.

176

Dennis, on top at the moment, methodically pummeling Jimmy, was suddenly submerged by an eight-year-old Forrest astride his shoulders trying to throttle him, a twin pulling each ear, other twins hanging on his feet, another Forrest kicking his knees, any number of Agneses taking handfuls of his hair, beating him with a slab — and all howling like banshees.

Dennis no longer had a choice. He was obliged to let go of Jimmy and try to get up to defend himself from his new attackers. But they would not let him.

It was Jimmy on his feet, who said, "Leggo of him! Leggo, I tell you!"

The horde of Browns fused into one Agnes, one Forrest, one pair of twins, and drew back, staring at Jimmy all scratched and bleeding. Both his eyes were swollen nearly shut.

"Who asked you into this?" he demanded. "I can handle him without no help from you. Mind your own business, can't you?"

"But he was killin' of you, Jimmy," Forrest croaked.

"Killin' *me?*" growled Jimmy. "I was killin' *him!* If you'da give me a chance."

He turned his head, looking for his adversary through the slits in his puffed face.

"But his knife," Agnes cried. "Jimmy, you know he's got a knife!"

The twins, who were only five, began to cry. I put my arms around them.

Dennis seemed to have forgotten us all. He was on his hands and knees, feeling through the bushes.

"No more, he ain't," Jimmy said. "You ain't got no knife now, have you, Dennis? What you lookin' for? Lookin' for your knife? Well, you won't find it. It's gone.

And if you should find it, I'd take it away from you. I'd throw it in the river. You won't never have a knife again. You ain't fit to have a knife. You ain't fit for nuthin', and what do you say to that? Want to fight some more or have you had enough?"

Dennis got up slowly and looked at us in a dazed way, as if he had never seen us before. His face was gray-white around the blood streaming from the corner of his mouth, and one of his front teeth lay loosely on his lip. Grass and moss was tangled in his long hair, and his arms hung limp and useless, his big, bare hands reaching to his knees. I held the twins closer. What would happen now?

He did not answer Jimmy. After looking at us for a minute in that dazed way, he started walking up the road. I thought that he walked like a gorilla.

"You're yeller, Dennis Daley," Jimmy called after him contemptuously. "Yeller all through. Take away your knife and your rocks, and you couldn't win a fight with a flea."

Dennis kept on going. We watched his back until he disappeared.

We did not notice until then that the other Daleys were there too. Hannah and Julie stood across the road, staring at us as they always did, with no expression. Kathleen was running back and forth on one railing of the bridge. Charles sat on the opposite railing, dropping crumpled bits of paper into the water in midstream, between the borders of shelly ice along the river banks, and watching them swept away.

"Well, come on," Jimmy muttered. "Nothing more to hang around here for. Be getting dark."

The twins and I followed close behind him. Forrest ran to catch up with him, marching proudly beside him. We

178

did not miss Agnes until we had left the woods behind, and heard her running.

"What did you stop for, Aggie?" I asked softly.

The whole world seemed hushed.

"His cap," she said. "Dennis's cap. I saw it in the bushes."

"What did you do with it?"

"I gave it to Hannah."

"Did she say anything?"

"No. . . . I didn't give her this. It was right by the cap. Funny he didn't see either one of them."

She held out Dennis's knife.

"I'll take that," Jimmy said sharply.

She gave it to him without a word, as if he were now in command of us all. He dropped it into his pocket.

"So we know where *that* is," he said. "Never need to worry about *that* guy again."

"No, nor any of the rest of 'em," Agnes said.

"Why? What do you mean?" I asked her, though I felt it too.

"Because — didn't you see? — *they don't hang together.* We'll never have to take on more than one of them at once. Whatever one of them does, he does alone. And whatever happens to him, he's got to handle it alone. I never thought they'd be that way."

We went on silently until we were at the end of the lane. The light had been lit in the kitchen for my mother to see to get the supper. It blinked at us as the lilac bushes stirred in the wind.

"Well, that's so," Jimmy said, as if Agnes had just spoken. "They *don't* hang together, do they?"

He looked at his brothers and sisters through his eye-

179

slits, and began to smile a tortured but happy smile. He struck Forrest a light, brotherly blow on the shoulder.

"Go on home with the kids, Aggie. I'll be along as soon as I go up with Althea."

"You needn't, Jimmy," I said quickly. "You ought to get something done for your face —"

"Face'll wait," he said. "I'm only going because it's so near dark."

"We can go up, too," Agnes offered.

"You put for home," he told her. "I ain't been out alone for a dog's age. Going to feel good."

When we were halfway up the lane, we saw Edith coming down.

"That you, Althea?" she called through the dusk. "Where on earth have you been?"

"She's been watching a fight," Jimmy answered. "A danged good one, too."

He gave me a little push toward Edith and struck off across the field, trying to whistle. The sound was like the squeaking of a mouse.

"Who fought?" asked Edith.

"Jimmy," I told her proudly. "With Dennis Daley. And Jimmy beat! He 'most killed Dennis. He's got Dennis's knife. And you know what we found out? *The Daleys don't hang together!* So nobody needs to be afraid of them any more, ever again."

Edith was incredulous and full of questions, which I did not have time to answer until after we had gone to bed, for when we reached the house my mother, having seen Lottie Fernald ride by with Bert Anthony, was talking to her on the telephone. Until bedtime my mother was repeating to my father what Lottie had said, describing how she had sounded, and speculating on what it meant, what

Lottie's state of mind really was now that she had come home without Eddie, what a widow's way of life would be in the valley.

On Saturday, while the beans were baking, my mother took Edith and me over to see Lottie, and while the older people talked I took care of Della's little boy. He was only two years old, and I was surprised by how much he knew. He could tell me the name of every animal in his picture book, and make the sounds they made; he knew all the primary colors; he named and pointed to all his features and clothes and toys. So we played school. I thought of how I had gone to school to Owen. I thought that Mrs. Carter would be astonished by Wayne when he was old enough to go to her school, and I made the first plan I had made in months because now I was not afraid to make plans. My world was steady again. I planned that I would often go to Della's, as Owen had come to my house, and I would teach Wayne as Owen had taught me. I would be Wayne's first teacher.

"What is your name, Girl?" he asked me.

Owen had come to me as a Boy.

"My name is Althea," I told Wayne. "But you must call me 'Teacher.'"

This was a new word to him, and he liked it. He said it over and over, smiling broadly, his eyes twinkling. He was a round little boy and his stomach pushed out the front of the red smock he wore over his cotton flannel blouse and pants. He looked like Santa Claus, and I hugged him as I had seen Mrs. Carter hug the Brown twins and the littlest Luneaus, remembering that when Mrs. Carter did it she looked over their heads at her older pupils in a way which included us all. But she had never hugged Julie Daley, who disappeared headfirst into Hannah's skirt when anyone was near enough to touch her; nor anyone else at school since the Daleys came. I sighed, thinking that, though there was now nothing to fear, school would never be the same as it had been last year.

"Why do you breave so long, Teacher?" asked Wayne.

I hugged him again and said, "Because my mother's putting on her shawl and I have to go now. But I'll come again, and we'll have school again. Like this. Just you and me."

The next day we went to church and Lottie came with Bert. After the service everyone gathered around her, saying how glad they were to have her back, but there was pity in their eyes. Lottie looked smaller and younger than when she went away, perhaps because she was in mourning. Her black silk dress and thick black cape stood out stiffly around her like clothes on a clothespin doll, and smelled new. Her black hat had a heavy black veil which her eyes seemed to strain to see through, and it had a black rose on the front. I thought a black rose was too impossibly sad for a flower to be. All the rest of the day my mother's manner toward my father told me she could never bear to live without him, and I knew I could never bear it either. Yet, at the thought, my lips kept twisting into a nervous smile, and I wondered what was the matter with me. I went up to my room to pray, and stayed until my mother called me to come down out of the cold. She was looking through an album full of shiny photographs, and showed me the Fernalds' wedding pictures.

"How much Della takes after her mother," she said.

I thought Lottie looked younger in the picture than Della did now, like a little girl who had put on a woman's wedding dress and pinned up her hair like a woman. Eddie looked thin and hard, in a high collar and bow tie.

My mother turned the heavy pages slowly, telling me who had sat for the other pictures; her grandfather on his seventieth birthday, her parents on a wedding anniversary, valley young people of long ago grouped for a tintype taken at a country fair, a little girl with long curls who had not lived to grow up. At last she closed the book. It had a dark cover with a silver bee on it, and silver clasps. I wondered if it could happen that someday I would sit and look at pictures of people I had loved and belonged to but whom my children never knew, at schoolmates since grown old, at a child I had played with who did not live to grow up. I touched the bee and the clasps; and the whole valley, its past and its future, seemed to lie under a shroud on which were printed the mathematics of time, figures estimating its toll. I wanted to run away, but did not know where to run to.

My mother rose briskly.

"Well, time to start supper," she said.

She put the album into a drawer, and lit the lamp. As she mixed batter, I heard her humming.

"They get used to it," I realized. "By the time you're old, you don't let yourself dwell on it. You think of it, but then you put it out of your mind. It's only when you first think of it that you are frightened."

When we went up the hill toward the schoolhouse Monday morning, I had scarcely thought of the Daleys for twenty-four hours. But as soon as I saw the crowded schoolyard, I knew that the Daleys were not in it, though it was nearly time for the bell to ring because Edith had done her hair three times before she would leave home.

"The Daleys!" I cried. "They're not there!"

I began to run, which Edith was too dignified to do —

though now Mrs. Carter was ringing the bell. Panting, I squeezed into my place in line beside Agnes.

"Where are the Daleys?" I whispered.

"Haven't come," Agnes answered.

"No talking in the line, girls," said Mrs. Carter, but she did not sound severe. "Joe, you may put up the flag."

When we were all in our places — fourteen Luneaus, five Browns, and two McIntires — she smiled at us from behind her desk as if we shared a lovely secret, as if an iridescent bubble floated in the air above us, a bubble which would burst if other eyes than ours should see it.

"Shall we choose our first hymn, children?" she asked in a soft, light voice.

It was like that all day, for the Daleys did not come. Nor did they come the next day, and none of us spoke of them. It was as if they had never really existed, except that Jimmy sometimes gave me a triumphant look, to remind me that it was he who had vanquished the big dragon and so the whole dragon family.

My mother was not at home that Tuesday. Lottie had called her in the night to say Della was feeling "miserable," that she had telephoned the doctor but he did not think he would be needed until morning, so could my mother come? Mother was gone until Tuesday evening, and, when she came while I was getting ready for bed in the shelter of the oven door, she told us that Della had a fine little girl, a sister for Wayne, and that Bert and Della were going to name her Ruth. Mother looked pale and tired, but excited and proud. After we had all gone to bed I could hear her, through the thin partition, telling my father that Lottie had come in the nick of time, for Della had clung to her mother until Lottie all but had that baby herself.

"Poor soul," said my mother. "After all Lottie has been through, to have this added on so quick! I finally had to step in and tell Della to show a little spunk and let her poor mother get a few minutes' rest. Thank the Lord, Lottie was so worn out she dropped sound asleep and didn't wake up until she heard the baby squall, so she missed the worst of it. But she'll have her hands full now for the rest of this week anyway and as long as she can carry the load, I think likely. Della's acted ever since her mother came as though she was about twelve years old. If Lottie's willing to take over the reins in that house, she's more than welcome to for all of Della, so I guess Lottie's future is cut out for her and no picnic either. I know one thing, when my girls get married, they'd better be more capable than Dell is, for I'm not going to live their lives for them. Matter of fact, both Lucy and Edith can cook and clean better than Dell, and I wouldn't wonder if even Althea could take better care of Wayne right now than Dell does. She was real handy with him over there the other day."

I went to sleep thinking smugly of how neat a house my mother's youngest daughter would keep for Jimmy by and by, what delicious meals she would prepare for him, how bravely she would bear him children, and how well she would bring them up. I thought, too, of what a different way of life this would be for Jimmy from the way he had known so far; and I saw him tall, broad-shouldered, in clean, well-fitting clothes, sitting beside me at the wheel of an automobile as we rode to church.

The rest of the week at school was as peaceful as the first two days; and after-school time was peaceful, too, because I went every afternoon to stay with Wayne while Lottie and Della and the baby slept. I took him for walks

185

before the sun went down, showing him the different kinds of bark on trees, the golden tears of pitch on the pines, woodchuck holes, and the first star in the evening sky. Then we tiptoed back into the house and had more lessons there. Every night he was in his footed sleepers before the baby woke to be fed, Lottie came downstairs to get supper, and Bert came from work to take me home. Every night I saw Bert toss his little boy into the air, then go through the open door into Della's room and stoop over the bed to take her in his arms.

I thought, "This is what I want. I must grow older as fast as I can."

It was not until we were ready to be dismissed Friday afternoon that Mrs. Carter asked, in an overly casual voice:

"Has anyone seen any of the Daley children this week?"

We stared at her. None of us had. We had almost forgotten them.

Someone said, "Maybe they've moved away."

"But no one has seen them go?"

No one had.

"That's all, then," said Mrs. Carter. "School dismissed. Good night."

The next day she took her courage in both hands and my mother on the wagon seat beside her and rode over to the Daley place. Hannah stood looking at them through the window until Mrs. Carter beckoned her to the door. Mrs Carter asked her, from the wagon, why they had not been to school. Hannah said her father was at home, sick in bed, and she had to look after him. Mrs. Carter asked why the others had not come. Hannah said she did not know. Mrs. Carter said that unless the boys and Kathleen came the next week, it would be her duty to notify the school authorities and there would be an investigation. Hannah closed the door.

"What will happen now?" asked my mother as they rode home.

Mrs. Carter did not know. She did not even know what she hoped would happen.

What did happen, no one could have foreseen.

We had only three days of school the following week. Thursday morning valley kitchens were rich with the smell of pork baking, roosters stewing, hot cranberry and cold barberry sauce, mustard pickle, stuffing and biscuits and mince pie and Indian pudding. At noon, each valley family sat down together and gave thanks. Della not only came to the table but had made the biscuits, because Bert said he had waited for some of her biscuits as long as he could. There was a special contentment even in the outlines of the hills against the gray sky, in the interlocked, bare branches of trees, and in the watchful waiting of dogs and cats who had no doubt that they would get their bountiful share when their turn came.

But before the doctor had finished his Thanksgiving dinner in the village he had to leave it to speak to a man who called at his door. The man was Sean Daley, saying he was on his way back to work on the railroad in Massachusetts, but that one of his children, staying on the old Burnham place, was sick and he wanted the doctor to get out there before dark if he could.

Luneaus, Browns, Anthonys, Carters, Dennetts, and McIntires were happily doing the few dishes which are used by families making a supper on chicken and pork sandwiches, crisp stalks of celery, a spoonful of this and that, a wedge of pie held in the hand, when the doctor telephoned the only Fernald in the valley.

187

He talked to Lottie a long time. He said he had been out on calls all the night before and most of the day and had to get some sleep, but he could not go to bed until he had a plan for the next day. He asked her if she could advise him. Five children were alone on the old Burnham place, and the youngest one was very sick. Their father was away at work, would not be back for a week, and no one knew where to reach him. The house was a shambles, cluttered, dirty, drafty, and its only heat was from green wood sizzling in the kitchen stove. The children were living mainly on potatoes. The sick one had a bad throat and a high fever. It looked something like diphtheria, but the doctor was not sure of his diagnosis. Mr. Daley said he had had the same symptoms last week and cured them by sweating. Whatever the child had had clearly been contracted from the father, and so certainly was contagious. If it looked like diphtheria in the morning, the doctor might have to operate. The child was too sick to be moved. The doctor could not operate alone. Anyone who went there to help him might be taking a grave risk, both to herself and to any family she returned to. What was really needed was a housekeeper-nurse who would stay with the Daley children at least until the father returned. Was there, by any chance, a woman in the neighborhood who could and would do it?

"Yes," said Lottie Fernald. "Stop in here on your way by in the morning, and I'll go with you."

Until that Thanksgiving night, Lottie had not heard of the Daleys. Della and Bert had heard very little, and when Della was told what her mother had decided to do, she could think only of the risk, and of how difficult it would be for her to manage alone. Lottie said quietly that the baby was ten days old and healthy, the house was in order,

the Thanksgiving leftovers would last through the week-
end, and she thought it was time Bert had his little family
to himself, especially since she was needed much more
somewhere else. She called Mrs. Carter to ask the children's names and ages, and if Frank would deliver a load
of dry stovewood to the Burnham place the next morning
early.

"Tell him to have the boys put it under cover as quick
as they can," she said.

"I'll tell him," said Mrs. Carter. "But oh, Lottie, you
don't know those boys! You don't know what you're getting into! If you'd only asked me about those children before you promised! I can tell you that never in my
life —"

"It wouldn't make a mite of difference to me," Lottie
told her. "They're over there in the woods alone, all of
'em cold and hungry, and one of 'em sick. What better can
I do than go look after 'em, 'til their father gets home anyway? No use to talk, Liz. I said I would and I'm going to.
Ask Cora if she can't send over some cooked stuff by Frank
when he goes with the wood. I've got to leave what's here
for Della, and I may not have time to bake tomorrow.
Don't know how that oven works, either. I'm going to ask
Martha to send Brad over here with some bedding and
some fresh milk that I can take with me when I go."

Mrs. Carter said, "All right, Lottie. All right. We'll all
do anything we can to help. But you remember this: if you
find it's more than you can stand — and I'm afraid it will
be — let us know and I'll see if you can't go right over to
the Dennetts. That's in case the doctor says you can't go
where there are children. I couldn't bear it for you to feel
you *had* to stay."

"Well, thank you, Liz. I hope the wood'll be there before I am. I'll need all the heat I can get. Now I have to call up Martha before she goes to bed."

My mother was sharper with Lottie than Mrs. Carter had been. She said Lottie must be crazy, after all she had just been through; the State should have taken those children before this; it would be a miracle if Lottie didn't get down sick herself within twenty-four hours; my father would bring sheets, pillowcases, comforters, and milk as soon as she had it strained in the morning; she would send some apples, too, and goose grease and ipecac and liniment and woolen strips in case they were needed; she could see the corner of the shed on the Burnham place from her kitchen and if Lottie hung a cloth out there where it would wave in the wind, when she needed anything she didn't have, my mother or some one of us would come as soon as we could, and Lottie could shout from the door what she wanted; if the doctor had to have a woman to go into such a beartrap as that place was, why didn't he bring a strong young one from the village? Lottie was the *last* one he should have asked.

"He didn't exactly ask me," said Lottie. "But I told him I'd go, and I will. Now I'm going to box up some eggs. Della's hens have been laying real good for the season, so she can spare a couple of dozen, anyway, for me to take with me. Good night, Martha."

"Good night, Lottie. You're awful good. You're too good, that's all. I'll send some jelly by Brad. And some canned blueberries."

When Lottie and the doctor reached the Burnham place the next morning, Hannah told them Julie was asleep and she could not wake her up. Julie was dead. When Mr. Daley came home a week later, the burial had taken place in the old Burnham family cemetery in the pasture, at-

190

tended only by the village minister and the undertaker, for by then Kathleen was sick and Lottie said the other children should not be standing outside in the biting wind.

The kitchen Mr. Daley came into that night was clean and warm. The cookstove had a high polish, the teakettle was singing, the woodbox was full. A bright quilt covered the old couch, and a braided rug was spread before it. Hannah sat beside the table making calico covers for the cushions of the rocking-chair.

"I'm sorry to have to tell you such a hard thing, Mr. Daley," said Lottie, "but hard things happen to us all. I'm sorry we didn't know where to reach you. But valley folks are good neighbors, and we've done the best we could. My son-in-law and Frank Carter and Brad McIntire set up stoves in vacant rooms as soon as they could after I got here. The Dennetts sent some cot beds. The Luneaus have put sawdust banking all around the house, so we're as snug as we can be until you close up the stairwell in the hall and get some storm windows. Kathleen is better. Charles is just coming down with whatever it is — even the doctor don't know — but I've got him in bed. Hannah and Dennis are as good as another pair of hands to me. Now, the doctor says tain't likely you could pick this up again, being as you've just had it, but you might carry it on you, so you can't come and go here, but you'll probably want to stay around as long as you can, so Bill Brown has het a kettleful of water in his cellar where you can take a bath after you leave here. Here's a bottle of something the doctor left for you to put into the water. Mattie's put some clothes of Bill's in a box down there, for you to put on. They're the best he's got, so take care of 'em. Put your own clothes in the box and I'll wash them for you. Good thing you ain't wearing a suit. When you're ready to go back you can take 'em off the line and have 'em to wear home when you come next time. Now after you leave Bill's tonight, you go over to the Dennetts'. They've got plenty of spare rooms and one of 'em's all ready for you. Miss Hester sent word about it, and said they'd give you some breakfast in the morning. But, long as you're here now, you might as well have your supper."

Lottie had not waited for Mr. Daley to say a word. Now she pulled out a chair for him at the table and began dishing up hot food from the stove. He ate, she said afterward, as if it were the first full meal he had had in years, with Hannah sitting there quietly making covers for the rocking-chair cushions.

When he had finished, he said, "Good supper," stood up and reached for his jacket and cap.

Then, without quite looking at Lottie, he asked, "Anything you need I can get?"

"Two things right off," said Lottie promptly. "If we had them, to go with what we've got and the neighbors will bring, we could get by for quite a while. We need a telephone. It ain't safe to be without one, at a time like this, so far from folks. Besides, a telephone's company. The other thing's storm windows. I wish you'd measure for 'em tomorrow and get as many as you can afford and put 'em on when you come next week."

As no one else in the valley knew what words had passed between Lottie and Mr. Daley, my mother and Cora Carter and Mattie Brown could hardly believe their ears when Lottie telephoned them, in turn, Thursday morning.

"Lottie!" they cried. "This really you? Where are you?"

"Right where I've been for going on three weeks now."

"You've got a telephone *there?*"

"That's right. Just a temporary line, hitched to trees. Makes an awful scratching, don't it? But they can't set poles now until spring."

"Well, this is great, Lottie. How'd it happen?"

"Oh, I guess Mr. Daley wanted to fix it so we could get help quick if we needed it. Charles was just coming down sick when his father was here. He's getting over it, though. I'll probably let him get up tomorrow. The rest of us are fine so far. Mr. Daley said he'd bring storm windows for the kitchen and put 'em on when he comes Saturday; then he'll get more as he can. And he's going to fix the stairs. Well, I've got to get some dinner started. Hannah's hanging out the wash, and Kathleen's playing checkers with Charles. Dennis is splitting up some kindling. I just called so you'd know we're on the line. Our ring's nine. Tell Bill and the Dennetts Mr. Daley appreciated what they done for him."

"We only saw him come and go," said Mattie. "He only raised his hand. Bill didn't go out. . . . Didn't know as he'd feel like talkin'. But he left the cellar real neat."

"The Dennetts said he hardly spoke a word over there," said my mother. "To tell the truth, Miss Susan and Miss Mary was scared of him and stayed in their rooms. But Miss Hester claims not to be scared of anything, so she showed him in that night and put out his breakfast for him Sunday. Oddest man, she said, ever she saw."

Lottie laughed.

"Any man's always seemed odd to the Dennetts," she said. "There, let's hope they ain't listening in. Anyway, he told us here when he come to get his clothes and measure for the windows that he had a good bed and a nice breakfast and he was obliged to everybody in the valley for their kindness. I told him it was no more than we'd do for any-body in trouble like his.''

"Well, that's so, but — how long is the house going to be quarantined?''

"Six weeks after the last one's up and around,'' said Lottie. She sounded almost pleased, in a way triumphant. "The doctor says he'll take no chances. But I don't think we'll need so many favors as we've had, now Mr. Daley's kind of taking over. It'll set the young ones back in school awfully, but that can't be helped. If Liz can leave any lessons on paper for 'em, in the mailbox, they'll do 'em. I told 'em somebody would bring whatever is on the Christmas tree for 'em. They're tickled about that. Well, I've *got* to start dinner. Call up when you want to.''

After a flurry of incredulous astonishment, everyone drew a sigh of relief, and everything soon was as it had been before the Daleys came, before Lottie came back from the West. Except that Lottie talked every day with one or more of the womenfolk, telling them, as each told her, about what she was cooking, where she was cleaning, the sewing she was doing, how the children were, and what the plans were for Christmas. The other women told her of their troubles, and Lottie was sympathetic but seemed to have no troubles. Mr. Daley now spent his week ends at home, wearing different clothes from those he wore away. He had bought a cow and some hens. Dennis had learned to milk. Charles and Kathleen were fairly in love with the hens and would live in the barn cellar with them if Lottie would let them. Kathleen had a pretty voice to sing, and Hannah was getting to be a great hand with a needle.

We had a Christmas tree at school and another at church. At both there were as many gifts for the Daleys as

194

for the rest of us, and from both they were sent more than their share of oranges and red cheesecloth bags full of popcorn and candy. Lottie said Mr. Daley brought presents to fill all their stockings though this was the first time they had hung them up on Christmas Eve since their mother died. Hannah made a new dress for Kathleen and Lottie made one for Hannah, and they made shirts for the boys and Mr. Daley. Kathleen crocheted ties for the boys and made pincushions for Hannah and Lottie. The boys and their father built a new dish cupboard. They had a big turkey for dinner.

"Oh, I'll tell you," boasted Lottie, "we had a real frolic here Christmas Day!"

Imagine the Daleys frolicking!

School opened in January without Pete Luneau, but Hannah, Kathleen, Charles and Dennis came back. We still could not imagine Hannah or Dennis frolicking, but already there was a great change in them. Hannah, though quiet, no longer stared. She showed an interest in the youngest children and gradually they responded, letting her lift them in her strong arms to sit on a high post or tree branch or to write at the very top of the blackboard. Dennis, also quiet, was no longer surly, and seemed older by two years than when we had seen him last. He not only drew his remarkable pictures on paper, but let Mrs. Carter put them on the walls. When he was not drawing, he was studying, and made rapid progress. From Jimmy's and Marie's and Albert's class he came into mine. Charles and Kathleen, on the other hand, seemed younger than they had before, and their running about did seem more frolicsome than weird. Charles still picked up stones but, instead of throwing them, took them home for a collection.

They had a sled now, a fine new one varnished bright and with the name "Flexible Flyer" painted in red. It went faster than any of ours on the road, but cut through more on the crust of the field because its runners were narrower and sharper; so they gave us turns on their sled in the road, and we gave them turns on ours in the field. All clean and neatly dressed, the Daleys were no longer, at a stranger's glance, distinguishable from the rest of us.

"I suppose your mother'll be back with you now, won't she?" my mother asked Della.

Della said no, that Mr. Daley had asked Lottie to stay on as housekeeper through the winter anyway, and Lottie thought that was better all around.

"Mother feels needed over there," said Della.

Lottie was still there the next summer. Long before then, Mr. Daley and the boys had shingled and painted the house and put in a big vegetable garden. Lottie and the girls had the yard full of flowers, and curtains at all the windows. Both girls and both boys came to church with Lottie every Sunday. Through the summer, Lottie had brought Hannah and Kathleen to spend the afternoon several times with Agnes and me, and we had been over there. The dog was gentle and lay asleep in the sun. Charles and Dennis went swimming with Jimmy and the Luneau boys, played ball with them, and helped them in the hayfields.

One July day Jimmy — he told me about it afterward — had pulled Dennis's old knife from his pocket and held it out to him.

"Guess this is yours," he said.

Dennis glanced at it with little interest.

"You want it?" he asked.

"It's yours," said Jimmy.

"I don't want it. Dad gave me another one."

"You've got another one?"

"Sure."

Dennis took a knife from his pocket. It had a bone handle and four blades.

"How long you had it?"

"Since Christmas."

"Gee. That's a beaut. . . . How's it happen you ain't been carrying it?"

"Have."

"Don't play stick-knife like you used to?"

"No. Worries Aunt Lottie. Says it makes her sick to see blood. I was always sticking myself."

"Women are funny."

"Sure are."

"Honest Injun, you don't want your old knife? I never used it."

"Well, go ahead and use it."

Agnes had become very religious. A week-long series of evangelistic meetings had been held at the church in the early spring. I was not allowed to go because they were in the evening, but Agnes went to every one and told me about them. At the final one she had been the youngest among those who stood up while the congregation sang "Whosoever will may come," and then gone forward to accept Christ. As nearly as I could without having been there, I followed her closely through her week of slow, sweet conversion and rebirth, like a small virgin with lamp trimmed, filled, and at last lighted. Now she stayed after church every Sunday, with other new converts, for the lessons which prepared them for baptism and admission to membership in the Christian church. She told me what she could of what she learned. She was reading the Bible through, beginning with Genesis, and when she came to a section which she felt she understood and thought I might understand we read it together on Saturday. I taught Agnes to pray. Until then she had supposed that all prayers were written by ministers or memorized like the Lord's Prayer. I, who had knelt by my bed and talked to God every night as long as I could remember, knelt at the foot of a tree in our pasture and talked to him for Agnes to hear. But by the time the wild strawberries blossomed, Agnes could make a much finer-sounding prayer than any of mine. As I listened, kneeling beside her on a mossy bank, I thought her prayers sounded as beautiful as any I had heard from a pulpit.

Later I said, "Agnes, if you were a boy, you might be a minister when you grow up."

Agnes flushed. She was usually so pale that color looked strange spreading under her dark skin.

She said, "I've heard there are woman preachers. But I'll tell you something, Althea, if you'll promise not to tell anybody else. Of course I don't mean your mother. But I don't see why you would need to tell your mother."

I promised.

"Well — if I can, if I can get to be good enough, if I can learn how, I want to be a missionary."

I asked her what a missionary was, and after that I was much more interested in geography because all the farthest-flung corners of the earth were places where Agnes might go to teach little heathen children about Jesus, if she became good enough and could learn how.

One hot August Sunday afternoon there was a baptism in the river behind the church. The new converts sat at the water's edge and the rest of us in quiet rows behind them while the village minister talked. The sky was clear blue that day, without a cloud in it. The tall pines which had dropped the spills to carpet the ground stood motionless, their tops shining like church spires, many soft fingers pointing heavenward. Birds sang ecstatically.

The village minister, in his gray frock coat and black trousers, walked into the water.

"Deacon Carter," he said, "lead Sister Lottie to me."

I could not look at Lottie, nor at Della and Bert when they followed her, nor at the three young men from the other side of the mountain. My eyes were fixed on Agnes, who finally sat alone at the water's edge, wearing the white gown Hannah and Lottie had helped her make over from her mother's wedding dress, and a pair of white canvas slippers Edith had outgrown. All Agnes had new that day was the white hair-ribbon Mrs. Carter had given her — a white hair-ribbon, an inner ecstasy like that in the throats of happy birds, and a light on her face which seemed to set her so far apart from me that I thought I should never be able to touch her again.

"Deacon Carter," said the village minister, "lead Sister Agnes to me."

Sister Agnes!

She stood up and went into the water. It seemed to me that she walked not in but on it. She stood between the two men while the minister prayed, and I felt no need to bow my head. I thought I was looking at an angel. Then for an instant she disappeared.

I thought, "She has gone. She will never come back."

I glanced quickly at her family, sitting beside us. Tears were streaming down both her parents' faces. Jimmy was digging his heel into the soft, dark loam under the pine spills, staring at the hole he was making, and his brothers stared at it too, as if wondering what would come out of it. But Pauline looked at her mother and, seeing the tears, was frightened and began to scream, "Take me home, Mama. Take me home. Take me —"

I pulled her against me, muffling her voice in my shoulder, whispering, "Sh! Sh! We've got to wait for Agnes!"

When I could look again at the river, it was deserted, flowing its usual placid course, no longer holy. The baptism was over. The women were getting up, collecting from the wagons the baskets and bottles which held our supper. These were carried into the vestry and the contents spread on tables covered with oilcloth. Then all who were members of the church went upstairs to give the hand of fellowship to those who had been baptized.

"Pauline," said her mother, "why did you bawl out like that? Making such a rumpus at such a time."

"I didn't want to go into the river," said Pauline, calmly chewing on a pickle. "I didn't want to get *my* best dress all soaking wet."

Jimmy burst into a howl of laughter.

I knew then that I would never marry Jimmy Brown. I looked coldly at them both.

"You don't even know what Agnes has done today," I said. "Much less what she's going to do. You don't deserve such a sister as Agnes is. You and I weren't good enough to go into the river today. Agnes was. We don't know enough. Agnes did. If you're good enough you don't mind getting your dress wet. If you know enough, you don't even notice it. I hope someday we'll be as good and know as much as Agnes, but we won't if we don't do something besides cry and laugh. Look, they're coming downstairs."

I moved into a corner by myself. I wanted to be alone when Agnes passed me. She came just ahead of the minister. I reached out and touched a fold of the skirt of the faded school dress she had put on in the Sunday School room. She looked around, peering through the dusk until she saw me, and smiled. After another step or two, she turned and held out her hand. My heart seemed to stop beating, but somehow I crossed the space between us. Hand-in-hand we went to the table and side-by-side we sat at it, but neither of us could eat. In the growing, neighborly, worldly confusion of serving and talking and the clatter of dishes, we sat still, silent, not even looking at each other. I did not know what Agnes was thinking. I was thinking that the longer I could stay close to Agnes Brown the better I would be and the more I would know.

When school began again, Joe Luneau and Charles Daley did not come back, but the other Daleys played the same games as the rest of us, they knew the Lord's Prayer as well as anyone, Dennis demanded his turn at pulling up the flag and they all looked up at it, repeating the pledge, as solemnly and proudly as Armand did, and Armand had always been the solemnest and proudest of us all.

The last Sunday before Christmas Mr. Daley came to church, with his children and Lottie. Nobody knew what the sermon was about, except that it was a Christmas sermon. Everyone was thinking of the miracle Lottie had wrought. Mr. Daley, wearing a new dark suit and a white shirt with a handsome tie, sat very straight in the pew, looking neither to right nor to left, and they all went away hurriedly after the service was over.

My mother could hardly wait to call Lottie the next morning, when she was sure Mr. Daley would have gone back to work.

"How did you ever manage it, Lottie? Getting Mr. Daley to church?"

Lottie laughed.

"It was easy," she said. "He's got a job putting in new track on this line, so he can be at home. I told him that was fine, but Hannah would have to take over the housekeeping because it wouldn't look right for me to live week in week out in the same house with a man I wasn't married to. He said why didn't we get married then. I said oh, I couldn't marry a man that didn't go to church. So he went, and we got married here last night. I had the minister up to supper, and afterwards Della and Bert stood up with us. Hannah made my dress, every stitch, herself. Mr. Daley — Sean — bought the cloth. It's brown silk. Hannah covered forty-six buttons for it. Kathleen sung for us. Dennis painted a picture of the house for us — way it looked last summer — and he and Charlie made a frame for it, cut glass to fit and all. Oh, I tell you, we had a rinktum here. Kind of surprised you, didn't I? Well, I've got to go. Mr. Daley — Sean — is waiting for me to go to the village with him to finish up our Christmas shopping."

Now it was as plain to see as a nose on a face. The Daley dog could not turn friendly, Mr. Daley could not forget to hate, the Daley children could not be good pupils, play games, love the flag, hang together, make friends, or even feel close to God, the sad ghosts could not be laid nor the eerie witches banished, until there was a mother in the Daley house.

"It's too bad," I said, "Julie never had a mother."

A picture of Julie was in the album of my mind, and she was my schoolmate who never grew up.

"She is with her own mother now," my mother said. "So

it doesn't matter any more. And maybe she knows what her going brought to all the others. You know what the Elder always said. 'God's will *will* be done.' "

I thought about the Elder, and thinking about the Elder made me think of Owen. I had not thought of Owen for a long time. It was strange that I was thinking of him all the way to the mailbox that morning, for, when I opened it, in among the other Christmas cards there was one for me, from Owen.

He wrote:

> Merry Christmas, Althea McIntire! I am at Mass. Agricultural College. That makes me a Mass Aggie. I made the basketball team — only freshman on. I work in a one-arm restaurant evenings unless I'm playing basketball. Has Mrs. Carter told you you should go to college? If she hasn't, she will. So study hard.
>
> Owen
> *P.S.* Still have fogs? Anybody drop out of one lately?

That was all. No address. I had no more idea where he was than if he had said he was in Persia. But his card was my favorite Christmas gift that year. I have it still.

I was ten years old now and small for my age. My sister Lucy was clerking in a village store. My sister Edith roomed with her, and rode every day on the trolley to a business school in a nearby city, taking a year's course to become a stenographer. But I went back to Mrs. Carter after vacation determined to study hard to prepare for the day when she would tell me that I should go to college, though I did not know where colleges were nor what a child of the valley could do in college except play basketball and work in a one-arm restaurant, and I had never yet seen a basketball or a restaurant.

Mrs. Carter taught on as she had always taught, with no realization that district schools practiced what would soon become new educational theory; each of us, in each subject, proceeded at his own pace, classified by which reader he was using. The law required us to stay in school only until we were fifteen years old, though my sisters had stayed until they were sixteen. Pete and Joe worked with their father and brothers in the woods that winter, and Charles as timekeeper for his father's railroad crew. Armand had a ninth reader, though he was only twelve years old. Agnes, also twelve now, was in the eighth, with Dennis and me. Owen had written, "Study hard." I studied hard, at school and at home, and did little else except on Saturdays when I took care of Wayne for Della mornings and had long talks with Agnes in the afternoons.

We hardly noticed that Rose Luneau and Hannah Daley had not come back after Christmas, and that two little Luneaus were there for the first time. We did not hear, if we were told, that Miss Hester Dennett was sick in bed for seven weeks, tenderly nursed by her sisters. We were unconscious of the war going on in Europe, now in its third year, and did not read President Wilson's note to each of the militant powers, proposing "a League of Nations to insure peace and justice throughout the world." We did not know that Germany's reply was the statement that all sea traffic adjoining Great Britain, France, and Italy would be "prevented by all weapons," that our ambassador to Germany had been recalled, that Germany was said to be offering a military alliance to Mexico, promising Mexico the states of Texas, New Mexico, and Arizona

204

in the event of a successful war with the United States. The word did not reach us that within two days three American ships, all homeward bound, were sunk by German submarines.

Agnes had become a priestess, always at her devotions, and I was her handmaiden. We were apart from the world.

But one morning in April, as we went slowly into the schoolyard, as separate from Jimmy, Forrest, and the twins as if the circles they made racing around us were impenetrable, we blinked at the sight of Miss Hester beside Mrs. Carter in the doorway. Against the familiar black of her hat, cape, and dress, her face was like a big pearl, pale, smooth, cold, and yet with a glow underneath. We had never seen her, or anyone, look like that. She was unearthly. She stood as stiffly as we imagined statues did; we had never seen a statue.

"They are all here," said Mrs. Carter. "I'll have them in at once. Children, come and take your places."

"It can't be nine o'clock," said Jimmy. "It was only —"

"It's not nine o'clock," said Mrs. Carter. "But we are all here, and Miss Hester has come to speak to us."

"Don't we put up the flag?" asked Dennis.

"Later," said Mrs. Carter. "Miss Hester will speak to us first. She is not well, and we must not keep her waiting."

We bumped against one another in the entries, hanging up our jackets, and slid into our seats.

Miss Hester had not sat down. She stood ramrod straight before us as she did each time she came, but she was changed. The light in her eyes was that of one who sees something begun which he will not see the end of but which he will go with as far as he can.

"Children, I am going to ask you one question. How

205

many of you have a newspaper every day in your mail-box?"

Not one of us raised a hand. The only newspaper at our house was the county weekly.

"From now on," she said, "every family in the valley should. This is the paper which came to my mailbox yesterday."

She took a thick roll from beneath her cape, unfolded it, and held the front page facing us. The headlines were two inches high.

PRESIDENT ISSUES PROCLAMATION:
"A STATE OF WAR EXISTS BETWEEN U. S. AND
IMPERIAL GERMAN GOVERNMENT"

The room went so still that it seemed no one was in it. No one and nothing but big black letters. STATE OF WAR . . .

"You have studied about the Revolution," said Miss Hester's dry voice after a minute, "and the War of 1812, and the War Between the States, and the Spanish-American War. The first was fought for the freedom of our country from the mother country, England, the second for freedom of the seas around us, the third for the freedom of those among us who were slaves, the fourth for the freedom of the island of Cuba from her Spanish oppressors. We are now entering upon a World War, for the preservation of democracy, the chosen way of life of all free and enlightened men everywhere. We are a peace-loving people. We have never fought and shall never fight except against tyranny. This is what our President Wilson said to the Congress, when every other means had failed:

"*. . . With a profound sense of the solemn and even tragical character of the step I am taking and of the grave*

206

responsibilities which it involves, I advise that the Congress . . . formally accept the status of belligerent which has been thrust upon it. . . . A steadfast concert of peace can never be maintained except by a partnership of democratic nations . . .

It is a fearful thing to lead this great peaceful people into war. . . . To such a task we can dedicate our lives and our fortunes, everything that we are and everything that we have . . ."

Miss Hester refolded the paper neatly and laid it on Mrs. Carter's desk, not hurrying, giving us time to hear the President's words repeated by our own hearts.

Then she turned back to us and spoke again, more quickly now.

"The Congress has adopted the declaration of war," she said. "German submarines have sunk a million tons of British shipping since January and nearly as many of Allied and neutral shipping. There are people who fear that we cannot complete our preparation in time to rescue our friends and save ourselves from destruction. They are wrong, of course, as faint-hearted people usually are. Our merchant vessels, loaded with all which is so desperately needed by our friends abroad, will be camouflaged; that is, streaked and spotted every color of the rainbow so that they will appear to be part of the sea and sky and even of the sunrise and the sunset, as rainbows are. They will sail under convoy, guarded above by dirigible balloons and hydroplanes, and on the water itself by patrol boats. *They will get through.* And by summer American troops will be in France."

She paused. In the stillness, only the clock ticked,

hanging on the wall. I watched the brass pendulum swinging inside the glass.

"Now!" Miss Hester began again briskly. "About all this there is very little that you and I can do. And perhaps that is a good thing because so much else needs doing that we *can* do. Your part, right now, is to study your history and geography as you have never studied it before. I imagine you older children know your United States history quite well, though there is always more to be learned about it. I shall send you books on world history, so that you will know what has happened in Canada, Mexico, and South America while so much has been happening to us, and the relations we have established with our nearest neighbors. At the same time you will study, in outline, the histories of England, France, Italy, Germany, and other European countries to find out what their past has been to make them what they are now, and every single day you must read the latest news, for history is being made now very rapidly, and you must keep up with it. Our hills shut us off from the rest of the world only if we can and want to think so. We should never want to think so, and in the months to come no one will be able to think so. President Wilson said that to the task of winning this war 'we dedicate everything that we are and everything that we have.' That dedication is for every American citizen. And you are all American citizens."

She turned to Mrs. Carter.

"I should like to see them raise the flag."

She led the way outside. Jimmy brought the canvas bag. Armand pulled the Stars and Stripes to the top of the pole, and it stirred softly in the April air.

"Thirteen stripes were the beginning," said Miss Hester. "There were thirteen stars then too. Now there are forty-eight. In union there is strength. *United we stand, divided we fall.* We are not divided. Look at us there, row on row."

We raised our hands in salute and heard our voices.

I pledge allegiance to the flag . . . and to the republic for which it stands; one nation . . . , indivisible, with liberty and justice for all.

Owen had taught these words to me and I had learned them as magic words. *I pledga legions . . . indiwillable . . . libertenjustus* — hearing the brook in them, the wind, and the marching feet. The blue of the flag was for the truth we knew, the wonder of being free, the duty to be fair. Its red was for the courage we must show. The white was for our trust in God. Because of Owen, before I was old enough to go to school, I had saluted this flag from my own dooryard and seen beyond it the pillars and domes of a gleaming white-and-gold city in which our country's President lived and worked, and the Congress.

"I'll push you five times," Owen had said behind my swing in the apple tree. "I'll give you a good start, and then you can keep yourself going if you want to."

After all these years all he had taught me came back fused, and I began to understand what it meant.

As our hands came down from our foreheads we looked at Miss Hester. She had not moved. She still stood there with her black-gloved hand over her heart and her face lifted. Her deepset eyes burned like coals in white ashes. Red was for courage, and white was for faith. But I thought I saw her sway.

Mrs. Carter took her arm and said quickly, "Miss Hester drove herself over, but I should like to have you drive her home, Dennis. Dennis is very good with horses, Miss

Hester. He has one of his own. And we all thank you for bringing us the news. None of us will ever forget how we heard it."

We watched the little black-top buggy lurch slowly through the sand ruts and disappear over the hill.

"Come in, children," said Mrs. Carter with a shake of her head as if to rouse herself. "Agnes, please lead us in the Twenty-third Psalm."

As soon as the morning exercises were over, she asked me for my eighth reader and gave me the ninth. Perhaps she thought the distraction would be good for me, but I could not be distracted.

I opened the reader, out of politeness to Mrs. Carter and because once I had been so eager to have it, but the stories and poems could not hold my attention now. Though Mrs. Carter was hearing the first class, I raised my hand. She nodded and I went to her desk, putting my hand on Miss Hester's newspaper, asking silently if I might take it. She nodded again.

Back in my seat I spread it out, read to the bottom of the columns on the front page under the black headlines, and groped my way inside as if into a strange house in which I must contrive to make myself at home.

When Dennis came back, Mrs. Carter was about to dismiss us for recess.

Dennis raised his hand.

"Can I stay in? Miss Hester let me take this book. About England."

I raised my hand.

"Can I stay in? To finish the paper?"

"May I," Mrs. Carter corrected us. "Yes. Though I think it would be better for you to go out, Althea. But this once, if you wish —"

All recess I was submerged in crackling paper and small type. Once or twice I glanced timidly at Dennis to see if the noise I made disturbed him, but he was bent low over the book about England. As Mrs. Carter began to ring the bell, I tried desperately and in great haste to get the mass of paper back into its original neat folds.

"I'll do that," Dennis said from the other side of the room.

He came and took it from me.

"You through with it?" he asked, shaking it into place. "Can I read it now?"

I nodded. "Can I have the book a little while? The one about England?"

He put it on my desk as the others were coming in. He did not look at me, but as he dropped the book I saw a smile pass like a moving ray of light across his face, and he said low, "*May* I."

That afternoon we saw the first airplane to make a path through the primeval valley sky. Armand heard it first, and we all ran outside to watch it. It was flying low, we could see its wings and tail and propeller, and, perhaps, because he saw the schoolhouse flag and then the crowd of country children looking up, the pilot leaned from the open cockpit and waved his hand.

My father subscribed to the *Boston Herald*, Mr. Daley to the *Boston Post*, and the Carters to the *Portland Press Herald*. They came to our mailboxes at noon, were read by the women as soon as they had finished the dinner dishes and by the men in the evenings, and were brought to school the next morning. When Dennis and I had finished Miss Hester's book about England, he returned it to her and she let us take a book about France.

The British opened an offensive with the Battle of Arras. The French forces took the banks of the Aisne. In May Congress passed the Selective Service Act, and on June fifth all men in our country between the ages of twenty-one and thirty — nearly ten million — were registered.

When Dennis returned the book about France to Miss Hester, exchanging it for a book about Germany, she was lying on her bed in the small room off the sitting room where he had seen her before. But she was knitting with khaki yarn, and had him come in so that she could measure a sweater against his shoulders.

"You are growing fast, Dennis," she said. "You are going to be as big a man as your father one of these days. The number of stitches I have cast on will make a sweater just a little too large for you. I will make the next one larger. But this will fit someone. I've no doubt there will be American soldiers fighting in trenches next winter who, though of course older, will not have shoulders much broader than yours."

As he stood with his back to her while she measured once more, she put her hand on his arm.

"I am glad you are reading my books, Dennis Daley," she said. "Until now only women have read them since my father died."

On June 13, as we were having our Last Day exercises, General John J. Pershing, in command of a projected American Expeditionary Force abroad, arrived in Paris, and was followed twelve days later by the first contingent of American troops. It is all written in a big, round hand in the diary I began to keep the day Miss Hester told us that war had been declared.

The summer was strangely quiet in the valley. I grew

restless. It seemed to me that the hills were shutting me off, even though Miss Hester had said they could not and must not. I could find little in the newspapers. Miss Hester was so sick that my mother would not let me go there to borrow books. I had lost contact with Agnes in that other world from which nothing earthly could call her. Jimmy and Dennis were working every day on valley farms where the planted pieces were all twice as big as they had ever been. I was alone and conscious of it for the first time in my life. Frequently I became very childish. I often behaved badly at the table and when my mother corrected me I was impudent. When I was, my father would say, "Be careful, Allie, or I shall have to take you away from the table." Sometimes I did it again; my mother corrected me again, more sharply this time. I was impudent again, and then my father led me upstairs.

One night, when this happened, Dennis was having supper with us. A storm was coming up and he and my father had kept on drawing in hay until after seven o'clock. My mother had waited for them, and insisted that Dennis eat with us. I had resented waiting. Now I resented the pleasure the hungry men took in my mother's food and the pride she showed in their pleasure. I said the stew had a funny taste, and spat it out.

"Any more of that, miss," said my mother, "and you won't get any blackberry pie."

I said I hated blackberry pie. I added, "The way you make it."

"Do you want your father to take you away from the table?" she asked.

I said I didn't care.

My father pushed back his chair and we went upstairs.

A half-hour later we came down. I looked angrily at my mother, and went out to sit on the step. I suppose the others had their blackberry pie.

When Dennis came out a few minutes later, he passed me without speaking. Then he stopped, in the shadow of the maples where I could hardly see him.

"What did he do to you?" he asked.

"My father?" I laughed. "Nothing. My mother thinks he whips me, but he never did. He talks, and sometimes after that he plays his violin. Tonight, after he talked, we just sat and looked out the window. My father wouldn't do anything to me."

After a minute Dennis spoke out of the dark as if he had tried not to.

"If I was him, I would," he said hoarsely. "You ought to be ashamed of yourself."

Pete Luneau left for Quebec to enlist in a Canadian regiment.

All summer I watched for glimpses of Joe Luneau walking with Kathleen Daley, Charlie Daley with Rose Luneau. They canoed along the river on Sunday afternoons. They rode past in the early evenings in Charlie's Ford. They stood on the bridges in the moonlight.

That September Joe and Charles went into the Navy. Miss Hester died. Kathleen did not return to school. Agnes and Armand went to live in town to go to the Academy, Agnes working for our minister's wife who was not well and had a large family of children, Armand tending horses at the livery stable and sleeping in a small room finished off above their heads.

In October the first American shots were fired from European trenches. President Wilson's "Fourteen Points" became the charter for allied war aims.

The January headlines said:

**MORE BRITISH U-BOATS SUNK THAN BUILT IN
DECEMBER**

**AMERICA PLEDGED TO RUSH TROOPS
ABROAD**

**WITH FRANCE TO THE DEATH FOR
ALSACE-LORRAINE**

I began a headline scrapbook, using a book I found in
the shed chamber, empty except for a few pages of Sunday
School cards.

By February American troops were under heavy fire
and gas attack on the Lorraine front; the *Luscania,* carrying over two thousand of our troops, was sunk; bombs fell
on London.

In April black, two-inch headlines said:

**HOLD FAST AND FIGHT IT OUT TO THE LAST
MAN; OUR BACKS ARE TO THE WALL —
HAIG TELLS HIS ARMY —
THERE MUST BE NO RETIREMENT**

I wrote in my diary that day:

England's back is as stout as an oak tree. Besides, Pete
Luneau is over there somewhere, and I think Owen Perry
is too, though I do not know. Joe and Charlie are in the
Navy. Hold on, England. More Americans will come.
Owen said about the flag, "Men have fought and died for
it, and would again." Miss Hester said, "There are people
who fear that we cannot complete our preparation in
time to rescue our friends and save ourselves from destruction. They are wrong, of course." America has never
lost a war, and never will, because she fights only for the
right, which is freedom under God. My mother is teaching me to knit.

Three million Americans were under arms.

May came in. It was close to first pasturing day in the valley.

THIRTEEN VON ARNIM DIVISIONS SMASHED: AMERICANS WIN FIRST FIGHT ON AMIENS FRONT

PRESIDENT ASKS POWER TO RAISE OUR ARMY TO ANY SIZE

My father said, "Here's something to put into that scrapbook of yours, Allie. Who'd ever have thought the day would come when they'd fight in the sky as well as on land and sea?"

He read aloud:

Major Richard Lufbery, the foremost American air fighter, was killed today in a sensational combat with a German armored biplane back of the American sector north of Toul. Lufbery lost his life after six of our airmen had tried in vain to down the flying tank.

MILLION AMERICAN SOLDIERS READY TO SAIL

TRANSPORT MOLDAVIA SUNK; MANY SAVED BY CONVOY

AMERICANS DRIVE GERMANS BACK OVER MARNE

U-BOAT SINKS SHIP OFF CAPE COD

"His photograph, *with frame!*" exclaimed my mother. "For nine sons!" The blades of her scissors flashed and on their points she held out a bit of newspaper to me.

A German mother has received the following communication: "His Majesty the Kaiser hears that you have

216

sacrificed nine sons in defense of the Fatherland in the present war. His Majesty is immensely gratified by the fact, and in recognition is pleased to send you his photograph, with frame and autograph signature."

AMERICAN CROWDED HOSPITAL SHIP
TORPEDOED
GERMANS ATTACK ALONG THE VESLE; SEND
4,000,000 TO FRANCE AND END WAR
PRESIDENT WILL SIGN 18 TO 45 DRAFT BILL:
OVER 12,000,000 WILL REGISTER SEPT. 12

The word came at the end of August that Pete Luneau was missing in action. By ones and twos other valley mothers went to spend an afternoon with Pete's mother. They told her she must hope for better news soon. They told her she was a lucky woman to have so many children, Rose such fine help in the house, Joe who wrote either to his family or to Kathleen so often (Pete had never been much of a hand to write), Armand such a capable and ambitious boy, and so many younger ones still at home, one waiting to be born.

Mrs. Carter, who would never have another child, had her two boys — her only ones — somewhere in France. All the important stories in the newspapers began "With the American Army in France," and the date.

The day after Labor Day Mrs. Carter stood in the entry door, ringing the school bell and smiling at us as she had all the mornings before. Dennis had gone to take Armand's place at the livery stable and to enter the Academy. Armand was now working in a grocery store. With both their brothers gone, Hannah and Kathleen had be-

217

come Farmerettes, wearing overalls and working in the fields like men. Albert Luneau had not come back to school. Jimmy Brown was Mrs. Carter's oldest pupil. Marie Luneau and I were next, and I was ready for the Academy but could not go there yet because my mother said I was too young to be away from home.

"You may bring the flag, Forrest," said Mrs. Carter. "Jimmy will pull it up."

When we had saluted it, she said, "Now, all of us together, looking up at it, will say a silent prayer for Pete, and for Joe and Charlie, and for other boys who once went to the valley school — for all who are fighting bravely for the right."

Her voice was clear and strong.

When we had gone inside and she was passing out books and paper, she gave me a paper-covered composition book. All its blue-lined pages were empty.

She said, "Althea, Miss Hester's sisters have given us a large part of her library. See the new shelves we have had built to hold it? This year I want you to read as many of those books as you can, at least one every week. You will report to me each Friday on your reading. Also you are to write a theme every day and copy it into this composition book and leave it with me before you go home. It must cover at least one page. When this book is filled, I will give you another."

I began with the first book on the left of the top shelf. It was *Their Wedding Journey* by William Dean Howells, and the world and way of life it described seemed so idyllic to me that it was like reading a fairy story. My first composition in my first composition book had the title "Too Old for Fairy Stories."

OUR OVERSEAS ARMY NOW 1,750,000 MEN

HOOVER ASKS US TO TIGHTEN BELTS TO BEAT
   GERMANY

NEW LIBERTY LOAN DRIVE FOR $6,000,000,000

AMERICANS GAIN 7 MILES, TAKE 12 TOWNS,
   5000 PRISONERS

A note was handed to President Wilson in his box at
the Metropolitan Opera House in New York City.

GERMANY SAYS SHE ACCEPTS WILSON'S TERMS,
   IS READY TO EVACUATE TO GAIN AN
   ARMISTICE

NO PEACE, SAYS WILSON, TILL KAISERISM ENDS,
   NO ARMISTICE WHILE GERMANY'S CRIMES
   GO ON

ALLIES HAIL WILSON'S LAST WORD TO BERLIN

AMERICAN AND FRENCH ARMIES GAIN, HAIG
   DRIVES ON

Bert Anthony cut the top off a round yellow pumpkin,
dug out the pulp and seeds, cut eyes, nose, and grinning
toothy mouth in the side, put a lighted candle in it, and
brought Wayne over to set it on our kitchen window-
ledge. I put my mother's shawl over my head and went
out to find where they were hidden. They were behind a
stone wall, and I should never have found them if Wayne
had not been so excited by the Jack o'Lantern, the cold,
and the dark that he laughed aloud. I caught him then,
and hugged him so hard that he squealed.

Bert waited in the lane while Wayne came back to the
porch with me. He was nearly five years old. He set the
Jack o'Lantern on his head, its grinning face toward me,

and trotted away with it into the night. As it bobbed away out of sight, like a wicked elf running backward into the land of fantasy, I stood alone on the step and tried to remember when I had gone out with a lighted pumpkin on Halloween. It seemed I never had, that the little girl who had danced beside my father was some other little girl. There were no stars out, and the light of the moon behind the clouds was like the reflection of a monstrous, consuming fire.

OUR MEN BREAK ENEMY FRONT ON ARGONNE
ALLIES FIX TERMS GERMANY MUST TAKE
HAIG CAPTURES 10,000; OUR MEN NEAR
 SEDAN
FALSE PEACE REPORT ROUSES ALL AMERICA

The false peace report on November seventh did not rouse the valley because it did not reach the valley. We did not know of it until we saw the headlines the next day.

"All this backing and filling," said my mother. "It may go on for months. Last summer they told us it might end some time next year. I shan't expect it before then. Stood it so long guess we can stand it 'till then if the Germans can. It's their country that'll be taking the brunt of it from here on. I don't know what the reason is that I can't get a decent pot of tea lately. Steep it and steep it and it's still only water bewitched."

ARMISTICE ENVOYS DELAY ACTION ON TERMS

"There, what did I tell you yesterday?" asked my mother, glancing at the paper when I brought it in, and turning back to crimp the edge of a pie with her quick thumb. That was a Saturday.

But the next morning my father hitched up the horse and drove into the village to get the Sunday paper. He had never done that before.

KAISER AND CROWN PRINCE ABDICATE; NATION TO CHOOSE NEW GOVERNMENT

"Well, maybe we can do business faster with the new one," my father said.

"I'll believe that when it happens," said my mother, tossing her head.

On Monday when I came in from school I picked up the paper before I took off my coat, as I always did.

"No use to look at *that*," said my mother irritably. "All it says is, 'Armistice Delayed.' Looks like they'd delay it 'till kingdom come. That yard's full of clothes. Take the basket out and start taking them in. Soon as I can get rigged up, I'll come help you."

I went out to the clotheslines with the basket. I unpinned a roller towel full of the smell of the pines and the river and the frozen grass. Holding its roughness against my cheek, I thought, "That's strange. I don't remember noticing the smell of anything for a long time." I folded it, laid it neatly in the basket, and folded others to go with it. I remembered my mother had told me this basket was bought new for me to sleep in when I was a baby; she kept it for me behind the stove. "As if I had been a kitten," I thought, "or a loaf of bread rising." I looked at the lines, deciding what I should unpin next, and found that by taking off all the roller towels I had cleared one line, making a white-walled avenue open at each end, east and west. I was facing the west where the clouds, which had been heavy all day, were separating, tumbling about like playful, gray-furred animals. Between and above them the sky was pale pink and lemon color.

I thought, "How lovely it is! How still it is! It's as if — everything had stopped!"

I did not know what I meant by "everything." It did not occur to me that I should ever wish to explain my feeling or to ask that it be believed. I just stood there in our clean, frosty valley, my part of America, among my mother's clean clothes, and heard, smelled, felt the sudden, extraordinary soft stillness.

Then bells began to ring. At first I did not really believe this myself. I knew there were no bells in the valley except Mrs. Carter's school bell and the sleighbells. These were big bells. They did not clang or jingle. They pealed. They were far away, and slipped into my soft stillness as part of it. Perhaps — for a minute — I was not too old for fairy stories after all.

My mother came quickly through the yard, pulled the pins out of a sheet beside me, folded it expertly by holding one corner under her chin, and put it into the basket.

As she straightened up, she stiffened.

"What's that? . . . Sounds like bells. Church bells."

"Doesn't it?"

"I've heard them a few times. When the wind was right. But there's no wind —"

"It's so still, though. And there's so many of them. Sounds as though they're all ringing at the same —"

"Hark! . . . Now there's whistles! The mill and factory whistles all blowing! You don't s'pose — Brad! Brad!

222

They're ringing all the bells and blowing all the whistles in the village! Come hear 'em! Quick!"

My father came to the barn door, and stood there listening. He need not have hurried. The pealing and the whistling went on for a long time.

"I know what I'm going to do," said my mother. "I'm going to call Central. *She* ought to know what's going on."

She ran into the house like a girl.

My father and I stood listening. We did not move or speak.

My mother came back to the porch.

"It's the war," she said in a new voice. "The war — is over!"

A light breeze had sprung out of the west — bringing the sound of bells and whistles more clearly into the valley, so that they seemed to bounce between the mountains, and ruffling the short, silvery strands of hair across my mother's forehead. All the clouds had gone now. The half-sun above the pasture pines was crimson, and turned my mother's thin face rosy.

"Red at night, sailors' delight," said my father. He added, "I was thinking of Joe and Charlie . . . And the Carter boys . . . And Pete." After a minute he asked my mother, "Think you dast believe it?"

"It's so," she said quietly. "It was announced by the State Department about three o'clock. They said, 'The Armistice has been signed.' The war ended at six o'clock this morning."

Then why had I not heard the stillness until four o'clock in the afternoon? I can only think that I could not hear it until word of it had reached our town.

It seemed that there was nothing more to say, nothing to do. I thought that people who had just stepped through the gates of heaven must feel like this. My mother came down slowly from the porch and the clothes slid into her hands of themselves, to lie like thistledown in the basket. The sun had set. The whole horizon was a ring of gold and stars were coming out in the dusk. The sky was crowning the peaceful world.

The bells still rang, the whistles still blew when we went into the house. Dreamily my mother started supper. Dreamily I stared at the old newspapers in the rack, at the checked tablecloth, at the lamp with the pink font, at the calendar on the wall.

November 11, 1918.

"It'll be good to have a barrel of white flour under my cakeboard," said my mother, "after trying to make something fit to eat out of cornstarch and soya beans and barley and potato flour. But we've been a sight better off than a good many. Wonder what they're eating in Berlin tonight."

My father brought in the milk and my mother strained it.

Then the telephone began to ring. Armand had come home because there would be no school the next day and the Academy would be closed. He brought word to the Daleys from Dennis that there would be a big parade in the morning and he would drive one of the hacks all decorated with bunting and crepe paper. Lottie called my mother to say they were all going down to the parade. My mother called Mrs. Carter to ask if I would have to go to school. Mrs. Carter called the Superintendent, who said all schools in the country would be closed the next day, and all schoolchildren in town were asked to be in the parade. Mrs. Carter called my mother back, and called Jimmy asking him to take the message to the Luneaus, who had no telephone. My mother called Miss Susan Dennett to ask if she and Miss Mary would ride down to the parade with us.

Bedtime came and the bells were still ringing, but intermittently now. I pulled my bed close to an open west window and, huddled in blankets, went to sleep waiting for the valley silence and then waiting for the bells.

The next morning boys were selling newspapers to the people lining the street in cars and carriages as I walked proudly beside Agnes to the music of the Fife and Drum Corps.

ARMISTICE SIGNED, END OF THE WAR!
THE DAY HAS COME, THE BIG JOB DONE!

Agnes rode home with us, sitting between the Dennett sisters on the back seat of the democrat wagon as I sat between my father and mother in front. On the way we all sang, even Miss Susan and Miss Mary adding their tremulous voices. "It's a Long Way to Tipperary"; "Joan of Arc"; "America, Here's My Boy"; "Keep the Home Fires Burning"; "There's a Long, Long Trail"; "Till We Meet Again"; "Over There"; "Pack Up Your Troubles"; "Good Morning, Mr. Zip-Zip-Zip." The Daley, Anthony, and Carter cars blew their horns and, passing us, joined in the song we were singing and took it on with them. The Browns caught up with us and sang behind us. The Luneaus, far back in their carts, were still singing each song after we had finished it.

Miss Susan murmured, "Oh, if only Hester were here today!"

Miss Mary said earnestly, "I feel she is, Susan."

I said, "It was Miss Hester who taught us about the

225

country and the flag. And about the other countries too. She told us, 'Our ships will sail under convoy. They *will* get through.' "

Miss Mary patted my shoulder.

"Bless you, dear," she said.

After dinner I read the paper. It reported that as soon as word reached the Front that the Armistice had been signed, American soldiers marked their lines with stakes and ran up the Stars and Stripes. It was then about eleven o'clock and they were all hungry, having breakfasted early "in anticipation of the greatest day in American history." Young German soldiers came into the American lines and were offered cigarettes. They said their orders were to retire with as little delay as possible. They expected to be back in their homes by a week from Sunday.

But for the Americans home was not so near.

The United War Work Campaign Committee issued an appeal for continued support, illustrated by a photograph of an American soldier.

America, Here's Your Boy! Help Us To Give Him Back To You Just As You Gave Him To Us — Two Million Of Him — Three Thousand Miles From Home In A Foreign Land.

The next day's headlines filled half the front page.

PEACE!
A NEW WORLD WAS BORN YESTERDAY —
A WORLD BRIGHTER, HAPPIER, BETTER
THAN MEN HAVE EVER KNOWN BEFORE!

For the rest of that school year, my diary shows only that one by one all the valley boys came home except Pete, that the former Kaiser now spent his days sawing wood at Dusseldorf, the titles of the books I read and of the compositions I wrote, and what Mrs. Carter said to me one day in April.

"Althea, you are the best-prepared of any pupil I have sent to the Academy. I know it has been lonely for you, waiting to go, but I think your mother was wise in her decision. You will still be among the youngest in your class, but probably not the youngest member of it. We shall all expect you to do well. You will take the same course Armand and Agnes and Dennis have taken, I hope: the College Preparatory. When I went to the Academy, that was the only course offered there. It gives the best training for life and for the appreciation of the gift of life, even if you don't go on to college. But I hope you will go on, as Armand and Agnes and Dennis plan to do. If they can, surely you can. The interest in higher education being shown by valley young people recently is a great delight to me. I had a letter from Owen Perry yesterday."

"From *Owen?* . . . Has he — finished college?"

"No, and that is a pity; one of many sacrifices to the war. He left college in the spring of his sophomore year to enlist in the Signal Corps, and was one of the first volunteers to reach France. He was a sergeant first class at that time, and before he was discharged he was a captain. What a record that is! But not surprising, for Owen."

I shook my head. *Captain Owen Perry.*

Wherever I am, he had said, *I'll see the flag flying over the valley.*

"He had been out of the service only a short time when he wrote, but had taken a position with a big advertising agency and doubted that he would give that up to go back to college. At his age, he feels, and with this opportunity which came to him through a colonel he was associated with abroad, he should begin now his adult life. That was all he said about himself. But he sent his best, he said, to everyone in the valley, especially to you."

"To me!"

"He was very fond of you, Althea. You must have known that. He said he spent some months in England, and that he never walked through a London fog without half-expecting to find you, a tiny girl sitting on a door-step; and that he would never see goldenrod and wild asters without having a picture of them as they bloom in the valley flash before his eyes, with a little girl sitting among them making *O's* on the back of an envelope while she waited for the mailman. . . . I thought as I read what he had written that he is well placed in an advertising agency. . . . He wondered where you are in school now, and hopes you will go to college and stay to graduate."

Suddenly I wanted to see Owen more than I wanted anything else in the world. I needed him to explain everything to me which he had not already explained — all the headlines I had so carefully copied during the war; what it was that President Wilson did in Europe after the war; why other people did not want us to join his League of Nations; what I had read in Miss Hester's books; why Kathleen Daley did not come to the valley church any more but went into the village with the Luneaus instead; just what it was that he had done and I could do for the valley by leaving it.

We're going to do all we can for the valley, he had said. *We're going to do great things before we're through. Because what we do for the valley, you know, we do for the*

228

country, for the country is just one valley and one moun-
tain and one city and one prairie after another, over and
over and over. And all its people are our people.

I still wanted to do whatever he wanted me to do, but I
needed to know why.

"Where is he?" I asked. "Where is he *now?*"

Mrs. Carter shook her head.

"I don't know. He wrote from New York. The main office of the company, where he is being trained, is there,
but he expected to be transferred any day to some branch
office, probably in the Midwest. He said he would write
again when he had a permanent address. . . . Now about
your compositions this week, Althea. They have no people
in them. They are all about ideas. Perhaps you are too
young to think so much about big subjects. Try to *feel*
more, and write what you know and feel."

"Next week," I said, "I will write about Owen when
he was in the valley. Owen and the fog. Owen and school.
Owen and pond lilies. Owen and the flag. Owen and God.
Owen the night he came to our house with Mr. Carter
and the Luneaus. Owen and what he said to me by the
rosebushes where I was dressing my doll."

Perhaps by going back I would find the way to go forward.

In June there was what my mother called a spate of
weddings. First was Kathleen's to Joe. Kathleen had studied and been converted to Joe's faith, and they were married in the Catholic Church in the village. Nearly everyone in the valley went, I saw statues for the first time, and
we McIntires, Carters, Browns, and Daleys were all much
puzzled as to whether we should stand and kneel when

the Luneaus stood and knelt or should remain seated. I
thought I had never seen anything as beautiful as Kathleen
in the long white taffeta gown and lace veil which Hannah
and Lottie had made for her, as she walked down the aisle,
her hand on her father's arm, with her light step which
was still so much like flying; then, kneeling for a long time
while boys stood by with lighted candles and the priest
with his back to us spoke in Latin, and music played softly;
finally standing beside dear, sturdy Joe before the priest,
offering her small hand to Joe for the ring which meant
that she would belong to him forever.

Two weeks later Rose Luneau was married to Charlie.
As Charlie had not accepted Rose's faith for himself but
only agreed that their children would be brought up in
it, their wedding was in the vestry of the Catholic Church,
and only the immediate families were present. But Hannah and Lottie had made a dress for Rose, too, exactly
like Kathleen's except that it was a larger size. After Rose's
wedding, the two crisp white gowns hung side by side in
Kathleen's room at the Daleys', where they had a whole
closet to themselves. I went over to see them and Hannah
went up with me to show me where they were. As we
stood before the open closet door, I wondered if I would
ever have a dress like that, and I wondered what Hannah
was thinking, now that she was left alone with her father
and Lottie. I remembered Julie for the first time in years,
and wished that she were where Hannah could teach her
to sew, to go into the fields with Hannah, to sit beside
Hannah at the table, to sleep with Hannah.

"Awful lot of stitches," said Hannah, "for so little wear.
Well, I better go to the barn." She closed the closet door
with a snap. "Best cow's about to calve."

Joe and Kathleen were living in the village now, where

Joe drove the grocery delivery truck. Charlie was working on his father's crew — we sometimes saw him glide by on the sectionmen's handcar at the railroad crossing — and Rose cooked and waited on tables at the boardinghouse near Portland where they lived.

I thought it was very sad that my sister Lucy did not have a long white gown and lace veil for her wedding the last day of the month, but she did not want one and my mother agreed with her that it was neither necessary nor practical. She wore a green muslin dress with a white Peter Pan collar, tight bodice, and windabout belt of darker green, and her white shoes had pointed toes. In these she stood before the village minister in the parlor and was married to Carl West, a lean-faced, redheaded young man we hardly knew, but with whom she had corresponded during the war. He worked in the bank in the village. In the parlor that day there were only our family, Carl's mother, and the minister, but everyone in the valley waited under the trees in the yard, where the men had set up the tables and benches we used for church suppers. After the ceremony we had ice cream out there; three different flavors, from freezers which had been borrowed, filled, and churned early that morning, and left packed in pond ice. Everyone had brought frosted cakes, and there were too many kinds to count. When everyone had eaten a great deal — except Lucy and Carl, who only crumbled their cake and let their ice cream melt into pink pools in their sauce dishes — Lucy put on a white hat which shadowed her eyes, and white gloves, kissed her parents and Edith and me, and rode out of the valley beside a lean-faced, redheaded young man we hardly knew. Indeed, that day and for a long time before, I hardly knew Lucy, or for that matter Edith. They had grown up and gone away, seeming to take nothing from the valley or to bring anything back into it on their brief visits.

But my mother said that Lucy had done very well for herself, that Carl was an up-and-coming young man. He had bought a large house on Main Street in the village, and his mother lived in the ell of it, which had three rooms. The rest of the house was for himself and Lucy; a kitchen, laundry room, dining room, and two parlors downstairs, four big bedrooms and a bath upstairs. Lucy would have furnace heat, running hot and cold water, and electric lights. She would no longer have to work at the store.

"And a good thing, too," said my mother. "With a house like that to keep so it will be a credit to Carl. All hardwood floors to polish. And full of the handsomest furniture I ever saw. Chairs and sofas upholstered in velvet, mind you, or stuff that looks like it; tufted, with buttons; awful dust-catchers, I don't doubt. And even the bureaus have marble tops. Thirty-nine windows to wash, and a pair of curtains to do up for every one. All big panes, though. And if Carl keeps on the way he's going, likely Lucy'll have a hired girl before long to help her out. Shouldn't wonder if she's by way of living like a queen, first thing we know."

That fall Edith, employed in the office of one of the mills, and I, entering the Academy, became Lucy's first hired girls. Our hire was our board and room and the assurance to my mother that Lucy would keep a close eye on both of us. I suppose she did so, that Edith also kept an eye on me all those four years, and that I did enough work in the afternoons and evenings to earn the price of the coal to heat my room and the electric power for the lamp I studied by, perhaps also for part of the cost of my breakfasts and suppers — but I do not remember it now. All I recall clearly about the West house, while I lived there, was the almost sacrilegious excitement I felt during the first few months whenever I pulled a switch at the foot of the dark staircase and instantly flooded it with light; then, having reached the top, returned it to darkness.

As far as I knew then, or know now, I lived in the Academy five days of every school week, and in the valley over week ends and through vacations.

Every Friday afternoon, as surely as I came down Academy Avenue into Main Street I saw my father's wagon or sleigh waiting in front of the West house. I quickened my step and began to run, leaving behind whomever I had been walking with. I sped across the porch which Lucy called a veranda, found my father sitting with Lucy in one of her parlors, and threw myself into his arms. This always embarrassed him, and in his embarrassment his pats on my back were like a thumping. I had always left my box of laundry, neatly tied, in the front hall closet, and ran to get it. It was all I took home with me, except my books.

"Well, Lucy," my father always said, "guess we better be getting back up the line. Cows waiting to be milked." Or, "You know how your mother worries soon as it shows signs of getting dark."

"Yes," Lucy answered vaguely, thinking no doubt of Carl and Carl's supper. "Well, tell her to take care of herself. Althea's a good girl, you tell her, and we're getting along fine down here. Maybe Carl will drive us up tomorrow afternoon after Edith gets out of work. Or some time Sunday."

But they did not often come. Edith went out Saturday

nights with one of the foremen at the mill. Lucy and Carl belonged to a bridge club which met Saturday nights, and both were very active in the Baptist church. Carl was a deacon and superintendent of the Sunday School. Lucy and Edith both taught classes there, Edith sang in the choir, and Lucy was president of the Ladies' Guild.

They did not often come, and everything at home was the way it seemed to me it had always been, the way I remembered it whenever I thought of it between week ends. As we went down the last hill the smell of the river came up to me, heady as champagne, and I was enclosed by the mountains. We came out of the woods and I saw my mother's light in the kitchen window. To make light or heat in the valley, one struck a match. I could see the phosphorescent glow the striking left behind on a black stove cover. We turned up into the lane and its banks were splashed with the pale yellow of evening primroses, or fragrant with sweetfern, or buried under snow. The hardwood trees were turning red or brown, or the twigs were encased in ice, or the new leaves were budding. The pines never changed, except slowly to grow taller and spread wider, so slowly that no change was visible. We rode into the yard and my father stopped to let me out before he drove on to the barn. I took my box of laundry and went up the path, across the porch, into the kitchen.

My mother was at the stove or in the pantry.

She said, "Well, hello — you're back again."

I kissed her, and sometimes there was steam on her face. She often held her floury hands behind her or rolled them in her apron.

"Take your box right into the shedroom. I've got a pie cooling on the window sill out there. Careful you don't knock it off as you go by."

234

I smelled the woodsmoke, the kerosene, the vegetables, salt pork, and cider in the cellar, the cooling pie, the stewing meat, the starch, the naphtha soap, the barn when my father brought in the milk.

We sat down together at the table and everything was as it had been, as it should be. I was in the valley where I belonged, and often it seemed that I had never been away.

But on Monday mornings when my father let me out at the foot of Academy Hill and drove on to leave my box of clean clothes at the West house, I waved a quick good-bye and joined the group going up to school as if I had never been separated from it. The tarred walk felt familiar to my feet, the giant elms stood majestically all around, my great gray stone house with ivy climbing up its sides and wreathing its arched windows was waiting for me, the bell in the tower was saying, "Well, hello — you're back again," and the talk of theorems, participles, declensions, battles, experiments, play-casting, scores, club meetings, debate practice, styles, old favorites, old aggravations, new possibilities was delicious to my ears.

We went up the cement steps, the heavy door opened to us and closed behind us, we climbed the inside stairway to the main room, and I found my own desk, put my own books into it, watched the teachers seat themselves on the platform, and sat straight for the opening exercises. A breeze which had blown across the playing field came through the open window or the hot air from a floor register lifted my accordion-pleated skirt. Blind Milton dictating to his daughters was before me in a frame on the wall, and I was one of his daughters. Winged Mercury stood on his pedestal beside the door into the headmaster's office suggesting the free fight of a keen imagination, the vast scope of man's mind, and I restrained a smile at the sudden memory of the day one of the boys put the headmaster's felt hat on the small white marble head. Here was my home of arched ceilings, rooms full of books and maps and chalk and foreign words and mysterious equations, corridors alive with competition and mischief, dreams and schemes, bulletin boards and lockers, all smelling of time and varnish and rubber and perfume and shaving lotion and H_2SO_4 and the powder with which the janitor cleaned the floor at night.

I studied Latin Grammar and read Caesar's *Gallic Wars,* Cicero's *Orations,* Vergil's *Aeneid,* and my teacher was a master's wife, a frail lady with pale hair and rose-pink cheeks, and a soft voice. It was she, too, with whom I read Shakespeare's plays, *Paradise Lost* and the Sonnets, *David Copperfield, Life on the Mississippi,* the *Leather-Stocking Tales,* and many other books I should not have found or dared to begin to read alone. She coached our plays, and was the leader of our Camp Fire group. I studied Ancient History, English History, and finally American History; French Grammar and then read *Gil Blas* and modern French short stories. I went with fear and trembling into the laboratory and at the stern insistence of a half-bald man with thick lenses in his eyeglasses put on a canvas apron, mixed a frightening concoction in a glass measure, poured it into a slender test-tube, lit the flame of a Bunsen burner and waited for what I had mixed to reach the boiling point.

But more than I learned in the classrooms with their knife-roughened desks or in the laboratory with its stained sinks, pitted benches, and foul air, and more than I belonged there, I learned from and belonged to the crowded corridors, the deep window sills on which girls sat with boys between classes, the coatroom in which girls hid from boys between classes, the lunchroom and the candy counter, the stage and the typing room which served us as an anteroom, the dark closet where we kept our properties, the piano in the auditorium around which we stood to sing the postwar popular songs, the pillars which we wound with crepe paper and evergreen for dances, the bleachers on the playing field, and the library where I went nearly every day after school, tiptoeing through the silence and peering through the dimness to choose not only the reference books I had to study there but also the lighter books I could take home to read after I had gone to bed at night. There were books about girls like me who wanted to go to college; girls older than I who were in college; girls who, having helped to decorate halls for dancing, themselves went to dances; girls whom boys called for at their houses, walked beside them on the street, brought them home and kissed them good night; girls who were asked by men to marry them and so became women, wives, and mothers. None of these girls reminded me of Lucy or of Edith, or any of the girls and women I knew. None of the boys were like any boys I knew except Owen, and I did not know Owen now.

I had said, "I don't want to be like the Dennett sisters. I don't want to be old without any father or any — any —" Owen had said, "Don't worry. You won't."

Owen, where are you?

Agnes and Armand were juniors when I was a freshman, and Dennis a sophomore. I rarely saw the boys, or, if I did see them, did not notice them or feel I knew them better than any of the others. At first I sought out Agnes in the coatroom, or walked down with her after school to

237

the street where she turned off, but Agnes was as completely absorbed in her vocation as ever, if not more so. She was going to school only to prepare for a life of personal sacrifice. She felt no need of earthly friends. She wasted no time sitting in bleachers. She wore her hair pulled back straight from her brown face and pinned up on the back of her head. She had only one skirt, one jacket, one black corduroy tam, and two shirtwaists, and looked the same every day. She did not approve of plays, of clubs, of dances or of decorating for dances. I admired Agnes, I respected her, I wished fervently that I were like her. But I was not like her, and so I could not talk to her. Often there were weeks when we did not say more than "Hi" to each other.

At the end of my sophomore year, Agnes and Armand were graduated. Armand was the valedictorian, Agnes the only girl who did not wear a white dress. The next fall Armand went to the State University, and Agnes to Gordon College in Boston.

Mrs. Carter said to me, "Owen was the first from the valley — but he had not always lived in the valley. Armand and Agnes are the first of those I taught to read who have gone so far. You will be the next, won't you, Althea?"

I answered, "Mrs. Peabody has talked to me about it. She is my English and Latin teacher. She wishes my grades in mathematics were better. I got a C in Geometry. She says unless all my grades are good I may not be able to get into a good college."

"Oh," Mrs. Carter sighed, "I wish I could help you. Wouldn't Dennis? I think he is very good at figures."

"Dennis!" I snapped. "I don't *want* Dennis to help me. Besides, I never see him."

I sounded sharp, like my mother.

"Well, try hard," said Mrs. Carter gently. "Do your very best."

"It must cost a great deal to go to college," said my mother. "I don't see how Agnes is going to earn her own way. It may be some easier for a boy, but I know there's a limit to what Althea can do. She isn't very big and I don't believe she can be very strong. I don't know, I thought if amongst us we got her through the Academy, maybe she could take a business course like Edith. Edith is getting sixteen dollars a week, and Lucy don't charge a cent for her board, nor Althea's either. Of course both the girls help Lucy in that big house of hers, and we send down enough eggs, butter, pork, potatoes and like that for all four of them. We don't want Carl to think he's married three instead of one. Nobody ever had a better husband than Lucy has."

"Althea should go to college," insisted Mrs. Carter. "Even though she isn't big, I think she's healthy. She's hardly ever missed a day of school. She can help herself a good deal, and maybe other folks can help a little. She can go if she wants to enough. Where there's a will there's a way."

"And what would she do with all that education if she had it?"

I felt Mrs. Carter's eyes on my face but could not look up.

"Oh, Martha," she said, "nobody knows. Nobody knows what they will do with it if they get it. But we all know what we can't do because we haven't got it. It wasn't so important when we were growing up, or didn't seem so, but the world is moving fast now. There is so much to understand, so much to be done. Ones like Althea must hurry up and find out what it is and how to do it, and be ready to explain it to younger ones."

I did not feel qualified for any such high destiny, and did not wish to be. I did not look beyond my Junior Prom. I wanted to go to it. I wanted to be invited to go to it by Lenny Rossiter, son of the mill superintendent, president of our class, basketball star, a boy with a smile like Owen's. To this end I would devote my Junior year.

The morning of the second day of school, Dennis stopped me on the stairs and asked gruffly, "Got your algebra done?"

I stared at him. "Sure," I answered, shrugging.

"Let's see your paper."

"Why?"

"Let's see it."

I pulled it, folded, from my book and handed it to him. He squinted at the figures in the dim light.

"First one's wrong," he said. "I think."

His hair was black, thick, and crisp. It stood off, I thought, like porcupine quills, and he had a patch on one knee of his blue serge knickers.

"Maybe it is and maybe it isn't," I said. "Give it back."

"Not until I find out."

He took it over to the window. I was not going to be seen near any window with Dennis Daley. I walked — my mother would have said I switched — angrily into the coatroom and stayed until the bell rang.

After the opening exercises he went past my desk on his way to class and dropped my algebra paper on it. He had marked four of the ten calculations wrong, and checked the point at which I had made each mistake. Furious but convinced, I spent my only free period doing the whole paper over.

The next morning he stopped me again.

"Got your algebra done?"

"Yes, I have," I said. "And if it's wrong it's going to stay wrong. I'm not going to spend my free period doing it over again."

"If it's wrong, you *are*," he said grimly. *"And* your free period every morning, until you start getting it right. Come on. Let's have it."

"I will not," I screamed as loud as I could in a whisper. "What business is it of yours? I wish you'd leave me alone."

"Don't think I wouldn't like to, you spitting cat," he growled. "But Mrs. Carter and Mrs. Peabody want you to do better in math, and you can; so you're going to. They've spent a lot of time on you, and their time's too valuable to waste. Give me that paper or I'll take it."

He clutched the end of the paper as I started to turn away, and because I was afraid he would tear it, I opened the book.

After that, every morning I handed him my algebra paper without a word and he later returned it without a word. But gradually he could find fewer and fewer mistakes.

Peggy Lewis and Marge Hamilton were teaching me to dance in the coatroom. In the winter, after a play rehearsal in the auditorium, someone began to play dance music. Lenny Rossiter danced with several of the girls and then stood beside me near the piano.

"I wish I knew how to dance," I said softly.

He looked down at me in surprise, as if he had not known anyone was there.

"Don't you?" he asked.

"No." It was a half-truth. I had never danced with a boy.

241

"Well, well," he said; "has to be a beginning some-where."

He took my hand, put his arm around me, and we were on the floor moving together. Everything whirled. It seemed for a few minutes as if I had always danced with Lenny and would always dance with Lenny.

The music stopped.

"Not bad," he said. "Not bad for a beginning. I guess you could learn."

"Oh, Lenny," I said, "I'd love to."

He went off to dance with someone else, but surely he would not forget how it had been to dance with me. In the books I had read, if one remembered, the other remembered. I tried not to stop remembering, day or night.

A week later, something other than a corrected algebra paper was left on my desk, and by someone other than Dennis Daley. It was a ticket to a basketball game, and Lenny drew the edge of it across my forehead before dropping it on my book. I thought I was gloriously marked for life. I went to the game with Peggy and Marge, but I was sure I would not leave it with them. I sat on the edge of a hard chair, seeing my first basketball game — I had never before been out in the evening without my family, and only Edith's kind interference had won me permission this time — not understanding anything about it except when a ball went into a basket — and I yelled myself hoarse. Each time Lenny looked toward the balcony I thought he was looking for me and I leaned forward and smiled. When the game was over and the team disappeared, I told Peggy and Marge that I had to wait for someone. They looked at me curiously, laughed, and went away. I was one of the last to leave the balcony, and the very last to linger by the outside door. None of the players came out that way. I went home alone, running from the rug of light beneath each lamppost to the next, feeling as if my heart were tearing its way out through my chest. The following day, at play rehearsal, while I did my big scene with intensity of effort and Mrs. Peabody listened with shining eyes, Lenny was holding Mary Lou Wentworth in his arms, pretending that he was going to drop her out of the anteroom window.

I was sick with disappointment, but I knew that tragedy experienced added to a woman's inner beauty. I gave up expecting Lenny Rossiter to ask me to the Junior Prom. But I did not give up the Junior Prom.

Jimmy Brown had finished at the valley school the year before, and was working in the mill. He had bought a car, and one Sunday at church I asked his mother if she thought I could ride down with him the next morning. Jimmy was not there. He never came to church now. Mattie said of course I could, and told me what time he would be at the end of the lane. He went much earlier than I needed to, but I told my father it would save him a trip and besides I had forgotten to bring home a book I must study before school opened.

It was late March then, and as I waited at the end of the lane for Jimmy, the sun had hardly pulled itself all the way out of the sea, the ground was melting, and water ran in the wheel tracks like little brooks. I had not seen Jimmy since the Christmas party. I heard his car making the bridge rattle, and it stopped beside me. I climbed in, laying my books between us.

"Still fooling around with them things, are you?" he grinned. "I'm glad to be out of jail."

I sighed and said I was not quite fifteen.

"What a fool Aggie is! A glutton for punishment!"

I said I guess it was different with Agnes. With Armand, too. I asked him about his job. He said he was making pretty good money, enough to buy this car, and when he was not working he could go where he pleased and do what he pleased. He said that was the life. I nodded.

Jimmy was now as tall as his father, but still very thin. He wore long trousers, not knickers like the boys at school. His shirt was open at the throat and his cap set far back on his head, his hair, still the color of maple syrup, curling around the dark rim. I tried to believe that his head had once lain in my lap as we sat alone by a cranberry bed. His hands on the wheel were stained from working on his car, and I saw reddish hairs on the backs of them. Jimmy was a man, at sixteen.

I said, "We have kind of fun at school sometimes, though. We put on plays, you know. And there are dances. Can you dance?"

He grinned. "Sure can. Go 'most every Saturday night. Grange dances at Bryant Hill."

"I'm not much of a dancer yet."

"Nothing to it." Jimmy knocked his cap farther back. "Just keep walking, that's all."

We were coming into the village.

I forced out the words, "Have you got a girl, Jimmy?"

He grinned at me.

"Dozens. But nobody special. I'm taking my time. Looking 'em over. This where you want to get out?" He stopped in front of the West house, handed me my books, and touched my chin. "You had me first, you know, Allie. If that's any comfort to you."

I rode with him two Monday mornings in April, and on the second one I asked him to my Junior Prom.

He turned his head and looked me over lazily.

"Well, now, I don't know why not, kid. Pick you up here at Lucy's, shall I? And then never say I didn't do anything for you."

I snatched my books from him and ran.

My mother spent the first two weeks in May making me a dress of pink Paulette chiffon with short, puffed sleeves, a gathered round neck, a high waistline, and a black velvet sash. My father gave me the money to buy pink silk stockings and black pumps with Cuban heels.

"It still seems to me you are too young," my mother said several times. Lucy did not approve at all, any more than Agnes would have, but Edith had agreed with me that every Junior girl would go if she could. "I suppose, though, as long as it's with Jimmy — somebody we all know . . ."

The night came. I went up the hill with Jimmy, into the familiar auditorium with Jimmy, danced with Jimmy. It was bright and hot. Other girls' dance orders had been filled out by their escorts with many exchanges among Academy boys. My order, dangling by its silk cord from my finger, had no names or initials in it. At intermission the chaperones — teachers and mothers — formed a receiving line, and Lenny Rossiter as president of the class led the way along it, with Marge Hamilton on his arm.

"Let's get out of here," Jimmy said. "Hot as Tophet. We'll go for a ride and get cooled off."

I let him draw me down the stairs and out into the damp darkness under the elms, but I was frightened.

We had nearly reached the car when we were overtaken.

"Where do you think you're going?"

It was Dennis, glaring at me. He seized my arm. I shook it off fiercely. I was afraid, but I would not let Dennis Daley know it. He was the last person I would let know it.

"Where I please," I said. "And where did you come from?"

"I saw you leave the hall. And whatever you please, you're not going anywhere except back in, or home."

I drew myself up.

"And what on earth were you doing in the hall?"

"Dancing. More or less. Now are you coming back or —"

"She's not coming back," drawled Jimmy, putting his arm around me. "She's going where I go, and where that is is no business of yours. Now want to make something of it? If you do, she can wait a minute in my car. Seems to me I've licked you once over her, and I'll be tickled to do it again."

Dennis said to me, "If you get into that car, I'll stay with it till you get out of it. Your folks let you come to the Prom. I'll bet they never told you you could ride all over the county."

"Get in," Jimmy told me, opening the door. "Get in there out of the way, and I'll settle his hash."

"Wait a minute," I said, clinging desperately to my dignity. Haughtily I asked Dennis, "Did you come alone, or did you bring a girl like everybody else? If you brought a girl, for heaven's sake, where is she?"

"I brought Madeline Dunstan," answered Dennis. I swallowed a gasp, for Madeline Dunstan was his employer's daughter, and the most beautiful, most brilliant girl in the Senior Class. There was no reason why I had not seen them, except that, nursing my tragedy, I had not looked at anyone but Lenny and Marge. "I don't know where she is right now. I left her standing in the middle of the floor. But she's all right. She knows how to take care of herself. That's more than you do. Now what are you going to do? If you get into that car, I stay right here as long as it does. If it moves, I'll follow it in Mr. Dunstan's Packard and I don't think I'll have any trouble keeping up. If it goes anywhere but to let you out at home, I'll follow you when you do go home."

I looked at him and knew he meant it. I burst into tears.

"Take me home, Jimmy," I sobbed. "This minute. I hate you, Dennis Daley. I wish I'd never see you again as long as I live."

"Don't worry," Dennis growled. "I won't bother you if you'll behave yourself."

He never took my algebra paper again. I never spoke to him again in the Academy. While he received his diploma in June, I sat making pleats in my yellow organdy dress. I was at Graduation that day, in my yellow organdy dress, only because, for the first time, I was receiving a prize book for scholarship.

One day the next fall Mrs. Peabody gave me several college catalogues and asked me to read them through, then show them to Mrs. Carter and my mother.

"I don't want to influence you in your choice, Althea," she said, "but if you find you would like to know more about Whitaker than is in the catalogue, perhaps I can tell you. It is the college where I took my degree."

I did not yet know what it meant to take a degree, but I knew, without looking at the catalogues, that if I should go to college I wanted to go to Whitaker, where Mrs. Peabody had gone. I wanted to be able to read Shakespeare aloud as she read it, to read Latin aloud as if I loved it as she did; I wanted her handwriting, her soft voice, her patient hopefulness, and her gentle smile.

I asked her many questions about Whitaker, and she answered them with the late afternoon sunlight slanting across the empty rows of desks in her classroom, in the dusk of the auditorium when everyone else had gone home after a rehearsal, with the sodden leaves clinging to our feet as we went down the hill together, while wind whipped the darkness and hurling snow against her living room windows in the evenings. The more I watched and listened to Mrs. Peabody, the more I wanted to go to Whitaker.

"If you are sure you have made up your mind," she said at last, "I think we should send in your application."

"Liz," groaned my mother, "I *don't* think we should bite off more than we can chew. According to this book, it's going to cost six hundred dollars a year just for her to be there, to say nothing of her clothes and books and trainfare back and forth. Six hundred a year for four years — why, Brad and I don't see that much cash in ten!"

"She will help herself," said Mrs. Carter. "And other help may come along."

"I don't doubt Lucy would do what she could, but Carl's very careful of his money. And so should everybody be."

"She'd better send in her application, as Mrs. Peabody says. After she finds out whether she's admitted, we'll know better how to plan."

"Well, I don't suppose it will do any harm to see."

Mr. and Mrs. Peabody wrote letters of recommendation. So did Mrs. Carter. So did our minister. The Dean of Women wrote Mrs. Peabody that though my grades in mathematics and science were not high, they seemed to

248

be improving; I had done very well in English, history, and languages, and my range of extracurricular activities was promising. My application was accepted, and I was asked to send in a fifty-dollar registration fee.

"There you are, Liz," cried my mother. "Fifty dollars right off the bat! And all her graduation clothes to make or buy! She says she has to have a new dress and hat for Sunday —"

"Baccalaureate," nodded Mrs. Carter.

"And another dress for Class Day and still another one for Graduation."

"She doesn't *have* to," said Mrs. Carter. "Any of them. Agnes didn't."

"Well, she's going to! She's got this far down there looking as well as the rest as far as I know, and I'm not going to be made a laughing-stock now."

"Then Lottie and Hannah and I will help you make them. Pick out some nice, neat material. It needn't be expensive. And she can use them for best at college. There'll be times when all the girls dress up."

"Wouldn't be girls if they didn't," sighed my mother. "But there's no use talking about it any more, Liz. I haven't got fifty dollars now. Not unless I take it out of the bank. And what little we've got in the bank has to stay there in case of sickness. I didn't know they'd ask for money this soon. I thought maybe this summer —"

Mrs. Carter patted her arm.

"I know, Martha," she said. "I'm surprised, too. But don't you worry. I've got some money in the bank for Althea."

"*You've* got some money? Liz Carter, if you think I'd let you use your money —"

"It isn't mine, Martha. It's Althea's. It was sent to me to

use to help valley children get started in college. I'll draw out fifty dollars for her tomorrow."

"Who sent it?"

"I can't tell you that. I was bound to secrecy."

"Then I won't let her take it, not knowing who it's from. I won't have her beholden to a stranger."

"She won't be beholden. If she doesn't take her share it will go to Agnes or Armand or Dennis when they need it. They've all had some already."

"Dennis!" I almost shouted. I had not thought of him for months. "What's he done with anbody's college money?"

Mrs. Carter gave me a quiet, searching look.

"Dennis is in Normal School," she said, "preparing to be a teacher."

"A great teacher *he'll* make!" I snapped.

"That's enough from you, miss," said my mother.

Mrs. Carter added gravely, "From what I have heard — and not from him — Dennis Daley is a better friend to you than you are to him, and so perhaps a better friend than you deserve, Althea. But those who don't deserve their friends need them most. As you grow older, I hope you will learn to appreciate your friends, known and unknown."

She turned back to my mother.

"The reason you have never heard of this fund, Martha, is that all of us who know about it are not to speak of it to anyone. But every valley student who goes to college gets one hundred dollars. Althea's will cover this registration fee and she will have fifty dollars to take with her when she goes. According to the catalogue, the first college bill doesn't come until November. Perhaps by then you will see your way clear to let her stay. The fund is not large, for the purpose and the need, but at least it gets them started. Now I must go."

"You're awful good, Liz," my mother said, "to do so much for 'em."

She followed Mrs. Carter to the door. I followed her to the lane.

"It's Owen, isn't it?" I asked her. "The money came from Owen, didn't it?"

"I told you, Althea, I'm not allowed to say where it came from."

"I know it's Owen. It sounds like Owen. Do you know where he is now?"

"If I did," said Mrs. Carter, "I couldn't tell you. Good night, Althea. You are a very lucky girl."

I waited until she had gone several steps and then ran after her, threw my arms around her.

"I know I am," I whispered. "I do know it. I'll *try* to be like Owen — and you — and Mrs. Peabody —"

"Of course you will," Mrs. Carter soothed me. "You'll try to be like everyone you admire. And you will be. But it takes time."

I had the Honor Essay at Graduation. My subject was "The Day God Spoke to Me."

I began:

"One day when I was very small I knelt beside my mother's hundredleaf rosebushes and asked God how I should begin to live.

"He said: *First see the glory that is in this country of yours. See it in the sky, in the river flowing toward the sea, in the trees, in the grass, in the planted fields, in the animals coming from pasture, in the houses and barns, in the*

251

churches and schools, in the flags unfurled, in the smoke
pouring out of giant stacks, in the engines and the wheels
and the railroad. See it in all America has been and will
not be again, in all Americans remember and dream of,
in all Americans are born knowing and all they will learn.

"He said, And when you have seen it, sing it out.
Whatever you want to live and grow, sing of it. Not only
with your voice, but with your heart and hands. . . ."

This was what Owen had always done and was still doing, wherever he was. I wanted to do it, too.

I I I

A COLLEGE is like a thumbprint, in that there are no two alike in the world. My college was like a thumbprint in another way. It had too much respect for individuality to set the nonconformist on a block and chisel away at him for four years, adding plaster features here and there for better proportion and superficial charm; or to squeeze a pliant one into a mold and keep him imprisoned until, at Commencement, the breaking of the glass could be safely recommended because the mind, the attitudes, the manners inside had set according to specification. It was content to leave its indelible mark upon each in a secret place where only he could see it — if indeed he could — but where he would feel it as long as he lived.

The contribution of a college depends upon the students it admits and graduates. The students it admits and graduates depend upon the purposes of the college. The purpose of my college was to prepare young people for combined mental and spiritual service to their fellow men. It accepted any high school graduate who appeared to desire ardently this preparation and to be capable of acquiring and using it. That he came with only ten dollars in his pocket and did not know where his next dollar was coming from did not prevent his matriculation at Whitaker; Whitaker believed that with his desire and capacity he would come by the eleventh dollar soon enough, and then the twelfth; if he did not — with what Whitaker could and would do to help him — it must be that he lacked desire or capacity or both in sufficient degree to make him a Whitaker graduate. Failure to meet either scholastic or financial obligations at my college was very rare, and when it happened the whole campus seemed to slip under a cloud.

Whitaker was founded soon after the War Between the States as a theological seminary for young men of the Baptist denomination. Most of these young men were from Maine farms. They brought in on horse-drawn sleds wood to heat the rooms of the dormitory where they cooked their Maine potatoes, fried their home-cured bacon, and ate crisp Baldwin apples from their fathers' orchards. The recitation building was unheated. The first student body numbered less than a hundred, and the faculty five, of whom one was the president. Many of the sons of these first students became missionaries, and in the 1920's, many of their grandchildren came to Whitaker — now a nondenominational, coeducational, liberal arts college — from India, China, the international quarter of Shanghai, and Africa, so accustomed to life with other races than their own that they were not at all surprised to find themselves associated with Chinese, Japanese, Negro, and Indian students. To the rest of us — still mainly from Maine farms and villages — association with many races and many faiths was a natural part of a college education, like the study of subjects of which we had never before heard even the names, listening to speakers from all parts of our country and abroad, living constantly and exclusively with contemporaries, freedom from all controls over our personal activities except those imposed by a code of honor which we wrote for ourselves. Whitaker was a microcosm, the adult world made small and simple enough so that we could understand it and find and hold our places in it.

Owen had said long ago: *We all laugh in the same language.* . . .

To the first brick dormitory had been added three more for men and one for women; underclass women lived in frame houses on College Avenue and Campus Street. To the first recitation building had been added a library, a chapel, a laboratory, a science building, a social hall, an administration building, and a heating plant. An abandoned church was our gymnasium, and we watched football games and track meets on the playing field from uncovered bleachers. Hayfields had been disciplined to lawn, shadowed by giant oaks and elms grown from seedlings planted by the first faculty. Walks surfaced with cinders from the heating plant struck black lines across the green of spring and early fall, the stark white of winter. The cinders crunched like snow under our feet. The walk to the chapel was bordered by peonies which bloomed for Commencement. The bell in the tower of the first recitation building was rung to wake us in the morning, to call us to classes, to celebrate athletic victories.

Black, brown, white, red, and yellow, we slept two to a cubicle, took turns under the icy shower, halved oranges and poured milk for breakfast, washed and dried dishes, dashed upstairs to make our beds, crunched off in flapping overshoes to class, assembled every day at a quarter of nine for chapel — Catholics, Protestants, and Jews pressed

255

shoulder to shoulder in the crowded pews — and crunched off to the next class. Together those who returned from the laboratories smelling of formaldehyde lunched with history majors memorizing dates, and heard or half-heard the liberal and the literal-minded comparing Biblical Literature and Astronomy courses, government students discussing politics. In the afternoon we read books on reserve at the library, played team games — the girls for interclass, the men for intercollegiate competition — climbed the steep little hill behind the campus and sat in the crevices of the ledge to write letters home. Evenings were for play rehearsals, study in our rooms, club meetings. We had neither fraternities nor sororities to separate us socially, and were separated only briefly by special interests, some to sing, some for French conversation or to read Greek, some to write, some to discuss philosophical theories, and for required attendance each Sunday at the church of our choice. Red, white, yellow, black, brown, we snake-danced after winning a championship, cheered our sister classes in the dining room, waltzed in the gym, filed to candlelight services on Sunday evenings, skated and skiied and canoed on the Androscoggin in season, waited for mail, answered doorbells, counted sheets for the laundry, carried muffins in our pockets for those too sleepy to get up for breakfast, took turns going downtown for ice cream for everyone on the floor, shared our boxes of food from home, walked twenty miles each fall for sweet cider from a cider mill. It is the togetherness Whitaker men and women remember. Whatever separated us dims and is forgotten. We were together not only with one another but with the past as it had been described to us, and with the future as we believed it would be and as we were determined to help make it.

256

In the Maine farm and village homes of my fellow students, as in the valley, men had been either Democrats or Republicans. A woman — when she thought of politics — was loyal either to her husband's or to her father's political party. Hostilities between the factions were mild and expressed vehemently only during campaign periods. It was taken for granted that both parties sought the best possible candidates, especially for national office, that both worked earnestly for the good of the country, and that the President and the Congress represented the American people and served the minority as well as the majority. While I was in high school at least three events which were greatly to affect the nation, and therefore the world, had taken place without making more than a few ripples on the placid surface of rural American life.

The Eighteenth Amendment to the Constitution, outlawing the manufacture, sale, or transportation of intoxicating liquors, had been passed in 1917 and ratified in 1919, going into effect a year later.

"A good thing, too," said our fathers. "Strong drink was ruining the country. Ought to have took steps long ago."

Even men like Bill Brown said, "Thank God. It's what I needed. Can't get the stuff, won't drink it."

"Wouldn't be done now," boasted our mothers, "but for a few women that had the spunk to get after it. Small wonder it waited for women. They're the ones that've suffered most. Look at poor Mattie! Even good men are too willing to let things slide. If this world is going to be decent, women have got to take a hand. Why, chances are the war would never have been won without 'em."

The Nineteenth Amendment, declaring that the right of

257

citizens to vote must not be abridged on account of sex, had been passed in 1919, and ratified in 1920.

"Know what that'll mean," chuckled our fathers. "They'll be wanting Easter bonnets early so's to wear 'em to Town Meeting."

"You going to vote like Frank?" my mother asked Mrs. Carter.

"I'll vote as I believe is right," said Mrs. Carter quietly. "But Frank and I generally agree."

"If you ask me," my mother told us at supper, "Frank has been voting the way Liz believes for years. Liz does the thinking and the talking over there. Only right she should help with the voting."

"Frank don't say much," observed my father mildly. "But nobody has ever seen which side of the ballot he put his checkmark on. Nor ever will."

"And no more will you see where I put mine!" cried my mother triumphantly.

"Don't need to," said my father good-naturedly. "Here on, either I'll haul you down to the Town Hall to cancel out my vote, or we can stay to home, get just as fur, and be just as well off."

"Did you vote for Teddy Roosevelt?" I asked suddenly, seeing the clothesline hung full of rugs, hearing my own childish voice, and remembering the minnows Owen gave me.

"Never told yet how I voted," my father answered, his eyes twinkling over the rim of his cup.

"Well, I'll tell you," my mother said. "He voted for Roosevelt when Roosevelt was a Republican. Not when he split the Grand Old Party. Your father's a dyed-in-the-wool Republican. But I say that split was the best thing that ever happened. It's how President Wilson got elected, and no knowing what the world would be like now if he hadn't. I only hope they don't kill him off before he finishes the job he started. He's the greatest man that ever was in the White House."

"See?" my father said to me. "She's a red-hot Democrat."

Woodrow Wilson died in the vain defense, at home and abroad, of his Fourteen Points, of a treaty with Germany in tolerable terms which the vanquished nation could reasonably be expected and required to fulfil, and of the United States' active, responsible membership in the League of Nations.

Out of his lingering, final illness, he said:

They will have to learn now by bitter experience just what they have lost. . . . We had a chance to gain the leadership of the world. We have lost it, and soon shall be witnessing the tragedy of it all.

All over America men and women looked at each other, perplexed and uneasy.

"If he was right, why didn't the Senate do as he asked? Just because he was a Democrat?"

"No. Many Republicans, including ex-President Taft, agreed with the President on this and supported him. Some Democratic leaders didn't. If we had joined the League of Nations, the United States would have been bound to defend European boundaries with American lives."

"But if we don't help them keep the peace they'll be at war, and we'll be drawn in anyway, as we were before."

"Only in a major war. Europe is constantly in little wars. It's chaos over there. Worst of all, there's this Communism that's started in Russia, and no knowing where else it has got a toehold or how far it will spread. Besides, there's Asia on our other side."

"President Wilson thinks if we joined the League we could establish democracy all over the world. Why can't we have the faith and courage to try?"

"Maybe because he's wrong. Sometimes a good man expects too much too soon of the human race. You might say he's ahead of his time."

"Well . . . maybe . . ."

American men returned gratefully to their fields, barns, offices, pulpits, courtrooms, machines, and laboratories; and American women to their sinks, desks, hospitals, machines, and interest in social reform.

In 1920, women voted for the first time in the United States.

We who were then in high school had returned to our textbooks, our basketball courts, our morning prayers, our Latin mottoes, our Scout meetings, and our plans for college.

But even before we left home, President Harding had died, a Vermont farmer had administered the oath of presidential office, by the light of a kerosene lamp, to his son — Calvin Coolidge — and the scandals of the brief Harding Administration began to be revealed. Thereafter, even the quiet, busy, happy, and comparatively austere atmosphere of Whitaker was rudely shaken from time to time by strange gusts born of the political whirlwind which followed the World War.

In our freshman course in American History, we were asked to read metropolitan newspapers which told of the misuse of naval oil reserves and of indictments for conspiracy and bribery.

But President Harding was dead. President Coolidge was a man of integrity. American production was expanding, standards of living were rising, and even abroad tensions seemed to be relaxing.

"We've made some mistakes," we said. "Every country — like every person — makes mistakes sometimes. When you have made them, you can correct them. But you can't correct them all at once. It takes time."

I roomed with Anne Reaves our sophomore year. Anne was a statuesque blonde from Houlton, and her father was a potato grower. I learned from Anne that an Aroostook potato-grower was not a farmer like the valley farmers, but a Big Business man, in a sense a gambler, rich in the years when his crops were good — especially if other men's crops were poor — deeply in debt when his crops failed, and ill off when potatoes everywhere ripened in abundance. Anne's father was also interested in racing horses. He had wanted Anne to go to Vassar or to Bryn Mawr, but Whitaker had been Anne's choice, for she was deeply religious and wanted to marry a man who would be a missionary. Anne's mother, on trips to Boston or New York, often sent Anne several dresses or hats or pairs of shoes from which to choose as many as she liked. Once three fur coats came, and all the girls on our floor sat around and stroked them. But Anne sent back all the coats, and never kept more than one of the simplest of the hats and dresses or a sensible pair of shoes she needed.

"I wish Mother wouldn't do this," she said. "I don't want luxuries. I want to get used to living without them. It's a horrible waste to be longing for silk and fur, to be miserable if you don't have it, and, if you do have it, to spend time and thought on putting exactly the right combinations together. I want my life to be simple. I want to care only about what is important. I've seen enough of time and energy being frittered away."

"I don't see why it wastes your time," I said. "They're so beautiful, Anne. And they're here. Why don't you just keep them? Or, anyway, some of them. It would please your mother."

Anne shook her head.

"You don't understand, Althea. This is something I have to get away from. I mustn't let it pull me down and drag me back. It's materialism and I hate it. Too many Americans have too much, and always want more — while in other parts of the world people are hungry and cold."

I didn't understand, as I had not understood my mother when she told me that it was wicked not to eat the crust of my bread when less fortunate children were crying for crusts of bread. I knew that the crust I ate would be no more helpful to those crying children than the crust I did not eat, and the one I did not eat would be soaked in milk for the cat. For me to eat too much and let my cat go hungry would not feed the children in city slums, nor in teeming Asia, nor in darkest Africa. Just so it seemed to me that the pretty clothes Anne did not wear would be worn by other American college girls, not by ragged young women on the banks of the Ganges nor by shivering brides in Siberia; and that the money Mrs. Reaves could not spend on one daughter probably would be spent on herself or on other daughters.

"There must be better ways to help," I said, "than to refuse your share of what your mother is going to buy anyway."

"I know there are," Anne agreed. "And I mean to find them. But this is where I have to begin. I've tried to change my family, but I can't. So I have to begin with myself. I must learn to do away with nonessentials. That isn't hard. I must learn to live without even some things most of us here consider essential. That will be harder. But I think I can do it."

"Why, of course you can, Anne," I said in surprise. "Most of us consider what we have here is essential to a good way of life. Oranges in the morning, salad at noon, meat or fish every night. Warm skirts and jackets and boots. Sizzling radiators; screens in the windows, toothbrushes, bathtubs and electricity. Books and music and plays. But most of us have lived and been healthy and happy in faded cotton flannel, with oranges only at Christmas, lettuce only in summer, meat once a week, heat only in the cookstove, water brought in pails from a well in the yard. We had baths in the washtub on Saturday nights, and studied by oil lamps. My parents live that way now, and I don't think they would want to change much. They didn't *always* have screens in all their windows, nor even toothbrushes. But why should we go without these things when they are here for us? Or even without a silk dress or a fur coat or a pair of high-heeled slippers if someone wanted to give them to us?"

"You shouldn't," Anne agreed. "Because you have. So you know how much you could do without if you had to — or if you wanted to in order to give real essentials to other people. But I have to prove myself to myself. That's how I'm different from the rest of you. I have more to — overcome."

I sat watching her as she stood brushing her long, heavy hair and pinning it into a smooth crown around her head, as she shrugged off her long, bulky beacon blanket bathrobe and reached for a skirt she had bought of Connie

263

Thurston because Connie needed the price of it to pay her laboratory fee. Anne had knit her gray sweater herself. It did not fit her and had dropped stitches, puckered rows, and twisting seams.

"I want to reach a state of mind, a state of grace," said Anne, "where I would not hesitate to give away anything I had, because faith would be all I needed and the more of that one gives away, the more one has."

I admired Anne, as I did Agnes Brown, for pursuing the stony path to self-renunciation. I admired Anne even more because she was renouncing so much more. But I was likewise more exasperated with her, for it seemed to me that the world had none too much beauty, taste, and lighthearted gaiety, that it needed more of these as well as of sterner virtues and more practical traits and skills, and I thought that Anne Reaves with her hair fluffed to catch the light, wearing a well-chosen, well-cut dress and a bright smile, would be a more welcome missionary and a better spokesman for democracy than an Anne made to look as much as possible like Agnes Brown. I thought the cold and hungry and ragged would prefer to be fed by one who did not have to become cold and hungry and unkempt herself in order to do it, that it was too bad for the heathen to get the impression that all Christians are solemn and intense, and that perhaps the world as a whole would not begin to come out into the light until submerged peoples discovered the existence of man-made beauty, learned to appreciate it, and began to want a few luxuries as well as the necessities of life.

I was not sure, but it was what I thought. I was not sure of this, as I was not sure when Howard Delle, a senior, began walking with Anne and me along the cinder paths, to sit with us on the dormitory steps and in the reception room, whether he was right or wrong in saying that Western civilization was following the trail of decadent Rome, with the widespread disregard of the Prohibition law — speak-easies, moonshine, bootlegging, rumrunning — with dances called the Charleston, the black bottom, the shimmy, with chorus girls bathing in gin, with city girls everywhere smoking, bobbing their hair, drinking champagne from their slippers, with women neglecting their homes and families for clubs and cards and going about in broad daylight with painted faces, with men writing articles on the advantages of free love, with so many people staying away from church to play golf and ride to the beaches, with everyone mad for money and more money. If what Howard said was true — and I knew he believed it to be true — of course he was right. But at Whitaker I saw, every day, ten times as many people as lived in the valley, all of them between the ages of eighteen and twenty-five, and none of them bathed in gin, drank champagne, stayed away from church, used make-up except at night, or had a high regard for money. I had missed the article on free love; and never heard it mentioned except by Howard. We danced only waltzes and foxtrots, and the Dean of Women spoke quietly to any couple dancing less than four inches apart. We had made a rule against women smoking on campus, and no one had broken it — though two girls whispered to their intimate friends that once over on the riverbank they had tried their escorts' cigarettes, on a dare, and found they tasted vile. A few groups did play bridge on Saturday evenings. It appeared to be an innocent game. A few girls had had their hair cut, and I thought the style very becoming.

I was not sure that Howard Delle — tall, dark, hollow-cheeked, with a long, high-bridged nose and a voice like an avenging angel's — was exaggerating the degree to which so-called "flaming youth" represented the young people of America and was undermining the future, but it seemed to me that he must be; and I could not agree that the activities of which he talked so ominously were equally sinister. But I knew from living with Anne and seeing the adoration in her face as she listened to him that Howard was the man she had come to Whitaker to find, and I ceased to sit on the steps or in the reception room with Anne and Howard. I let them crunch the cinder walks by themselves, and began coming home from class most often with Bunny Lambert. Flapping along behind them, sometimes, Bunny and I noticed that now Anne's overshoes were always neatly buckled. She was avoiding the very appearance of evil.

Howard was graduated from Whitaker in June, having worked his way through by preaching in neighboring rural churches through the college year and substituting for ministers on summer vacations. He and Anne were married that summer and went together to Boston, where Howard began a three-year course of study to become a missionary in the Far East and Anne took nurse's training. I never heard directly from Anne after we separated between the peony borders in front of the chapel after watching Howard and the other seniors march out to the strains of "Auld Lang Syne," but Agnes told me that she often saw them both at meetings and lectures and that they were completely dedicated to the ideals of foreign service. I never doubted that they were.

I think the reason Anne did not write to me was that she had felt estranged from me by my friendship with Bunny. Bunny was as tiny and blithe as Anne was regal and solemn. She wore her pleated skirts shorter than the average and her dark eyelashes fluttered devastatingly whenever she smiled or spoke — which was almost constantly, even in class. She had a friend at Ballard, a men's college not far away, who wrote her every day, invited her to fraternity house parties, sent her violets in January and sweet peas in March — and the last time he came to take her out, in our sophomore year, he brought his roommate for me. We went downtown to dinner and to what they laughingly called "the cinema," and took so long returning that Bunny and I were fifteen minutes late signing in and gave ourselves two demerits each. Not only that. The very next day Bunny and I went to the barbershop to have our hair cut short and shingled in the back. I remember something like despair in the way Anne looked at me that afternoon, but I remember better the crisp, delicious coolness of the pillow against my bare neck as I lay down to sleep that night.

This was a year in which we read in metropolitan newspapers and reported in Government class about rampant gangsterism; of strikes led by a group of secessionists from the Socialist Party who had become the American Communist Party, affiliated with the Russian-controlled Third International.

I was back in the valley in July when a young man named Scopes was brought to trial in Dayton, Tennessee, accused of having taught *that the earth was once a hot, molten mass, too hot for man or animal life to exist upon it; in the sea the earth cooled off; there was a little germ of one-cell organism formed, and this organism kept evolving until it got to be a land animal, and it kept on evolving and from this was man.* He was prosecuted by William Jennings Bryan of Nebraska, defeated Democratic nominee

267

for the Presidency in 1896, 1900, and 1908, and defended by Clarence Darrow, America's most famous criminal lawyer. Bryan declared that he had no doubt that the whale had swallowed Jonah, Joshua had made the sun stand still, and that the world was created in seven days in the year 4004 B.C. Darrow proposed calling to the stand scientists, who might have testified that the theory of evolution was wholly consistent with Christianity, but the judge ruled that the only question was whether or not Scopes had taught evolution, which he could not and did not wish to deny.

"What difference does it make?" my father asked. "A man has to believe what he believes. A good many things is known now that wasn't known in Bible times."

"Well, God knew it all then, didn't He?" demanded my mother. "And the Bible is God's Word."

"Nobody ever claimed He wrote it down. There's many a slip 'twixt the cup and the lip, used to say in the copybooks."

"I don't like Darrow calling Adam and Eve a fool idea."

"It's awful hot down there in Tennessee this time of year, I guess. Tempers are flying. Got to take that into account."

"I s'pose you like to think you're descended from a monkey, Brad McIntire."

"Well, it wouldn't bother me none. Monkeys are a sight smarter'n some folks I know. Come to think of it, Marthy, way you go around this house when company's coming, using both feet and both hands to once, I don't know but maybe —"

She snatched his hat off a hook and threw it at him.

"There now," he said. "I see an organ-grinder down in Portsmouth once got served just that way. My, how that monkey's eyes did pucker up. Look in the glass, Marthy."

John Thomas Scopes was convicted and fined a hundred dollars. The Supreme Court of Tennessee upheld the anti-evolution law, but set aside the fine. Bryan died a week after the trial ended, exhausted by his effort but firm in his faith.

It was blackberry time that same summer when we heard a knock at the door about ten o'clock one night. We should have been in bed and asleep, but it had been the best haying day of the season and my father and I had cut and dried and hauled and stowed away in the top loft four loads of meadow grass. My skirt still smelled of the sweet-grass that grows in our meadow, and I still shivered at the thought of the snakeskin we had found in one of the ditches, a black, sequinned gown five feet long which the wearer had slithered out of. But my mother had gone blackberrying all afternoon and come home with enough for more jam than would be eaten in one winter. My father and I had picked them over after supper. Now we had made the jam — she liked to make it, she said, before the berries had lost the heat of the sun — and my father and I were watching her pour the wax which sealed the glasses.

A knock at a valley door was surprising at any time of year, but on a summer evening when only an unhooked screen separated outside from inside, and especially at ten o'clock at night, it was unheard of.

"What in tunket!" my father exclaimed.

He had taken off his boots and was cooling his stock-inged feet on the window sill. They struck the floor with an unwilling thump, and he padded through the entry.

"Somebody must be sick," I said.

"Nobody would knock for that," my mother answered. "Must be strangers lost their bearings. Happens sometimes late years. Folks at the beaches wandering around in cars, no more idea where they are than if they was on the moon. Last ones that spoke to your father asked him if he knew where they was. He said yes, he knew, but he couldn't very well tell them; best he could do was tell them how to get out of here."

"Oh, so that's it," we heard my father say. "Looks to me like Halloween in August. Always a passel of young ones likes to rig up that way for Halloween. Well, what you pounding on my door for, middle of the night?"

"Want you to join up," rumbled another voice. "Look better if you did. Everybody round here has, just about, except the Catholics."

I shaded my eyes at the window. There was a draped and hooded figure on the porch, and in a silent car beside the lane I could see other hooded heads as awesome as skulls in the moonlight.

"Mama," I whispered, terror-stricken. "It's the Ku Klux Klan!"

"What on earth's that?" my mother asked. She put down the kettle of wax, but not before she had sealed the last jar of her precious jam, and came to look out with me. "Good land! Somebody six feet tall dressed up like a ghost. He must be daft."

"There are more of them in the car," I whispered. "I've read about them. It started in the South and it's spreading all over. They preach what they call 'Christian' hatred of Jews, white hatred of Negroes, Protestant hatred of Catholics. They do terrible things to people. I wish he would just lock the door."

"Hark!"

"You join up now, and I'll tell you where the next Konklave's going to be. Nobody but members s'posed to know time or place."

"What would I have to do to join up?" my father asked. *Oh, Father . . .*

"Gimme ten dollars. I'm the local Kleagle of the Klan."

"Give you ten dollars? What would you do with it?"

"We keep four out of every ten for the work right here. A dollar goes to the King Kleagle, fifty cents to the Grand Goblin, and the rest to the Imperial Wizard, the Emperor, and the Imperial Kleagle. They're the heads of the outfit."

"So what's the work right here that my four dollars would do, and what do the Goblins and Gizzards and all them high mucka-mucks do with my six dollars if they get it?"

"Plenty to do, I can tell you that. You'll find out at the Konklave. What would you say if I told you the Catholic Pope is going to move to Washington, and they've got all their blasted cathedrals stuffed with ammunition to take over the American Government soon as he gets there? What would you say if I told you the Catholic church right in this town has got its basement full of dynamite, and the Luneaus helped to pile it in there and will be amongst them that'll drag it out and blow up every Protestant church and public school in this town if we don't hand the buildings over to them, unless we clean it out first?"

"What would I say? I'd say you'd lost your mind or else you never had any. It must be one or the other, anyway, a feller to come into my dooryard all covered up in sheets. What's the idea of that rig?"

"Nobody's s'posed to know who is Klansmen. And, look here, I don't like the way you're talking. I come here as a friend. To warn you you'd better join up and take a stand

271

for the right, and keep away from them Luneaus. Folks seeing you with them might get the idea you was on the wrong side of the fence. Nothing happens, see, the Klan don't know about. Them as ain't with us is against us, way we look at it. Either you're a good American or you ain't. You —"

"Well, now, you can stop right there. I'm a good American as fur as I know. I'm a durn sight better American than what you be, and so are the Luneaus. I don't care whether you like the way I talk or not. I don't like the way *you* talk, and I'm not going to hear any more of it on my place. I can't stop you playing hobgoblin and having Konklaves with Beagles and Gizzards and the rest of it, but you can't Konklave on my porch, so get off!"

"Hold on now. You can't rastle me, and if you could, that car out there is full of Klansmen —"

The screen door slammed.

"I said get off my porch, or I'll wind that sheet around your neck. You won't get a cent of my money and you won't never get *me* rigged up in a sheet. Get OFF, I said."

I could not believe it was my father. I trembled all over. But the Klansman moved off the porch and into the shadow of the trees.

"No wonder you fellers don't want decent folks to know who you are," my father called. "But I know who you are. I'd know that voice in Timbuctoo, and if ever the Klan does any harm in this town, I'll tell the Luneaus and the Carters and the Daleys and Bert Anthony and your father who I know that belongs to it, and we'll take you down and dip you in the river if we have to cut a hole in the ice to do it. You used to be as good a boy as any of 'em, but you've been in bad company for some time now, and

272

you're in pretty deep. All I can think is you don't know any better. But you see you find out before you come around me again. And just you see to it your hobgoblins don't do anything rash before you've pulled out lock, stock, and barrel and told everybody you was in but ain't in any longer. Because if there's trouble, the valley will make you pay for it. We don't aim to breed Gizzards nor Goblins nor Emperors here — just people that can live and let live, don't lie, and ain't ashamed to show their faces. Now get out of my yard. This is my stamping ground."

I could hardly believe my ears. Nor my eyes, for the shrouded figure backed away as my father advanced, and finally turned, retreating in a long, loping stride to the car. My father waited until the car moved off. Then he came slowly back to the porch, stood on the top step for a few minutes, looking at the stars, and then padded back in.

"My gracious, Brad," my mother said, staring at him. "How did you dare?"

"Dare? He knew better than to lay a hand on me or let anybody else."

"It was Jimmy Brown, wasn't it?"

Jimmy!

"Never mind who it was. Don't say a word of this to anybody unless they speak first. Don't matter who it was as long as they only play games with money from ones that's fool enough to give it to 'em. But if there's trouble, he'll get it double and he knows it now. So maybe there won't be."

But my mother knew Jimmy's voice as well as he did. I had never heard it since the night he took me to my Junior Prom, for he did not live at home long after that. I had forgotten his voice, and the way his damp hair had felt

273

against my fingers as his head lay in my lap, the steely glint of his eyes in his hard, brown, boy's face, the drinking cup he had once held to my mouth, and the present he had made to me in a dream instead of a ring for my finger. Now I remembered it all as if it were yesterday.

"What would Agnes say?" my mother wondered. "It would break her heart. Poor child, she's had so much to put up with in that family. So much to learn that they never knew and never will know. She's done it all alone. If she ain't a saint, I don't know who is."

Not all alone, I thought. None of us ever had to do good things alone. Agnes had the Elder to help her, and Mrs. Carter, and well — everybody in the valley in little ways, and later people in town too. But so did Jimmy. Why did Agnes find so much that was good, and Jimmy so little? . . . Maybe it was Owen who helped Agnes most, because he was the last from the valley to help her, the only one then who could help her.

I realized guiltily that I had not thought of Owen for months, though each year Mrs. Carter gave me a hundred dollars which I knew must have come from him. Now it was a comfort to think of him in a personal way, to superimpose his picture upon that of the glinting-eyed boy in the cranberry bed who had grown into a sheeted member of the Ku Klux Klan and spoke in a surly, threatening rumble. Owen smiled down at me out of a small clearing in the fog, across a tubful of pond lilies, a blue mass of wild asters, a hundredleaf rose bush vivid with bloom.

He said, *You're Althea McIntire . . . You look pretty. Everything in the valley is pretty. . . .*

The Ku Klux Klan was never known to do violence to anyone in our town. Within a year, the truth of its intent and the falsity of its claims, the poverty of its ideals and the scandal of its corrupt practices were recognized through most of the country. I was proud that my father had known and denounced it for what it was within five minutes of the first time he heard of it, but he was only one of many. To menace the freedom of thought, religion, and personal safety of other citizens is not long permitted by a nation of free men, for freedom is their dearest possession, dearer even than life itself.

All that summer Bunny's friend's roommate, T. Weston Palmer, was mailing me postcards from most of the big cities and many odd corners of the United States, and at least once a week sent me a long letter. The letters were extraordinary, for Wes was a brilliant and extraordinary young man. In his twentieth year, while still a college junior, he had had a novel accepted for publication, and his father, a manufacturer of radios, was so proud that he at once offered to buy his son whatever he wanted most. What Wes wanted most — among objects money could buy, he said — was a Stutz bearcat, a coonskin coat, and a black beret. Mr. Palmer cheerfully provided the car, and promised that if Wes would use it during the summer "to tour this great country of ours and see what we've got here, my son," the coonskin coat would be forthcoming before the snow flew again.

Dad would have naught to do with the black beret. I doubt if he knows what a beret is (do you, my chick?) but obviously it sounded sinister to him. Maybe the old boy thinks it's a Bolshevik uniform. He doesn't know what Bolshevism is, either, but he hates it. So I squared my shoulders, drew myself to my full 5′11″, said it was very decent of him to give me the car, the trip, and the coat, and that I would show I was a chip off the old block by providing myself with the black beret. (It's a round French cap, cherie, renowned for staying on when the wind blows.) I must say the old boy looked mighty proud of this display of resourcefulness on the part of his offspring. So out I marched in a blaze of glory, picked up a couple of fraternity brothers who needed a summer away from yacht clubs, and bravely across the land we came, packed like sardines into our uncovered wagon, peering conscientiously through our goggles at American scenery (it's overrated), American mansions (they're ugly), American corn (it's not all in the fields of Kansas; a lot of it is in greasy cellars you get into if you say Joe sent you), and American hogs (they don't all have four feet and some of their snouts are as short as my nose). I don't know what you'll make of all this, petite. I don't know what I'll make of it myself, but a new novel I hope. I'll drop you another line soon. Not that I wouldn't rather drop you a kiss or two, but you Whitaker girls are so-o-o repressed. Puritans, every one of you. It matters little how Puritanical the rest of them are. But you — couldn't you resolve this summer to be less Whitakerish come fall? Couldn't you at least relax as much as Bunny? See you in September.

Wherever Wes went, he found much to laugh at, and little to admire. He zigzagged at top speed through the Loop in Chicago to avoid the machine-gun bullets of gangsters, but the police were ahead of him all the way, so far ahead that he never saw one. Had I read *Main Street?* I should, but it was too kind to small Midwestern cities. Lewis's *Babbitt* was better, stronger, but the businessmen who should see themselves in it read only sales reports and the *Wall Street Journal.* "Dreiser is a wise old bird." Dreiser's *American Tragedy* was the best new novel out. Wes's publishers had sent him an advance copy.

I think they hope I'll do something like that, but I should live long enough! A guy named Wright is designing some marvelous buildings out here. If you saw them, I wonder if you would think it was a dream or a nightmare. The few people who live in his houses are looked upon as freaks by their neighbors. He is really appreciated only abroad. And we consider ourselves such a dynamic, progressive country! But if anybody has a really new idea people think he's crazy. I expect three Palmers and the family doctor to sign papers consigning me to some luxurious sanatorium when my book comes out. Will you bake me a cake with a file in it, cherie? You know who this country counts as its real current heroes? Not artists, not philosophers, not poets, not statesmen (if any). Nope. Babe Ruth, the man who hit 59 homers in 1921; Red Grange, a football player; Jack Dempsey, the heavyweight champion of the world with dynamite in his gloves. The U.S. is sports mad. I yawn. Ever hear of S. Freud? It's high time you did. He's been trying to free the libido since the turn of the century, and some people are beginning to think it might be a good idea. I've decided to make you a present. I'm ordering for you a year's subscription to the *American Mercury*. The more boobs, morons, and yokels we encounter — dozens of new ones every day — the more I love H. L. Mencken.

I could not reply to these letters for I had no address. I read them at first with amusement and a feeling that I, too, was careening lightly across state boundaries and intellectual boundaries, alerted and instructed in sophistication, but as the pile in my bureau drawer mounted, the postmarks traveled eastward, and August slid into Labor Day, I felt that I was being carried beyond my depth and perhaps Wes was, too. I wondered how much Mr. Palmer knew of what his son had found in his voyage of discovery, and whether he would be sorry that he had bought the Stutz and promised the coonskin coat on condition that this journey was made. I was not eager to see Wes again. Actually, I was afraid to. And I was grateful that I had been unable to reply to his letters and so had not committed myself to anything, even inadvertently.

But when Tim Gilmartin and Wes appeared to take Bunny and me to the Ballard-Whitaker game, each of them with a handful of huge golden chrysanthemums and a fringed stadium blanket, Wes looked so dashing in his black beret, sang both Alma Maters with such boyish abandon, and looked so rueful when Whitaker won over Ballard for the first time in five years, that I decided his letters had been a pose and almost forgot them. After the game we all squeezed into the one seat of the Bearcat, Bunny on Tim's knees, and rode ninety miles for hot dogs at a roadside stand which the boys said served the best hot dogs in the world. We ate three apiece, along with mugs of thick black coffee, sitting wrapped in the stadium blankets on the shore of a pond where cattails grew. The sun was going down across the water and after a while the stars came out. All the time Wes was telling funny stories about his summer trip — what he said to the Amish couple riding in a buggy; the family who insisted that he take a snapshot of them sitting around a table floating in the Great Salt Lake; the flock of sheep he had to ride behind for hours on Raton Pass, until it occurred to Butch Evans to bribe the old shepherd with a drink from his pocket flask; and dozens of other anecdotes. Wes told stories very well, with lively imitations of dialect, accompanied by sounds of steel-rimmed wheels turning, geese squawking, shots being fired, girls screaming, and laundry flapping on a line. No matter how much we laughed, Wes talked on with pretended earnestness, and every time his dimples deepened he smoothed them out and frowned. Wes was not a handsome boy, but those dimples were a constant fascination, and the way he kept tossing back a heavy lock

278

of hair which was always falling over his forehead made him as endearing as a pony.

We sang all the way back to Whitaker, but I can think while I am singing. I thought over the hours Wes had talked, what he had said and what he had not said.

At the dormitory Bunny and Tim paused in the shadow of the stone steps, but I went straight in and Wes followed me. At the door of the reception room he put his hand on my shoulder and drew me in.

"It's 9:45," I said. "Any minute the proctor will blink the lights, and the boys will have to go."

"Just until then," he said.

The sofas were all occupied by other couples, but he pushed me down on one arm of a big chair and sat on the other arm himself, holding his black beret between his knees.

"What's the matter, Thea? I can tell something's the matter. Didn't you have fun?"

"Of course I had fun."

"Then what's the matter?"

"Fun isn't everything."

"It sure isn't. But I thought it was all you were ready to have with me. Did I get you wrong, baby — I hope?"

He leaned toward me and took my hand.

"I didn't mean that," I said. "I mean — your letters — and the way you talked tonight. You poke fun at everybody and everything. You've been in forty-four states, and all I've seen is part of two, but all you do is laugh at them, or make other people laugh. A little of that is enough for me. I don't believe this country is a joke. I think it's a great country. You must have worked at not seeing anything beautiful to tell us about, anything to be proud of, anything to make you glad and thankful you're an American. I suppose that sounds naïve to you. I suppose you'll tell Tim on the way back to Ballard that I'm Whitakerish. I've heard you use that word and I know it's no compliment. Well, go ahead and say it if you want to. I don't care. I suppose I bore you. Well, the more I think of it, you make me just plain mad."

I felt my lips tremble. I was afraid I was going to burst into tears.

Wes did not let go my hand.

The lights blinked. The other boys stood up. There was no waiting upon an order in the girls' reception room at Whitaker.

Wes leaned closer.

"Listen, Thea," he said in my ear. "You don't bore me. Sometimes I wonder why you don't, but you don't. And nothing I say about you anywhere is meant to be anything but complimentary. I agree with you that America is no joke. I've been playing the fool about it because it seemed safer. I haven't dared to say what I really think. But I will after this — if it won't make you madder than you are now. I want to. I need to. I need to tell it to somebody, and you're the only one who would listen. If you will."

All the other couples had gone. The proctor stood meaningfully beside the door with her finger on the light switch.

"I'll listen," I said. "I won't get mad if you're fair."

"I'll be as fair as I know how," he promised. "You have to believe that."

He pulled me so hard against him that it hurt, released me so suddenly that I swayed, and went out the front door as Bunny came in. I stood in the hall looking after him. I had never seen him so serious, so intense, before. It was a new Wes.

Bunny linked her arm in mine on our way upstairs to our room.

"Wes is a scream, isn't he?" she asked. "I never knew such a funny guy. Aren't you beginning to like him?"

"I like him," I said. "I may even get to like him a lot."

Bunny was so pleased she jumped up and down on the landing.

"Oh, goody, goody. A girl who's never been mad about a Ballard boy hasn't lived. They're so much more exciting than Whitaker boys. You know what Whitaker boys are going to do — be ministers or teachers or doctors — you almost know what they think before they tell you. Ballard boys keep you guessing. You never know what they're going to say next. Timmy's cute. And so's Wes."

All that year college students were reading Lewis's *Arrowsmith,* which criticized the medical profession; Hemingway's *The Sun Also Rises,* which ignored ideals and social problems, indicating that pleasure was all, and only to be found in physical sensation; Fitzgerald's *The Great Gatsby* and his "lost generation"; O'Neill's *Desire under the Elms* and *The Great God Brown*; Eliot's *The Wasteland* and Millay's *A Few Figs from Thistles*; Hughes's debunking biography of Washington. Many of us also read the poetry of Robert Frost, Edwin Arlington Robinson, Carl Sandburg, and Vachel Lindsay, the novels of Willa Cather, Ellen Glasgow, and Edith Wharton, Sandburg's *Abraham Lincoln: The Prairie Years.* All these latter writers deplored human shortsightedness, injustice and cruelty without themselves losing or destroying in others a deep love for America and confidence in its future. They saw all sides where too many saw only one, sensed purpose where others found only futility, climbed hills toward the sky while others scribbled in damp and dusky caves.

One evening in June 1928 I was alone in my dormitory room, packing my trunk. It was the same trunk I had brought to Whitaker as a freshman, the one my mother had brought to my father's house when they were married. I remembered her packing it for me the first time — how she had knelt before it on the parlor floor, folding and placing deftly my clothing, quilts and toilet things. Before she finished I brought a small pillow to cushion her knees. She had looked up and smiled, and my tears — all too ready — started.

"Well, for goodness' sake, don't cry, Althea," she said briskly. "You wanted to go to college, and you're going."

Yes. I had wanted to go to college, but that night I could not have said why, except that a boy had come out of the fog long ago and told me to go. Standing beside my mother while she packed my trunk, I could see this only as an absurd and insufficient reason for leaving her, my father, the house where I was born, and the valley which I loved.

She turned the key in the lock, and gave it to me, rising stiffly.

"Put it in your handbag," she said, "and don't lose it. You have to keep your wits about you from here on."

Now I had been to college. In the morning I would be one of a long line going down the chapel center aisle to receive my degree. Tonight I was alone, for Anna-Marie Gonzales, my roommate, had gone to the Commencement Ball, as had all the other girls I knew well in the dormitory. The building seemed deserted. Every step I took had an echo. The sound dragged at my feet. I perched on the window seat, hugging my knees, and looked out at the deserted campus where the colored lights of Commencement time danced in the wind against the black backdrop of the little hill I had climbed so often for so many reasons that I felt I could not leave it behind but must pack it in a corner of my trunk. I could smell the peonies blooming for the Class of '28.

Suddenly the call bell rang in the corridor. Three short buzzes. That was my number. I listened, disbelieving, while it rang twice more. It must be a mistake. As it rang the fourth time, I sprang up and ran to the stairwell.

"Is that for me?" I called down.

"I don't know," answered a man's voice. "Who are you? Girl or angel?"

"I'm Althea McIntire. Three is my ring."

"Well, if three is your ring, Althea McIntire, come down and answer it."

I did not recognize this voice, to name it, but it had an urgency for me, a familiar magnetism, which took me down three flights as if they had been a ski-slide.

He stood framed in the open French doors of the reception room, his feet planted wide apart, his hands deep in the pockets of his gray flannel trousers, his dark blue flannel coat thrust back so that the full, white square of his shirt front showed, and the full length of a crisp blue and white tie held in place by a gold clasp. He was looking up, watching me come, and his smile spread from the rim of his collar all over his bright, ruddy face up into his thick, curling, touseled sulphur-and-molasses hair.

At the foot of the stairs I held to the newel post with both hands, staring at him. He did not move and his smile did not fade or falter.

He said, "I take it you think we haven't met before."

We had met before. He was the Boy who had come to me out of the fog; the stranger who kept on smiling; the one who showed me that I *was*, who gave me my name;

283

the teacher who did not care about shoes and who taught me all I still cherished most, of what I knew.

I said, "Owen," feeling my lips form the word, but hearing no sound.

It must be a dream. I had no sense of contact with reality.

But then he laughed, was across to me in two strides, swung me to a seat on the newel post I had been clutching and held me there.

"By golly," he said, exultantly, "time and all that happens doesn't make much difference in people, does it? The way they begin is pretty much the way they hold out — inside. I ought to know that — it's been proved to me so many times — but when it's more than fifteen years since you've seen a person, and that person has grown to a woman or a man, you do wonder, don't you?" You're just taller, that's all, Althea. Taller and older. But you're the same Althea."

"Where did you come from?" I asked. "Where have you been?"

"Why, up in the fog," he laughed. Then he said, "No, there's more to it than that. I want to tell you all about it. And hear all about you. But, first, isn't there a dance? I'm sure I heard dance music when I got off the streetcar."

"The Commencement Ball. But I didn't want to go. I'd much rather talk. How long do we have? I mean, how long can you stay?"

I did not breathe until he answered. How long he could stay was more important to me then than anything else in the world.

He let me slide down from the newel post.

"We have as much of tonight as you want to use. Any

way you want to use it. I came to see you graduate tomorrow — if you can get me in."

"I'll get you in. I had tickets for Lucy and Carl, but they found they couldn't come."

"Nobody from your family coming?"

"No. In April my mother —"

"I know. Mrs. Carter wrote me. I thought of writing you then, but I had about made up my mind I'd be seeing you. . . . You know, your Commencement is going to be quite a thing for me, Althea. The first one I've ever been to. I'll be proud enough for a family of ten even if I need only one of your tickets. Now what do you want to do?"

"Oh — talk," I said. "Talk. And hear you talk."

"Where? Here?"

"No. No, I think — on the mountain."

I went ahead of him out into the soft dark and the fragrance of the peonies. There were no rules for seniors that night, and it was the first time I had ever left the dormitory without signing a slip saying when I would be in. I was wearing a sleeveless white pique dress I had worn to dinner and the night breeze was wonderfully cool on my bare arms. I felt a sudden, complete freedom from supervision, restraint, tension, as if the world had once more come back to me all new, and as if, in it, I were invisible.

Going in among the scrub pines at the foot of the hill, we left the dancing Commencement lights behind us, and Owen took my hand. We walked side by side, for the rough path had been made by couples, but I was half a step ahead for my feet were finding our way. It was so dark that, even that close, I could not see him, only felt his hand over mine.

We reached the peak and crossed it in the starlight to the farther side, where from a ledge we could look out

285

over the little city which was Whitaker's neighbor. We sat down in a crevice, and it was like sitting on a balcony overlooking a continent motionless in sleep.

"How does it happen," Owen asked, "that I am this lucky? Why aren't you out with some classmate tonight?"

"I might have been, except that I didn't feel like dancing. . . . I'm glad I wasn't."

I still could see only the outline of his face. His voice was just as it had been so many years before, light, boyish, eager. The feeling between us was exactly as it had been when we sat on a grassy bank, among the goldenrod and wild asters, watching two clouds come together to make a *W;* when he pushed me in a swing; when he pulled me on a sled; when I sat in the tree hammock and he on a branch beside me, and, looking down at his pond lilies in a tub, we sat on a boatside with our feet in the water, and I had baked him a cake. Again we were in a garden which no one else could enter.

"There is some special boy, Althea?"

I shook my head.

He took my hand again and put it, palm up, on his knee. He bent each of my fingers gently.

"You should find one soon," he said. "Find him and marry him. Only be sure he is the right guy. It is the most wonderful thing that can happen to anyone."

Nothing had ever come into our garden which was disturbing. It did not now.

"Has it happened to you, Owen?"

He laughed.

"Honey, how else would I know it is the most wonderful thing?"

He told me how he had found her. On a business trip West, his train had been derailed in the outskirts of a lit-

286

tle Ohio town. During the two hours he had to wait, he walked through the town, and saw her sitting on a porch talking with a young man. It was a hot afternoon and they were drinking lemonade. There was frost on the pitcher and on the tall glasses. She wore a long, thin dress with little roses printed all over it and her dark hair was fluffed out over her ears. A little later he walked back by and the young man was still with her. The third time he passed, the young man had left, but the girl was still there. Owen folded his arms on the gatepost and asked if the lemonade was all gone. She said she had saved some for him for she could see he looked thirstier each time he went by. As he sat in the wicker chair next to hers, she asked if he lived in the town. He said he was just passing through. "So many times?" she asked. He said his life so far had been all passing through, but now the idea had struck him that perhaps it was time to settle down. When he went to the station where he had left his valise, the train was long gone. He stayed a week in the little town's one hotel, and the fact that it was a very bad hotel was only one of the minor reasons why he was glad he did not have to stay longer. Corinne was a stranger in the town, too, a girl from the East stopping over to visit a grandmother, and on the way to Chicago where an uncle who was a newspaper editor had sons with friends who were to inherit meat-packing industries.

"She's never been to Chicago," Owen said. "Before I left, I put her on an eastbound train to break the news to her poor, proud mother in upstate New York that the meat-packing industry had suffered a serious setback, for Corinne was going to marry a brash fellow with no inheritance, no pull, no college degree, various obligations, and only one foot precariously placed on the bottom rung of the advertising ladder. . . . We took the plunge that fall, in 1921, and had our first son within the year. It was hard sledding for a while. We didn't have much money, and I was traveling a good part of the time. But that's all over now. I'm permanently located in New York, we have a nice home in White Plains, and two more sons. We named the first one Granville for Corinne's father, who died when she was a little girl; it's also a family name, and the name of the town where she grew up, where her mother lives still. The second one is Daniel for Gramp. The newest one, poor little chap, is Junior. We're hoping for a girl next. Seem to have run out of names for boys."

"In 1921 . . ." I said. "While you and Corinne were having hard sledding . . . you were helping Armand and Agnes through college. You must have helped Dennis Daley too — though you never saw him. Then I came along."

"You came along first. Remember? Or rather, I came along and you and your folks and the valley took me in. You'll never know what that meant, and I'll never forget it. When I left the valley, I meant to do something for it, over the years, not only because of what it did for me, but for what it did for Gramp. After I left college to go into the service, while I was overseas and pretty sure I wasn't going back to college, I made up my mind what I could and would do — just give the little push that might make all the difference to any valley youngster who was college material. At first, I'll admit, I was thinking only of you. Then I remembered Agnes. When I wrote to Mrs. Carter about her she told me about Armand. Then I saw a kind of pattern. I didn't have much money then, but I was pretty sure I would have in time. Money and excitement is what a man gets from the advertising business. One thing he gives is an impetus to business all over the country; that's important in a democracy, but it's not enough. The country needs more than things which can be bought and the money to buy them with. It needs physical, mental, spiritual, and social health. So it needs doctors, lawyers, teachers, ministers; the money from business has to help provide them, I figure, or how are we going to get them? The training they need is expensive. . . . When I met Corinne, my only family was in the valley and I told her about the obligation I felt toward them. Corinne understood. She's a Barnard graduate, but wouldn't be if she hadn't had that editor-uncle in Chicago to help her through. He didn't need to be repaid, she said, but it was a debt to be repaid some way, in one coin or another. . . . We're mighty proud, Corinne and I, you know, that we've had something to do with Armand Luneau's being at Cornell Law School now. He's on the *Law Review,* and has spent a week end with us twice; a brilliant fellow. And with Agnes Brown's leaving for Burma in August. (Corinne and I'll be on the dock to see her off.) And with Dennis Daley's finishing his first year of teaching an eighth grade, in Lipton Falls, New Hampshire, at the same time that he is taking courses toward a degree at the University, which will qualify him for high school teaching or educational administration. A lawyer, a missionary, and an educator out of the valley already! Corinne and I feel that's enough to justify the merry-go-round I'm on. And this is only the beginning. You graduate tomorrow. Who's next, I wonder?"

I told him it would be a little while, but I thought Bert and Della Anthony's son Wayne would be the next. Wayne would enter the Academy in the fall. During the summer after my Junior year at Whitaker, Mrs. Carter had been sent to Boston for major surgery and needed several months for convalescence. To meet this emergency and to finance my Senior year I had substituted for her in the valley school. Wayne, his little sister Ruth, and Joe and Kathleen Luneau's son Noel had been my best pupils, as Mrs. Carter said they were hers, but Ruth was only in the fourth grade and Noel in the first. Wayne had finished the eighth grade at the age of eleven, and waited — as Armand and I had waited — to be old enough to go into town to school. Wayne was quick intellectually, and a conscientious student, but devoted to his father and a great lover of physical work and the outdoors. He did not yet feel sure that he needed or wanted higher education, and Bert and Della were not ambitious in that way for him. What he did with his life would depend upon the influences of the next few years, while school attendance was required of him.

Owen wrote their names in a little book he took from his inside coat pocket, though neither of us could see the writing.

"Bert and Della," he said. "They were married about the time I came to the valley. . . . I played ball with Joe in the field across the lane from your house and you watched from the hammock in the tree. . . . Who is Kathleen?"

"She was Kathleen Daley. Dennis's sister."

"If Armand and Dennis are in that first-grader, Noel, he's of good stock." He put the little book back into his pocket. I knew he was smiling. "Now tell me about you," he said. "And what is the matter with all these Whitaker men, Althea?"

I said slowly that I admired Whitaker men and felt I had many friends among them, that in my first two years at college I had had dates and good times with several of them, but that all my dating during my Junior year had been with a Ballard Senior. When I came back, after my year in the valley, most of the Whitaker men seemed like boys to me. Besides, I had been preoccupied with my studies and with concern for my mother who had not been well during my year at home but would not admit it for fear I would stay on with her and perhaps never finish my education. To please her, I had come back, but I had gone home for scattered weeks during the fall and winter, and was there all the last month before she died. Between times and since April I had had a heavy schedule of make-up work to do, and no time to think of men.

"Not even of that Ballard Senior?"

I said I never thought of him now if I could help it.

I shifted my position, for the ledge was growing cold and hard. Owen's arm slipped behind me and his hand on my arm drew me back against it, cushioning me. We sat silently looking off at the lights of the little city, like heavy-lidded eyes. The breeze had gone down. It was very still. It seemed as natural as breathing to be there in the dark with Owen.

After a while he said, "Corinne isn't like you in any way I know. At first I thought that was strange, for I had always taken it for granted that somewhere another Althea, of my own age, was waiting for me. That probably was what prevented me from making any serious mistake."

"The same as knowing you has kept me from making any serious mistake. . . . But I wasted time on Wes Palmer. I wasted a whole year."

"I refuse to believe that time a girl like you would spend with anyone is wasted."

"This was."

Then I heard my voice begin about Wes, the first time I had ever said more than a few words about him to anyone. I told Owen how innocently and lightheartedly my relationship with Wes had begun, how his letters had puzzled me while he was traveling about the country, but how I had grown to believe that because he had such a brilliant mind and wrote so charmingly, so amusingly, with so much facility, he was destined to become a figure in American literary life, capable of widespread influence. I had liked everything about Wes Palmer except his ideas, and I had felt challenged to change his ideas.

"I never changed one. Wes despised his father because he was a businessman, and his whole family because they had money; yet he took their money and threw it around as if the only duty he recognized was to get rid of as much of it as he could. He scorned American educational institutions because of their low standards as compared with European institutions, but, with all his brilliance, he was only a C student at Ballard. He was an atheist and said men had dreamed up God because they were afraid to stand on their own two feet and face facts; he claimed that the church would still be using the tortures of the Inquisition if it were not prevented by law; yet he thought it was amusing to break laws, boasted of the number of traffic tickets he had and of the night he spent in jail for disturbing the peace after he had been drinking. He said men were not ready for any high degree of civilization, much less of governing themselves, and wished we all lived as savages do, but he had never used a tool larger than a pen, would not walk two blocks, and if he had a flat tire on his Stutz, drove it to a garage to have it changed even if he ruined the tire as well as the inner tube. He had a low opinion of all mankind, but particularly of the white race, and most particularly of Americans. He laughed at our foreign policy, sneered at our history, and was horrified by every move our government made. We could do no right, in Wes's eyes. We could only do wrong. . . . Before the end of his Senior year, Wes had lost patience with all of us, completely. He was an only son. His father said he must either go into the family firm or settle down to the study of law. He replied that he would do neither. His book was published. His father read it and told him that after June he would have no money except what he earned. Wes was failing two subjects in the last semester of his Senior year. He told me he was going to be a citizen-of-the-world and camp out on the bank of the Seine. He used his first royalty check to buy passage to Europe. I saw his ticket. It was first-class. I've never seen or heard from him since."

"Still," Owen said, "I don't believe the year was wasted. Whether or not it did him any good — and you never know — it must have taught you a good deal. . . . You remember Teddy Roosevelt was always a hero of mine?"

I remembered.

"He said something once which I memorized. It seems to fit in here. He said: *The professed internationalist usually sneers at nationalism, at patriotism, and at what we call Americanism. He bids us forswear our love of country in the name of love of the world at large. We nationalists answer that he has begun at the wrong end; we say that, as the world now is, it is only the man who ardently loves his country first who in actual practice can help any other country at all.*"

I knew that was true.

But I said, "You give Wes Palmer too much credit. I

293

don't think he has ever loved or ever will love anything or anyone, or that anyone can ever love him."

It seemed as if I had tossed down the cliff a pebble which would never reach bottom, but spin forever in space.

"Then a year was full time enough for you to spend with him," Owen said gravely. "But when the right guy comes, you will know him, as I knew Corinne. He almost certainly won't come out of a fog. He may have red hair or dark, be tall and thin, have a voice that rumbles or rings like a bell. But you'll know him when you see him."

"I can't imagine where he'll come from."

"It doesn't matter, does it? Where will he come to, is the question. Where will you be?"

I was slow to answer. We were the only people in the world.

"It may be a disappointment to you, Owen."

"I'll never be disappointed in anything you do."

"I'm going back to the valley. My father needs me. Mrs. Carter wants to retire. I'm going to keep house for my father and teach the valley school."

Owen put his hand under my chin and lifted my face. Behind his head the rim of the moon was climbing out of the pines.

"Disappointed?" he repeated. "Why, we always talked about what we were going to do for the valley! You're the one who is *really* going to do it. The rest of us have mostly taken out of it. You're taking back into the valley everything you've found and learned and are. Nobody could do more than that. . . . You and the valley. That will be quite a combination for Wayne and Ruth, and Joe's little boy! You know what I wish? I wish I could bring Gran and Danny and Junior home to the valley to go to school to you."

He stood up, and drew me up, and kissed my forehead.

"I have to take you down now. It's nearly morning, and you're going to graduate in a little while. You're going to graduate, and I'll be the proudest man in the whole audience."

We groped our way off the mountain, leaving the ghost of our garden behind. But it will always be there, moonlit, riotous with goldenrod and wild blue asters, hundredleaf roses, and waxen-petaled, gold-stamened pond lilies.

I V

I HAD come home. I was the valley teacher. It had been one thing to substitute for Mrs. Carter, and it was quite another to replace her in valley children's lives.

That first morning in September, I set out early to walk slowly and alone the familiar half-mile to the schoolhouse. Lemon-colored evening primroses on the banks of the lane had paled at their first glimpse of the sun and withdrawn into themselves, as I should have liked to do. Wild asters and goldenrod, heavy with the dampness of the night, stood as straight and sturdily as I could have if I had still been in the kitchen at work my mother had taught me to do, as other valley women were at that hour in their kitchens. I broke off a branch of sweetfern and crushed the soft leaves in my hand, calling on their spicy fragrance for courage.

I wore a dark, accordion-pleated skirt, a white blouse with a ruffled front, a cherry-colored cardigan, and it was not a cold morning but I shivered as I turned into the main road. My fingers felt stiff. I looked up at the twin mountains, and over the mountains. I prayed.

"Show me how, oh, God . . . Oh, God, show me how."

We had lived here with Indians. Denmark had sent us cows. We had moved from cabins into frame houses, and the children ran up like steps. We fought against tyranny from without for the freedom of our new country. We built a church. We built a school. We fought against tyranny from within, for the freedom of a subject race, for a stronger union. Stoves were brought in, machinery, and engines. We sent boys to the frontier and girls waited for them to come back or joined them to settle the Great Plains. The frosts came, and the floods, the dry times, the fog; and each in its season the peepers sang, or the whippoorwills, or the wind in the pines; the stacked corn rustled or the ice cracked or the flowers bloomed. Todd Perry took everything the Elder owned, but left him Owen in exchange. The sawmills stripped the valley of much of its source of wealth, but gave Bert Anthony to Della and to all of us the Luneaus, their merriment, their childlike generosity, their faith which we respected though we did not share it. The railroad with its cries in the night, its rumble and roar, brought Sean Daley to Lottie, Kathleen to Joe, Hannah — dear Hannah! — to be the valley saint. It was Hannah who had seen Mrs. Carter through her convalescence, and helped me care for my mother in her last illness. We all turned now to Hannah in time of trouble, and Hannah's face was more beautiful to us than the Mona Lisa's.

The Elder had said:

Everything that happens, everything we do or don't do, has a reason. A good reason, though often we can't see it. Good will come even of evil in time, but it may be a long time. Everything is according to God's plan, but we don't know what the plan is. We only know it must be good, because God made it.

The Elder was dead, but his teachings lived among us. His grandson, far off in a great city, had another Daniel Perry, and did not forget the valley. The Elder's teachings and Owen's ambition and vision had given us Agnes Brown, out of a drunkard's family, to be sent to Burma with a Christian message.

Miss Hester had said:

We are now entering upon a World War for the preservation of democracy, the chosen way of life of all free and enlightened people everywhere. We are a peace-loving people. We have never fought and shall never fight except against tyranny. . . . To the task of winning this war we dedicate everything that we are and everything that we have.

Miss Hester died fighting that war, and so did Pete Luneau; but the rest of us lived through it, and it was won.

Mrs. Carter, growing old in the valley school, had taught most of those who lived now in the valley all they knew which could best be learned from books. She had set Owen on the path which led him to the place where he was now. Together she and Owen had made a lawyer of Armand Luneau and a teacher even of Dennis Daley. . . . A teacher, even of me.

"The past has been given to us," Miss Hester said. "The future must be built, as others have built our past."

The future we must build, as others have built our past . . .

I turned the key in the lock of the schoolhouse door, warm as if I hugged about myself one of the khaki scarves

Miss Hester had knit for the soldiers. The impression was so strong that I actually made a motion as if to take it off and hang it on a peg in the entry. But it was not a scarf which could be removed. It was an invisible, intangible mantle which enveloped me; my shield and buckler; my inheritance from those who had come before. It would never leave me, as long as I did my duty, whether great or small, as they had taught me, by precept and example, to see it.

I stood for a few minutes behind Mrs. Carter's desk, which was now my desk, and looked around the quiet room. I saw the green globe box on which Miss Hester had sat, listening to our opening exercises and awaiting her time to speak, and I wondered who would come to speak to my children. I saw the blackboards on which Dennis had drawn the Atlantic Ocean and the Eastern shore, the other Daleys their ships with sails and smokestacks, and Mrs. Carter her tiny flags for Jamestown, Plymouth, Boston, New Amsterdam, Philadelphia.

New Amsterdam, now the great city of New York, where Owen spent his days . . . .

All the blackboards were as clean as new sheets of paper, for Hannah and I had scrubbed them on Saturday, when we washed the erasers and dried them in the sun, laid out the new sticks of white and colored chalk, washed and oiled the floor, mopped and waxed the desk, polished the stove.

The room was waiting for the future. I went steadily from one window to another, opening them wide to let it in.

I took the canvas bag from a peg in the boys' entry, ran into the yard, fastened the flag to the rope and drew it to the top of the pole which had once been the tallest, straightest tree in the Dennett pasture. I had not noticed a wind stirring, but in the upper air it caught the red, white and blue folds and flung them out against the sky.

I pledge allegiance to . . . one nation . . . with liberty and justice for all.

Then I went back inside and stood by the open window behind my desk, watching the children come.

During the forty years Mrs. Carter had taught here, she had sometimes had as many as thirty pupils and sometimes as few as five. When there were thirty, they were all valley-born and their parents valley-born before them. Boards were laid across the seats, children took turns using the ten double-desks, the only aisles were along the walls, and all drank from a long-handled dipper which floated in the wooden water bucket. The year before I went to school was the year when there were only five pupils to the ten double-desks, and the School Committee would have sent them by wagon into the next district if any man in the valley would have undertaken to transport them, and if Mrs. Carter had not agreed to teach for half-salary, which was five dollars a week.

But when it was time for me to go, seven Luneaus were enrolled, and faster than Luneaus grew too old for school other Luneaus became old enough. My sister Edith finished, but the Brown twins came the next fall, one on each side of Agnes; and then the Daleys. We had two zinc water pails and Mrs. Carter gave each of us at Christmas a folding tin drinking cup; after that we were expected to use the dipper only for dipping, though sometimes the boys drank from it. The double-desks were removed that year, and the room filled with thirty single desks and with seats which could be folded. We had aisles, but they were narrow. Twenty or more of the seats were occupied.

The thirty seats were still there on the morning I became Teacher, and when I had rung the bell, every one was filled. Two of the oldest boys, Ernie and Dick Luneau, stood by the door.

The automobile had come to the valley, frightening the horses, making the roads unsafe for hens, dogs, cats, and children, rattling the loose planks in the bridges, hurling dust against the lace curtains in parlor windows, and mixing gasoline fumes into the fresh valley air. They brought the snowplows which took away our bobsledding, and relegated sleighs to empty barn lofts, the jingle of winter bells to memory. They took away mud and sand and ruts, and gave us a smooth, graveled surface highway with a stone foundation. They brought us new settlers, men who could live in the country and work in the town, and their wives who might keep their friends, their recreation, their church in the town where they came from, but whose children came to the valley school.

The future we must build . . .

"Ernie," I said, "please put my desk chair beside the globe box. Those are the only seats I can offer you and Dick for our opening exercises. After the exercises you may, if you will, go to my house and ask my father for the two black-painted chairs from the shed-chamber, and for my mother's sewing table. I am sorry you will have to carry them so far, but they are not heavy. They are all of pine, which you know is light weight. . . . Good morning, children. I shall now read you the first psalm. Tomorrow one of you will read for us. After that we'll sing *America.* Tomorrow one of you will choose the hymn.

'Next, I will lead the Lord's Prayer. Tomorrow one of you will lead us. Finally, we'll go out to give the pledge of allegiance to the flag. I put up the flag this morning so that you could all see it as you came to school. Tomorrow one of you will put it up."

School had begun. It was 1928, and we had a water cooler with a faucet. To the wall beside it was screwed a container holding two hundred paper cups.

Twelve new houses had been built in the valley; every old one was in good repair and inhabited. We had seventeen automobiles, all Model T Fords; and fifteen telephones on one line. There was electric power in the village, but we still brought our water from wells in the yard, lit our houses with kerosene, cooked and kept warm by wood or coal stoves, and had three battery radio sets among us. My father and Frank Carter were our only full-time farmers, and they sold little of what they produced except eggs, butter and potatoes. All the other men — even Bill Brown — were woodsmen, or construction workers, or railroaded, or were employed in the village shoeshop; but every one had a cow or two, a few hens, a pig, and a garden. We did not receive a large share of the nation's income. None of us could think in terms of billions or even millions. But we were content and comfortable. We had come a long way from the time when we cut down virgin pine to make clearings for our cabins, the river and footpaths through the woods were our thoroughfares, and we depended on fish and wild meat for our provision.

Mrs. Carter transferred to me the bankbook in which were recorded the amounts of money Owen had deposited, and the amounts she had withdrawn. The fact that Owen Perry contributed to the higher education of the valley

302

young people was no longer a secret; he had helped too many of us too much, and the valley was too small, too closely integrated, for long keeping of such secrecy. But the amount presently available was never disclosed. Only Mrs. Carter and I knew that he had so far deposited a total of three thousand dollars, and that twenty-five hundred had been spent for Armand, Agnes, Dennis, and me. Only I myself knew that, in the spring of 1929, he deposited five thousand dollars in one check, and that none of this was withdrawn, but waited in the security of the bank for Wayne to decide how he would spend his life, for Ruth to prepare for the Academy, for Noel to learn his multiplication tables.

No one else in the valley had been to college. No one else knew what a college education cost, understood about scholarships and deferred tuition plans, or knew what Armand, Agnes, Dennis or I had done to help ourselves, what my parents had sacrificed to help me. It was now generally taken for granted that Owen Perry had put us all through college and would do the same for any other valley boy or girl who wanted to go. He was the valley symbol of success.

"Know what Armand figured out from what he heard when he was at the Perrys' — not from anything they said, but the way folks there talked?" Joe Luneau asked Bert Anthony. "Figured Owen's getting paid right around fifteen thousand dollars a year. I figure that's 'most fifty dollars every day he works."

"They say Owen Perry gets fifty dollars a day down there in New York," Bert told Frank Carter.

"Don't doubt it. Owen's smart. Has to be doing well to keep his family and help other ones the way he does. Must cost a mint to live in a city place, best you can do."

When they told my father, he said, "Shows what can happen in a country like this. It's happened a good many times before, and will again to boys with Owen's git-up-and-git. Lucky for folks here he was one that had it."

Joe and Bert found themselves hoping that their children had it, too. Bert had never carried fifty dollars in his pocket in his life, nor felt the need of it; would not have changed places with Owen, he said, for a barn all stocked with cattle; but it would be a fine thing to have an Owen in the family. Joe now owned a grocery store and meat market in the village, and two of his younger brothers and Marie worked for him there. It was a thriving business, and sometimes Joe had to bring his accounts to me to get them straightened out. It had not seemed to him that a person should have to go to college to know how to keep accounts; he had not gone even to the Academy, and even Owen Perry had not gone far beyond; but if a college education would make Noel better able to take over, in his turn, the business Joe was building, Joe was now willing to have him go there as soon as he was old enough.

Noel Luneau was in my third grade in 1929, a little boy with his father's swarthy complexion, his mother's shy ways and haunting eyes, his Uncle Armand's speed of learning; but already I could see that his intelligence was verbal, not mathematical; he did not have Armand's sober concentration or tireless industry, and flitted from story to story, from picture to poem, from thought to fantasy as Kathleen had once from fence to tree and from tree to tree. Ruth Anthony was now in my eighth grade, and would be ready for the Academy the next fall, though she was only twelve years old; a bright, sturdy capable girl, she could go on to school earlier than I had because she could live at home and ride to and from town with

Wayne. Wayne was a Junior at the Academy that year, riding with the Luneaus, and next summer he would have a driver's license and the use of his father's car. Wayne was a handsome boy, serious, quiet, an excellent student and a star athlete in both basketball and baseball. Owen was greatly interested in all I could write him about Wayne. Wayne had, I felt, everything Owen considered most promising in a boy, what he hoped his own sons would have. I was happy to be able to write Owen in October that Wayne had at last talked to me about college, saying that he was taking all the science courses the Academy offered and believed he would try to prepare for medical school.

"If so, your first doctor is coming round the bend," I wrote. "Can you advise us as to what colleges offer the best pre-medical training?"

I was surprised that so many weeks passed without an answer to this letter. I thought perhaps it had miscarried. I wrote again during the Christmas vacation.

Even I did not in any way associate with Owen what we had read in Boston newspapers of fluctuations in the Stock Exchange which, beginning in September, had gone into a dizzy spiral by the end of October. Certainly no one else in the valley did. To us Wall Street was another Gay White Way, the Stock Exchange was a gambling casino, and those who bought and sold stocks were all immensely rich or incredibly wild and foolish. It had nothing to do with us, we thought, or with the lives of sensible people anywhere. Most of us owned a few Liberty Bonds and had a bankbook to which we sometimes added a small deposit but from which we rarely made a withdrawal. We did not know that Liberty Bonds had given many thousands of our fellow Americans their first interest in varied investments.

It meant nothing to us that on September 3, over eight million shares of stock were traded; for we had never traded anything but cows and horses and sometimes eggs and butter for tea and sugar and molasses. When we read headlines at the end of November about men who saw their life savings disappear overnight and committed suicide in the morning, we were sorry for their families and shocked to think that money could hold so important a place in anyone's life. We looked about us at the everlasting hills, at the river flowing its placid course, at wood lots which, once cut off, were dark again in twenty years with good pine growth, at the cows which fed our fields and the fields which fed our cows and would feed us as long as we saved back seed for the spring sowing; and we felt secure — particularly blessed — and, I suppose, proud that we did not expect more of life than we could earn from day to day, owing no man and owed by none.

Life in the valley was a small, simple wheel which, for the most part, we still turned as we always had with our own hands and feet. We had no conception of the vast, intricate system of cogs and wheels which interlocked to turn one another in modern American economy, and spanned the ocean to connect with similar systems all over the world; and so we did not realize how widespread the results would be of a semiparalysis of the Stock Exchange.

Owen wrote me in late January:

Did you think I was lost in another fog? It isn't that I wasn't glad to hear how well Wayne is doing. He must be quite a lad. Della and Bert ought to be mighty proud of him, and you and I are going to be too. Any good Liberal Arts college would do for pre-med, wouldn't it? But I'd like to see Wayne at Harvard, if he could get admitted, and from what you say I'll bet he could. We'll see. If he has to go to a less expensive school for his un-

306

dergraduate work, maybe he can go on to Harvard Medical. You're all set to start him somewhere as soon as he is ready, aren't you? And that's lucky. I must have had a premonition to make that last deposit right when the experts were saying that American business would remain on a "permanently high plateau." That plateau, as no doubt you know, has gone down like the lost continent of Atlantis. The sinking not only left my security box stuffed with a lot of worthless paper; it practically wiped out the company I was with. Its nose is now just above water, and I don't know how long it will stay that high, for manufacturers have no money to put into advertising products which nobody has the money to buy. As soon as I saw the handwriting on the wall (I must have been blind not to see it sooner), we moved into a little farmhouse in Connecticut. It makes me think of valley houses, only we do have a pump in the sink and a coal furnace in the cellar. It's quite an adjustment for Corinne, because she never lived without gas or electricity before, or tended a furnace, and three small boys dirt up a lot of clothes, but she is a good scout. The boys love it out here, of course, and I shall when I get some time to enjoy it. Right now I'm doing what I can for the company I've been with and trying to get into another one, but the prospects are poor in all of them. They're worse than running scared. They're *sitting* scared — petrified. What I'd like is to start a little advertising business of my own, but it would certainly have to be on a shoestring, and even my shoestrings are broke! Don't worry. The sun will come out again. It always has. In the meantime, you keep on getting valley kids ready for the Academy, and pushing them through into college. We're ready for Wayne now, and Ruth too. The next one in due course. In the meantime, Althea McIntire, are you keeping a sharp lookout for that right man?

Appalled, I wrote Owen urging him to take the money he had deposited, since Wayne would not need any of it for another year and a half, and use it to start his business.

I assumed that five thousand dollars would start anyone in any business anywhere. I added that the house, the school, and the valley kept me too busy to think of men, right or wrong. Besides, I did not know a man who was not married.

Owen replied promptly that the money on my account at the bank was for education, that education was the only safe investment, that if he had not put it there it would have gone down the drain with other investments. He said:

> I went skating today for the first time in ten years. On the frog pond back of the house. I had Danny on his sled, and thought of how I used to spin you that way on the marshes. Only I didn't have skates then, did I? Now I do! And much besides! The years have been far from wasted.

He added:

> A girl should never be too busy to look. And the right man for you is not married. Come, come, Althea. I want to dance at the wedding.

By spring of 1930, the village shoeshop was closed, except for a day or two now and then when a small order trickled in; the price of lumber was so low that it seemed wiser to let the trees grow until times were better, and Joe and Marie had no more to do at the store than they could do by themselves. All the other Luneau men and Bert Anthony plowed by the acre instead of by the square yard, and the rich smell of newly turned ground and commercial fertilizer filled the valley. Women walked beside their men in the fields, covering the seed their children dropped. There was someone to speak to across every fence. Even the newcomers to the valley had asked farmers to plow for them and been taught to plant and cover, and then to hoe. The smell of the potato blossoms was so sweet I thought of what it must be in Aroostook County, which I had never seen.

That summer we made our own social life. We churned ice cream for children's parties and took them on a Fourth of July picnic on the mountain, taught them to swim in the river, used the gasoline to take them all for one glorious day at the beach. The women met to sew together in the afternoons, making men's shirts, our own dresses, clothing for the children. There was a drought, drying up the wells, and we did our laundry at the river, speaking of women on the other side of the world who always washed that way. Boys wore yokes to bring drinking water from a spring in the woods on the hillside. We had community suppers on the church lawn, and other evenings we sat on porches to sing, or met in houses where there were radios or victrolas, and I taught the older boys and girls to dance while the other women visited in the kitchens, babies slept in clothes-baskets, men stood talking and smoking in barn doorways, and children of eight and nine and ten played hide-and-go-seek in the dark. We filled every glass jar and crock we owned, that year, with the produce from our gardens, so that by fall the shelves as well as the bins in our cellars were filled. As soon as the harvest was in, the pigs were butchered, the fresh meat eaten, the hams smoked, the pork put down in brine, the sausage and hogshead cheese made, the fat tried out and put away in old lard pails. Then the men went hunting for deer and rabbit and even squirrels, for they could get a little money for antlers and fur, and wild meat was tasty. Every flock had enough roosters so that one could be spared at Thanksgiving and again at Christmas for every family in the valley. We were fortunate, we knew. We felt fortunate. We only wished we could bring back into the security of the valley those who had left it for the more complicated world outside.

Armand came home for a few days that fall, with his bride, before leaving to take a position with a law firm in the Midwest. He had been studying all summer for his bar examinations, while his wife worked as a waitress in a restaurant. They looked pale and thin to us. We wished we could put them to bed where the southwest wind laden with the smell of the first hard frost, of fallen leaves, of wet pine and cornhusks, blew out the curtains; fatten them with rich milk, beaten eggs, New England boiled dinners, and Baldwin apple pie; then send them out to bring home nuts, sawdust to bank the house, and frostfish caught through the ice. But this was not their work, and they had to go where it was, in their little old car which did not look as if it would hold together to cross the Hudson River and the Alleghenies.

I had told no one except my father what Owen had written of his situation but everyone realized, now, that any man in business was under heavy pressure in these times. The Carters said they wished he would bring his family to the valley for a real vacation.

"It's no bed of roses out there," my father answered. "Even for a boy as smart as Owen. He's got a lot of courage, though. He'll make out. I guess they need ones like him, now, to hold things together. I guess he won't come this way until he's got it straightened out."

The only one nobody worried about was Agnes, not only because Agnes was surely in the palm of God's hand, but because she was the one away whom we could do the most to help. She wrote to her mother every Wednesday, telling of the journeys she made by foot and by two-wheeled cart, of the people she saw along the way, of those who came to her meetings, and of those associated with her in the work. Every Sunday the letter was read aloud in church, and Mattie listened with hardly more pride and no less eagerness than the rest of us, for Agnes wrote with the pen of an angel and had also a loving spirit, a complete lack of self-concern. She was well, she was happy, she was safe, but this came through only between the lines. In the next barrel, could we send her long black knitted wool socks in children's sizes, old sheets for bandages, lard in sealed tins for inflamed chests, hard candies? And would the children in the valley school paste little pictures on pasteboard to make merit cards for Burmese children?

"Sometimes I think Ruth may want to be a missionary like Agnes," Della said. "I don't see how I could stand it for her to be so far away, but if Mattie can I suppose I could. I don't know what better a young person can do than give his life to the service of the Lord. That's as near to heaven as anyone can get in this world."

Hannah worried about Dennis, but no one else did.

"Can't see for the life of me how he knows enough," Hannah grumbled. "Even if he has been to two colleges. Ain't old enough for one thing. Don't see what they was thinking of to hire him. Must have been hard up, is all I can say."

Privately, I agreed with Hannah that the Academy trustees must indeed have been short of applicants to engage Dennis Daley as headmaster. He did not get his A.B. degree until the June before he became headmaster in September, and his teaching experience had been in grade schools. He was only twenty-six years old, and Hannah, with whom he had spent a week end in the summer, said he did not look that much. Though I had not seen him for nearly ten years, when I had imagined all the changes which they could conceivably have made in him it was still impossible for me to visualize him in the office presided over in the early days by graduates of Boston Latin School and Harvard, and in my time by tall, elegant, gentle Mr. Farraday, who wore the only Vandyke beard I had ever seen except in pictures.

But I did not consciously devote time to trying to visualize Dennis, and I certainly did not worry about him or about the Academy. I took it for granted that if he did not do well there, he would not be reappointed.

Few in the valley gave any thought to him, for none of us had known him well, many of us had not known him at all, and since he went away to school he had rarely come back — only for his father's and Lottie's funerals, and one week end with Hannah. We assumed that the valley meant little or nothing to him, and so he meant little or nothing to us.

Mrs. Carter said stubbornly, "Whatever Dennis set out to do well, he always did," and my father added, "Best help here of any age I ever had. Always liked him. Can't see why he never comes around, though. Seems as if he would, now he's so near, if he thought anything of us."

I asked Wayne how he liked Mr. Daley. Wayne shrugged and said he hardly ever saw him except at morning assemblies.

"Always seems to be busy in the office. Don't know what there is to do in there all the time. Fellows that get sent in there for discipline don't like him, though, I can tell you. Easier to face the Old Boy himself, they say."

I could believe that.

The placid current of self-containment in the valley was no more than ruffled by the closure, that fall, of a Portland bank of which our village bank was the smallest branch. All of us except the Browns had a little money; none of us, as individuals or families, had much; nobody except me knew the amount on the book in Owen's and my names. As we were not accustomed to withdrawing, the fact that we were now unable to do so was no hardship. All of us assumed that such a great bank as a Portland bank could be only temporarily embarrassed, and that by and by we would be notified of its reopening or at least that our money was now available.

I was much surprised and my father was delighted when he answered a knock at our door one evening during the Christmas holidays and saw Dennis Daley standing there.

"Well, Dennis! Come in, come in. By zounds, no need for you to knock at this door. Take off your coat and set down. How've you been, boy?"

I looked at them across my mending. The palms of the thick red mittens my mother had knit for my father had long ago worn out, and small patches been replaced by larger ones until the whole inside, from wrist to finger tip, was of navy blue flannel. He would wear the mittens as long as the backs lasted.

Dennis was taller and thinner than when he was a student at the Academy. His black hair was as thick and heavy as ever, but neatly trimmed now, and lay in crisp waves on either side of a straight side part. His gray tweed suit, well cut, made him look heavier set than he was, and instead of a vest he wore a cable-knit gray pullover. I supposed it was sleeveless, but I could not be sure. He was as serious as ever, perhaps more so, but no sulkiness remained in his face or resentment in his eyes. He gave the impression of great intensity, like a fire burning where it cannot be seen or heard but giving off heat waves. He sat with one knee lifted, his hands clasped around it, talking with my father about the weather, the hunting season, the luck of the trappers. I noticed that his hands were big, bony, and very clean, an almost pearly cleanliness that valley men's hands never had even in church. I noticed too, with mild surprise, that his voice was deep and rather musical.

He and my father talked as easily as if they were together every day.

But when at last he turned toward me he cleared his throat before he spoke.

"Would you ride downtown with me, Althea?"

I was astonished, but I asked quietly, "Why, Dennis?"

He said it was a nice night out, and he had to go to the Academy office for some records. He had happened to think as he was driving by that I might like to ride along.

I thanked him, but said my father and I had planned to make some cornballs. The children liked them when they stopped in during winter holidays.

"Well, now," my father said, "I can get the corn popped while you're gone. Won't take long after you get back to make the syrup."

I said I liked the smell and sound of corn popping, and, no, I thought I would stay in that night.

Dennis cleared his throat again and said, "This is really business, Althea. Quite important. I want to show you some records which I'm not supposed to take out of the office. If you won't come tonight, will you come tomorrow? It is a matter you should be interested in, and I think you will be."

I said, "In that case, I will come now. I have a washing to do tomorrow if it's fair."

I went into the front entry for my coat and overshoes, and walked ahead of him through the yard to the car, opening the door before he could reach it.

We were halfway to the village before either of us spoke.

Then I said, "Are you going to tell me what these records are I have to see?"

"If you ask me," he replied coldly. "I don't want to intrude on your thoughts."

"Of course I want to know why I'm doing this," I snapped.

"Obviously not for pleasure."

"Obviously," I agreed. "When was it ever a pleasure to either of us to be together?"

"It never was for you, I know. I wonder why."

"As far back as I remember you, Dennis, you were always forcing me — or trying to force me — or wanting to force me to do something I didn't want to. I hadn't seen you for ten years until tonight, and I had almost forgotten it. Now here it is again. I didn't want to ride down here with you tonight, and you know it."

"That's true. But it's not important. Everybody has an unpleasant duty once in a while. It won't take long. I'll have you home within an hour."

"Well, what records do I have to see? Is somebody from the valley failing a course? I can't help that. I've done what I could for all of them. Now it's your turn."

"Nobody from the valley is failing a course. I want you to see Wayne's record."

"It's good, isn't it?"

"Extremely good."

315

"Then why do I have to come all the way down here to see it?"

Suddenly he laughed. There was no bitterness in the sound. It was like a boy's laugh.

"I can't say why you felt you had to. I felt you had to because I wanted you to."

"Even though I didn't want to."

"Even though you didn't want to."

We were riding up Academy hill, and the wheels began to spin. I hoped they would keep on spinning, and then slip back all the way to the foot. I hoped he could not get me to his office under the bell tower. I certainly had no intention of walking. I was angrier than I had ever been in my life with anyone except Dennis Daley.

But the wheels caught, we reached the top of the hill, Dennis sprang out, jangling keys, unlocked the school door, turned on the lights, and stood waiting for me. I passed without looking at him, and hurried toward the office. Despite my anger, I was conscious of the hollows in the stairs, worn by many teenage feet including my own, and of the familiar smell of mingled plaster, varnish, oil, and chalk dust which is a part of every school yet not alike in any two. It was a welcome home, and I wondered at myself for having stayed away so long.

I stood in the office doorway looking down the shadowy center hall between the rows of classrooms, only half-hearing the filing case unlocked and a drawer pulled open. But when there had been no sound for a minute or two, I turned. Dennis stood by Mr. Farraday's desk, burning eyes fixed on a card he held in one hand. He had loosened the knot of his tie and pulled at it until it lay on his cable-knit sweater, and unfastened a button so that his collar fell open. He was running his free hand through his hair,

which now stood up in shaggy peaks. . . . Dennis Daley
. . . I stood staring at him and slowly realized where we
were, who we were, what time it was. . . . Mr. Farraday
was dead. Mrs. Peabody was no longer down the hall in
Room Four. Mrs. Carter came to the valley school only
once a year, as Miss Hester had. Owen was in Connecticut,
with a family of his own. Armand was in Kansas. Agnes
was in Burma. There was nobody here but Dennis Daley
and me. Nobody at all.

I went over to him and asked, low, "Is this what you
wanted me to see?"

He started, as if he had forgotten I was there, dropped
the card on the desk, and threw himself into his chair,
then spun in it to look up at me from under his heavy eyebrows, his shaggy peaks of hair. He was looking at me, but
without recognition. He was like a man alone, speaking to
himself.

"It doesn't matter," he said. "It's Wayne's record, but it
tells a small part of the story. It's all A's, because A's are
as high as we go. I watch these students, discuss every one
of them separately with their teachers. I've read Wayne's
examination papers. I've listened to him outside the laboratory door and classroom doors. I eavesdrop on him in the
halls. He not only will be valedictorian of his class, he
has the best mind that has worked in this school for many
years, among students or faculty. He would be among the
top students in any preparatory school in the country.
That alone would make him a problem in a school like
this. But he has other problems, and they make problems
for us, too. He has no real intellectual contact with anyone
he knows, because our minds aren't equal to meeting his.
So he reads. He reads good books and bad books, old
books and new books, wise books and foolish books, and

317

everything he reads influences him in a different direction. He is like some men with women, led by the nose by every pretty one they see. Or like a dog barking up trees, sometimes wrong trees and sometimes right trees, but every night a different tree. Something has to be done. *Someone* has to take that boy in hand quick, before he's lost to himself and everyone else."

Surely we were not talking about the Wayne I thought I knew, Della's sturdy, handsome son I had taken care of when he was a little boy, whose maps and themes I had put on the bulletin board when I substituted for Mrs. Carter, whom I had taught to dance last summer. Not Wayne Anthony. Some other boy.

"Who?" I whispered. "Who can take him in hand, Dennis?"

"Nobody we know. Somebody somewhere." He pulled me into a straight chair by his desk. He saw me now, but not as Althea McIntire. "Wayne Anthony has to go to college. Not only that, he has to go to a college where there are men he can respect and trust, and who will understand him. . . . This is what I brought you down here to tell you. I couldn't ask in front of your father. I don't know what you've told him, what you are supposed to tell anyone. But you have to tell me the truth. How much education money has been deposited which has not been used?"

"Five thousand, five hundred dollars."

". . . As much as that! . . . Is it — was it — in the bank here?"

"Yes."

"All of it?"

"Yes."

He had been sitting forward in his chair, his hand grip-

ping the corner of the desk so hard that the cords and
knuckles gleamed white in the light from a swinging electric bulb. Now he slid back, and his chin sank into his
open collar. His hair put his face in shadow.

"So — it's all gone. . . . That's what I was afraid of.
Does Mr. Perry know the bank failed?"

"No. And it hasn't really failed, has it? It's supposed to
be reorganizing. Surely by next fall I'll be able to get at
least what Wayne will need to start with?"

Dennis lifted his head and smiled at me. The almost
tender smile on his mouth and the anxiety, the incredu-
lity, the faint scorn in his eyes made a strange, disjointed
combination.

"That's the valley talking, isn't it?" he said gently. "You
never got it out of you, did you? You never really went
away from it. And I guess everybody's glad of that. . . .
But listen to me, Althea. That Portland bank and all its
branches are not only closed. They're through. They're
dead ducks. If they're ever sold for their feathers, the de-
positors will get their share of the price of feathers for
which the demand is slight and the price accordingly low.
In the course of the next several years, you may get scattered checks amounting to a tenth of what was on your
bankbook, and you may not. You won't know when or if
you're going to get one. You may never get one. . . . It's
fine to be patient and optimistic; but Wayne must go to
college and he can't go on patience and optimism. . . . I
know it won't be easy, but there's no way out of it. You
will have to let Mr. Perry know what has happened to his
money."

"I can't do that."

"You have to."

"I can't."

"He would want you to."

"Maybe. But I can't."

"Will you give me his address?"

"No."

"Why not?"

All the words were staccato, like the ticking of a big clock in an empty room.

"I can't tell you that."

The clock stopped. In the long silence Dennis bent forward again, staring at the clean, bare surface of his desk.

"All right," he said slowly. "You don't need to. I see how it is. He's caught in the toils of this thing himself, and couldn't help now, however much he wanted to."

"He thinks," I whispered, "that at least we are provided for, and off his mind."

Dennis nodded. The light on his face was reflected from the bulb above the shining desktop, but the coals in his eyes were fired by inner intensity.

At last he turned toward me again, his big hand clutching the corner of the desk again.

"Well, so we are, Althea," he said. "Mr. Perry has seen four of us through. Agnes is doing her giving on the other side of the world. Armand may be able to help later, but a lawyer starting out in times like these has a long wait between cases, and lives from deed to deed. I made some discreet inquiries of Joe and Kathleen. Joe had to lend Armand some money to get to Kansas. Armand's wife is expecting a baby this spring. They'll likely have a big family, and Armand is still carrying debt for money he borrowed to finish his law course. I still owe a few hundred dollars, too; do you?"

I shook my head.

"Then we should consider that we owe Wayne as much

as we had from Mr. Perry, shouldn't we? . . . I wish I didn't have to put it this way, Althea. I wouldn't if up to now I had been able to save anything at all. I figure that, with what I have to pay on my other debts, I can save about two hundred dollars by June. I'm going to move in with Hannah because it will be cheaper, but of course I'll have to pay her something for board, beside what I can do to help her on the farm. I'll try to get a summer job but they're hard to find now. . . . I suppose you have saved — and put your savings in the bank."

I nodded.

"Do you want to help? With what you can save from now on, I mean? . . . I know what I'm asking, Althea. A district schoolteacher's pay is mighty small. But we're all there is. I've talked with Bert, and he can't help. He has lost his savings; Della isn't well and may have to go to the hospital; they have three other children coming along. It's as much as they can do not to ask anything for themselves from Wayne. At least, you and I are financially responsible only for ourselves. If Wayne were a different boy, I'd say he could wait a year or two. But it isn't safe for Wayne to wait."

There was nobody here but Dennis and me. Dennis Daley and me.

I said, "Of course I want to help. I don't need much of what I earn. But how would Bert and Della feel about Wayne's accepting it from us? It was different with Owen. Everyone thought of Owen as rich. But they know we aren't."

"Stupid," Dennis said gently. "How will they know it is from us? We'll put it in the Barclay bank in your name, and they'll think Mr. Perry put it there after our bank failed. That's better all around."

I nodded. He stood up. It was like the links of a chain tightening and rising upright.

"That's it, then. I promised to have you home within an hour, didn't I?"

We went down the hollowed stairs, the lights going out behind us. It was very dark outside. We groped our way to the car. He had difficulty cranking it, for the engine was ice-cold. I slid over and finally caught the coughing motor with the spark lever.

"Thanks," Dennis said, getting in and pulling his long legs in after him. "You're a good scout, Althea."

I remembered that Owen had said Corinne was a good scout.

"That," I said, "is the first kind thing you ever said to me."

"Are you sure?"

"Sure enough to bet on it."

"You've got no money to use on bets," he reminded me. "Or any other nonsense. And may not have for a long time to come. Something's been started in the valley that has to go on. Nobody can see the end of it."

"Owen will help when he can."

"I hope he can. But whether he can or not, it has to go on."

"That's what he would say. Because he loves the valley. Why do you say it? Because your conscience tells you you should make returns for whatever Owen did for you?"

"Partly that. Partly because I am a teacher —"

"Not in the valley."

"The valley has a teacher. It doesn't need me. Or hasn't until now. . . . Do you have an idea I don't love the valley?"

"You've hardly been in it since you left the valley school."

"Has Mr. Perry?"

"No. But he never forgot it."

It was a minute or two before he answered. His eyes were on the road ahead.

"Well, I suppose you won't believe this, but I never forgot it either. It did at least as much for me as it ever did for Mr. Perry. You know that. Do you think I don't? . . . It took him a while to get ready to do something for the valley, didn't it? Well, it took me a while too."

Bitterness was back in his voice. I had put it there.

The car was turning into the lane when I said, "Dennis, I have hurt you. I suppose I meant to. I must have meant to. But not consciously. I admire you very much for what you have done for Wayne, and want to do. I am grateful to you for showing me how I can help. I complained on the way down that you were always trying to make me do something I didn't want to do. You really weren't, to-night. I have some uncontrollable urge to oppose you, to criticize you. I've always had it, whenever I saw you. I wish I didn't. I don't understand why I do."

We were in my dooryard, under the tree from which Owen had first looked down at me. Dennis shut off the engine and turned in his seat. It was so dark that I could not see his face.

"It may surprise you to know that I've done some thinking along that line. Quite a bit, in fact. And I think I know the answer. But I don't think you would like to hear it. Or would believe it if you did. So I'm not going to tell you. At least, not now."

I did not urge him.

"Whatever the reason is," I said, "I don't think it's fair to you, Dennis. You shouldn't have to put up with it. If we are going to work together for Wayne, we must do it separately, and talk, if we have to talk, by telephone or by mail. I don't like what I do to you when I see you. I don't like the kind of person I am when I'm with you. Please don't come here again — anyhow when I'm here — if you can possibly avoid it. Hannah is my dearest friend. She is your sister, and you are coming back to live with her for a while. That will make Hannah very happy. But I'm not going to her house as long as you live there. Please explain to her, in any way you can, that I hope she will come to see me."

"Doesn't sound very neighborly."

"It isn't. But you and I can't be neighbors. Something between us prevents it."

"We might overcome it."

"I don't think so. It's too much of a risk to take, for the faint possibility of what isn't necessary. . . . It's agreed that we'll do what we can for Wayne. Otherwise, let's go our separate ways."

"You insist?"

"I insist."

He startled me by laughing suddenly, in that boyish tone, and dropping his hand on my shoulder. I drew back as if struck, opened the car door, and stepped out in the snow.

I was halfway to the door when he spoke my name through the open window, and I stopped against my will.

"Althea . . . I'd better warn you. You can try. But it won't work."

I made some small, exasperated sound, and ran up the steps, across the porch, into the kitchen which smelled of

324

hot popcorn. My father sat at the end of the stove, drawing the last white popperful so fast across the ruddy covers that it danced all over, outside and in. I kicked off my overshoes, dropped my coat on the couch, and went into the pantry to pour molasses for the syrup.

"Why didn't Dennis come in?" my father asked. "Don't he like popcorn?"

"I don't know. He and Hannah can pop some, if he does. She raised more than any of us."

He snapped back the hot catch, and turned the corn into a milk pan. As I stirred the molasses at the stove, he sat smoking his pipe, watching me. He had taken off his boots, and I could see his toes, inside his heavy wool socks, stretching to enjoy the heat as he rested his feet on the lacy iron shelf of the stove. I had never known anyone so capable of enjoying physical comfort as my father, no doubt because he never took it for granted, and because comfort — not discomfort — was what he noticed. You could tell that he liked to wash his face, to blow his nose, to scratch the back of his neck, to ease off his suspenders. He never drank without saying, as soon as he finished, while his mouth was still cool and wet, before he rubbed his sleeve across it, "Good water!"

I poured the syrup over the two heaping pans of popcorn, dividing it evenly, and began making handfuls into balls quickly, vehemently, as if they were weapons with which I must defend myself at once and with deadly intent. I knew my motions were like my mother's. I wondered if my father thought of it.

"Pretty secret, I s'pose," he said. "Them records Dennis wanted to show you."

"No. Well, the records may be secret, but the facts aren't. They were Wayne Anthony's records. He's doing very well at the Academy. He'll be the valedictorian this year."

"Smart boy. Everybody knows that."

"Dennis wanted to talk about — what college Wayne should go to, to learn to be a doctor."

"That all?"

"Isn't it enough, even for Wayne? To be a doctor?"

"Didn't mean that. Meant, was that all Dennis wanted? Never mind. None of my business. Time I was going to bed."

He stood up, and knocked out his pipe. I looked at him curiously.

"What made you think that might not be all Dennis wanted?"

"Oh, I dunno."

He padded as far as the sitting-room door, paused with a hand high on each side of the doorframe, and glanced over his shoulder. His eyes twinkled at me exactly as I had seen them twinkle at my mother when she was in what he called "a high dudgeon," or sometimes being "on her high horse."

"None of my business," he said again. "Only, seems as though it would take more than school records and talk about Bert's boy to set the sparks flying way they have around this kitchen ever sence you came in."

He disappeared, catlike, and the bedroom closed behind him. I heard the springs squeak as he sat on the side of his bed. I knew he was easing off his suspenders, sighing with the pleasure of it, pulling off his socks and rubbing his toes with his callused fingers. I knew he would hang his trousers on the bedpost and sleep in his flannel shirt.

I thought, choked with love and sorrow, "My father is

326

the dearest, bravest, kindest, wisest, most wonderful man in the world even if he didn't go to school four years all put together. I wish he weren't — alone in there."

I kept on thinking this, while I wrapped the cornballs in oil paper, washed the pans and spoons, brought the plants from the window sill to the table, shut the drafts in the stove, blew out the light, and climbed the stairs in the dark to my room. I clung to the thought, unwilling to let it go. After I was in bed, I cried a little, and supposed I was crying for my mother, because I longed to see her and hear her voice and because I could not take her place in my father's life.

All September Della Anthony was in the hospital and could not be at the station to see Wayne off for Root College in Boston, but she was proud to be able to tell her nurses and the other patients that her son was preparing to be a doctor. Dennis's investigations had shown that high-ranking graduates of Root, if personable, were certain of admission to Harvard Medical School. I had a letter from Owen, enclosing a check for a hundred dollars, saying he did not know when he could send more as he had started his agency, but business was slow and highly uncertain — and advising me to transfer part of our account to a New Hampshire bank.

Good New England bankers are conservative [Owen wrote], so very likely they will pull through, but all banks now are having hard sledding. It's safer not to have — what shall I say? — all our cordwood on one sled. What's new in the valley?

I wrote him that I had taken his advice and opened an account at Barclay. I told him Wayne had entered Root, after earning enough in the bowling alleys to buy his books. His admission fee had been paid. After his November bill had been covered, he might be able to take a part-time job to help himself, but Dennis felt it was important that Wayne use the full first semester to adjust himself to college as, for a pre-medical student, every course counted and laboratory courses took a great deal of time. I said Della had come home, but would need a long period of convalescence; Hannah Daley was staying with her while the children were in school, whenever Bert could not be in or close to the house. I told him that Wayne's sister Ruth, while not the student Wayne was, had been on the Honor Roll since entering the Academy, and that Joe's Noel was continuing to astonish me, particularly by his poems, which were uncanny for a boy his age, acutely sensitive, beautifully phrased, written apparently with the speed of light and no effort at all.

I did not tell Owen that I was also astonished by Noel's Uncle Dennis, who had become so active in the valley and in the town that it was impossible to avoid him, and I was the only one who tried to. He never came to our house but often talked with my father in the field, as he did with all the other men he saw as he drove up and down the road. Though the Academy was technically a private school, he showed daily interest in the public schools and analyzed their needs so effectively in town meetings that he was elected to the School Committee. New reference books, especially encyclopedias, found their way even into the district schools, along with sky charts, modern world maps, work books and germicides. He joined the valley church and organized young married people into a Couples Club which met once a month with the Couples Club of a village church where they played Ping Pong and bridge. He organized a valley troop of Boy Scouts, and when he asked me to take a troop of valley girls I could not refuse, nor could I refuse to let my girls meet sometimes with the boys' troop for a social evening, though it meant that Dennis and I were jointly responsible for the program and I had to spend the evening in the same room with him. From a headmaster whom only Wayne and Ruth and a few others from the valley ever saw, he had become the hero of every child in the valley and the familiar friend of every older person except me. He still drew extraordinary pictures with chalk, a crayon, or the stub of a pencil, even with a stick in wet sand; and he knew more games, more tricks, more stories than anyone else, and passed them on as if there were no end to the source. He went fishing, hunting, skating, tobogganing, swimming — and everywhere he was followed by men, boys, girls. People said it was fun to be where he was, yet one always felt that his lightheartedness was on the surface; below and behind that, he was deeply concerned about serious and important matters. Sometimes he talked about these serious and important matters; and, when he did, people listened closely, their eyes fixed on his thin face.

"Guess there ought to be something we could do about that," they said to one another. "Don't know what. Maybe Dennis can figure out a way."

"Keep trying to think," my father said, "who 'tis Dennis makes me think of. . . . Only one that comes to me is Abe Lincoln."

During the summer of 1931, Wayne did not work away, for he could find no work. He helped his father on the farm, and spent nearly every evening for weeks with Dennis.

One night in July, as I sat in the swing chair under the maples, after my father had gone to bed, I heard our number ring and went into the house to answer it. Dennis's voice came over the line.

"Althea?"

"Yes."

"I know it's late. Hope I didn't wake you."

"No."

"This may be a shock, but I have to see you. Right away. Alone."

"Children are taught to say 'May I.'"

"How true. But adults learn it is no use to ask for permission which won't be granted. Whether I may or not, I'm coming. I'll be there in five minutes. Time to get dressed, if you aren't."

"I am."

I went back to the swing chair and sat moving it just enough to stir the air and keep off the mosquitoes. It was very dark and still. I heard my mother's clock in the kitchen strike ten. A few minutes later I heard Dennis's footsteps as he turned into the lane, and thought how rarely now we heard footsteps on the road. I stopped swinging and watched him pass me like a shadow.

I let him go all the way to the porch before I said, "I'm here."

He turned.

"Are you really? Some people would have sung out before and saved me a few steps."

"I thought you enjoyed exercise."

"Not right now, thanks."

Some swing chairs were double, but ours had two single

330

seats facing each other. He dropped into the empty one opposite me, sighed, and rested his head against the back.

"First time I've stopped today except to eat. Been doing Hannah's hand-mowing. First time I've seen the stars tonight, though I've been out since dusk fell. Funny how they show even through these branches, isn't it?"

"Been driving?"

"No. Been walking. With Wayne. In the woods. Had to keep on walking until I tired him out, so he would go home to bed. Takes a lot of walking to tire Wayne out, at his age, and in his state of mind."

"Why didn't you drive over here?"

I knew as well as if I could see them that he was raising his eyebrows.

"Well, Hannah might have heard me leave and come back, even though she had gone to bed upstairs when I called you. Other people might have heard me go by, and noticed where I went. I didn't think you'd like that."

"It was nice of you to take that into consideration," I said grudgingly.

"I think so myself. I do it all the time, and always think it's darned nice of me, considering. Sorry I had to take the chance of using the telephone. But all the lights were out up and down the road. I guess we're the only ones awake in the valley."

"Why are we awake?"

"Because of Wayne. We're at a crisis point with that boy, Althea."

"What's the matter?"

"I can only tell you what I've been able to find out. You aren't going to like it. I don't like it. But it doesn't matter much now what we like. . . . You know how well he did at Root last year. Close to the top of his class, and would have been top man if he could have applied himself better. But he was worried. Now he thinks he has solved his problem. He says he is not going back to college."

"Why?"

"Because — it's funny in a way — he refuses to use any more of Mr. Perry's money. Not only that. He has made up his mind to take the first paying job he can get, and return to Mr. Perry the money he used during his freshman year."

"What on earth — what earthly objection —"

"I warned you you wouldn't like this. And it's not easy to explain, but I'll try."

He bent forward, his elbows on his knees, his eyes lower than mine but looking up at me intently, and in a gentle, deep, earnest voice began a story which at first made no sense to me whatever. Under the tree in which I had first seen Owen Perry, his laughing mouth, his faded overalls, his bare legs, the man whom Owen Perry had helped to become an academy headmaster sat in the dark telling the woman Owen Perry had helped to learn how to teach valley children that Bert and Della's son Wayne, born and brought up in the valley, would not let Owen Perry help him to become the first doctor from the valley. And the reason was that Owen was a rich businessman. Wayne, at eighteen, had no respect for Big Business. Wayne had seen jobless men selling apples on freezing city street corners. He had walked along riverbanks where hundreds of families lived in shacks of old crates and tar paper which were washed away in flood season, sometimes taking the occupants too, if they were not quick enough to reach high ground. Wayne had spent in the study of economics many hours which we might have preferred he had given to biology and other sciences. He had read that some six hundred thousand families in the United States lumped together had a larger income than the total earned by sixteen million other families.

"Wayne thinks this is terribly unfair," Dennis said. "He thinks it is wicked. He broods on it, and on the faces of children he has seen in the settlements they call Hoovervilles, in the windows of crumbling tenements beside railroad tracks, and on what he has read of the way miners and other laborers live. He thinks about the sanitary conditions, the diseases poor people get and spread and die of. He has walked, sometimes all day long, through the fine residential sections in and around Boston and compared them with what he has seen of slum districts. He is horrified and ashamed by this comparison, and feels driven to do something about it. All he can think of to do is to refuse to use Mr. Perry's money!"

"But what has all this to do with Owen?"

"Nothing, of course. I've tried to show Wayne this summer that everything we know of Mr. Perry shows him to be the kind of businessman all businessmen should be. Whatever money has come to Mr. Perry — and nothing has come which he didn't earn himself — he has clearly been trying to use in ways that will benefit society. And of course he is far from the only businessman who thinks and plans and feels that way. But Wayne has seen and read so much that hurt him that he's totally blind to the possibility that some men who have money use it well, and he is convinced that nobody has the right to control large funds. To be blunt, he thinks every rich man must be a scoundrel. No matter what a man might have been before he became rich, if he is rich Wayne has him written off as a scoundrel. He wishes he never had to use money. He vows he never will use money for anything but necessities. And he is determined not to be indebted to Mr. Perry in any way."

"How ridiculous!" I said. "When he will always be indebted, whether he knows it or not, to Owen for what he did for you and for me — and, so far at least, not for a cent of what I suppose he considers Owen's dirty money. . . . I think it might be just as well if Wayne doesn't go back to college."

"I was afraid you would feel that way, Althea. But listen."

He went on talking, as if he were drawing a picture, about a boy who had grown up in the valley, in what many called a substandard way of life. It had not seemed substandard to his parents, for they had never known either a higher or a much lower standard. It was not substandard to us, for we knew how rich it was and how much richer it could be, with or without money. Perhaps Wayne had always felt differently about it. Anyhow, he had gone to a big city and made comparisons before he was old enough to see all the meanings, all the ramifications, all the shadings between black and white. Now he was caught in the brambles of his own thorny thinking and feeling. He felt he had to strike out against personal wealth, and Owen was the only person he knew to strike out against. It was absurd and tiresome, but Wayne was resolved to keep his self-respect by having no association with the wealthy. Wasn't that better, healthier, than for him to follow the other possible line — to feel that he was justified in taking all he could get, regardless of the way it came and of his opinion — however unfounded — of those it came from? His mind could not be changed now. He had made it up too painfully, walking between

"Hoovervilles" and fine residential areas, and reading books on economics, poems like *The Wasteland,* novels like *Babbitt,* until his eyes were hot in their sockets. Nothing could change Wayne's ideas but time and experience and mature insight. And the place for Wayne to spend his time, get his experience, develop his insight now was in college. If he left college, he would never go back, but sink deeper and deeper into misunderstanding and hate.

I asked, "What do you want to do about it?"

I thought I knew. Still I asked.

"We have to tell Wayne the whole truth. He needs the truth to tide him over. We have to tell him that Mr. Perry is not now a rich man, if he ever was; that because of what Mr. Perry did for us, and because of our admiration and respect for him and for valley children, we are doing as much as we can of what he wanted to do; that the money Wayne has had and will have for college has come from us, and that the only way he can repay it is to finish his education and help others in the best way he knows. What way that is, only he can decide."

"We didn't want anyone to know!"

"Wayne has to know. I'll bind him to secrecy. I can make him see, I think, that it might be as hard for his parents to let him accept this kind of help from us as it has been for him to accept it from Mr. Perry."

"But will Wayne accept it from us?"

Dennis laughed. I had never heard a man laugh so much like a boy as Dennis. But a boy who laughs like that laughs often. Dennis's laughter was rare.

"Well — he certainly can't have the *same* objection! . . . I think he will accept it. I'll try to show him that, if he wants to help those children on the riverbanks and

335

along the railroad tracks, this is the way for him to begin. . . . It's not the same at all with Wayne as it was with the rest of us who went away to school, Althea. I told you that a year ago. It's nip and tuck with Wayne. The rest of us knew what we wanted. He only knows what he doesn't want."

"But we can do so little. Compared with what Owen might have done."

"With money, yes. But what we can do that way will have to be enough to get him by. He wants to help himself all he can. He wants that very much. But his judgment isn't good. Maybe gradually we can improve his judgment."

"Maybe you can. I have the feeling now that I'll never understand him at all. But you have made me feel — sympathy for him."

"I doubt if I could feel sympathy for him if I didn't understand him at all. That must be very hard to do. Maybe only a woman could do it."

A light wind had come up and blown away the mosquitoes. We were not moving the swing. There was no sound anywhere for a minute or two, except the soft rustle of leaves above our heads. Then a whippoorwill spoke beside the lane. It is said that a whippoorwill speaks only when standing still, but hops between each note. He spoke again, quickly, three times. Then there was the flutter of wings, and silence.

I said, "Dennis —"

My voice sounded as if it came from a distance. Everything seemed separated by space and the dark. I was not sure whether I had spoken or was only thinking.

But he said, almost drowsily, *"Hmm?"*

"You are a very understanding person. I don't see why

I didn't know that long ago. Why I needed to have it spelled out all this year."

"You told me why."

"What did I say?"

"You said I had been trying, as long as you had known me, to make you do things you didn't want to do. It's hard to know much about a person who makes you feel that way."

"I — don't feel that way now. You haven't done that for a long time. I tried to feel it when you telephoned to-night, and when you first came. But I didn't. Because I couldn't."

"I warned you of that. Remember? I said you could try. But it wouldn't work."

Our words floated on the stillness like half-closed lilies on a millpond.

"That same night you said you thought you knew the reason why I felt as I did, but you wouldn't tell me what it was.

"Tell me now."

"You sure you're ready for it?"

"I don't know."

He leaned forward, slowly.

"Let's see."

He took my hand between his. We sat quietly like that for a few minutes.

Then he said, "Maybe you're ready. . . . I'll take the chance. . . . Althea, you didn't feel that way toward Owen Perry, did you?"

"Oh, no."

"I never met him, but I've heard a great deal about him. He certainly was — is — quite a guy. He was a very special friend of yours when you were a little girl. You always felt that you wanted to do whatever he wanted you to do, didn't you?"

"Yes."

"Yes. . . . A lot of people don't agree with me, but I think even a little girl can fall in love. . . . So can a very young boy. . . . That's not to say they'll stay that way, but sometimes they do. . . . Did you feel you wanted to do whatever Jimmy Brown wanted you to do?"

"No. If I did, it was only for a few weeks. I don't think I ever did, really."

"Did you ever feel that he was trying to make you do what you didn't want to?"

"No. I didn't feel he wanted anything of me that mattered. To either of us. And of course he didn't."

"What about the men you knew in college?"

"No. Whatever they wanted, I gave only what I wanted to give. I didn't resent them. I wasn't — afraid of them."

"But you resented me, and were afraid of me, even during the years when we never saw each other. . . . Only I don't think it was me, Althea. . . . Believe me, this isn't easy to say. . . . But I think you sensed, unconsciously, that I loved you, and that — you had to fight against my making you love me. . . . I think it was loving anyone more than, as a little girl, you loved Owen Perry, that you resented and feared. . . . And I didn't help matters by showing, in a blundering boy's way, that I felt driven to overcome that resistance. . . . For a long time I hated Owen Perry, maybe as much as Wayne does now, only because he stood, unknowingly, between me and what I wanted most — everything I wanted of life for myself — and because I had to accept his help (knowing that you knew I was accepting it) as the only way I had of becoming the kind of man who might — please you. . . . An

338

emotional boy's reasoning can be very faulty, and at the same time honest and painful. So, I assume, can a girl's. But if it gets better as we grow older, maybe it's the best possible training; at least for a teacher, or a parent. . . . So that's the reason I figured out. Maybe it's the wrong one, Althea. I don't claim to be telepathic."

"Perhaps you are."

"Wrong?"

". . . Telepathic."

Clearly, this was more of an admission than he had expected. He sat thinking about it, looking down at my hand between his. It was fortunate for me — for both of us, I think — that Dennis was not an impulsive man.

"Well, we'll find out more about that. Later," he said gently. And then, "You never really expected, after you began to grow up, to marry Owen Perry, did you? But it was supposed to be someone much like him, wasn't it? A lively, laughing Tom Sawyer kind of boy who liked everybody, and grew into a man who never worried, carried responsibilities easily, lit up a room whenever he came into it, had sweethearts of all ages wherever he went and never took advantage of any of them? . . . Not a dark, hulking fellow who stayed by himself; played stick-knife — badly; drew pictures he didn't want anyone to see; threatened you when you were rude to your mother; grabbed your algebra papers and marked them up so that you had not only to do over some of the problems but to copy over the papers; followed you and threatened you again at your Junior Prom; and, even when you were woman-grown, dragged you out of your own house to go downtown with him for reasons you didn't know until you got there, and this very night called you up and told you you had to see him whether you wanted to or not?

339

. . . I wonder that you ever stopped holding me off, Althea. I really do. When I told you that you couldn't keep it up, I was only whistling in the dark. . . . It's very late, you know. On toward morning. You should go in."

I stood up obediently and stepped out of the swing. He walked beside me to the door. I had not been so light, so free, since childhood, and never so happy.

I said, "I've had many teachers, all good, but the most important ones have been men. I wonder if it is like that with every woman. . . . More than anyone else, my father taught me about home, the valley, what it is and what it has. He made me secure. Owen taught me to want to know about the outside world and what connection it has with us. He gave me — well, an easy word for it is inspiration. Now I think you are teaching me to know myself. It seems — sort of like walking backward, doesn't it? Surely I should have learned that first. Owen tried once to tell me what you have told me tonight, but I did not understand it until now. It seems a pity that I can't learn anything by myself. But I'm grateful to you — all of you — for taking the trouble to teach me."

"No," Dennis said. "No, it isn't walking backward. Knowing ourselves is a very advanced course. That's why so many never achieve it. And no, you mustn't be grateful to men for teaching you. Don't you think your father and Owen Perry considered it a privilege — as well as only fair — to teach you? Women taught them, and you were one of those women, even when you were only four years old. As for me — who do you think taught me the best I know? Aunt Lottie and Mrs. Carter and — you. I hope you and I are going on teaching each other for a long time . . . Althea."

He kissed me.

I went into the kitchen and blew out the light. The front hall was dark, but up in my room the silvered pink of dawn came through the east window and touched the mirror. In it I could see my face. I stood and stared as if I had never seen it before.

Wayne went back to college that fall. Ruth was now a senior at the Academy. Noel was in the sixth grade at the age of ten, and reading *Robinson Crusoe*, *The Three Musketeers*, Carl Sandburg's *The Prairie Years*, Bruce Barton's *The Man Nobody Knows*, and everything in verse which he could find from Edgar Guest to Shakespeare's sonnets. Owen sent another hundred dollars for the Barclay account. Agnes wrote that in two more years she would be sent back to the States for a year of study. Armand had a baby daughter, and Marie knit a small pink sweater and matching bootees to send to Kansas. Christmas in the valley was hushed and sad, for Mrs. Carter died the day before. After that, once or twice a year Dennis found time to stop in at the valley school and talk to the children.

In 1932, the national income of the United States was less than half that of three years before. We had sixteen million unemployed. Nearly six thousand banks had failed. Breadlines formed outside every relief agency, private funds for charity were nearly exhausted, and local and state governments were scraping the bottom of the barrel.

Countries of western Europe and South America, terrified by what had happened in our country and caught in the undertow, struggled for economic security, each according to the disposition of its people. Only the Soviet Union, now close to the completion of its Five Year Plan, seemed to be avoiding all crises. This was said to be the result of intelligently planned economy for a classless society. Many idealistic, well-meaning citizens of democratic countries — as well as some not so well-meaning — began to write, speak, teach, and preach the admirability, the desirability of similar planning for a similar society in every country, addressing themselves to those they called "the little people." We looked at one another and wondered who the little people were. We felt as big as anybody. Told that we were underprivileged, we counted our privileges and found them too many and too sweet to gamble with. We wanted more of the luxuries of life for ourselves, and even more we wanted the necessities of life for anyone who lacked them; but we wanted nothing which had been taken away from anyone to whom it belonged. Whatever we had, we wanted to earn, and we hoped those who were wiser than we would find a way for the unfortunate to earn what they needed and wanted. In the meantime, we went on doing what we could see to do in the places where we were.

Dennis and I were married in June of 1932, standing in the parlor among the horsehair-covered chairs, below enlarged, heavy-framed photographs of my grandparents on their Golden Wedding day. Only our families and oldest friends were with us, but Owen and his Corinne were among them, and after supper under the maples we all danced in the grass to the records my father played on the Victrola.

"Got a jig tune, Brad?" old Frank Carter called. "Bet you could step it out a mite. Show the young folks how."

So my father stepped out a jig on the porch, and everyone clapped. Then Kathleen, still light as thistledown, did what she said she guessed was a Highland fling.

"There's so much here that's bright and good and lasting," Owen said to me. "I'm glad you and Dennis are in it. I'm glad you're going to stay in it."

The next spring, while I was waiting for Martha, Franklin D. Roosevelt was inaugurated President. On the day he took office hardly a bank in the country was operating normally. At his inauguration he said, "The only thing we have to fear is fear itself." The following day he issued a proclamation ordering a "bank holiday," and all banking transactions were suspended. Institutions found to be sound in twelve Federal Reserve bank cities were opened a week later, but our Barclay bank was not among these.

Martha was born in April. Ruth Anthony was substituting for me in the valley school and the town had no funds available for her salary, or Dennis's, or any other teacher's. Martha was born at home and Hannah, who took care of us, would not let us speak of pay. My father offered the doctor a gold piece from the green box under the husk mattress of his four-poster bed.

The doctor laughed, tossing the gold piece, and said, "First money I've seen for some time. You're a shrewd man, Mr. McIntire."

"I've always kep' a few of them on hand," my father chuckled. "Like a few spoonsful of whisky, in case of sickness."

A week after Martha was born, the President, empowered by the Emergency Banking Act, ordered all privately owned gold coins, gold bullion, and gold certificates to be exchanged at a Federal Reserve bank for other currency. My father ruefully opened his green box.

"Well," he said. "Git me silver, Dennis. 'Taint so pretty, but it clanks better."

Later on, when the Barclay bank reopened and Dennis

was paid again, he took his money to it as he had before; and I wrote a check to Root College for Wayne's tuition during the last semester of his Senior year.

Early that fall, Wayne entered Tufts Medical School, and, as soon as her crop was harvested, Hannah, who had come to live with us, sold the Daley farm to the Chernocks, a Polish family from Western Massachusetts. Without Hannah to be with Martha while I was away, I could not have continued to teach the valley school. Wayne's sister Ruth had not returned to Normal School after coming home to substitute for me, but was taking nurse's training in Boston.

"I don't know whatever makes mine take so to hospitals and the like of that," said Della. "Nothing I ever expected. But such ones are needed. I found that out when I had my operation. They get good pay too. And they're respected. I must say I'm thankful Ruth is where she can kind of look after Wayne. Don't seem as though he knows how to look after himself. Didn't you think, last time he was home, he looked awful peaked?"

We did, and, more than about his physical condition Dennis and I were concerned about a side of Wayne which, as far as we knew, his parents had not seen. Though he had done well scholastically at Root, he had not fulfilled the promise of his Academy years, and apparently he had cared little for college life, made few friends there. The only friends he spoke of to us were young men he had met in places where he worked week ends and on vacations, young men as bitter, as vaguely idealistic, as impractical as himself. He had spent that summer in a CCC camp, building public parks along the sides of heavily traveled thoroughfares, but the work and his associates had hardened his heart as well as his hands,

344

and the brown color of his skin struck deeper. He refused our help now as definitely as he had always refused Owen's, giving as his reason that he would not take our children's birthright. Then, grim, distraught, he entered medical school.

At the end of that year he left it, disappeared to the West, and was not seen again in the valley. He sent a letter once in a while, from Cincinnati where he was working in a factory, from Arkansas where he was following the harvest, from a shack in Arizona where he was "getting over a cough and doing some writing," from Detroit where he was on WPA and "doing some speaking."

Though Owen continued to deposit money with me for the college education of valley children, it lay undisturbed in the Barclay bank, waiting for Noel. Dennis and I watched his progress with almost feverish eagerness, seeing him get A's without effort in languages and social studies, D's for lack of effort in sciences and mathematics.

And our Denny was born.

There were long-drawn-out and violent strikes in many great cities during 1936 and 1937. By 1940, labor's work week was only forty hours long, and one who worked more than that received pay for time-and-a-half.

My father, Hannah, Dennis and I, who rarely rested except during the night's sleep, and never without a baby, or some mending of clothes or linen or harness or pot, or reading material in our hands, looked at one another and smiled.

"Forty hours is a small part of a week," said my father.

"Good land," cried Hannah, "who could bear to set and twiddle their thumbs?"

"Not you, that's sure," I told her. "Well, I suppose a good many who never could before will fix up their houses, raise fruit and vegetables, get the reading habit, listen to music —"

"But a good many won't," Dennis said. "People who've always worked only for money and done what others told them to may not know what to do with free time. They may not know what to wish for except more money. It will take them a long while to find good ways to use their leisure. Every change — even a change for the better — brings new problems."

Abroad Italy had attacked Ethiopia, and Hitler invaded the Rhineland. Spain was rent by civil war between Loyalists, aided by Russia, and supporters of a totalitarian regime, aided by fascist Germany and Italy. Hostilities had broken out between Japan and China.

President Roosevelt said: *If we are to have a world in which we can breathe freely and live in amity without fear — the peace-loving nations must make a concerted effort to uphold laws and principles on which alone peace can rest secure . . . America hates war. America hopes for peace.*

Wayne Anthony wrote to his mother from Spain, saying that he was driving an ambulance for the Loyalists, "which is the only way I know to live with the shame I feel that the country in which I was born and raised has passed the Neutrality Act and prefers the comfort of noninterference to taking its rightful place as the champion of Spanish people who are fighting and dying for democracy."

Hitler moved into Austria. Violent persecution of Jews was taking place in Germany. Hitler invaded Czechoslovakia. Mussolini attacked Albania. Germany and Russia signed a nonaggression pact in August, 1939.

346

On the first day of September, Dennis received a letter from Wayne. The envelope had a Cambridge, Massachusetts, postmark.

My dad used to say somebody had been to hell and gone [wrote Wayne]. I used to wonder what he meant. Well, I know what I mean. I've been. Sometime maybe I'll tell you all about it. Some of it you may have guessed. I must have done by now almost everything you warned me against without naming it. I beat my head against stone. I turned my back on the valley. I put God out of my life. I joined the American Communist Party. I went to Spain to fight against fascism. Communism was my religion. I crawled through the mud for it, hid under bridges until they were blown up, made bandages out of my shirt, carried the wounded to shelter and saw their dead faces when I laid them down, got shrapnel in my leg and in my shoulder, hunted for food for children with swollen bellies. I'm glad of everything I did in Spain. But the day Russia signed a pact with Germany was the end for me.

I'm here with Ruth now. She says I look like a walking skeleton, so I don't dare come home. I don't have time anyway. I have two weeks for earning a little money. I got here dead broke. But I've transferred my credits to Harvard, and am going on with my medical course there. I can live with Ruthie in her apartment. I don't want to be a millstone around her neck, but I'll take any help I can get for the next few years. I'd say I was a fool to feel that way I did about Mr. Perry's money except that, if I'd had it then, it would have done me no good. If there is any of his money available now, and you can bring yourself to let me have it, I'll use it to the best advantage I know how, and pay back every cent to your fund some day. There is going to be a desperate need for doctors in this world. Doctors, and God. How did I ever get so far away that anybody could convince me I could live without God?

On that same day Hitler's armies crossed the Polish border.

Dennis wrote to Wayne that night and I wrote to Owen. For the first time, I told him of the failure of the Portland bank, and of the exact remaining amount of our fund, which appeared to be only enough to see Noel through the State University where he would be a Sophomore that year. Noel needed more than the rest of us had, for costs were rising and he seemed unable — perhaps unwilling — to help himself. Joe and Kathleen were doing what they could for him, but they had a large family of younger children. Then I told Owen all we knew that he had never known about Wayne, and enclosed Wayne's letter, asking him to return it.

Owen's reply was dated September 3, 1939 — the day Great Britain and France went to the aid of Poland, and the Second World War began.

Owen wrote that he had reached Wayne by telephone and would go to Boston that week end to see him.

Bert's and Della's boy is now a man, not a child to have money doled out to him. If he will agree — and I gather he will — we shall open an account together in Cambridge and from it he can take care of his expenses for the next two years. I hope we shall be friends and that I can see him often. Corinne and I want him to visit us. This fellow and his experience and conclusions are a great asset to this country, and we must make him realize that. It may well be the biggest thing yet to come out of the valley. Wayne will need Dennis's friendship and yours, but he will need nothing more from the fund. God bless you both for what you have done and are doing to keep this country stable in the face of the greatest peril it has ever seen.

When I left Gramp to go downtown to school, he gave

348

me a few of his books which were my favorites. I'll never part with them as long as Perrys have clothes to their backs and soles to their shoes. Wayne's letter sent me to a page in one of them which I read at least a dozen times before I left the valley and at least as many times since. The name of it is *The Witchcraft Delusion*. It was published in 1868. A very small, brown book on the Salem witch trials.

Wayne says the day Russia signed a pact with Germany was the end for him, and how did he ever get so far away (from the valley) that anyone could convince him, etc.

Gramp's little brown book answers that question, near the end, as Gramp would have. I can hear his voice saying the words as I copy them from the discolored page.

". . . And what was God's good design in permitting this outbreak of a fatal superstition? For our answer to such an inquiry, we are pointed at once to a great fact which soon became apparent: *by that very fury the superstition itself was forever exploded.* No gentler means than this, perhaps could have accomplished such a happy end. It may be that those appalling enormities were necessary to drive out the deeply lodged error from human beliefs. We of the present day need not treat it with ridicule or reproaches. In the seventeenth century it was invested with an awful solemnity. It is not for us to denounce that generation. All delusion has not yet departed from the earth. There are false and fatal systems of belief among many men today. . . . Arguments seem powerless to destroy them. . . . 'Error is seldom overthrown by mere reasoning. It yields only to the logic of events.' The learning and wit of all the world could not have rooted the witchcraft delusion out of the minds of men. A practical demonstration . . . alone could give it a deathblow. . . . It makes it one of the greatest landmarks in the moral history of mankind. It makes it a fair and trustful augury that God is leading humanity, by every providence, out of the gloom of ages into the cloudless lustre of the 'golden year.' "

349

Owen had enclosed Wayne's letter, as I had asked him to, and I put away the two together to keep.

In April 1940, Hitler took over Denmark and his troops invaded Norway. In May the blitzkrieg struck Holland, Belgium, Luxembourg, and France. The Maginot Line was bypassed by German armies; the British forces, pinned against the Channel, were evacuated from Dunkirk.

Our Brad was born that May.

In June Mussolini's armies attacked France from the east. Twelve days later the French surrendered. Our Congress passed a conscription act, providing for the registration of seventeen million young men.

The President said, *We must become the arsenal for democracy.*

As Wayne began his interneship, the United States signed a pact with the Danish Minister in Washington agreeing to the defense of Greenland, took over "any foreign vessel . . . lying idle . . ." in our waters, occupied Iceland, and agreed with England on the Atlantic Charter.

Their countries seek no aggrandizement, territorial or other; they desire to see no territorial changes that do not accord with the freely expressed wishes of all the people concerned; they respect the right of all peoples to choose the form of government under which they will live . . . they believe that all the nations of the world, for realistic as well as spiritual reasons, must come to the abandonment of the use of force . . .

At 7:50 A.M., December 7, 1941, a rain of Japanese bombs fell without warning on Pearl Harbor where a

350

great part of the American Fleet lay at anchor. The next morning our President appeared before the Congress to say that yesterday "the United States was suddenly and deliberately attacked by naval and air forces of the Empire of Japan."

Within four hours the Congress had approved a declaration of war. Before nightfall Britain had declared war against Japan. Three days later Germany and Italy had declared war against the United States. Wayne Anthony had enlisted in the Medical Corps of the United States Army.

During those three days, Dennis had talked to the children of every school in our three-town union, and heard their pledges to the flag. He quoted the President's words and asked that they be memorized:

The true goal we seek is far above and beyond the ugly field of battle. . . . We Americans are not destroyers but builders. . . . We are now in the midst of a war, not for conquest, not for vengeance, but for a world which . . . will be safe for children. . . . In the dark of this day — and through dark days . . . to come — we will know that the vast majority of the members of the human race are on our side. Many of them are fighting with us. All of them are praying for us. For, in representing our cause, we represent theirs as well — our hope and their hope for liberty under God.

Manila and the Naval bases of Cavite and Singapore fell to the Japanese. We lost the battle of the Java Sea. The fortress of Corregidor, after heroic defense, surrendered in April. The enemy controlled the Dutch East Indies, Malaya, Thailand, Burma, western Pacific Islands, and threatened Australia. The valley had lost touch with Agnes.

British and American ships landed in North Africa 400,000 men commanded by General Dwight D. Eisenhower. Algiers, Oran, Casablanca, and Dakar . . . Bizerte, Tunis, and the Kasserine Pass . . .

Midway, Guadalcanal, and the Solomons. Bismarck Sea, Kula, and Vella Gulf. Kwajalein, the Admiralty Islands, the Marianas, Guam, and Leyte . . . Lingayen Gulf, Manila, Bataan, Corregidor, Iwo Jima, and Okinawa. The Burma Road was opened — but not until, in one of an infinite number of dangerous flights over the Himalayas which pilots called The Hump, the plane had crashed in which Wayne Anthony was a passenger.

When this news reached the valley, I sent it on to Owen, who replied:

> He — and we — always knew he had a mission. Somehow, through all his uncertainty, he found his way to the fulfilling of it. I am writing to Della and Bert. This is a tremendous sacrifice for them, and for the valley. But valley people know that great achievements require great sacrifices. Our job now is to be worthy of Wayne.

General Eaker's American Eighth Air Force did round-the-clock bombing of Germany. American and British airborne troops directed by General Eisenhower landed on Normandy beaches and were reinforced. By September 1944 most of France was free, and Allied armies moved through Luxembourg and Belgium. The Americans crossed the Waal and the Meuse. Aachen, the Battle of the Bulge, the Saar Basin . . . In March 1945 the Allied Armies had reached the bank of the Rhine. In April General Patton's tanks reached Czechoslovakia, Russian forces from the east joined Americans from the west at Torgau on the Elbe, and the Italian people executed Benito Mussolini. On May 7, the German chief-of-staff signed the Act of Military Surrender.

In these times, among these people and place names, valley children, including my own, were growing up. We talked together every day of leaders who would forever be a race apart to me, and of parts of the world forever foreign to me, but to them more familiar, better known than many people and places only a few miles away. When I shuddered to think of what the German people were suffering they reminded me, "It's because they let this thing happen. Remember what the Luftwaffe did to England. Remember *We shall fight on the beaches, we shall fight on the landing grounds, we shall fight in the fields and on the streets, we shall fight in the hills; we shall never surrender;* and *If we fail then the whole world . . . will sink into the abyss of a new Dark Age.*"

They loved England as if it were another home, and I remembered the old man in the valley who had said when he heard the first whistle of a train in the night, "I wisht I was aboard of her, a-going to England." Now the schoolroom ceiling hung thick with model airplanes, and when the Pacific war was over their builders expected to fly to England and hear Big Ben strike the hours.

On August 6 a new weapon razed Hiroshima. Three days later another destroyed Nagasaki. Soviet troops entered Manchuria and Korea, and all Japan was swept by bombing. The following day the Japanese government began surrender negotiations, and on August 14 accepted the Allied terms — unconditional surrender, occupation by the Allies, free elections by the Japanese people to choose their leader and their preferred type of government.

In cities and towns of the United States there were celebrations, but the valley was very quiet. Our country alone had suffered over a million casualties, lost nearly twelve hundred ships, spent $330,000,000,000, drawn deeply on reserves of commodities needed for the future, in a war which we had sought in every way we knew to prevent, to postpone, or to shorten. Our buildings stood roofed, four-walled, painted, with flowers blooming under their unbroken windows, but all around the horizon we sensed ruins. Only one valley boy was known to have died on military duty, two were missing and five had been wounded; yet the fields seemed filled with wooden crosses marking the graves of servicemen and women, of civilians of every race, even of children . . .

We had done what we had done, not because we loved war, but because we hated it. Now all we wanted was a just and lasting peace for every country in the world.

That fall the valley school and all district schools in our union were closed. Buses took our children to a new consolidated school in town, and I became its principal.

V

IT IS twelve years now since the end of the Second World War.

One day last summer I stared at my address on a letter I had just taken from our mailbox. It was written in a hand I had never before seen except, now and then, at Christmas. I sat down on the bank of the lane and tore open the envelope, though it has always been my habit, as it was my mother's, to open a letter neatly with a stroke of the scissors.

After I had read the letter I sat looking at it for a long time, but did not see it. By and by the world came back, as out of a fog, but it was not the same world and never would be quite the same again for me.

When I went up the porch steps, my daughter Martha, who was visiting us for a few weeks while her husband was away on Army Reserve duty, looked up from sunbathing her baby and asked anxiously, "What's the matter, Mother?"

"Nothing," I answered. "Here's your letter from Milt."

I gave the paper to my father and reached for the knob of the screen door.

"Something is too the matter," Martha insisted. She stood up. "Did you hear from — Denny?"

Her brother Denny is in the Air Force.

I shook my head.

"She just heard from Denny yesterday, didn't she?" my father asked, taking his glasses from his shirt pocket. "May be a month before she hears again. Don't all do like Milt, Marthy, write every single —"

The screen door closed behind me.

"Will you watch the baby, Gramps? I've got to try to find out what's the matter."

"No. Don't. She'll tell you when she's ready."

"But didn't you see, Gramps? She's pale. She's positively white. I never saw her look like that before."

"Didn't? Well, I have. Better let her alone, Marthy. Better that way. She'll be all right."

I went into the pantry and began making biscuits to serve with cold meat and salad for the noon meal. The spoon, the bowl, the breadboard, the rolling pin, the pan felt good in my hands.

When Martha brought the baby in, after a while, I was setting the table, and I asked her to mix the salad — for she is more skillful at that than I am. I took the baby, washed his face and hands, and put him in the old high chair. I can never tie his bib without kissing the back of his neck, though I try to do this when no one is looking.

Dennis came in with a basket of tomatoes, summer squash, and broccoli which he set in the dark cellarway to cool, and said there would be enough peas for supper. He had a bunch of roses, too, and I asked Martha to put them in water while I brought the baby his milk.

"What's this, old man?" Dennis asked. "Does your grandmother like you better than roses?"

He looked at me oddly.

"Can't beat grandparents for foolishness," my father said. "Here comes Brad with the tractor. Can't get over it.

Mows the whole farm in one forenoon. Haying's done in two days. Used to take me all summer."

Brad came in, big and hot. I am always amazed by the breadth of his shoulders. Only last week, it seems, he used the high chair. Now he is a Sophomore at Whitaker.

Though we have a lavatory off the kitchen, he likes to wash up at the kitchen sink as his grandfather does. From childhood he has copied his grandfather, as Denny always has his father. Martha has copied no one, but in all the ways that I am not, is like my mother, for whom she was named but whom she never saw.

"You okay, Mom?" Brad asked, low, as he emerged from the roller towel and I passed him on the way to the refrigerator.

I nodded and smiled.

We sat down at the table and, after the baby and I had played for a few minutes with our food, I fed him. We talked about the heat. Martha read us parts of Milt's letter. My father said, "See by the papers they're going to take our troops out of Japan," and Dennis and Brad discussed the probably mixed feelings of the Japanese people about this separation from those whom they had once regarded as enemies and many of whom they had later come to think of as friends.

While the others had their blueberry pie, I asked Martha if I might put the baby to bed for his nap.

"Yes. Thanks. And while you're up there, why don't you take a nap yourself? I'll do the dishes."

But when I had sung to Stevie until his eyes closed, I went into the attic and was there for an hour or more, hardly aware of the high sun or of the cobwebs it shone through.

The next morning the men went early into the field,

and as Martha and I cleared away breakfast, I said quietly: "There is something I have wanted to do all my life. It's strange I've never done it. I've kept putting it off. If I put it off much longer I'll never do it. I'm going to climb the mountain today. The higher mountain."

"Oh, Mother! Not alone?"

"Why do daughters so often say, "Oh, Mother!"? Sons never do.

"Wait until Saturday. Lorraine won't be working and I can get her to stay with the baby. The haying will be done, and we can all go. We'll take a lunch —"

"Maybe we can. Saturday or some other day. But I always thought that when the time came for me to climb that mountain — I would climb it alone."

I felt as if I were already alone, already climbing and filled with a blind urgency to reach the top. It was difficult to come back to Martha, but for a mother — as Martha already knew, though she could not suspect that it would be true all her life — her child's smallest need takes precedence over her own greatest need, and she will fight her way back from the gates of Paradise to meet it. I had not nearly that far to retrace my steps, but the path seemed to have grown up to alders as swamp trails do between berry seasons.

I shook cleaning powder into the sink and scrubbed, feeling Martha's eyes on me but not looking at her. I washed and rinsed the cloth, and took it with the dish towels to pin to the porch line. Hanging in a row, they danced in the morning breeze.

When I came back into the kitchen, I was ready.

"Martha, dear," I said cheerfully, "I suppose my plan for the day sounds odd. Come to think of it, I suppose it

358

is because you are here that I made it. I doubt if I'd have the courage to tell anyone else about it, and I certainly wouldn't dare to go without letting someone know where I was. But I do want to see the valley from up there before I'm too old. Call it a notion or a whim. When you're my age you may have one. This is mine. Let me go. Please? I'll be very sensible. I know it's quite a way, and steep in places, and I'm not used to climbing. But if it's too much for me, I'll stop and rest, and then come back. If I'm not home by five o'clock, you can send Brad to look for me." I laughed. "Or a whole posse, if you like. There'll be three hours or so of daylight after that. But I'll be home by five, if not sooner."

To reassure Martha, I had thought of much I did not want to think of. My mind struggled, frustrated as a child's eager feet that want to run but are stayed by adult worry about what the child knows will never happen.

"Well," Martha said, exactly as my mother might have, "if you're sure you know what you're doing, go ahead. I guess nothing will happen to you if you really will stop when you're tired. Just don't pretend you're a Girl Scout. And the sooner you start, the better, if you're going. Before it gets too hot. I'll pack your lunch."

"No. You go get the baby's bath ready. I'll pack my lunch. I know just what I want. Run along, dear. I'll see you by five."

". . . What'll I tell the men?"

"Anything. I don't mind they're knowing where I am. After I've gone."

From halfway up the stairs she called, "Wear a hat!"

"I will."

I did, but as soon as I was among the trees at the foot of the mountain, I left it on a bush and shook out my hair, already damp and sticking to my neck and forehead. Now I could feel the shadow of the pines. I had thought I would stop to rest after the walk in the sun, but the cool dampness of the woods was invigorating, and I went steadily on. There was no path — though once there had been — for few people walk for pleasure nowadays except Scouts, who take each time a different route; but I knew that as long as I was climbing I was going toward the top. At the foot of steep, bare ledges I did not dare to rest; the need to know that I could scale them drove me on. Near the summit I clung to a bush to fill a bottle at the spring from which a brook was leaping. Breathing hard, exultant, on my hands and knees with the folded top of a paper bag between my teeth, the bottle in one pocket of my slacks, I crawled until I saw thin, wild, sunlit grass stirring in the wind just ahead of me, reached turf, and lay on it, my arms outflung, my forehead pressed hard against it. I had reached the top of the valley's higher mountain, and felt myself becoming part of it, one with it.

I don't know how long I lay there. I had not looked at my watch, nor thought of it, since I left home.

When I stood up, I could see one tree ahead of me. It was an ancient beech, with leaves only on its lower branches, the top dead and ragged from the winds. I went to it and found, as I had known I would, that it grew at one end of the long, rough slab of granite which covered the tomb of Saint Aspinquid, the valley's Indian chief who had become a Christian.

I took from my paper bag one of the roses Dennis had brought me the day before, and laid it in a crevice of the stone. I should not have wanted anyone in my family to know that I did this, but it was a tribute I had wanted to pay since childhood. And today my rose was not only for Saint Aspinquid.

At last I sat down, with my back against the gnarled trunk of the old tree, and looked off over the valley, over the years.

I saw the wilderness with a river running through it for miles, and Indians in canoes on the river. The white settlers came, the cabins, the cows, the sheep, the fields of grain, the wheels. Fog closed in, and war. Men left this lovely valley to fight and die. Some of them came back to peace and freedom. Cabins gave way to frame. The church appeared, and the school. Another fog, and through it great words reverberated.

A new nation, conceived in liberty, and dedicated to the proposition that all men are created equal. . . .

The endurance of the nation established, machinery hummed, and the whistles of wood-burning engines cut the night silences, but machinery did not always hum nor engines whistle, while always in their seasons there were the songs of peepers, whippoorwills, wind in the pines, running water, rustling corn.

I saw Elder Perry picking apples, and again in his pulpit; Owen laughing down from the hammock in the maple tree; the Dennett sisters among the treasures of their great house; the Browns, the Fernalds, the Anthonys, the Carters, the Burnhams, the McIntires, the flag flying over the schoolhouse and the vision in the sky above it of the White City of Washington. Then I saw Mrs. Carter behind her desk, and the Fernalds and Perrys replaced by Luneaus, the Burnhams by Daleys.

All this I saw most clearly because one remembers in exquisite detail what first touches deeply the mind and the heart.

But I saw, too, quite clearly enough to recognize them, one after another of us creeping shyly, half unwillingly, out of the valley's shelter into the town — afraid of its strangeness, humble before its challenge, and even more afraid of the world beyond and more humble in the face of what might be demanded of us by it. We wanted to stay hidden, but could not, because we were a part of the world and its work had to be done.

A steadfast concert of peace can never be maintained except by a partnership of democratic nations. . . .

The First World War . . .

The Second World War . . . I thought of Wayne. And I thought of Noel Luneau, who had escaped the draft because of poor physical condition and had graduated from the State University, but never found employment which seemed to him worth doing. He flitted from bookkeeping to news reporting to broadcasting to selling to free-lance writing to figurine painting and back to bookkeeping. With a college education he had done nothing he could not have done without a college education. He had made two unsuccessful marriages, ignoring the tenets of his parents' faith, and time and experience had seemed to bring him no real maturity. Sometimes between jobs he stayed for months with his parents, letting Joe go alone to the store, criticizing Kathleen's cooking, canoeing lazily on the river, lying in a hammock, or drinking and sleeping beside the fire. Yet he was charming — and this frightened us. No girl in the valley refused an invitation from Noel without regret. They said he was fun to be with, spent his money freely — too freely —and paid delightful compliments. Our boys gathered round him wherever he went and heard his stories of famous people he had seen here and there, heard him say that the only reason for living was the pleasure of each day as it came, listened to him laugh at industry, duty, honor, morality, sobriety, frugality, loyalty, patriotism, faith, and love — everything good they had been taught to believe in.

We dreaded to see Noel come home. We were thankful to see him go. We pitied Joe and Kathleen with all our hearts, and we fought with all our might what often looked like losing battles against his influence. From knowing Noel, valley parents came to lack confidence in the value of higher education, and some children with the capacity for it failed to develop a sense of its desirability and importance.

"If that's the way colleges turn them out," parents said, "just as well if mine never see the inside of one."

"Why bother?" our young people asked. "Driving a truck and even waiting on tables pays better than teaching school like the Daleys, or being a missionary like Miss Brown. That Mr. Perry we hear so much about didn't graduate from any college."

We told the young people there were better rewards than money. We also reminded them of Armand, who was now a judge, drove a Cadillac, and had lately had a new home built for his parents. We asked them why they supposed Mr. Perry had set up a fund to help them go on to school, unless he believed that higher education was important.

There were years when we had wondered if the future of all Owen, Dennis and I had tried to do would go down to defeat before one Noel.

And still we had kept a troubled eye on the world.

The United Nations had been organized. Allied occupation of Japan and of West Germany had proceeded smoothly and our relations with the peoples of these countries were good. But Soviet Russia had incorporated the Baltic states and part of Poland, was supporting Communist regimes in the Balkans and neighboring states, attempting to coerce Turkey, interfering in the politics of the Middle and Far East. The North Atlantic Treaty Organization had been set up, and General Eisenhower appointed Supreme Commander of its military force. In 1950, the armies of Communist North Korea, occupied for a time after the Second World War by Soviet troops, invaded South Korea which had been occupied by American troops while its democratic government was established under the guidance of the United Nations.

Owen had written me:

I've been looking through another of Gramp's books tonight. It is *Democracy in America,* written by one Alexis de Tocqueville in 1835. He said:

"There are at the present time two great nations in the world which seem to tend toward the same end, although they started from different points. I allude to the Russians and the Americans. Both of them have grown up unnoticed; and while the attention of mankind was directed elsewhere, they have suddenly assumed a most prominent place among the nations; and the world learned of their existence and their greatness at almost the same time.

"All other nations seem to have nearly reached their

364

natural limits, and only to be charged with the maintenance of their power; but these are still in the act of growth; and all the others are stopped, or continue to advance with extreme difficulty; these are proceeding with ease and celerity along a path to which the human eye can assign no term. The American struggles against the natural obstacles which oppose him; the adversaries of the Russian are men; the former combats the wilderness and savage life; the latter civilization with all its weapons and its arts; the conquests of the one are therefore gained by the ploughshare; those of the other by the sword. The Anglo-American relies upon personal interest to accomplish his ends, and gives free scope to the unguided exertions and common sense of the citizens; the Russian centres all the authority of society in a single arm; the principal instrument of the former is freedom; of the latter servitude. Their starting point is different, and their courses are not the same; yet each of them seems to be marked out by the will of Heaven to sway the destinies of half the globe."

Against the trunk of an ancient beech tree, with my hand on Saint Aspinquid's tomb and a small bundle of Owen's old letters in my lap, I was swept by wave after wave of ideas, feelings, memories, which I half-tried to push back but could not.

Pusan. Inchon. Seoul. Pyongyang. Hungnam. The Yalu.

Hannah had died in 1951, and four of her nephews, in Army uniform, carried her coffin to the cemetery on the old Burnham place which now belonged to the Chernocks, and placed it beside Julie's small grave.

There were months of negotiation at Panmunjom, while the air war continued vigorously between American Sabre Jets and Russian MIGs.

General Eisenhower had become our President, and the shooting and bombing finally stopped, after two years of death, injury, and widespread destruction; but in 1956, valley boys in Army uniforms still shivered in unheated shelters or paced up and down, beating their hands, looking across a three-mile strip of no man's land, while on the other side of it young Communists likewise shivered, paced, and looked across. What were they thinking, those young Communists? Did they, like our valley boys, long to go home? Or had they no word meaning what the word "home" means to us?

I asked myself if all America had accomplished "by the ploughshare" — by its struggle against "the wilderness," and against savagery not only of nature but of human nature in ourselves, among those we knew, and throughout the world — by its faith in the "exertion and common sense" of free men and women everywhere — could go down to defeat before that other vast nation whose "adversaries are free men," who "centres all the authority of society in a single arm" and "the sword," whose principal instrument is "servitude," and who "seems to be marked out by the will of Heaven to sway the destinies of half the globe."

The answer was in the Elder's *Witchcraft Delusion.*

And what was God's good design in permitting this outbreak of a fatal superstition? . . . By that very fury the superstition itself was forever exploded. . . . It may be that those appalling enormities were necessary to drive out the deeply-lodged errors of human beliefs. . . . There are false and fatal systems of belief among many men today. . . . Arguments seem powerless to destroy them. . . . "Error is seldom overthrown by mere reasoning. It yields only to the logic of events." . . . A practical demonstration . . . alone could give it a death-blow.

366

What had happened to Wayne, when Communists signed a pact with Fascists, had happened to others; it happened later to many more, when the Soviet drew an Iron Curtain between its persecutions and the free world, when it did not cooperate with the United Nations, when it aided the invasion of South Korea, and when it crushed with tanks a new government struggling to be born.

We have now withdrawn our troops from every country except where the native peoples need and want them for defense. It is our way to fight only for freedom, and not because we love war but because we hate it. But we, with other free nations, are welcoming constantly refugees from behind the Iron Curtain, our armed forces and air power are kept at the peak of efficiency, and we continue to stockpile military weapons, including the most lethal devised by the horrified mind of man, awaiting Communist agreement on a system of free international inspection to make disarmament worldwide. We keep our promises to friends and to enemies. We have great patience, but we are neither weak nor foolish. We hate war, but we have never lost one. High over the valley, where once there were only the stars, the sun, the moon, and cloud formations, American boys fly jet planes like sky toboggans, and feather fans of rosy light spray out beside and behind them as the snow used to from my sled at sunset time.

On the higher mountain I said aloud: "No, Owen. . . . Noel could not stop us. In the last seven years, five more valley boys and girls have gone to college and three have their degrees. One of these is now in graduate school preparing to be a professor of American history. Another is becoming a nuclear physicist, and that is Ivan Chernock, whose parents took him out of Poland, a little boy, during the Second World War, and brought him to his grandparents on the old Burnham place. The third is our Denny, now in the Air Force.

"Of the two now in college, one is Della's youngest, Brooke — who may be an artist, Owen. Dennis feels she has great promise. She may one day put the valley on canvas and send it out into the world. The other is our Brad. Brad is a big boy with broad shoulders, strong hands on a tractor wheel, the mechanic of our family; but the Elder is in him, and he will be the valley's first minister. I say this low, Owen, because I am humble before the fact, and yet mightily proud.

"Noel could not defeat the valley. The valley may yet, by some miracle, save him. . . . And no more can the Communist sword defeat our American ploughshare, if every one of us puts his shoulder to it. As we will."

The sun was low when I made my way down the mountain and back into the valley.

As I went through the dooryard at home, Brad looked up from where he lounged beside the baby's play pen on the porch, and grinned.

"Just in time," he said. "Or Martha would have had me mountain climbing — after all the hay we've put in today."

I picked up the baby and carried him into the house, kissing his neck as we went through the entry.

In the kitchen Martha was getting supper.

She said, "Hail to the wanderer! Do you feel better now? Or worse?"

I said I felt fine.

That was all. Everything was as if I had never been away, except within myself. What had happened there must not have shown, for no one noticed it.

368

Later that night, when Dennis and I were alone in our room, I asked, "Do you remember thinking I didn't seem quite myself yesterday?"

He glanced at me in surprise.

"I remember now. I had forgotten. You seemed all right this morning."

"I am all right. It took a little time. I only needed time. I had a letter from Corinne. Owen is dead."

He reached for my hand.

"I said that," I added slowly, "because it is what people say. I don't believe it. Owen couldn't die."

"No," Dennis agreed gently. "Not Owen . . . nor Wayne . . . nor anyone who has really lived."

"Corinne said the Valley Fund was included in his will."

"I would be sure of that without being told."

"Yes. . . . And Armand is helping now, of course. The younger ones will in their turn, if they can. Besides, people in many places are helping as they didn't use to, with scholarships."

He knew all that, of course. He knew I was thinking aloud.

I said, "There must be something more we can do. Something else. Something different."

Dennis waited.

"I wonder — if I should try to write a book. . . . It seems — presumptuous. . . . So many books have been written and are being written, by people with more talent than I have. . . . But no one has told the valley story, and perhaps no one will, if I don't. What I could say, if I can find a way to say it, might show what 'the American experiment' means to people like us, who have been called the 'little people,' the 'underprivileged,' the 'backward.' It means the opportunity to make our own mistakes and to correct them.

"Owen told me once, 'We're going to do all we can.' Then he said — or was it God? — 'See the glory that is here. Then sing it out. Whatever you want to see live and grow, sing of it.' . . . I'm not at all sure I can sing, but I do hear a kind of music, faintly. . . . Owen has done all he could. I'd like to do more than I have. . . . Even the words to begin with came to me on the mountains."

Dennis waited again, his hand warm over mine, his eyes on my face.

When I said nothing more, he took his pen from his pocket, unscrewed the cap, and handed it to me.

"If they have come to you, Althea, write them down."

I stood by the bureau and wrote:

I have yarn to spin, colors to blend, a pattern to weave, and edges to bind securely for the preservation of the whole. I cannot promise that the yarn will not be loose, the colors too pale or too strong or ill-matched; please be tolerant of the workmanship. The wool is of the best quality, clean and sturdy, springy to the touch, native grown, product of snug shelter, rocky pasture, and the narrow, sweetfern-bordered lanes which wind forever between the all-but-forgotten beginning and the unforeseeable end.

In my basket the carded and rolled shearings, all alive and billowing, are heaped bottomside up. I attach the top roll to the spindle and strike the great wheel with a wooden pin. It begins to turn, and I am startled by my own temerity in setting it in motion. . . .

370